and all the stars

by Andrea K Höst

And All the Stars
© 2012 Andrea K Höst. All rights reserved.
ISBN: 978-0-9872651-3-5
EBook ISBN: 978-0-9872651-4-2
www.andreakhost.com
Cover design using stock art by Andrea K Höst

Acknowledgements

I BLAME THIS BOOK ON
FLANNERY AND WENDY DARLING
and thank them for it.

Additional thanks to Dr Jennifer Elliman, Dr Chris Fellows,
Julie Dillon, Lexie Cenni, and Estara Swanberg.

Author's Note

Spelling is Australian English.

Chapter One

Madeleine Cost's world was a tight, close space, a triangular tube tilted so her head lay lower than her feet. Light reflected off metal, not enough to give any detail, and there was barely room to squeeze one hand past the slick surface, to explore face and skull and find powdery dust and a throbbing lump. Dull pain also marked upper shoulder, hip, thigh. She felt dusty all over, grimed with it, except her lower half, which was wet. Free-flowing liquid drained past her head.

She could smell blood.

Ticket barrier. Those were the rectangles of metal above and beside her. Madeleine could remember reaching for her returned ticket as the red gates snapped back and then – then a blank space between there and here. Thursday lunchtime and she'd been at St James Station, planning to walk down to Woolloomooloo to wait for Tyler, just off the plane and sure to be strained and tired and all the more interesting for it.

The noise the water made suggested a long fall before it hit somewhere past her feet, close enough to spatter her ankles before draining past her. The ticket barriers were a generous double flight of stairs above the platforms, or had been. How far above them was she now? Had it been a bomb? Gas explosion? She could smell smoke, but it wasn't overwhelming. The blood was stronger. Smoke and blood and falling water, and how far was it falling? How big was the drop, and how—

"Hello?" Madeleine called, just a croak of a voice, anything to shut off that line of thought. The effort made her cough.

There wasn't room enough to shift to hands and knees. She could barely squirm onto her stomach, the small pack she wore catching on the withdrawn gates. Stretching one arm forward, she followed the path of the water down, and found an edge. But she had no way to measure the size of any gap beyond. Reaching back with one sandalled foot, she explored damp channels in powder, and grainy concrete. No edge. Not willing to just lie there, she tucked her elbows in close and wriggled back an inch.

The ground shifted.

Freezing, Madeleine waited for the plunge, but nothing followed except a faint rocking motion. She – the slab of concrete with its burden of ticket barriers and girl – was balanced on a downward slope. Another shift of position and she could send the whole thing plunging, and would fall and fall, and then the blood would be hers.

Eyes squeezed shut, Madeleine tried to calm herself down. She'd always thought herself a composed sort of person, but black panic clawed, demanding an urgent response – screaming, running, leaping – however impossible that might be. It was only the itching in her throat, setting her coughing again, which pulled her back.

Could she drink the thin flow of water running past her? It didn't smell – not stronger than the blood and smoke, at any rate. The tumbling splash was so loud, a solid belt as it hit the concrete near her feet. St James Station was underneath Hyde Park, the ticket barrier level just a few metres below grass and trees. The strength of the water's impact suggested a drop to the platform level.

Up. Down. Stay. Three choices which felt like none in the blood-scented dark.

Her phone, tucked in the outer pocket of her backpack, let out the opening notes of her favourite song. Prone, elbows tucked in, hands beneath her chin, she couldn't just reach back. By the time she'd scrunched herself into the tiny extra space on the tilted border of her world, and worked her opposite arm back, the smoky voice had eased into silence. She still scrabbled for the pack's zip, ignoring the burning protest of her bruised shoulder and side, and caught the heavy rectangle between two reaching fingers.

As Madeleine brought her arm painfully forward, the clear white light from the phone conjured hazy reflections of girl in the silver-metal sides of the two ticket barriers. These faded as she turned the makeshift torch forward to reveal whiteness and a crosshatching of dark lines. Bars.

Madeleine stared, confused, until she recognised the green-painted railing which edged the upper level and the stairs to the platform. They were warped and twisted, but still looked thoroughly solid, forming another wall to the cage capping the slab of concrete. There was no way forward.

It was difficult to see beyond the railing, but the white resolved itself into dust, pale mounds of it, through which she could glimpse a third silver rectangle, this one twisted and torn, the tickets it had swallowed spewing from its innards across dust and chunks of concrete.

Her raft lay on one of the flights of stairs, which did not make sense. St James Station had only two lines. The tracks sat parallel, perhaps fifty metres apart, their platforms joined by a broad expanse of concrete full of pillars which held up the ticket barrier area. The ticket barriers sat over this central area, while the stairs were to either side of it, close to the tracks. To be on the stairs she and her metal cocoon would have had to fall sideways.

Whatever the case, at least she was near the bottom, even if she would still need to risk moving backward to get out.

But before that… Turning her phone around, Madeleine found a missed call from her mother. Her parents thought she was at school, and had no idea she was skipping to start work on the portrait of Tyler. There'd been no point embarking on Round Five Thousand of the Grades v Art argument when Tyler's mild willingness to oblige a cousin didn't extend to altering his schedule in any way, and the cut-off date for the 2016 Archibald was in less than a week.

The phone's clock told her it was nearly one pm – maybe fifteen minutes since she'd arrived at St James – and the signal was strong, but she couldn't get through to her parents. It wasn't till she called triple zero that she had any kind of response, and that was a canned message which boiled down to "Everyone is calling emergency".

Trying to reach her voicemail messages didn't work, so she gave up and texted: "Can't get through – will talk later".

Without knowing more about what happened, she couldn't be sure whether it was more sensible to wait for rescue, or try to make her own way. Shifting about could trigger a slide or collapse.

Out in the dark someone else's phone rang – one of those joke ring tones, growing louder until the phone was shrieking. No-one picked up. How many people were in the station, lying in the dusty dark? Calling out brought no response, but the ringing told her there must be someone.

Tucking her phone into her bra, Madeleine explored behind her again, cautious toes still finding only dust turning to mud, and wet concrete. An inch back, and nothing. Another inch, and the ground shifted as it had before, but this time Madeleine didn't freeze against the see-saw's tilt, and almost immediately it settled. The settling didn't surprise her – resting on rubble on a stairway, her raft was hardly going to tip upright – but the sensation of it was strange, not as firmly solid as she would expect from concrete stairs.

Feeling a sudden urgency, she wriggled several inches, her feet pelted by liquid as she moved closer to the falling water. And then her questing toes found the far border of her raft, another rough edge. She slowed down, backing inch by inch, until she was half out of her metal tube, part-lying and part-kneeling, then reached with her foot hoping to find the straight edge of a step, or at least firmly packed rubble.

Tickling softness.

She jerked her foot away, gasping and then coughing. Brief and strange as that contact was, she'd recognised instantly what her foot had touched. Hair.

It was a person, and all around her was the scent of their blood, and whoever it was had not moved, or spoken, or reacted at all to Madeleine's foot in their face. She and her raft were on top of someone's body.

The chance that this was not so, that she was crushing someone too badly injured to react, made it impossible for Madeleine to stay, to quiver or quibble or spend one moment longer where she was. She stretched out her other leg, trying to reach as far as possible, and this time met cloth, and a warm and yielding wetness, and though this left Madeleine in no doubt that the person beneath her was not alive, it gave her even less reason to slow down, as her foot found something solid beyond and she thrust herself up and back, with a temporary agility worthy of a gymnast, onto something which was step and only step, with a railing she could clutch while she sobbed and gulped to keep down the scalding liquid which rose in her throat.

Her foot, the whole lower part of her leg, was sticky-wet, and when she could move at all the first thing she did was hold it out, back towards her raft, and the water which fell so steadily. She wanted to stand in the narrow stream, to be certain nothing remained, and to be free of her thick coating of dust. But she couldn't bring herself to cross over the crushed, mangled thing lying invisible in the dark, any more than she could turn her phone on it and capture a sight to burn her mind.

Still clutching her railing, Madeleine looked about for the source of light which made the darkness not quite complete. There were no sturdy exit signs or miraculously enduring fluorescents: instead a field, a wall, of luminous motes, shining and glittering.

It made her dizzy, for it was the sky, the sky at night with muted stars and yet it was here and to her right, not above, despite the direction gravity proclaimed to be down.

These wrong-way stars did not produce nearly enough illumination to truly see through the thin mist of settling dust, but she could make out shapes, black against coal grey. The ticket barriers. The railing. The stair which had been severed above the wide mid-flight step where she stood.

The glimmer was not enough to reveal any details of the platform below, so Madeleine had to resort to her phone, to gauge the eight-foot drop and then decide to work her way along the outside of the railing, keeping her head turned away from what lay upon the stair. She looked for the reflective strip which lined the edge of the platform instead, but couldn't make it out through the powdery white mounded everywhere.

The climb down was relatively easy, the severed railing firm despite the absence of the upper half of the stair, and then she was on the flat expanse of the platform, a treacherous landscape of concrete and projecting rods of metal beneath concealing dust. Ridiculous amounts of it, some piles higher than she stood, and even the gullies between those mountains were knee-deep.

Madeleine guessed the entire ticket level had fallen down, but that did not explain what looked like an explosion in a chalk factory. Nor the stars. They drew her, a moth to the moon, her free hand held over her mouth and nose to keep out the fine haze of floating particles. Up close, unobscured, the stars blazed in a wall of black: galaxies and nebulae and fiery novae, stretching up and to either side of her in a faintly curving wall which bisected the broad lower expanse of the station and disappeared through the cracked and buckled cement at her feet.

Tucking her phone away again, Madeleine lifted both hands and brushed cautious fingertips against the surface. She expected it to be cool, slick and damp, like limestone in caves, but what she touched was velvet. Astonished, she pressed her hands against warm, smooth stone, sensuous against her skin. It felt as solid as marble, but somehow alive, as if waiting would bring a pulse, the beat of a buried heart.

And then light flashed, and she was picked up and thrown backward into the dark.

Chapter Two

Madeleine lay suffocating in dust and near misses. Broken leg. Steel bar through her back. Broken neck. So many things she could have done to herself. Worse was measuring what damage she had actually done. She'd landed flat on her back, fortunately square on one of the deeper piles of dust, which had erupted like a geyser around her. Her already-painful skull was screaming protest at new abuse. But it was a reluctance in her arms and legs, a disconnect between want and ability to move, which spun her into terror. Paralysed. Was she paralysed?

Pins and needles. They arrived in force, swept through her, the whole of her body jolting with a hornet swarm's stinging assault, but her spasmodic curl in reaction showed her that she could move, even though the most she could manage at first was to curl further, to clutch knees, elbows, and try to breathe through lungs which buzzed and burned, while somehow not inhaling powder. It smelled like an approaching rainstorm.

Madeleine did not quite lose consciousness, but when the stinging receded she lay numb while a new layer of dust sifted down. She'd nearly killed herself. Thrown away the unspeakable good fortune which had given her a protective cocoon of metal when however many others at the station had nothing to shield them. She had too much to do, too many images in her head which deserved release, and she had almost denied herself that. Sabotaged her own future just because of something strange and beautiful, velvet beneath her touch.

Her phone, still tucked behind the padding of her bra, lit up. The singer's crooning murmur was far from a spur to action, but Madeleine did manage to pluck the device from her chest and tell it hello.

Her mother's crisp voice, crackling with static. "Finally! Maddie, I'm on my way to the school. *Stay inside.* They say the cloud's heading our way, but we should have time to get you home and seal the doors. Don't hang up – I'll let you know when I'm there."

"Cloud?" Madeleine blinked. "What are you talking about?"

A familiar, exasperated sigh. "Always in your own world. Look, they think it's some kind of bio-weapon. A cloud of dust, coming from a black tower in Hyde Park. It's happening all over the world – black towers and dust. They're saying it's aliens or – oh, what does it matter? Just stay where you are until I get there. Are you closer to the Strickland or Walpole Street entrance?"

The glow of Madeleine's phone lit up glittering swirls in the powder still settling after her fall. Her throat itched, and she wanted nothing more than to be saved. And her mother was out trying to do exactly that, driving to school instead of home keeping herself safe. Riding to the rescue.

"I'm at the Gallery, Mum."

The background noise of the call changed abruptly, and then her mother's voice came clearer, no longer on the hands-free set. "You're where?"

"The Art Gallery of New South Wales," Madeleine said, making the lie resigned, apologetic, with no hint of dark and bruises, of broken things and dust. "I was waiting here till Tyler's plane got in."

"You..." The word trailed away on a small shaking note, as unlike Victoria Cost as it was possible to be.

"I'm probably safer than you," Madeleine said, to fill the silence, to hear something other than that strangled word. Her eyes stung and she had to swallow, to work to make her voice sound casual, a little guilty, a touch disbelieving, as if she couldn't credit the idea of black towers or bio-weapon attacks. "I'm in the Asian art section – it doesn't even have windows. Are the animals okay?"

"That damn painting," Madeleine's mother said. "You – Madeleine, why do you always..."

"Is Dad home?"

"He's on his way." Her mother's voice was regaining its usual brisk pace. "You stay where you are. *Don't* go to have a look outside. Find the door to that section and shut it. Don't worry about what the Gallery staff say. Stay as far away from outside doors and windows as possible, for as long as you can. Even when the air seems clear, use something to cover your mouth and nose. The roads are going insane, so I'm not sure when I'll be able to get in to where you are, but I'll call you back when there's news and you can head to Tyler's. You've still got that pass-key?"

"Yes, Mum." The familiar reeling off of instructions helped Madeleine conjure a shadow of a smile, made it possible to respond with the right note of weary patience.

"Good. I'll call you when it sounds like it's safer for you to head to Tyler's. Or if it looks like you should try to spend the night there. Don't let anyone try to make you leave before it's clear."

"I won't. Mum..."

But her mother had hung up. Madeleine laughed, then coughed, and gingerly levered herself into a sitting position. Her back and head did not love her, but her mother did, even if they'd had a lot of trouble talking to each other the last few years. Now all she had to do was overcome a little matter of collapsed exits, and get herself down to Tyler's.

And then? She could pretend to her mother all she liked, but whatever the dust did, Madeleine was surely going to find out. She must have exceeded any minimum dose a thousand times over. Breathed it, swallowed it, had it in her eyes, ground it into her skin.

But that only made her want a bath, to clean herself off, to not be this filthy, fumbling, near-blind creature. "If you want B, finish A," her goal-oriented mother was always saying, and just now that was advice Madeleine was willing to take. Time to get out.

"But first check for other people," Madeleine reminded herself, and sighed.

Lifting her phone, she used it again as a torch, surveying a dim landscape of severed support pillars, broken stairs, and deceptively soft mounds below a wall of stars. Her train had departed as she'd walked up the stairs, and both platforms – what remained of them short of the wall of stars – stood empty. In the middle of the day the station had been far from busy, but there'd been a few people about. She could start with the small control rooms where the station staff retreated after signalling trains to depart, and the elevator–

No, not the elevator. Nothing could be alive in that compressed wedge of glass and metal.

The platform control rooms were double-entrance boxes, not much larger than the elevator. Madeleine headed left, focusing on the nearest doorway: a dark, empty square. A phone began to ring as she approached, and Madeleine edged into the room to a jaunty proclamation of *I'm Too Sexy*. A man lay near-buried in the dust, sprawled face-down across the threshold of the far doorway. Madeleine couldn't see any blood, any obvious injury, but the layer of dust didn't seem disturbed by any rise or fall of chest.

As the phone switched to screaming about messages, she made herself touch his shoulder, shake him, press her fingers to his throat, but chose not to turn him over, to discover what had left him so still. Instead, she moved to the edge of the platform, raising her phone to peer up at the shadowy curve above and the darkness which swallowed the track in either direction.

"Anyone there?" Madeleine called. "Hell–" A new spasm of coughing ripped through her, reviving the pounding in her head. It was impossible not to kick up fresh clouds of dust as she waded through it, and inhaling sharply had been a definite mistake.

If anyone was going to call for help, they would have done so already. All she could hear was falling water. Best to be methodical.

Reluctant to go near the starry wall again, Madeleine merely peered along the shortened platform, then turned to begin picking her way in the other direction. Almost immediately a rounded shape turned under her foot and she nearly went down, dropping her phone into a drift which glowed and sparkled unexpectedly.

"Welcome to the Glitter Mines," Madeleine muttered, digging to retrieve her phone and then investigate what she'd stood on. A scatter of soft drinks, escapees from a tumbled vending machine. That was serendipity, and Madeleine immediately picked up the nearest bottle and twisted the cap. The contents erupted into her face, but even a sticky orange bath was better than dust on dust, and she gulped down the remainder, till her throat no longer felt coated. Discarding the bottle, she wiped her phone, then tucked a few spare drinks into her backpack.

Moving more cautiously, she decided to follow the very edge of the platform, since little of the rubble had reached the track itself, and the curved arch above it was still intact. The platform extended further than the central connecting section, and she walked all the way down to the end and peered along the track as it disappeared into the tunnel to Circular Quay.

No visible damage, and far less dust. The twin overhead lines which powered Sydney trains seemed intact, though she supposed they must be severed by the starry wall. It would be easy for her to climb down and walk out, but she still had a lot of area to check.

About to turn away, Madeleine caught sight of a depression in the dust and, disbelieving, angled her phone for a better look. Footprints. Barely visible, since another layer of pale powder had settled on top, but definitely footprints. Three, maybe four people, had climbed down to the tracks here.

She wasn't angry at being left. People were like that. And it released her from further searching.

The drop to the track was nearly as tall as Madeleine, but it wasn't difficult to lower herself off the edge to the chunky gravel which surrounded the rails. Then she hesitated at the mouth of the tunnel, trying to see more than a few feet along the track before turning to stare back at distant pinpricks, remembering the feel of velvet beneath her fingertips, and then the jolt. Her hands weren't damaged.

"Focus." Now was the time for getting out, not speculating.

Madeleine began to walk, holding her phone up high in case of something more unexpected than dust. The area between the rails was easy to walk on, with only stray lumps of clinker to look out for, and she followed the gentle curve until the only sign of dust were sprinkles which may have come from those who'd gone before her. Stopping to study a dusty print, she suddenly found her coating of grime intolerable.

Shedding her backpack, Madeleine pulled loose the wooden pin she used to hold her crinkle-curling brown hair in a knot at the nape of her neck, and ran her fingers through it over and over, showering an enormous amount of dust onto the rails. She was wearing a strappy sun dress, chosen because of Tyler, and not something she'd ordinarily wear while painting. Shaking and patting it with her hands added to the cloud around her, and she moved a few metres further before trying to beat her backpack clean.

It was impossible to get it all off, but she did manage to reduce her coating to a light powder, and cracked another bottle of soft drink to sip as she walked, fighting off the persistent itch in her throat. The clinker crunched beneath her feet, and occasionally she heard sounds which made her pause, poised to run, telling herself it was only rats, and far from reassured by that since she *hated* rats.

Aliens or rats, whatever it was stayed away, and eventually a point of light appeared ahead and the tunnel began to lighten. Soon Madeleine didn't need her phone to find her way, and she picked up her pace even as she noticed a fine layer of powder covering the track and clinging to the walls. Circular Quay was not an underground station, and a thin coating of dust had settled over it, including on the train – a double-decker Tangara type, big and blocky – which sat on the track at the station platform. Fortunately it was not right up against the tunnel exit: first came a short section of track like a bridge, with a walkway along the side. Madeleine stepped up on this, and immediately looked out to what should be a sweeping view to the Sydney Harbour Bridge across the ferry terminals.

The only trace of the Bridge was a dim grey line. Years ago a great storm of red dust had picked up in Australia's desert heart and swept across New South Wales all the way to Sydney, blanketing the city in a fiery haze. Madeleine had missed it, had woken only to a family car which needed a good wash, but she'd seen pictures of the Bridge hidden almost as completely as this. When her mother had told her that a tower in Hyde Park had let out a cloud of dust, she'd imagined a billow of smoke building to a cumulonimbus, something with edges. Not an entire desert's worth of haze, to hide all landmarks and coat every surface white.

In the muted sunlight she noticed a faint purple tint to the cloud, and the whole thing sparkled, brighter motes catching the eye as they drifted. An alien attack which came in shades of lavender. Beneath this pastel blanket lay a city hushed, unmoving. Usually there were buskers playing down in front of the ferry terminals, their music threading through the chunk and clatter of trains and the rush of cars from the Cahill Expressway above. Today Madeleine could hear only a hum from the Tangara sitting at the platform, and maybe one or two cars creeping at a snail's pace along the road overhead.

Slipping around the metal gate which divided the walkway from the platform, Madeleine headed for the escalators to ground level, glancing at the train's lower row of windows as she moved. Through the film of dust she met the eyes of a half-dozen people staring up at her.

Their open horror made her flinch and for a moment she had a clear and exact picture of how they must see her. Not a skinny teen with big green eyes and hair on a life mission to frizz, but someone coated head to foot in unknown doom. Dead girl walking.

What was the dust doing to her? It itched against her skin, tickled her throat. Did her back and head ache because of bruises, or was that the first symptom?

But Madeleine was almost glad not to be like those who stared up at her. She had escaped the wreck of St James, and in a way gained a second release due to the certainty of her level of exposure. The dust cloud was not a barrier to someone who had waded through the stuff, and she was not locked in an air-conditioned bubble, hoping the train's guard had closed the doors before any dust drifted inside. Would air-conditioning filter the dust out? How long would they stay there, unable to do anything but wait?

Head held high, Madeleine walked past two more carriages, and took the escalator down to street level. She'd lost her ticket, and had a moment as she wriggled past the barrier where she thought she could remember being thrust sideways, falling, and then she was out, walking through a ghost town powdered white.

In the hour since a tower of black had arrived at St James, the usual crowds of Circular Quay – tourists, office-workers, shop staff, ferry passengers – had vanished. Only the seagulls were out, shaking pale lavender wings and fighting over a spill of abandoned potato chips. But, as Madeleine found her way below the overpass and headed east, she realised that there were people everywhere. In cars, the windows wound up tight. Peering out of hastily closed shop fronts and restaurants. Crowded in tight, anywhere there was a door which could be shut, where gaps could be blocked with t-shirts or newspaper, where they could pretend the drift of white-purple had been safely kept at bay. Like the train passengers, waiting out some unlikely Sydney snowstorm. Trying not to breathe.

With visibility of no more than a few metres, it was disorienting walking through the cloud, but Madeleine was fairly certain she was heading in the right direction. A siren made her jump, and she turned sharply, only seeing the cloud and her footprints in the settling layer of powder. The blast didn't belong to any vehicle, but seemed to be coming from all around her. As she moved on, she began to make out words, and realised it was some kind of emergency broadcast, though she couldn't see the loudspeakers.

"...side...threat has been...panic...to seal...shut down...do not go...hospital...damp cloth..."

The snatches of instruction came and went, following Madeleine up to Macquarie Street, trailing her along the spiked metal fence of the Botanic Gardens, and fading completely as she neared the eastern border of the parkland known as The Domain and found the stairs leading off the promontory down to Woolloomooloo. The dust cloud was starting to thin and she could see a good portion of the seaside suburb below. Bracketed by two peninsulas – one park and one naval base – the bay was narrow and entirely dominated by Finger Wharf, with its long stretch of teal and white apartments, and row of impressive boats moored alongside. The water was as pale as the choking sky, a sluggish swell only occasionally breaking the surface layer of dust apart. It made Madeleine wonder how far west Sydney's dams were.

A row of compact, expensive restaurants sat at the street end of the Wharf, their outdoor seating areas an icing-dusted display of half-eaten meals and overturned chairs. Every shutter was closed, every door sealed, and through the glass she could see more collections of the trapped, crowded together, sitting on the floor, huddled in despairing clumps. Staring back at her.

Even when the cloud settled, the dust would still be everywhere. How would anyone get home without kicking it up? How could they get rid of it all?

There was at least no difficulty getting into Tyler's apartment. The electronic key to the residents' section of the central walkway gave her no trouble, and then she was unlocking his door, dropping her backpack, suddenly in a hurry to turn on the shower, to stand fully clothed in a blast of steaming water and watch her violet dress return to its original white and blue. A trembling weakness followed, because shedding that powder coat left her like the others: trapped and fearful. All she had now was the wait for the dying to start.

Shaking, Madeleine stared down at the tinted water draining away, and her attention was caught by her feet, narrow in strappy sandals. There was a crescent of carmine beneath the nail of her right big toe and for a moment she could only stare at it blankly, but then she was curling down, hitting her shoulder on the tap in her haste, scrabbling for soap, a nail brush, needing to erase a thing far more immediate than suspicious powder.

By the time no hint of blood remained, her toe was scoured red and her breath came in short, sharp pants. And then she coughed and spat glittering flecks, and laughed, and sobbed. Lucky! She was so lucky! She was not lying broken, was not a wet, shapeless bundle, a leaking horror to be crawled across and left behind in the dark. She had received a gift of life, a mayfly fortune, precious however temporary.

She would not waste it.

Chapter Three

On non-dusty days Tyler's three-bedroom corner apartment commanded a spectacular view of water, park and city skyline, though the headland blocked any glimpse of the Opera House or Harbour Bridge. The previous weekend, when Madeleine's father had driven her in to drop off her supplies, she hadn't dared do more than tuck easel, canvas stretchers and paints against the near wall of the sunny main room. She'd only met Tyler a handful of times since he'd returned to Australia and found massive success playing a witch on a new TV series about vampire detectives. She'd had no intention of jeopardising their sittings by prying.

Now, hair wrapped in a towel, she took his cordless phone and dialled and redialled while glancing around the open lounge and dining area, then checking out the two spare bedrooms, one utilitarian and the other converted into a shelf-lined office. The master bedroom was spare and tidy and looked like something out of a designer's catalogue. It was only in the massive walk-in wardrobe that she found any sign of personality, and there it overflowed.

One of her earliest memories was of Tyler in a sunhat, face hidden by the broad brim. He obviously still favoured them, had a dozen variations on hooks high around the room. Below was a profusion of jewel-tone scarves, glimmering gowns, and plenty of the skinny jeans and shirtdresses he was commonly photographed in. Gaps here and there – he'd been filming overseas for the past two months – but still a bountiful range of possibilities.

Her own clothes drip-drying in the shower, Madeleine fingered a flower-spattered shirtdress. She was shorter and narrower of shoulder than Tyler, but had the same curveless figure, so likely some of his clothes would fit. A pattern in black and gold caught her eye and she lifted out a silken dressing-gown. Koi carp in an *irezumi* style: brilliant golds and iridescent green against black. She slipped it on, and hit redial once again.

"Give it up, Michael," sighed a warm, throaty voice. "There's nothing you can do about it."

"Tyler."

"Leina?" Tyler laughed, that infamous burble capped with a soft intake of breath, a tiny, shiver-worthy *ah!* "I think I'm going to be a little late, kiddo. Are you at my place?"

Only Tyler had taken seriously her five year-old self's insistence not to be called Maddie. She'd long ago given up that fight, but enjoyed the fact that he remembered.

"Yes. Are you–?"

"Still on the plane. We were just coming in to land. And now, well, there's been an informative lecture on something called bleed air, which apparently requires running engines. And much debate on whether all this floating muck rules out a dash to New Zealand or the bright lights of Tasmania." The amused voice grew serious. "Please tell me you were safely flipping through my dirty picture collection when this happened."

"You have a dirty picture collection?"

"A most graphic one: best you don't look. Now tell me."

"I – almost." There was a wobble threatening her voice, and she knew if she tried to explain St James she'd fall to pieces, so she hurried on. "My parents think I'm at the Art Gallery. I didn't want them to try calling here till I arrived. I...well, I guess I'll know sooner than most what the dust does."

"Any symptoms?"

She hadn't heard her cousin so grave since her broken arm. And what could she tell him? That she was tired, and her back hurt, though the shower had helped her headache. That the dust surely had to be some kind of attack?

"Tyler, I wanted you to do something."

She could almost hear the smile. "If it involves annoying stewardesses I'm all over it. Otherwise—"

"Get someone to take a photograph of you, just as you are now, and email it to me."

"Leina..."

"I came here to paint you, Tyler. I want to—" Her voice had risen, and she swallowed the rest of the sentence, staring out of the window at an only faintly hazy sky, and a talcum-dusted world. Sydney's familiar skyline was made unreal not just because of its powder coating, but by a black lance dwarfing skyscrapers and Sydney Tower. At least double the height of its nearest rival, it thinned to a needle point.

"I want to be painting right now."

"...I'll see what I can do." Tyler paused to murmur to someone off the phone, then added: "I'll call you back if there's any developments here. Take care of yourself, Leina."

There'd been a large laptop in the office, which Madeleine fetched out and was glad to find required no passwords to access the net. She put down her drop-cloth and set up the easel, then went and dug through Tyler's wardrobe until she unearthed an old tracksuit, since it would be a crime to get paint on that dressing-gown. No new email had arrived so she tried to ring her parents and, finally, with a certain level of reluctance, figured out how to make a large screen rise out of a cabinet, and settled down to watch the apocalypse.

"...too early to call this any kind of catastrophe. We are facing something new and unknown, but one thing that leaps out is the placement of these towers: Hyde Park in London and Sydney, Melbourne Park, Central Park, New York, Shinjuku Gyoen, Tokyo. In every city, no matter how densely crowded, the Spire has been placed so as to minimise damage—"

"Still at the expense of dozens, if not hundreds of lives around the world. If this isn't an attack, then it's negligence of—"

The terse, combative words reawakened Madeleine's headache, and she flipped channels until she found a picture of one of the black needles piercing a grassy park. No sign of windows, doors, openings of any kind: just a round, black column narrowing to a point. From a distance you couldn't even see the stars.

The picture changed, showing the park without the tower, with a couple of joggers pounding across it. And then a blink-and-you-miss it moment, an almost instantaneous arrival which was then played again, slowed down to demonstrate that the Spire had *risen*, not landed, and with far less damage than anyone would expect from such an event.

Aliens from underground?

"...clear from viewing the Tokyo, Manila, and Sydney Spires that they are not identical. A comparison to nearby buildings shows the Sydney Spire to be some six hundred metres in height. The Manila spire is more than three times this size, rising over a kilometre and a half above Villamor Golf Course. The narrow base of the Spires compared to their height – in some cases not more than a hundred metres across – suggests that they extend deep underground. At least one hundred – closer to one hundred and fifty cities..."

The Spire currently on-screen – Madeleine had no idea what city it belonged to – began to vanish behind a haze, a vagueness which thickened, extended, became a plume, a cloud, an immensity which grew so quickly that Madeleine wondered how the entire underground of St James Station had not been packed solid. It was clear, though, that the majority of the dust was coming through at the top.

The camera recording the scene had to be kilometres away, but it soon showed nothing but purple-tinted white, and then there was a time-jump in the playback and the Spire began to appear again, looming out of the thinning cloud. Madeleine wondered how many people had been coated as completely as her, and how many were still crammed into the nearest shelter, waiting for the dust to settle. Searching themselves for the any sign of what would happen next.

Singing, slow and sultry. Madeleine shifted, then realised she'd dozed off, and reached for her mobile, murmuring a response.

"Maddie? Sweetheart, are you okay?"

"Dad." Madeleine sat up, rubbing her eyes. "Fine – I was just resting. Did you and Mum get home in time?"

"Don't worry about us: we're all tucked up. Even got the animals in. Listen, you're going to have to sit tight there, at least till it rains. Don't go out while that stuff's still all over the ground. And drink bottled water."

"Lucky there's a coffee shop here." Madeleine muted the television, hoping her father hadn't picked up on the noise, then poked at laptop keys, trying to bring the screen to life. "How long till they know what the dust does?"

"That's anyone's guess. I doubt a visual examination will tell us anything – unless it's bacterial and already known. Smaller animals would react to it first, but of course not necessarily in the same way as humans." Her father, a devoted vet, sighed. "I have a great view of the Nguyens' retriever. Racing up and down, showing no signs of anything yet. It's nothing like so bad out here though – you can only see the dust on dark surfaces."

"But it blew all the way to Leumeah." Her family currently lived in an outlying Sydney suburb, more than fifty kilometres from the city centre. "Dad...I'm sorry. I–"

"All that matters is that you're safe inside." Her father's voice had thickened. "Though once this is all over, you're grounded till you're twenty."

Madeleine kept him on the phone, asking questions he didn't have answers to, then talked to her mother, making up more lies about the Art Gallery, and conversations she hadn't had with Gallery staff. She'd been lying to her mother too often lately, and usually felt quietly guilty about needing to, but was glad for the moment to concoct a reassuring fiction about a highly militant curator holding back any threat of dust with ingenuity and sheer force of will. She was privately sure the Art Gallery of New South Wales would be full of dusty people – it was too close to Hyde Park, and every jogger and lunchtime soccer player in The Domain would have run for it as soon as the dust started drifting down.

As Madeleine finally ended the call, the television switched from something about the Olympics which weren't likely to happen, to a diagram of Sydney, of the cloud spreading south and west, leaving much of the far northern and north-western suburbs untouched. But by then she'd opened her email, and was flipping through a dozen photographs sent by someone called Michael. Tyler Vaughn in a Hunter green shirtdress and black jeans, his long auburn hair gleaming, makeup subdued, lips berry-dark and perfect, giving the photographer a Mona Lisa smile.

Even against a backdrop of airplane seats he looked both inviting and untouchable, rich with mystery. It was Tyler's public face, and nothing like the image Madeleine had wanted to create. But there was a last picture, one obviously captured earlier, of Tyler seated by an airplane window, lipstick chewed to traces, strands of hair caught by the weave of the seat's cover. He must have been staring out the window at the dust, toying with a long topaz necklace, and just turned his head toward the person seated next to him. The green eyes which came from Madeleine's father's family were tired, lids drooping, and his mouth was stern.

And Madeleine was lost to anything but the fragile skin beneath his eyes, the tangled hair, the chips in the polish on his nails. This was just what she'd wanted, and she began sketching furiously, small compositions at first, and then a more detailed piece, before transferring the lines to one of the pre-prepared canvas stretchers.

The Archibald Prize, the focus of all Madeleine's recent ambition, required that portraits be painted from life. Even if that wasn't a rule, Madeleine would normally never consider painting from a flattened image on a computer screen, and she would have aimed for four or more sittings. But this wasn't about proving a point any more, was not about prize money, schools or careers.

It was just the rest of her life.

ooOoo

Tyler had a few thousand litres of hair product. What he lacked was anything resembling food. The refrigerator was empty, unplugged. Every shelf of the tall pantry cupboard was packed solid with boxes of the same brand of shampoo, along with neatly-labelled boxes of junk Tyler had collected over the years: clippings, ticket stubs, even a box dutifully inscribed "Dirty Pictures".

At other times Madeleine would have stopped to look, or at least smiled, but she only bit back a growl of frustration and turned to fling open the doors beneath the kitchen cabinets. The hunger had hit her as an absolute imperative. Not you-haven't-eaten-since-breakfast pangs, but shooting pain, a frightening urgency which left room for nothing but the need to fill her stomach. The cabinets offered only a token collection of saucepans and more boxes of hair product, all of it the brand Tyler had done a commercial for last year.

The upper cabinets. Plates, mugs, glasses, half a jar of instant coffee. And sugar. A kaleidoscope of paper tube packets advertising different cafes, scattered any-which-way across the shelf. Madeleine grabbed a handful, roughly aligned, and tore them open, pouring the contents into her mouth. Again. Again. Struggling to swallow the grainy bounty as discarded packets dropped to the floor, and then there were no more, and she was scratching among the fallen paper, hunting out fragments she'd dropped before fully emptying.

The kitchen floor was a black slate tile, and specked across it were granules of white and brown, lost to her haste. Madeleine, on her hands and knees, contemplated the tiny crystals, then levered herself shakily to her feet and ran a glass of water, then another, drinking until her breathing had slowed.

A few dozen packets of sugar weren't nearly enough, but now that the keenest edge of her hunger had been dulled it occurred to Madeleine to pull out several of the boxes of shampoo, revealing a small supply of packets and tins at the back of the pantry cupboard. It seemed Tyler didn't live completely on take-out.

"Thank you for not making me lick the floor," Madeleine muttered, and wondered how many planeloads of people were arguing over their last packet of peanuts.

She ate a tin of pineapple chunks while heating pumpkin soup, and drank the soup lukewarm while heating a second can. It had stopped hurting by then, so she poured the second serving into her mug to sip at a less frantic pace.

The still-muted television was showing a smothered road, cars creeping along, and one racing as if it could outpace the air itself. Slow or fast, they lifted a trail of dust. Madeleine had deliberately angled her canvas away from the screen, not willing to either watch it or turn it off. Finding that feeling had not changed she unlocked the sliding door to the balcony and stepped out into cool autumn sunset, the city skyline outlined against crimson. The air itself occasionally caught alight, motes of glitter blazing fiery warning of their presence. She drank her soup and watched them drift.

Shutting the hushed world back outside, Madeleine scrupulously cleaned up the mess she'd made in the kitchen, then hesitated between canvas and TV. She would have chosen canvas, but the presenter was holding up his wrist, his face stiff with suppressed emotion as he unbuttoned his cuff and pulled it back, displaying what looked like an old bruise, a flush of green beneath the skin. Then there were other people, men and women who usually stayed behind the camera, leaning forward to show more wrists, green and blue, and their faces were the same as the presenter's – tight with distress and determination.

"...in our Sydney studio at the time of the Spire's arrival. We could not have been quicker sealing the doors, and the Building Manager shut down the air-conditioning plant as a matter of priority, and closed every vent possible. It made no difference. Every single person in the building has begun exhibiting the symptoms observed in the heavy-exposure group broadcasting from Seoul. We can only repeat the medical advisory. Do not travel. If you are infected, do not attempt to reach a hospital. Even if you are indoors, cover both mouth and nose with multiple layers of damp..."

Madeleine was in the bathroom, pulling the oversized tracksuit top over her head, shucking the pants, staring at herself in the mirrored wall. Blue wrists. Not a flush of colour beneath the skin, but bold streaks extending to the inside of her elbows. More at armpit and groin, midnight blue. She turned, considering the true bruises on her back, dim by comparison, and spotted more midnight blue at the back of her knees.

Pressing the skin of her right wrist produced none of the pain response of a bruise. The skin was warm, soft, normal. She didn't feel sick, beyond having eaten far too much too quickly.

"...just in," the presenter was saying as Madeleine returned. "The Seoul group has reported intense, urgent hunger, an almost crippling–"

Madeleine hit Mute and turned away. If anything worse happened, she'd know it as soon as anyone, and she didn't like the way the presenter kept having to stop and swallow, didn't like what his voice rather than his words were telling her. It pulled her into thinking of a whole world looking at their wrists, clogging the phone lines, melting down Twitter and Tumblr and Facebook, comparing symptoms, reaching out in their overwhelming need to know what it all meant, how far it would spread, what would come next, after the hunger. If she spent her time thinking about how she would die, she wouldn't finish.

Thankfully she was working with quick-drying acrylics, had already laid down the base colours, and could now build detail. The clothes, necklace, hair, polish, and blue seat made a vivid mix, and she would have to work to stop Tyler's skin from receding, or losing the magnetic quality of pale green eyes.

Racing symptom three.

ooOoo

Drumming rain, lukewarm and persistent.

Sitting tilted in a corner, Madeleine puzzled over why she felt the rain should be hotter, and turned her head away from slick tiles. She'd been leaning against them so long it felt like her skin was peeling out of a mould. Lifting a hand she could trace the indentation of grouting below her eye. Velvet.

She blinked, saw tinted glass, and recognised the outer wall of Tyler's enormous shower, and then looked at her foot, her leg, all the way up to the sodden hem of the tracksuit top. Midnight blue. With stars.

What surprise she felt was for the lack of pain. Pain had been the constant, the dominating force which had overtaken every other consideration. It had started in her lower back, tiny twinges, and she'd thought it just another consequence of her marathon at the canvas, a companion to the stretched ache between her shoulder-blades. The pangs had spread to her legs, her arms. Not too bad at first, an intermittent ache that made her want to shift and move. But then sharp, deep pains along her bones, making her gasp and jerk and stamp about.

For a while she'd been able to work through, but one jolt had taken her at a bad moment and she'd slashed a fine line of white across half the canvas. After quickly repairing what she could, she'd had to step away. Better to leave the piece unfinished than destroy what she'd achieved. Particularly Tyler's hand, toying with the long topaz necklace. That was some of the best work she'd ever done.

Her memories were hazy after the last of the painting. Another patch of extreme hunger, and a long time on the couch, shifting and twisting. Random images from the television: black towers and people in Hazmat suits. Roadblocks. Blue and green animals, everything warm-blooded showing stain. Crackling feedback on her phone when she tried to answer a call.

It had been daylight when the tremors and cramps started, knots beneath her skin which made her cry out and whimper. That was why she'd ended up in the shower, needle-hard water stitching her skin because the heat and the pulsing force had been the only thing which had helped at all.

She pulled off the sopping tracksuit and by slow degrees drew her feet up, levered herself on to them, and shut the water off. Then she shuffled with geriatric gait to lean against the mirrored wall. This time she didn't need to look for patches of blue skin, but catalogued instead what was familiar. Her head, barring a patch below her right eye, remained its usual untanned self. Her neck, except for a line up the back. Some of her right hand and the thumb and two fingers of her left. That was all Madeleine.

The rest, from just below her collarbone down, was an unbroken dark blue, studded with motes of light. Galaxies, nebulae and fiery novae. They weren't on the surface of her skin, but seemed to float below it, as if she had become a window on a night sky at the centre of the universe.

And the way it felt! The mirror she leaned against, the tiles beneath her feet. Everything she touched was a confusing mix of the texture she expected, but also velvet. And when she ran blue palm along blue arm, it was velvet on velvet.

There were still fine hairs along her forearm. Peering close she could make out the faint lines and ridges at her wrist, and her fingers showed the prune effect of long exposure to water. If it wasn't for the shimmering light beneath, and the feeling of velvet, she could tell herself that she'd simply been stained blue. But her skin was not her skin.

Was she turning into the tower?

Memory of warm stone, wondrous and strange, flooded through her. Touching it had sent a tingle all through her, but then it had thrown her away, blasted her–

The mirror shattered, and Madeleine was tossed forward, bouncing off the basin and falling to her hands and knees. Fragments of glass and tile rained down around her as she cowered, hands over her head, but none of it touched her, and she was aware of strength flowing out of her in a way which felt as uncontrolled as a throat wound. She was doing this, destroying everything around her even as she shielded herself.

Madeleine pulled it back, an effort which left her limp, barely able to lift her head to survey her handiwork in a room suddenly dim, lit only through the open door. Shards of glass and ceramic lay everywhere. The mirrored wall, ceiling light, the basin, shower screen, even the tiles – all looked like someone had taken a sledgehammer to them. But she wasn't injured at all. Not even the smallest fragment had reached her, though she would now have to find some way to move without cutting herself to shreds.

The television was still on. Madeleine could hear a voice with a British accent, talking about death tolls. About 'blues' and 'greens', a mandatory no travel order, and the possibility of person-to-person transmission.

She was hungry again.

Chapter Four

Tyler's inadequate pantry finally drove Madeleine outside. It was Saturday morning, four days after the arrival of the Spires, and she no longer felt like she would keel over if she walked any distance, but she might if she didn't find something to eat soon. Whatever else being blue meant for her, it made skipping a meal a major problem.

Overnight rain had washed Woolloomooloo clean of obvious dust. High white clouds studded a ceiling of dazzling azure, and the sun's warmth tempered a fresh wind. She could hear some kind of electronic music, but it was too faint and distant to identify the source. Otherwise, silence. The long row of boats bobbed lazily in unshrouded water, and high fencing hid the lower apartments' patio gardens, so it wasn't until she reached the restaurants, their outdoor eating areas still in disarray, that Madeleine had any reminder of disaster beyond the clean black shaft of the Spire dominating the cityscape.

She'd hoped to find the restaurants – well, not open for business, but perhaps one or two of the dozen with doors ajar. But a line of shutters and solid glass doors greeted her, and she'd collected too many cuts in awkward places making her way out of the wrecked bathroom to be eager about breaking in. There was, however, something unexpected where the wharf widened and curved around to its second mooring. A café table set with a brilliant white tablecloth. Seated very upright beside it was a girl, pouring herself a cup of tea.

And eating scones. Scones with jam and cream.

The girl looked around as Madeleine approached, providing a glimpse of starry blue streaks marking her throat. She was short, curvy, her eyes and light brown skin suggesting Asian heritage, though her hair was a wild mass of spiral curls, held back from her face by a red tartan bandanna. Her eyes were swollen, but she managed a crooked sort of smile.

"Table for one?"

Madeleine laughed, and then stopped because her laughter worked as well as the girl's smile. "I'm having to hold myself back from mugging you for your little pot of jam."

"Ha." This time the smile worked, warm with wry edges. "I could tip you into the bay before you got so much as a spoonful. Sit down, I'll bring some more out."

Hunger overrode any pretence of restraint, and Madeleine swallowed the remaining half-scone before the girl had taken two steps, then quickly emptied what was left of the little serving pot of jam and cream, running her finger around the interior to catch the last traces. The tea was sugarless, but Madeleine drank it anyway, and finished off the milk. Then she pulled off her backpack and sat down, embarrassed, staring at her sandals poking from beneath the hem of the green maxi-dress she'd liberated from Tyler's closet.

Her toes glimmered back at her.

"One Devonshire tea, special Blue serving," the girl said, putting down a tray holding a half-dozen scones, whipped cream, and a jar of plum jam. She picked up the teapot and left again, and by the time she was back, lugging a chair while balancing a tray, Madeleine had inhaled four still-warm scones and was spreading jam on the fifth.

"Sorry." Madeleine had recovered enough to put down the jam and make room for a larger teapot and accompanying cups and milk. "Thanks."

"No problem – it keeps hitting me like that. You've got to stay ahead of it." She surveyed Madeleine frankly, gaze lingering on her face and hands, and Madeleine, uncomfortable with the extent of her blueness, was glad she'd worn a long-sleeved shirt knotted over the dress. "I'm Noi."

"Madeleine."

They drank tea in silence. Madeleine, who constantly received report cards declaring "does not work well with others" and "does not participate in group activities", searched for the right thing to say. With a glance toward the restaurant, *Nikosia*, she tried: "Did you stay in there the entire time?"

"No." Noi's voice dropped. "Once the stain started showing, everybody went home. I...there's no-one at my home now, so I came back to check on Niko."

Madeleine awkwardly took another bite of scone, giving the girl time to take a few deep breaths. "Niko?"

"My boss. I knew he lived alone, that no-one would be around to check on him." Her voice wavered again, then firmed, and a ghost of a smile emerged. "I've only been here a few months – first year of my apprenticeship – and he was a little tin-pot dictator who had me on prep and cleaning for forever. But he took me on, so I owed him for that, and, well. He was in his apartment."

Madeleine didn't need to ask for details: television had fed her more than enough statistics. In the areas of heaviest dust exposure the first deaths had been recorded within twenty-four hours of the darkening of wrists, though for most the crisis point was after the two to three day point. Green stains were slower to regain strength, but so far had a much higher survival rate. Even among Greens it still took the very young, the sick and weak, the elderly – and a great many others who were none of these. Surviving Blues were rare. Noi had stayed at her home till everyone there died, and then returned to find this Niko dead as well. Making scones and drinking tea in the sun was a better response than Madeleine would likely have managed.

"My parents haven't shown any signs yet," she said, glad and guilty to be able to say that. "They live at Leumeah, and had a little time to prepare."

"That's southwest, right? Are you going to head out there?"

"And risk letting in the dust – or infecting them if this *is* infectious?" Madeleine shook her head. "I'm borrowing my cousin's apartment. I'll stick there until–" She stopped, unsure what limit there was to 'until'. Tyler had sent her a text two days ago, letting her know he was still at Sydney Airport, no longer on the plane. Then, nothing.

"Want to go look at it?"

Noi was gazing up at the Spire, and Madeleine suddenly regretted not bringing her sketchpad, and then was overwhelmingly glad for that reaction. Since she'd woken she'd spent hours staring at Tyler's portrait, but had inexplicably lacked any urge to complete it. She'd thought she'd lost something, but with Noi her usual drive to capture people around her had revived.

But Madeleine also wanted to see the Spire again up close, to compare skin to stone, so she finished off the last of the scones, and helped Noi put her table away and lock up. Noi had obviously been tidying earlier – *Nikosia* was the only restaurant where the outside tables had been cleared of dusted food. Then they started up the curving multi-flight stair to The Domain.

Noi stopped abruptly, and Madeleine barely avoided running into her. Then she saw the reason: an ungainly tumble of school uniform and blue-patched limbs sprawled at the foot of the next flight of stairs. The second body Madeleine had seen in person.

"He has stars," Noi said, fingers digging into Madeleine's arm.

After a beat, Madeleine understood Noi's reaction. The stars developed after the cramps, at what the TV was calling the survival point for Blues.

"Maybe there's a stage we haven't hit yet," she said, approaching the body reluctantly.

He'd been around her own age, and what she thought of as half-made: someone who'd shot up in height recently, and was all bony wrists and coat-hanger shoulders, not yet fully filled out. Wide mouth, strong nose, and very straight, dark brows below a mop of black hair which didn't quite curl. Madeleine immediately wanted to draw him as well, which felt a wildly inappropriate thing to do with the body of some poor random boy who had died of being Blue.

"I think he's breathing," Noi said.

"Could he have fainted from hunger?" Madeleine reached down to press fingers to the boy's throat, and easily found a pulse.

Noi joined the examination. "There's an enormous lump on the side of his head," she said, and showed Madeleine red-streaked fingers. "I guess we better take him back to the restaurant. This should be interesting."

Madeleine rescued a pair of rimless glasses about to slide out the boy's pocket, then she and Noi carefully straightened him and tried to work out how to get someone taller than either of them down several unforgiving flights of stairs.

"If I go first, with his knees hooked over my shoulders, and you lift him under the armpits?" Noi suggested.

They experimented with this, and eventually managed to get enough of the boy off the ground to move down. The steep, lowest flight was hardest, both of them struggling, but not daring to stop. It wasn't that he was impossibly heavy, but they needed to keep pace with each other or be pulled off balance. The last few steps were particularly wobbly.

"I don't think I've recovered as much as I thought," Madeleine panted, as they propped him against the end of the railing.

"In future, I'm only rescuing people who faint at the bottom of stairs." Noi looked down at the boy doubtfully. "Maybe I should go find some sort of cart."

"Hey! HEY!"

The shout came from above, heralding three more boys stampeding down the stair.

"If you're the cavalry, your timing sucks," Noi said, unimpressed by their rapid approach.

"What happened?" asked the tallest boy, and Madeleine had to blink because he was movie-star handsome: precisely symmetrical features, flawless brown skin, silky black hair, athletic build. Even his voice was fantastic: a mix of Indian and plummy English accent which was candy to the ear.

"We found him on the stair," she said, and felt silly for her defensive tone. "He's hit his head."

"Told you Fish was pushing himself too hard," said the boy nearest Madeleine, a strawberry blond well-furnished with freckles. His blue eyes sloped down at the corners, giving him a weary look, but his hands moved briskly over the unconscious boy's head, locating the lump as if he could learn something from it.

The third boy was the shortest, his face fashioned from an imp template, with pointed chin and fly-away eyebrows which darted toward the sandy-blond hair at his temples. He might as well have 'Mischief' stamped on his forehead.

"You two carried him down the stair?" His grin took up half his face. "Damn, I'm sorry I missed that."

"Yeah, yeah, the floor show's at eleven," Noi replied. "Maybe we should get your friend out of the sun. We were taking him to the wharf."

"Lead the way. I'm Pan. This is Nash and Gav. Looks like you met Fish already."

As Madeleine and Noi introduced themselves, the first two boys hoisted Fish up on linked arms.

"Was there anyone nearby?" Nash, the tallest one, asked. "Could someone have attacked him?"

"I haven't seen anyone but Madeleine," Noi said. "We were going up to look at the Spire."

"We've just been." Pan glanced over his shoulder, and up. "Fish wanted to do some comparisons of our stars to the ones of the Spire. You seriously think someone hit him, Nash?"

"It would be stupid to ignore the possibility. We still haven't the least idea what is going on."

"Why compare your stars to the Spires'?" Noi also looked over her shoulder, craning back to sight the tip of the Spire.

"To see if they matched in pattern, or even reacted." He glanced down at Fish, at the patches of blue on his exposed arms. "And to see if having stars would let us through the barrier around it."

"Did it?" Madeleine asked, interested. "Did you touch it?"

"No. The barrier remains. But it was only a first look."

Unlocking the sliding entrance door of *Nikosia*, Noi led them into the small indoor dining area, pulling one of the tables aside to clear access to the long, padded seat which ran up the right wall.

"There's a first aid kit somewhere. Be right back."

"Have you been cooking?" Pan asked, sniffing the restaurant's fresh-baked aroma as his friends manoeuvred Fish onto the too-narrow seat. Then he laughed: "Man, you won't even have to look at people to tell which ones are Blues – just wave something edible and we'll come running."

"Are you all–?" Madeleine asked, and Pan held his arms out, showing starry blue palms and a thick stripe disappearing under the sleeves of his jacket.

Nash was more obviously Blue, with all of the back of his neck that shade, the stars rather faint, and Gav – wearing a black blazer over a school uniform similar to Fish's – stripped it off to reveal all of his left arm and most of his right was blazing with light against a midnight field.

"Only Blues are out and about, I think," he said, hooking the blazer over a chair. "We fell over quickest, once the stain showed up, but the Greens at school can still barely get out of bed."

"School? You stayed at your school?"

"We're from Rushies," Pan explained, gesturing at an embroidered gold crest on the blazer. "Rushcutters Bay Grammar. It's one of the biggest boarding schools in Sydney. Two-thirds of the students are day boys, but the rest of us are either from out of town, or overseas. No way to get–"

He broke off as Noi emerged from the kitchen, first aid kit in one hand, and a baking tray half-full of scones balanced on the other.

"One of you grab the jam and butter I set out," she said. "There's drinks in the walk-in to the right."

She handed the tray off to Nash and then began sorting through the first aid kit while everyone else attacked the scones. Even Madeleine had another, surprised at herself.

"Is this extreme appetite thing going to keep up, do you think?" she asked Nash.

"Who can tell?" He didn't seem as hungry as his friends, only eating one scone for the pile they'd inhaled. "*BlueGreen* – one of the data compilation sites – is suggesting that the stars indicate some level of stored energy, and that is why there's a need for increased food intake. Did both of you experience the surge after the stars developed?"

"Surge?" Noi paused, holding a pad of antiseptic-soaked cotton wool. "The poltergeist imitation? Yeah, I sent our coffee table flying."

Madeleine nodded, and rubbed her arm where her shirt hid a plaster-treated cut.

"It may relate to the field which stops anyone from approaching the Spires," Nash said. "The Spire has stars. Blues have stars. The Spire has a shield. Blues experience the surge. And only Blues are so ridiculously hungry. So far." He sighed, and looked quickly at Noi's patient, who had shifted in response to her dabbing. "We went down to Circular Quay after trying the Spire, because someone had reported a Blue dog, and small animals surviving are so rare we wanted to document it."

"An exercise in futility, with bonus rotting seagulls," Pan said. "Gav, you have a car, right? I don't think Fish is going to be up to a walk even if he does wake up."

"Right." Gav grabbed his blazer and another scone and headed to the door. "See you soon."

"I think he'll be okay," Noi said, as Pan hovered at her elbow. "He at least reacts to the antiseptic, and there wasn't that much bleeding. Is he a good friend of yours?"

"Fish? Never even spoke to him before Friday. I think I might have seen him once or twice, but he's in year eleven – Nash and I are year ten – and Fish is a day boy."

"Then why was *he* still at the school?" Madeleine asked, reasonably. School was the last place she would have wanted to hang out.

"Microscopes. Rushies is big on Theatre and Science, so the school's all auditoriums and laboratories. Fish stayed up Thursday night studying himself. Then he moved on to everyone else. Did I tell you I went off at him, Nash?"

"It does not surprise me, temper-boy," Nash said, brows lifting.

"After he recovered from the surge, he divided everyone up," Pan explained. "So now we have Greens Dorm, Blues Dorm, and the big one for those who didn't make it. Fish broke the Greens up into groups and tried different things on them. Aspirin, heat packs, cold packs, sugary drinks, water only. Teddy – Teddy Rasmussen from 10B – he was doing so bad, and Fish told me to switch him from hot packs to cold packs and keep checking his pulse and writing down all the changes and I just started shouting. Told him I never knew anyone better suited to their name, that fish were warm in comparison. He just waited until I wound down and then asked me if I knew the best way to take out a zombie."

"Head shot," Noi said promptly.

Pan nodded at her. "And wooden stakes for vampires, and silver bullets for werewolves. And penicillin for bacteria. But we don't have the slightest idea what to do about dust and starry towers. Information is a weapon, a defence, a first step to everything according to Fish, and we need to gather as much as possible before the next wave of infections, so we can act rather than react. He and the other big contributors on *BlueGreen* even think they've found a way to increase Green survival rates. So I've wanted to punch him a few times, but I'm feeling a bit 'Oh, Captain! My Captain!' at the moment as well. All the teachers left, y'know? Had their own families to look after, though I guess some of them meant to come back. Fish stayed, and now he's gone and fallen down some stairs. Which is distinctly uncool of him, really."

Nash reached out and put a calming hand on the shorter boy's shoulder, and Pan let out his breath.

"End soliloquy," he muttered. "But, damn, it would be stupid to die from falling down, after all this."

"Seriously, I don't think he's that bad," Noi said, snapping the kit shut. "His heart rate and breathing seem to be normal, anyway, and that's as far as my basic first aid is going to take us. We'll put some ice on the lump, see if that helps. How many are left at that school of yours? Do you need food to take back?"

They moved to the kitchen, discussing the boarding school's catering resources, and perishable food which should be eaten first. Of the three hundred boarders at the school, sixty-two were still alive. Twelve Blues, and the rest Greens not ready to look after themselves. The Fish boy had probably collapsed from exhaustion, rather than hunger or mystery attacks.

"Is your name really Pan?" Noi asked, hunting out a box to hold milk and meat while Madeleine wrapped ice in a cloth serviette.

"Lee Rickard, at your service," Pan said, with a little bow.

"Then why Pan?"

"Can't you guess? Should I go find some green tights? I've played him three times – totally typecast." He mimed a quick sword fight, dancing around the cramped kitchen. "And this is Avinash Sharma. Gav is Gavin Wells, and sleeping beauty out there is Fisher Charteris."

Madeleine glanced through the one-way panel set in the kitchen door and started, because 'sleeping beauty' was gone. She pushed the door open, and spotted him standing in the outdoor eating section. As she watched he lifted a shaky hand to his head, and sat down on the nearest chair.

Fish – Fisher – didn't react as she approached, all his attention focused out, and up. Madeleine paused before speaking because she still didn't have her sketch pad and she badly wanted to draw all five of her new acquaintances, but this one most of all. With those dark, straight brows he must always appear a trifle severe, but right now, his light brown eyes fixed on the Spire, he looked positively murderous.

"Plotting revenge?" Her attempt at lightness fell flat as he jumped, then clutched his head all the harder. "Sorry. Try this." She pressed the serviette against his head, then almost dropped it when he tried to bat it away. Once he'd realised what it was and took hold, she stepped back because now his glare was directed at her.

"What are you talking about?" he asked.

"I just – well, you looked angry."

The glare faded, and he glanced back at the Spire. "Aren't you? All this useless death. Don't you want to tear that down and stamp on the pieces?"

"I–" Madeleine felt off-balance, and wondered if there was something wrong with her for not feeling that way. "I guess I've been thinking of it as a natural disaster," she said. "Though I suppose 'natural' is entirely the wrong word for giant starry towers."

"Fish!" Pan led the others out of the restaurant, and slid a box of food onto a nearby table. "Damn, you had us worried. What happened? Were you attacked?"

The older boy stared at him blankly, then his mouth twisted with sudden amusement. "Did he fall or was he pushed?" he asked. "I wish I could pretend to something less feeble than feeling dizzy. Where's Gavin?"

"Gone to get his car. Madeleine and Noi here found you."

Fisher seemed a unhurried sort of person, taking his time looking first Noi and then Madeleine up and down. His gaze lingered on Madeleine's starry feet and she self-consciously tucked them beneath the hem of her dress, prompting a quick look of comprehension.

"You both have stain covering at least a quarter of your bodies, yes?" he said, with an air of a theory confirmed. "Only the stronger Blues seem to be fully recovered, even though the surge initially left us barely able to move."

"Lucky us." Noi held up her hands, the palms glimmering with light. "I can't stand not knowing what comes next. Will that thing spit out more dust? Will we keep changing?"

"What happens next is rotting corpses," Fisher said, surveying the city skyline, window upon mute window. "Because people went home to die, it isn't as bad as it could be, but at the very least it will be unpleasant. It may even be a bigger problem around the city fringes, where the survival rate is higher, and the living are more thoroughly mixed with the dead. The government needs to stop futilely trying to ban travel, and start finding a way to arrange corpse disposal. Or at least ensure that the water supply isn't compromised, so we don't exchange one sickness for another."

"They'll stop flailing eventually," Pan said. "Maybe. It's better to still have the government than be like the US, anyway, with all its new presidents. And China. And Pakistan and...and...hey, nuclear weapons aren't kept near big cities, right?"

"If it's nuclear you're worried about, concentrate on power plants," Nash put in. "And, see that?" He pointed at a distant thread of smoke rising beyond the parkland which blocked their view of the harbour centre and the North Shore. "That is our now. Non-automated, high manpower vital services, like fire fighters and doctors – none of those are here. International transport is...not necessarily gone, just limited. In the medium term we will see fuel rationing. At this time there are thousands of functioning towns and cities worldwide, with police and hospitals and all that we're used to, but they're overwhelmed by all the people who've fled out of the Spire cities, and transport of food will be limited. Add to that the dust still circulating on the wind, meaning there will continue to be outbreaks, anywhere and everywhere. But...so far there has been no sign that this is transmissible person-to-person, so we are not beyond the point of recovery."

Nash glanced up at the Spire, not adding the obvious caveat, then turned his gaze on the long wharf stretching out into the water.

"Tyler Vaughn lives here," he remarked, giving Madeleine a tiny shock.

"So do Nikki Zee and Jason Kadia," Noi said, nodding. "I think only Nikki Zee's in residence right now, though. I saw Tyler Vaughn a few times when I first started working here, since he uses the restaurants a lot. But not lately."

"Filming *Five Blades* in LA," Pan said knowledgably. "Which, dammit, I was looking forward to."

Not at all wanting to talk about Tyler, Madeleine unhooked the pair of glasses she'd rescued and handed them to Fisher. "We managed not to stand on these," she said.

"Thanks." He held them up so he could look through the lenses, then tucked them away. "Something far from easily replaced."

"Food does not worry me as much as medicine," Nash said. "Any kind of–" He looked down, eyes widening, and fished a phone from a pocket, glanced at the screen and was beaming by the time he brought it to his ear.

"Saashi!" With an apologetic gesture he turned, talking rapidly in a language Madeleine didn't recognise, and walked a little way down the wharf.

"His sister," Pan explained. "He hasn't been able to get through to her, and wasn't sure if she was in Mumbai or still on location." At Noi's confused look he added: "Nash is from a big-time Bollywood film family. Mum's an actress, Dad is a producer. Saashi's just starting out as a director."

"So which one is Nash aiming to be?" Noi asked, with an appreciative glance at the tall, well-made boy. "Are they the singing, dancing kinds of Bollywood movies?"

"Most of them. Nash dances like a dream, but he's a horrible singer. Not that he'll let that stop him – he'll probably end up directing after a few years acting, then h-he'll–" Pan stuttered to a halt, his lively features falling still.

After a moment, Noi began deliberately peppering Fisher with questions, producing a brief lecture on decomposition, cholera and quicklime. Madeleine found herself watching, aware of a familiar sense of withdrawal and disliking herself for it. For the last few years people had been something she loved to draw, but no longer allowed herself to be drawn to, which was not an attitude suited to current circumstances. But still she felt that distance.

The arrival of an apple-green Volkswagen – the curve-top model from the 2000s – was a welcome distraction. Madeleine took a box, and followed along behind Fisher, glad to see that while he moved with care he was no longer wobbly.

"What the hell is with your taste in cars, Gav?" Pan asked as they reached the roadside.

The strawberry blond boy grinned as he popped open the compact boot. "Girls love it," he explained, and mock-leered at Noi and Madeleine. "Suddenly inspired to get to know me better, right?"

"Maybe," Madeleine said, unable to not smile a little.

"Cheerful, compact and zippy?" Noi asked, tucking the food box in the boot. "Is that what you're trying to tell me?"

"Fuel-efficient, can go for hours," Gav responded, blush competing with an ever-widening grin. But that faded to solemn consideration. "Want me to come back for you two? We're getting pretty well organised, and we've sworn off re-enacting *Lord of the Flies*. You can even have an exemption to the uniform rules."

"I'm waiting for my cousin," Madeleine said, and was horrified to find tears suddenly pricking her eyes. "He was – I should wait a couple more days."

"I'll stick with Madeleine," Noi said immediately. "It'll give me a chance to go through the kitchens here."

"Exchange numbers," Fisher ordered, sitting sideways on one of the front seats.

"And call us without delay if there is a need," Nash added, his candy-cream voice rich with concern and reassurance.

It took only a few moments to bump phones and contact-pass numbers, Twitter handles, email addresses. Pan added a quick explanation of their school's location, perhaps fifteen minutes away by foot.

"All right now?" Noi asked, waving as Gav pulled his apple-green chick magnet away from the curb.

"Yeah. Sorry – I really hero-worshipped my cousin when I was a kid, and I...just wish I knew."

Noi was silent and, aware of inadvertently prodding a wound, Madeleine turned and surveyed the long building jutting out into the bay. She wasn't quite sure why Noi had stayed with her, and, as usual, she had an overwhelming desire to find some space to herself and draw. But Noi and her reasons for being there brought forth a competing impulse.

"How many apartments are there on this wharf?"

"Not a clue. A few hundred, I guess."

"If around a quarter of that school survived, there must be other people here. Probably Greens who can't get about yet."

"Probably."

"Is there some kind of security office which would have keys?"

The shorter girl stared at the enormity of the wharf, then let out her breath and resurrected her wry smile. "Never pictured myself as a ministering angel. But I'm game if you are."

"Last thing I want to do," Madeleine said. "We'd better get started."

Chapter Five

"Science Boy must live on this site," Noi said, as Madeleine fumbled with keys. The girl waved the tablet computer she'd brought along. "No wonder he fell down – no sleep."

"Did you find what's the best thing for Greens?"

"I found a big argument over it." Noi fell silent as Madeleine slotted one of the master keys into the lock and turned. The door opened an inch, then caught on a chain as sound spilled out: a television, the now-familiar voice of an Australian Broadcasting Corporation presenter based in Canberra. And a smell.

"Should we knock again?"

"Not if you want to get through this entire building this century. Watch out." After the Building Manager's office, they'd taken a side-trip to a maintenance room in the garage for, as Noi put it, a Ministering Angel Toolkit. This included an upright, three-shelf trolley they'd stacked with food, and a red and black pair of bolt cutters, which nipped through the chain effortlessly.

Madeleine pushed the door open, but neither of them made any move. The full impact of the smell was enough to guess what was inside.

"We're going to have to check," Noi said. "If we're doing this properly."

Before Madeleine could say anything the girl lifted her chin and walked into the apartment. Madeleine followed, calling out "Hello?" in case the smell hadn't told the whole story.

Two people were on the couch, sitting snugged together beneath a blanket, one man's head resting on the other's shoulder. They looked to have been in their fifties or sixties, and Madeleine could almost think them peacefully asleep if not for the waxy pallor, and the single fly which had found its way into the apartment, to spin joyfully in the corner of the smaller man's mouth.

Gulping, and then trying not to breathe, Madeleine looked away and found Noi opening the nearest door.

"Look in all the rooms, check the hot plates, turn off any running water, the TV, then out," the girl said, with a fixed determination.

"Hot plates?"

"Kitchen rules," Noi replied, shrugging. "But it's worth thinking fire prevention."

Madeleine moved to obey, finding no active hot plates, no running water, and no visible way to turn the television off. The remote was probably somewhere on the couch, and she felt bizarrely that it would be impolite to go hunting for it, disrespectful to disturb the dead. And she didn't want to touch. But Noi spotted a discreet cord, a wall switch, and was reaching for that when Madeleine said:

"Wait."

The TV showed a van crammed full of people and personal belongings driving toward a roadblock. The thin hum of the engine dropped, then picked up again. Then a tinkle, breaking glass, and the van screeched to a stop. Little chopped-off noises followed as it hastily reversed, turned, and accelerated away, one headlight punched out.

"Where is that?" Madeleine asked. "That's not here, is it?"

"That's everywhere," Noi flicked the power switch. "Come on."

Madeleine wanted to protest that Australians wouldn't do that, but couldn't. She followed Noi out and closed the door as the shorter girl wrote "D2" on a diagram she'd found in the building manager's office.

"I guess so long as we stay in the city centre we won't have to worry about that," Madeleine said. "Everyone here would have to already be infected. Teaming up with that school is probably still a good idea, though."

"No, I'm glad you said no to that. Here." Noi picked up the tablet computer and passed it to Madeleine, then began pushing their trolley toward the next door.

The tablet was displaying a very recent post on the *BlueGreen* site titled "Blues dangerous?" It was a summary of stories of Blues hurting people, with repeats of the surge, or jolts of 'invisible lightning'. And two incidents, one in Singapore, the other in Norway, of Green survivors, thought to be recovering, who had been found dead after coming into contact with a Blue.

"I'd rather give it a few days," Noi said, as she rapped on the new door. "See what happens."

Madeleine read through the article in silence, then fumbled for the keys, painfully conscious of the patch of midnight and stars below her left eye, of the whole of her body feeling like velvet beneath the concealing dress. There was a lot still to learn about being Blue.

ooOoo

The apartments at Finger Wharf were grouped into two long parallel buildings, joined by a connecting roof over a massive central throughway where modern metal and glass sat strangely mixed with wooden walkways and arching old-fashioned conveyer belts preserved as decorations. There was a hotel nearest the street, and a smaller separate building enjoying the prime views at the northern end. Three hundred apartments, a hundred hotel rooms. Noi and Madeleine rapped on doors until their knuckles were sore, and then they used the blunt end of the keys, their shouts "hello?" becoming cursory as they toured through death.

Most of the world – or at least this portion of Sydney – had died curled up on the couch, watching television. These were much easier to deal with than the handful who, like Madeleine, had ended up in their showers, finding some comfort from the pelting water. They were usually at least partially naked, the marbling of flesh and the beginnings of bloat difficult not to look at when reaching to shut off the water. The splashing left Madeleine feeling contaminated.

In one apartment the windows and door were so effectively sealed with tape and plastic that Madeleine swore she could hear the room inhale when they broke through. She had to wonder whether it was the stain or suffocation which had killed the small family inside. In a different apartment there were nearly a dozen people, with empty bottles – champagne, beer – everywhere, and a partially-eaten sheet cake where someone had roughly scrubbed off 'Birthday', and spelled out 'Apocalypse' with shining silver cachous.

Death had not come all at once. Most Blues had died quickly, but many of the Greens had obviously lingered over the past three days, so the sick-sweet aroma of rot was not always present, though there were often other smells. Bowels relaxed in death. A couple of times pungent incense made their eyes sting. In one bedroom scented candles still burned, set all around three little beds and three tiny occupants tucked up with toys, and favourite books. Noi and Madeleine blew out the candles, and found the mother in a bathtub of blood.

Out in the hall, Noi marked off the apartment, then slumped to the ground, and Madeleine joined her, shuddering.

"How long ago do you think she did that?" she asked the shorter girl. "An hour? Two? If we'd started at the other end of the building we could have saved her."

"Or just delayed her."

Madeleine hunched her shoulders, then pulled off her sandals and massaged her arches. Velvet against velvet. Over two hours, and so much more left.

"I thought we'd find more people. How can they have had one in five come through at that boarding school, while in forty apartments we were too late for the sole survivor?"

"One in five healthy teenagers with Science Boy playing head nurse," Noi pointed out. "We're trying to Nightingale the wrong demographic."

"Do you want to go on?"

With a sigh, Noi nodded. "Yeah. I'd obsess about it if we stopped now. About things like that family, except with one of the kids still alive instead. But eat something – don't let the hunger catch up."

They snacked on some of the nuts and dried fruit they'd brought along to offer to survivors, and Madeleine browsed *BlueGreen* while Noi sent some texts. There was an entire section devoted to Rushcutters Bay Grammar, one of a half-dozen 'major studies' cobbled together by whoever happened to have access to a large number of infected people.

"Looks like we're not being very original," Noi said, and held up her phone to show a Twitter feed for #checkyourneighbors.

Madeleine could wish for fewer neighbours, but nodded and stood up. "My cousin's apartment's the last on this row. We can put me down as a survivor."

"One less door to thump on, anyway."

There was a merciful run of empty apartments, and they moved on to the next level up.

"Who is it?"

The words had a horror movie quality, the barely audible sound sending Madeleine flinching backward, the keys she'd been lifting to the lock jangling.

"Hello!" Noi called out, with only a suggestion of a gulp. "We're checking for sur – for anyone who needs help. We have some food and bottled water, or we can bring milk if you want it."

"I don't need anything."

It was a woman, her voice hoarse, frantic. Madeleine and Noi exchanged worried glances.

"We can leave some things out here for you, if you'd like," Madeleine offered. "You don't have to open the door while we're here."

"Go *away*."

"All right. Sorry for – uh, we'll be in apartment 222 later, if you, um..." Madeleine trailed off as a thump made the door shake, as if the woman had hit it. "We're going now."

Noi hurriedly pushed the trolley down the walkway to the next door, then clutched Madeleine's arm.

"I don't know whether to laugh or scream," she whispered. "What the hell?"

"Maybe she somehow managed to avoid the stain. Of course she wouldn't want to open the door."

"She could have just said that." But Noi shrugged off her annoyance. "I guess we can at least chalk up another survivor."

"We still don't know everything that the dust does to people. She could be something new, changed in other ways."

"Don't say that after you told her your apartment number. Let's get on – I'm wanting some distance."

Madeleine rapped at the new door, far less casually, and called for longer than had become habit, before making a quick, nervous sortie and heading for the next apartment.

"Wait."

The strained voice was worse for being louder, sharper, and it was impossible not to jump, Noi even letting out a tiny, cut-off shriek as they spun in unison to see the previous door had opened, though there was no sign of a person.

"Take him away."

The faintest suggestion of movement followed, then nothing.

"I am freaking the shit out right now," Noi said, under her voice. "Are you freaking the shit out?"

"I'm...really looking for an excuse not to go in there," Madeleine said.

They approached the door like nervous horses, ready to shy at a moment's notice. Madeleine moved to peer around the corner, changed her mind and backed to the limit of the walkway, against the railing, so she wouldn't be in reach of anything which might be just inside the door.

"Can't see anyone," Noi murmured, craning for a look down an airy, white hall. She hefted the bolt cutters, adding: "It's going to turn out to be some scared little old lady and I'm going to look like the bad guy waving these around, and yet..."

"Let's get this over with."

Madeleine picked up a bottle of water, on the theory that it might make a distracting projectile, and followed Noi in. One of the smaller apartments, very neat and tidy, with the windows wide open, sheer curtains rippling. No-one in sight. Two doors shut, one open. Competing scents: pine, and rot.

"Oh."

Noi lowered the bolt cutter, gazing into a room dominated by a king-sized bed. A pale cream spread had been drawn over the occupant. Two steps and a twitch of the cloth and they had found an obvious candidate for 'him'.

"I almost wish she'd come at us yelling 'Brainnnsss!'. Then I could justify running away."

Madeleine nodded, staring at a thick-set man in his sixties, whose cheery strawberry-striped pyjama pants cut into a swelling stomach, the skin unpleasantly mottled. Probably one of those who had died the very first night.

"Could we even lift him?" she asked. "Where would we take him *to*?"

"One of the other apartments?" Noi was frowning, but no longer held the bolt cutters at ready as she worked through the problem. "I think it's doable. We'll need something to shift him with, but I've got an idea for that. Come on."

Calling out that they were going to get something to help, Noi led the way down to the wharf's echoing central hall.

"You head back to the restaurant and grab a couple of pairs of gloves. They should be in the box in the storage room to the left in the kitchen. Meet back at the elevator."

That was easily accomplished, and Madeleine found Noi had beaten her, and was lazily spinning a wheeled platform topped with a gilt metal framework.

"Luggage thing from the hotel," she explained. "All we have to do is get him off the bed."

The mystery woman hadn't shut them out. The dead man was still large and unwieldy.

"His arms and legs will trail off the sides," Madeleine pointed out, reluctant to touch the man even with gloves.

"How about this?"

Noi dragged the cover fully off the bed, then pulled out the near corners of the blue bed sheet. Catching on, Madeleine lifted the section of cloth nearest her.

"Hold your side a little lower," Noi instructed, then lifted hers, straining, and flopped the man onto his side in the very centre of the sheet. "Now if we tie the corners across, they'll be like handles."

It was still awkward, and moving him made the smell worse, but they managed to haul the sheet-bag to the side of the bed, and line the baggage cart up so the man could be pulled through the tubular metal frame to lie more on than off. They exposed a large stain on the mattress in the process, and Madeleine gagged at the stench of it, and hastily followed Noi as she pushed the cart effortlessly out of the apartment. After a moment's debate they returned and hauled the mattress out as well

"He's gone now," Madeleine called back from the doorway. "We...let us know if you need anything else."

She pulled the door closed and caught up with Noi and the cart, two doors down at one of the apartments they'd cleared already, to help her slide the heavy bundle to the floor. After bringing the mattress, and a quick detour to the apartment bathroom to abandon gloves and wash hands, they left the empty cart still in the room and shut themselves outside, heading back to their trolley of supplies.

"Time out for existential crisis," Noi said, sitting down. The words were light, but the girl grey, eyes squeezed shut, arms wrapped around her knees.

Madeleine sat down to wait, understanding that Noi was here because her home was filled with the bodies of her family, her wry good humour a façade of normality plastered over extreme grief. Madeleine's ongoing worry about her parents was a minor thing by comparison, and had lessened after last night's rain, though she wished she could get through to Tyler. Her phone was on its last legs, too, nearly out of charge.

A distant shout: "Are you two okay?"

Across the central hall, standing on the matching walkway of the parallel southern apartment building, was a girl in a dark purple gown and violet hijab, and a tall, hollow-cheeked man with a neatly trimmed beard, both of them loaded down with shopping bags. It was such an everyday, ordinary sight that Madeleine had a moment's dislocation, and told herself that there was no chance at all that they'd found an open supermarket.

"Yes!" Noi called. "Glad to see you! We've just been going door to door checking on people."

The man said something to the girl, who nodded, and called: "Good idea! Wait a sec and we'll come across!"

"I think our luck's turned," Noi murmured, as the pair took their bags into a nearby apartment – greeted by a weary, green-stained woman – and then made their way over.

"I'm Faliha Jabbour, and this is my Dad," the girl said, when they arrived. She was about fifteen, round-cheeked and blue-palmed. "What's the plan?"

Noi introduced herself and Madeleine, and explained their progress so far.

"So few?" Mr Jabbour asked, his English slow and heavily accented but understandable. "We must hope for better."

"We should do our floor first," Faliha said. "Check on Penny and Tesh."

Her father shook his head. "For the sake of safety, it is perhaps best to remain within quick reach of each other." He gave Madeleine and Noi a grave glance, clearly not wanting his daughter to face the apartment of friends.

"We can leap-frog," Noi said. "There's only one bolt cutter anyway."

Leap-frogging worked well, vastly speeding up their progress. Faliha knocked, called out, and unlocked the doors, but waited outside while her father checked the apartments. And soon they were joined by Carl, then Asha and Annie, Mr Lassiter, and Sang-Kyu: all the Blues in three hundred apartments and a hotel. There were also twenty-four Greens, most of them barely able to shuffle to their doors. Asha and Annie brought back to their apartment a Green boy only eleven or so – the youngest survivor Madeleine had seen so far – while Mr Lassiter, supplementing rusty high school French with a translation app, took in a very ill tourist who could barely speak English. The baggage cart was called into use again and again.

Once every room had been checked, all the Blues went down to the restaurants and sorted through them while Noi and Sang-Kyu cooked up a couple of massive vats of curry – one chicken, one vegetarian – discussing what constituted Halal with Faliha and what was vegan with Asha. And what their food prospects would be in a few weeks.

Madeleine helped clean up, watching their faces. Everyone red-eyed, smiles fragile. The sun was setting by the time they broke up to deliver curry and head to their respective homes. A gorgeous autumn evening, with a ribbon of smoke smudging the northern sky, and a mute tower of black watching, and waiting.

ooOoo

"What's your cousin like?" Noi asked, as Madeleine unlocked the apartment door. "Worth the hero-worship?"

"I guess. I don't know anyone else who is so resolutely…his own self, which is an odd thing to say about an actor. He says he only ever plays himself, though, just in very strange situations."

"An actor? Anyone I'd have heard of?" Noi parked the trolley of food, glanced around Tyler's spacious apartment, and fixed on the portrait. She gave Madeleine an incredulous glance, looked back, then said: "Okay, I so should have realised that. You've the same colour eyes. Why didn't you say anything when we were talking about him before?"

"Habit? Once people know I'm Tyler's cousin, that's all they see me as. My parents moved to Sydney so I could get away from people trying to be my friend or picking fights with me because of Tyler."

"Did you actually *paint* this?" Noi asked, picking up a brush.

"Yeah." Madeleine tried to sound casual, to not show how closely she was watching Noi's face.

"Shit, why would you need to worry about being thought of as just someone's cousin?"

"I think I'd have to do something pretty spectacular to overcome Tyler," Madeleine said, and laughed quietly at herself for liking Noi more because of the way she was looking at the painting, impossible as it was not to be that way. "I've been sleeping on the couch so I could see the TV," she added. "But there's a spare room if you want it."

"Couch is good," Noi said, glancing at the large leather half-square. "I don't suppose your cousin runs to enormous vats of bubble bath? I want to soak, but after this morning I need bubbles to make it not like that woman."

"There might be, but I should clean the floor again. I broke the mirror."

Noi followed Madeleine to the bathroom, stared but did not comment on the amount of damage, and opted to re-purpose some of Tyler's enormous supply of shampoo. While the older girl was in the bath, Madeleine found herself fussing about, fixing pillows and blankets, hunting through Tyler's clothes for things Noi could wear, anxious to please. Not her usual behaviour, especially when she was itching to get at her sketch pad, but nothing was usual. She moved about restlessly, spent a few minutes on the phone to her parents, then let herself do what she'd wanted for hours.

So many people. Small, quick sketches at first. Noi holding a cup of tea with little finger raised, outwardly serene. Fisher tumbled on the stair. Nash, head thrown back, ready for action. Pan, all grin. Gav, blushing but sure of himself. The woman in the bath, naked breasts bobbing in crimson. Faliha, knocking on a door, eager and afraid. Mr Jabbour, his smile sad. Carl, with an Iron Man physique, but hesitant, looking down and away. Asha, short blond hair sticking up, checking warily over her shoulder. Annie, shoulders sagging. Mr Lassiter, superbly neat, running an absent hand over the close-cropped black fuzz on his head. Sang-Kyu, giving a thumbs-up signal.

This first rush done, she came up for air and discovered Noi curled beneath the quilt on the other half of the couch, already asleep despite the early hour. Madeleine hadn't even heard her come into the room, and wondered why she hadn't said anything. Or perhaps Noi had, and been ignored, as Madeleine was too used to doing when interruptions came when she was drawing. Stupid and rude of her, and not how she wanted to treat Noi.

The girl had pulled her mass of curling hair up into a topknot, but a few black spirals escaped to spring across her face and, captured by the image, Madeleine shrugged off her annoyance and began a new sketch, a very detailed one. Then she moved on to more pictures of Noi, and of the four boys and their apple-green car, and tried to decide if they were as likeable as they'd seemed, or if she was just reacting to the situation. Madeleine was used to distrusting people and holding herself in reserve, and yet she'd met Noi and teamed up instantly, and did not want that to end. She didn't even dislike the idea of joining the four boys at their school. Still, she could surely accept the need for allies without forgetting to be wary about relying on others.

When hunger and weariness finally broke through she snacked and showered, then killed all but the hall light. With the TV off, the city skyline became more dominant, blazing away at however many kilowatts per hour, keeping the corpses lit. Once again she heard a weird electronic music, almost like an untuned radio.

Had her mother sounded strange? Even though her eyes were sandy-tired, Madeleine couldn't make herself stop analysing their brief discussion. Had there really been something there, or was she just looking for the next disaster? The day's activity should have left her feeling, if not cheerful, at least hopeful. There were people around her who were friendly, and she'd solved the problem of food for a solid chunk of time. Instead of reassured, she was on edge.

A noise in the dark. Madeleine shifted, unsure if she'd been sleeping, and tried to process what she'd heard. A close sound, stifled and secret. A minute or more passed before she realised it was Noi, crying.

Pinned between a desire to do something, and knowing that nothing she might do could make any real difference, Madeleine lay listening to the muted betrayal of pain. If Noi was anything like Madeleine, she wouldn't want anyone to know she was crying anyway, so it was better to stay still and quiet, not go blundering in.

The question of whether that was the right way to treat Noi occupied her until long after the last tiny sob had faded.

Chapter Six

Sunlight crept beneath Madeleine's eyelids, but it was a sumptuous roil of cinnamon and chocolate which woke her. She scrubbed a hand across her face, stretching, and blinked at a man on television filming himself in front of a Spire. The only sound was from Noi clunking something in the kitchen.

For some minutes Madeleine didn't move, watching the man holding up a star-studded arm, displaying it as best he could next to the Spire's whorl of light. Then she shifted her attention to the easel, to Tyler who was somewhere out there probably dead. Painted eyes gazed back at her, uncompromising, and she realised that she felt no impulse to return to the portrait because it didn't need it. The roughly blocked background, the quick strokes she'd used for everything except the highlight points of head, hand and hair, worked perfectly.

"Which do you prefer for shops: King's Cross or Bondi Junction?" Noi asked as Madeleine sat up. "There's a fair few things I need, and from what Faliha was telling me it's probably not a good idea to wait too long."

"I've never been shopping at either of them," Madeleine said. Finding the room unexpectedly chilly, she pulled the koi dressing gown around her. "What on earth are you cooking?"

"Fudge, and caramel squares. I figure we need to always carry something with a big sugar hit – little blocks of emergency energy. There's pancakes for breakfast, or will be by the time you're dressed."

"Can I *keep* you?" Madeleine asked wonderingly, and then laughed with Noi at how that sounded. "I'm guessing you get that a lot. It must be nice to be good at something so useful."

"What, and you aren't?" Noi said, looking pleased. "I'd kill to be able to draw like that." She nodded toward Madeleine's sketchbook on the coffee table. "I can't believe you did those from memory."

"Not a useful skill," Madeleine muttered, and shrugged at Noi's questioning look. "My mother wants me to be a vet. There's no money in art. I need a real career, need to be *practical*, can still paint in my spare time." She pulled herself up, hearing the resentment leaking into her voice. "Guess none of that matters now. Did you always want to cook?"

"Hell, no. I was destined to be a pro basketball player." All of five foot nothing, she grinned blithely. "Well, okay, maybe I did watch a few too many episodes of *Masterchef* when I was a kid. And food's a big thing in my family – I'm Thai-Italian, so I'm like Aussie fusion cooking incarnate. My Dad would have preferred I finished Year Twelve before starting my apprenticeship, but he knew it was the only thing I wanted to do." Her smile faded, and she stirred the bubbling pot of fudge.

"I'll go get dressed," Madeleine said, hesitated, then murmured "Thanks," and left it at that.

After another raid on Tyler's closet, they disposed of the pancakes and found a second backpack for carrying supplies. Madeleine took a moment to remove the boring print over Tyler's bed and hang his portrait, balancing the frame of the stretcher on the hook. She refused to acknowledge any symbolism to the gesture.

"We'll have to search some of the apartments for car keys later," Noi said as they headed down. "But my bike should be enough for this trip. Meet me out front."

It was still early, a breezy and overcast day with a chill southern breeze. Madeleine wished she'd added a jacket to her ensemble, and tucked her hands into her armpits as she walked slowly down the wharf, attention on the Spire flirting with the clouds. Every velvet step reminded her of warm, unnatural stone.

A tutting motor warned her of Noi's emergence from the driveway on the eastern side of the wharf. Her curls foamed beneath a white helmet and she rode a cream moped, speeding to a precipitous stop at the curb.

"I've only the one helmet, sorry," she said. "The Cross is closer, so we'll head there. Anything you particularly need?"

"Underwear," Madeleine said, sliding onto the seat behind the shorter girl and feeling a little ridiculous.

"Underwear it is!" Noi said, and shot them across the street, past the Woolloomooloo Bay Hotel, and by a collection of tiny terrace houses. She rode with verve and obvious pleasure at having no competition for the road, but it was the shortest of trips, and when they reached the shop-lined streets around King's Cross Station she slowed to a crawl, staring at ragged holes and spills of safety glass.

"Looks like we're late to the party," Noi said. "Looting: the new economy."

Madeleine was shocked by the destruction: there was hardly a shopfront intact. King's Cross had a certain reputation for a drugs-and-prostitution nightlife, but it was an ordinary enough inner-city suburb otherwise.

"What would anyone need from a nail salon?" she wondered.

"Cuticle crisis? Hangnail emergency?" Noi shook her head. "Let's do this quickly."

Tucking her moped between two cars, she led the way into a *Best & Less*, snagging a couple of enviro-bags from a checkout. The store offered a full range of cheap, serviceable clothing, and there was no sign of whoever had broken the door open, so Madeleine quickly stuffed bags with clothing suitable for a Sydney winter, and slipped on a plum-coloured coat with a white lined hood.

"Did you see a shoe store?" Noi asked, joining her at the door. "I want some serious boots."

"Next to the chemists?"

They left the unwieldy bags at the moped, and headed to an up-market shoe store, with a brief detour for chargers from a phone specialty shop. Madeleine quickly found sneakers and some comfortable slip-ons, then told Noi she'd be next door.

The chemists was a disaster zone, and she hesitated at the door, not overly surprised at the mess. The scatter of items in the front of the store was nothing compared to the complete shambles at the back, where a pharmacist would dispense prescription medicine. But Madeleine didn't need anything serious, and slipped off her backpack to do a cautious tour, collecting aspirin, toothbrushes, tampons, and a couple of bottles of cough mixture in anticipation of flu season. Heading out, she paused and picked a box off a shelf, reading the label doubtfully.

"They were four very fanciable boys weren't they?"

Madeleine hastily tried to put the box back, but Noi plucked it from her hand.

"No, no, it's just what I was thinking. Though I see this packet has Science Boy's name written all over it."

Madeleine stared. "I didn't–"

"Oh, come on. I looked at that sketch pad of yours. Some nice pictures of me and the other three, and about a thousand of he-who-dives-down-stairs. You couldn't have been more obvious if you'd drawn love hearts around each one."

"He's just a good sub – what are you doing?!"

Noi, attempting to shovel an entire shelf of condom packets into Madeleine's backpack, sent half of them scattering to the ground, but tucked in the rest. "No, don't back down on good sense. Even if not Science Boy, it can't hurt to put in a supply. There's got to be a few thousand reasons why getting preggers during a starry blue apocalypse is a bad idea. Better yet–"

She slung the black boots she was carrying around her neck and waded into the mess in the pharmacy section.

"Drugs, drugs, damn, someone really cracked a rage fit back here, didn't they? I should have put the boots on first." Glass crunched. "Hmm, that might be useful. Hey, does your phone have enough juice to Google the name of – oh, wait, that looks right..."

Arms full of boxes, Noi waded back and tumbled her load into what little space was left in Madeleine's backpack, scrunching them down so she could zip the bag up. "Painkillers, antibiotics and the Pill. Probably. We'll look them up when we get back. All done?"

Madeleine considered the backpack uncertainly, thinking Noi's practicality immensely premature given that Madeleine had never even kissed anyone, and Fisher hadn't looked at her twice. Then she sighed and slipped the bag over one shoulder. "Which of them is it you keep texting?"

Noi's grin broadened. "Pan. Which, damn, is giving me fits because, seriously, a Year Ten boy? He's got to be only sixteen. Or fifteen. I don't know if I could handle fifteen. I don't think fifteen's even *legal*."

"How old are you?"

"Eighteen! And, yeah, I know – no-one would think it strange if our ages were the other way around but it's a big mental adjustment for me to be chatting up someone in Year Ten."

"Half the world is dead, we just robbed four stores, and you're worried about liking a guy two years younger than you?"

"Priorities, I have them."

They headed out, Noi swinging her new boots by their tied laces as they debated the best way to occupy the rest of the day, and then puzzled over transporting so many stuffed bags on a moped.

"Hey, hey, more damsels in distress! You two want a hand?"

Three people were walking toward them: two guys in their early twenties and a younger girl.

"No, we're good," Noi said. "We don't have far to go."

"You sure?" asked the one in the lead, tall and blond with a surfer tan. "It's no problem."

"Yeah. Thanks anyway."

The blond guy shrugged and waved, but his friend, short and sandy, gave them a dirty look as he turned away which made Madeleine glad Noi had refused. The girl, between the two men, hesitated, fine pale hair drifting across her face. She looked painfully young and overwhelmed, and Madeleine felt suddenly sick.

"You okay?" Noi called.

The girl's eyes widened, sending a frantic message which she stopped short of saying aloud.

"Hey, what's the problem?" surfer guy said. "This is our friend Emily. We're taking care of her."

"You need a place, come with us," Noi said, speaking directly to the girl.

"Mind your own business, bitch," snapped sandy guy.

"Just walk over here," Noi said, still talking straight to the girl. She swung her pair of boots lightly.

"Little girl, you think you can fight us with those?" Surfer guy sounded pleased by the idea. "Man, even in the old world you wouldn't have a hope. But this is the new world! The Blue world!" He laughed, bubbling over with good humour, then lifted an arm and pointed his palm at a nearby shop window.

Nothing visible came out of his hand, but the window still shattered, a wide round hole punched through the safety glass, little crystalline squares showering the display.

"Shit, all of us can do that," Noi said. "You think you're special?"

"Uh-huh. Big talk, shortie. I think you're the only fighter on your side. You might want to get out of here before you get hurt."

"No."

Madeleine wanted to run, but she stepped forward to Noi's side, gripping the metal pole of a parking sign for support.

"You're the ones who're outgunned," she said, putting as much quiet authority into her voice as she could manage. "Leave before I do this to you."

Lifting her free hand she aimed the palm at the windscreen of the nearest car, and pushed out with the strength which had been in her since the surge, giving her all in order to impress.

She'd kept her eyes on the leader, and only saw the result of her effort in peripheral vision as, with an enormous smash and scream of metal, the car shot back and then flipped up, setting off a cascade of collisions climaxing with the first car's descent, a smack-bang coda only a ton of metal falling out of the sky could provide. A half-dozen car alarms rose in discordant chorus.

The reaction of the two men was, thankfully, exactly as Madeleine had hoped. As she stood there, one hand wrapped around the metal pole and the other still pointed at the destruction she'd created, they turned tail and ran in the opposite direction, and did not look back to see that she still stood, hand out, head high, eyes fixed on the place they had been. Paralysed.

ooOoo

The aftermath followed the same course as the time at St James Station, with the added complication of Noi, who managed to lower Madeleine's arm, producing a burning sensation in her shoulder. When, soon after, Madeleine curled down to clutch her knees and gasp in pain, the girl hugged Madeleine protectively, not realising that made the pins and needles worse.

Despite the blaze of pain Madeleine could feel Noi shaking, so struggled to say through stinging lips: "S'okay. Jus' tempry."

"I reserve the right to panic," Noi replied, with a gasp of relief. "I've called the apple-green cavalry to give us a lift."

By the time the cheerful Volkswagen arrived, the worst had passed, and Madeleine was sitting almost upright, bracketed by Noi and the blond girl, Emily, all her limbs feeling disconnected and not quite hers. Recovered enough, though, to appreciate the stunned reaction of the four boys to the line of five cars rammed into each other, garnished with an upended sedan whose engine had been driven almost through to the boot.

"Questions later," Noi said, as the cavalry piled out of the car. "This is all way too noisy and attention-getting. Can you stand, Maddie?"

Standing wasn't much of a problem with so many hands ready to help, though Madeleine was feeling far too vague and floaty to navigate herself to the back seat of the Volkswagen, and yet found herself there, Emily on one side and Fisher on the other. As Gav was cheerfully exchanging names with Emily, Madeleine remembered the squares of fudge Noi had given her before they set out, tucked into the front pocket of her backpack. A backpack now sitting on Fisher's lap.

Painful heat washed through her as she stared at the overstuffed bag. He couldn't possibly know, had no reason to open it, but—

Fisher frowned. "What is it? Are you going to be sick?"

Madeleine looked away, head spinning. "Where's Noi?"

"Ferrying the court jester," Nash said, nodding ahead just as Noi's moped cut in front of them, Pan balanced precariously backward, indulging his inner hoon by holding arms and legs out at the same time. But it was Nash's expression which caught Madeleine's attention. Fond, indulgent. Enough to make Madeleine wonder if it was not Pan's age which would get in Noi's way.

Trying not to picture the contents of the bag spilling everywhere, Madeleine turned resolutely to the girl on her right. Tall, fine-boned and delicately pretty, with the kind of silken, straight hair which Madeleine sighed over on the days when her own was determined to imitate steel wool.

"Emily? Sorry, didn't mean to be so...over the top."

The girl ducked her head, colour flooding through porcelain skin, but then lifted her eyes and said fiercely. "I'm glad you did. They were such awful people, pretending they wanted to help. I couldn't find a way to leave without them getting angry."

"What more can we do to get the word out, Fish?" asked Gavin as he followed Noi onto the private road along the eastern side of Finger Wharf. "People are checking on each other, grouping up, but for kids like Emily here there's too big a chance they'll walk right into the wrong person. The site messages, Twitter, it's not enough."

"The Safe Zone model's gaining momentum," Fisher replied. "Melbourne Trish got through to the ABC, and once they start broadcasting links we'll catch the majority." He saw Madeleine's confused expression. "A sister site of *BlueGreen*, working a model which came out of Toronto. Establish safe zones, just as we have with Rushies. Remove corpses, manage food, identify survivors with expertise, like doctors, electricians, and then gradually clear outwards from your central point. We're looking at seventy to ninety per cent mortality in high exposure areas, while the fringe areas are full of people trapped in their houses. Even in cities which have had rain, like Sydney, they'd be risking everything to go outside. Once the Blues and Greens have established some organisation, we can look at trying to help the uninfected in the dust zones. Not to mention working on some kind of inoculation. There's Blue groups in Berkeley, Beijing and London who are the primary focus for that research, and we're feeding them as much information as we can."

His glance at Madeleine clearly put her in the category of information to be gathered, but questions were forestalled as they pulled up near the apartment elevator. Madeleine was by now piercingly hungry, but all her attention was focused on retrieving her backpack from Fisher, which she managed to do with minimum fuss as they waited for the lift, drawing a startled look and stifled cough of laughter from Noi.

"So are we all capable of trash compacting cars if we put our minds to it?" Pan asked, as they travelled upward. "I mean, I know I'm not the only one who's been playing with recreating the surge. I've felt tired afterwards, but haven't collapsed. Definitely haven't had any couldn't move moments."

"Do you get pins and needles after?" Madeleine asked, better able to engage with the situation now that her backpack was safely in her arms, and Fisher was carrying innocuous bags of clothing.

"Nope." Pan glanced around, but everyone shook their head.

"I haven't even tried," Noi said, unlocking Tyler's apartment with the master key.

"Do you react like that every time?" Fisher deposited the bags he was carrying by the couch, started to sit down, then said sharply: "Unmute that TV."

The television, which had been busily telling the world's story to an empty room, currently displayed an unsteady image of two men walking toward a Spire.

"What are they – is that a bazooka?" Gavin asked.

The pair had stopped, one man moving back to whoever was filming while the other dropped to one knee and lifted the bazooka to his shoulder. Noi found the remote in time to give them sound as the man fired, a plume of white followed swiftly by a sunburst of orange.

"That was perhaps not an entirely pointless exercise," Nash said, as the fiery bloom died to a drift of smoke, revealing a completely undisturbed Spire. "It gives us a gauge for what will *not* penetrate it, at least."

"Aliens always have impenetrable force fields," Pan said. "Must be some kind of industrial law. No invasions of Earth until force field technology achieved."

"You still think it's an alien invasion?" Noi asked, bringing water and a plate of sweets over to Madeleine, who gratefully tucked herself into one corner of the couch and stuffed her face.

"I sure don't think it's the judgment of God. Did you hear that dipweed calling himself Pope? The one in Vienna, I mean, not the one in Florence."

"No religion I've ever heard of has mentioned giant starry pointy things," Gavin said. He glanced at Nash, who looked amused.

"Technically, there is no reason why Shiva or Kali could not do such a thing. Why should any god tread old ground?"

"Divine retribution via aliens then," Pan said. "Still aliens.

"No, I don't mean about it being aliens," Noi said, offering Emily a chair and pointing people toward the trays of sweets in the kitchen as she muted the television again. "The secret government conspiracy idea never seemed likely, which does leave gods or aliens. It's the invasion part. If they're invading, where the hell are they?"

"Laying their plans? Waiting for more people to die so it's safe to come out?"

"Or just watching." Gavin shrugged at Noi. "There's the aliens doing experiments theory. Think *The Island of Doctor Moreau*, except we're the animals being made into 'people'. I think there's even a religion which already believed that – that humans were uplifted by aliens. So all this, the whole horrible thing, has been to make Greens and Blues, to create the next evolutionary step of the human race."

"A new world, a Blue world," Madeleine murmured, and felt sick.

"I agree with Fish that we should not rush to judgment," Nash said, paused, then repeated: "Fish?"

Fisher, who had been keeping a watchful, worried eye on the television, looked up, then let out his breath. "Sorry. I've been trying to find a way to ask Madeleine to take off her clothes. Everything I can think to say sounds impossibly wrong." One corner of his mouth twitched at their various reactions, then he added to Madeleine: "You're very blue, aren't you?"

"Yeah." Madeleine couldn't stop the rush of heat to her face, and wondered what the patch around her eye looked like when she blushed. "Just a minute – I actually anticipated that particular request."

"Oh, man, everything I can think to say right now sounds impossibly wrong as well," Pan said as she stood up, then added on a more serious note: "You want us to kick off, Maddie? Give you less of a crowd."

"It's okay." She collected the bags of looted clothing and, most importantly, the backpack of looted other things, and headed into Tyler's walk-in wardrobe.

Noi followed her to check that Madeleine was okay, turned to go, then returned to pick up the backpack and briefly clutch it to her chest, bouncing in a circle of silent hilarity.

That at least left Madeleine smiling as she dug through the bags to unearth a pair of very short shorts and a matching crochet halter top which was a mere inch or two from being a bikini. Something she would normally never consider wearing, since it made her look like a noodle, only emphasising her lack of hips and how little she had to fill the top. But looking in the mirror she saw neither abbreviated black cloth nor string-bean figure, only stars.

"Barely human," she murmured, and saw exactly the same thought in the faces of those who waited for her in Tyler's lounge room.

"Damn," Gavin said. "But – damn."

Madeleine, resisting the urge to clutch the coat she'd carried with her to her chest, turned so they could see her back, which had a particularly brilliant display: her own tiny nebulae. She looked down, the handful of sticking plasters on her arms and legs catching her eye.

"How are you still alive?" Fisher asked, sounding breathless. He came close, putting on his glasses, and she looked away as he bent to study her back. "Can I document this?"

"If you keep my face out of it," Madeleine said, and stood unhappily as he circled her, taking pictures with his phone. She hadn't really processed the impulse which had produced so many sketches of Fisher Charteris, but couldn't entirely deny Noi's conclusion, and so watched his face gravely as he angled his phone to take pictures of her stomach. He was someone she'd only just met, and she liked the bones of his face, and the cinnamon warmth of his light brown eyes, and she wanted to do more than just sketch him.

Finished, he looked up, brows drawn in thought, and Madeleine wondered if he made many enemies because the slightest frown made it seem like he was seriously annoyed. He caught her gaze, and paused to study her frankly in return, and that was a little too much for Madeleine in front of an audience, so she retrieved the plum-coloured coat and sat back down, trying not to curl protectively into a ball.

"I was at St James," she announced, wanting to limit questions about that time. "The dust was knee-deep. I walked out along the track. Higher exposure, more stain."

"I don't know of any other very high exposure cases who have survived," Fisher said, tucking phone and glasses away. "Did you eat anything unusual, take any medicines we could investigate?"

"I don't think so. I painted, and ate soup. I took some aspirin early on because I'd hit my head. But—" She grimaced. "If there's anything really different about me, it was that I'd touched the Spire."

Fisher paused in the act of sitting down, then completed the movement, the lowering frown reappearing.

"Something you might have mentioned earlier!" Pan said. "What was it like then?"

"Like us," Madeleine replied, uncomfortably. "Velvet. The same sensation as blue-stained skin. It was warm, too, and felt alive. Except solid as marble."

"That's...so not comforting to hear." Pan exchanged a glance with Nash, then tangled fingers in his hair, feeling the shape of his skull. "Not pointy yet."

"I'd only just touched it when the force field came up," Madeleine went on. "I was knocked back, paralysed like I was this morning. Then awful pins and needles. Today I was a lot hungrier afterwards, but otherwise it was the same."

"Did that happen during your surge?" Fisher asked, very intent.

"No."

"Go look at the bathroom," Noi said, and pointed the way. When they returned she added: "I was surprised you aren't more cut up, seeing all that."

Madeleine explained briefly how the shards of glass and tile had bounced off her during the surge, the cuts simply the result of picking herself off the floor afterwards.

"Personal force field," Pan said, excited. "Can we do that? Okay, yeah, it makes us even more like the Spire, but *so cool*. But why the paralysis?"

"Some controlled, less spectacular experiments might answer that," Fisher said, not taking his eyes off Madeleine. "Something I wanted to organise anyway, somewhere away from anything we can damage, but even more so hearing this. It's more than worth investigating whether your survival is intrinsic to you, or a result of the shock soon after exposure. Have you heard from your cousin?"

"No. But he had just flown in when the Spire arrived, and was safe from the dust for a long while. The last time I heard from him he didn't have the stain."

"Leave a note," suggested Pan. "Forward the apartment phone to your mobile." He grimaced. "The senior dorms are set a little apart, and it makes a real difference to know there's not a body in the next room. I'd be all manly now and say you girls should let us protect you, except you just gutted a car, and I think Noi would throw those boots at me. But we're good company, and wash most days."

"How're your Greens?" Noi asked, a note of regret in her voice.

"Up and about, all but a few of them. Not quite ready for a marathon, but you wouldn't be walking into playing nurse or anything."

"I mean how's their attitude? To you and your plans. To these stories of Blues killing Greens."

All four of them hesitated, which was answer enough.

Noi sighed. "Look, I'm all for teaming up, community, good company, whatever. But even if nothing else happens we're facing a world divided into three parts. The uninfected. People doing Kermit imitations. And people who can gut cars. Some of whom seem to think they've been promoted to the top of the heap. Give Maddie's cousin another couple of days and then we'll come over, but we need to think contingency plan."

"Fair point," Fisher conceded. "Any suggestions?"

"If nothing else, we'll try to find the keys to some of the spectacular array of boats lined up outside. Some of those things are practically floating mansions. Driving out of the city to any of the surrounding towns would mean competing with the thousands who've already done that – and potentially being isolated and locked up for being Blue. Not that I have the least idea of how to drive – or is it pilot? – a boat, or any suggestions on where to go. But it's a first step."

"Nash knows boats," Pan said.

"Sailing," Nash corrected, but they all stood and went out on the balcony to survey the gently bobbing array.

Madeleine stayed where she was, just turning so she could watch them. Fisher was self-contained, withholding judgment, while Gavin was clearly more optimistic, reassuring Emily. Nash's shoulders were slumped, and Pan was keeping a concerned eye on him. He reached up and put a hand on the taller boy's shoulder, and Nash seemed to gain strength from the gesture, straightening, but then moved away.

Noi came back inside, face pensive, but grinned when she spotted Madeleine drowsing. "Hey, it's barely midday! Not nap time yet." She sat down on the coffee table. "They want to get together day after tomorrow for some shiny new super powers tests. At a park or a beach, where there's lots of space. Okay with you?"

"Do you really think it'll turn into a Blues versus Greens kind of thing? Particularly at that school – they saved lives there."

"I don't think it's inevitable," Noi replied. "I just think it's..." She paused, deliberately inspecting Madeleine's glimmering legs. "I think it's human."

Chapter Seven

"Morning, kiddo."

"Tyler!" Madeleine almost dropped the phone. She settled for depositing her shoulder bag on the floor, and sitting beside it. "I'm – I'm so glad!"

His bubbling laughter enveloped her. "So am I. You didn't sound too hot last time we spoke."

"Are you okay? Are you–?"

"Now in technicolour? Very much so. Embarking on a brave blue world, or what have you. Have you noticed the potential for a soundtrack?" he added irrelevantly. "*Blue Hotel. Blue Velvet.* So many songs, such a dreadful wealth of puns."

"Where are you?"

"At a hotel, just by the airport. We walked here after the stain began to show."

"Do you want me to come pick you up? I, um, found your car keys."

"Did you? Felt like a drive in the country?"

"Went out to see Mum and Dad. They're still stuck in the house, and I took them some supplies."

Noi had driven, fast and confident, the M5 wide enough that even the occasional abandoned wreck was easily avoided. They'd stood tins and bags of rice on the front path of Madeleine's home, and hosed them off in case they'd brought any dust with them. Then they'd hosed the house, trying to get places the recent rain would have missed.

"How dusty is it out there now? Are they going to make a dash inland?"

"The cobwebs under the eaves were tinged purple. And you can see occasional flecks of sparkle in the grass. The inner city's the same, except more so." She sighed. "I don't see how the uninfected could ever risk going about without face masks. Dad said he and Mum are even sleeping with a sheer curtain over them, and that until there's been a heap more rain they're going to stick it out in the house. No-one had time to put in supplies, though. When we went to leave, the lady over the road waved at us madly through the window, and asked us to go get nappies and tins of baby formula. Your car doesn't have enough boot space."

"Well, I didn't really buy it with babies in mind." He chuckled. "Who are 'we'?"

Madeleine apologetically explained his extra house guests. "We were just off to Bondi," she added, mouthing 'Tyler' at Noi as she stuck a puzzled head around the door. "But that can wait till I collect you."

"No, I found a car. I'll head home tonight after taking a friend to check his family. Why in the world are you going to the beach?"

"For some Blue powers tests. We're trying to work out exactly what Blues can do so we can avoid doing it accidentally. We've ended up with a lot more people going than I expected, but I guess it is kind of a critical thing to know."

Tyler didn't respond, and she said his name, wondering if they'd been cut off.

"I'm here. I–" He paused, a completely uncharacteristic hesitation. "I can't do that, you know. Force punches. I don't seem to create energy, but I need it. I'm lucky I made a couple of good friends out here – they keep me on my feet."

"You *need* it?"

"Mm. Let's just say I was playing quite the wrong character on *Blood Mirror*."

"Seriously?"

"Giant dust-spewing towers, and you balk at some mild vampiric tendencies?"

"I...guess not. That explains some of the stories going around, at least."

When Tyler rang off, Madeleine grimaced apologetically at Noi, but only said that Tyler would be in that night, since she wanted more time to think over 'mild vampiric tendencies'. Grabbing the bag containing a portion of the lunch they'd packed, she headed down to the garage.

The Blues test session had spiralled into an event. Fisher's discussion on *BlueGreen* of Madeleine's experiences, and his plan to test and compare a range of Blues with different levels of stain, had swiftly been picked up by other Blues around the world, and multiple groups had organised to do the same thing – a couple of test sessions were already underway, and others were waiting for day wherever they were.

When the number of people wanting to join the Sydney test had risen to more than a hundred, Fisher had asked Madeleine, Noi and Emily to head to the beach a couple of hours early, to get Madeleine's testing out of the way before too many people were around. At a little after seven in the morning it was chill with a hint of mist above the water, but the sky was a pale blue wash which promised a day worth being outside.

The apple-green Volkswagen was waiting by a white hatchback as near as possible to the centre of the massive arc of beach, six boys leaning on the railing above the esplanade. Noi pulled Tyler's red convertible sports car in beside the hatchback, and grinned at Pan's expression.

"That's it, I'm riding back with Noi," Pan said. "I can't take this any longer."

"We've collected about a dozen sets of keys," Noi told him. "Come back after and you can pick one out. I'll throw in a couple of boats."

"You're on!"

"This is Nick, and Shaun," Gavin said, nodding first at a freckled blond boy and then a dark-skinned guy with cool mini-dreadlocks. "Part of our data collection team, and volunteer guinea pigs."

They were both Greens, and the brief discomfort that fact inspired bothered Madeleine inordinately. There was no reason to feel any different about

Greens, and certainly Nick and Shaun were nothing but nice as they showed off the stain-coverage diagrams they'd created – a front, back, left and right outline of a generic person – and enthusiastically highlighted almost all of hers.

"Thanks for keeping my name out of it," Madeleine told Fisher, as Noi and Emily filled out their sheets.

He nodded absently, surveying the beach. "Another advantage to starting this early. You followed the discussion on fields versus punches?"

"Yeah." Naturally many Blues hadn't waited for formal test sessions after his post on 'Subject M', and it had quickly been established that two different expressions of power were possible: 'punches' focused and pushed out, or protective fields. Fields seemed a lot harder to create, but within an hour of the post Blues began reporting that they'd successfully paralysed themselves by surrounding themselves entirely with a field, and then trying to throw it like a punch. "Nice to know I did that ass-backward," she muttered.

"You destroyed a car with a shield," he said. "I don't want anyone else on this beach when you try to punch. Let's see if we can get into the lifeguard tower."

This was easily accomplished with the aid of "Noi's Little Helper" – a small crowbar usually used to open delivery crates – and they explored the circular observation level, deciding to ignore the beach vehicles kept in a locked garage below.

Pan made a quick, efficient burglar. "Binoculars, first aid stuff – man, I keep expecting the lifeguards to show up and have a go at us."

"They might still," Nash said.

They moved down to the sand, Fisher leading Madeleine to the edge of the surf while the others waited by the stairs.

"The beach is a kilometre long, and we're halfway, so you've got five hundred metres of unbroken sand in either direction," Fisher said. "We'll do the tests right at the wave wash, so it'll be clear each time. Do you think you can punch instead of using the shield?"

"We practiced yesterday afternoon." Madeleine pointed at a shell and focused the roil of energy inside her into the tiniest little blip, sending the shell shooting away in a spray of sand. "No more dramatic collapses for me."

Fisher smiled. "At least a softer landing here. And a better setting." He gazed down the vast stretch of beach to the rocky rise of cliffs at the south-western end, his face contemplative. After a moment his determined brows lowered in remembered anger, and he turned toward the centre of the city, but they were too low and too far for the Spire to be visible. "Go all out, " he added. "And try to keep the punch flat, scoring the surface rather than digging into the sand."

He strode back up the beach while Madeleine hooked off her sandals and hitched up that day's maxi-dress. The damp sand felt incredible against her velvet skin, and she shivered when the water rushed up to caress her feet. The last trace of mist had already burned off, and the blues of sky and water were shifting, deepening. There were no seagulls, no voices, no cars; just the soughing of the waves.

Madeleine glanced back. They were all clustered together at the bottom of the tower stairs, more than fifty metres away, Nash and Shaun holding cameras at ready. The question of angles preoccupied her, and she eventually knelt, and cupped her hands before her knees, focused down the long, slightly curving line of surf, and poured everything inside her down through her arms, her palms, out.

THOOOOMMMMMM!!!

The noise shocked her, and she jerked. Since she'd angled a little low, gouging underground, this lifted the punch, sand exploding up for the whole of perhaps a hundred metres. The leading edge of water poured and foamed into the instant trench, and Madeleine took a deep, shuddering breath, wondering at the sudden rush of exultation.

"Damn, Maddie, I am *never* going to piss you off!"

Pan had run down, Noi and Shaun close behind. He was lit high with excitement, but paused to help her back to her feet and then pushed a brightly coloured stick into the ground a few metres to her right before trotting down the line of the trench with another.

"No pins and needles? Urge to imitate statues?"

"I'm fine." Breathing deeply, Madeleine took the sandals Noi held out, trying to reconcile the rush of excitement with a sick feeling in her stomach. "Like I'd run up a lot of stairs. Just...trying not to picture what would happen to any people in the way."

"If they were Blues, we think they'd auto-protect," Gavin said, coming up with the others.

"Auto-protect?" Noi repeated. "What's that supposed to mean?"

"Tap me with a finger-punch and I'll show you."

"Seriously?"

He gave her a mock-sultry look. "I know you'll be gentle with me Noi."

"I'm immune to your lash-batting," Noi told him. "Okay, you asked for it."

Waiting till Nick and Fisher had moved out of the way, she pointed at his shoulder. Madeleine couldn't see the punch, but she realised she was beginning to feel it happen. And she could just barely make out a visible ripple around Gavin's shoulder as he stood, unmoved.

"Now do it again, a good solid palm-shot."

Frowning, Noi obeyed, and this time the shield was obvious, making the air around Gavin shimmer.

"It doesn't work if you bean him with a cricket ball," Pan said, jogging up. "Not automatically anyway, though if you see one coming you can try to shield in time."

"While we just get punched," Nick said, pulling his shirt down so they could see a round, red mark above a patch of green. "Seriously cheated in the special abilities department."

"Could be we just haven't figured it out yet," Shaun put in, looking up as he tied the end of a colourful ball of wool to the first stick. "You Blueberries can be brute force, and Greens will be the brains."

He trailed off down the beach, unreeling the ball of wool, which switched colours at regular intervals, and Pan followed him, pushing a stick into the sand at each colour change.

Madeleine's punch had reached over one hundred and fifty metres. Her nearest rival was Gavin, managing fifty. Then Noi, Emily, Fisher and Pan, mildly indignant at measuring lowest. Madeleine spent her time on the lifeguard tower's steps, sketching, snacking, and watching Nash, not surprised when he kept to his role as cameraman and did not test.

Pan dealt with any disappointment by playing the fool for Emily, drawing her out until she was pink-cheeked and giggling, convincing her to put her fine pale hair in a bun and calling: "Come on Tink!" as they raced along the line of sticks to confirm the length of each punch.

It wasn't until they'd eaten a second breakfast, and Pan had led Nick and Shaun off to investigate the food opportunities of the Bondi Pavilion, that Madeleine had a chance to speak to Nash. He and Fisher had paused, as they all did eventually, to watch her sketch.

"Can I look—?" Fisher asked, pleasingly surprised and interested, and she handed the sketchpad to him, glad she'd taken the precaution of removing a couple of sheets before heading out.

Madeleine studied their faces as they turned over pages, stopping particularly at the portrait of Noi sleeping to say impressed things. Compliments were something she struggled with. Either she thought them over-effusive, a lie with ulterior motives, or she dismissed them as the opinions of people who didn't know what they were talking about. Better than the alternative, of course, but she never expected real appreciation.

She found herself thinking about Mrs Tucker, something she hadn't managed to do since she'd understood the amount of death a cloud of dust might bring. Mrs Tucker, who had been substitute art teacher for all of two weeks when Madeleine was in Year Ten, who had asked Madeleine to stay after class on her last day there and had mercilessly deflated an over-inflated bubble of pride, pointing out issues of composition, and Madeleine's complete absence of backgrounds. Cutting her to bits for deliberately avoiding areas she was weak in, for acting as if she had nothing to learn.

Mrs Tucker, a scrawny, wrinkled, grey-haired woman, the 'wrong demographic' for survival. She had given Madeleine the contact details of a talented university student willing to tutor cheaply, and left not the burgeoning art genius who had stayed back expecting praise, but a beginner, a pretender, overwhelmed by how far she had to go. Madeleine could only hope she'd been outside the dust zone.

And of course there were now new people to worry about, ones she didn't have the luxury of ignoring – nor even wanted to. Proving Madeleine's expectations wrong once again, Nash made several comments which showed he had a very good understanding. And Fisher – Fisher looked at her as if she had become suddenly real to him.

"I'm jealous," he said, handing the sketchbook back with a solemnity which lent the words weight. "I can't do anything like that. It's a revelatory skill, isn't it?"

"Revelatory?" It wasn't a word Madeleine associated with her work.

"You see Noi as beautiful, and when we look at these images, we realise that beauty as well."

"If we managed to miss it before now," Nash added, mouth curving.

Madeleine, suddenly very glad she'd taken out most of the sketches of Fisher, moved hastily on to another uncomfortable topic.

"I heard from my cousin before we left today. He'll be back this evening." She pushed on through the beginning of their congratulations. "He's a Blue, but he said that he doesn't create energy, he needs it. That two other Blues have been keeping him alive."

She kept her gaze steadily on Nash as she spoke, and saw how his face closed.

"A revelatory skill," Fisher repeated. Rather than disturbed, he sounded almost pleased. "Also a skill which involves paying attention to people. Is your cousin returning home? We're finding that it takes all three of us to keep Nash up – at least, without needing to frequently rest. Though he's highly stained, which must impact on the need."

"Can Greens gives you energy as well?" Madeleine asked Nash, and flushed at the flat, accusatory note in her voice. "Is this why there's been so many stories?"

"They can." Nash sounded resigned, then straightened, as if refusing to let himself be ashamed. "Shaun's a good friend – he volunteered to allow me to check. It's a different kind of energy." His candy-cream voice was grim. "And much less. If I had no other Blues around me, if I had spent the last few days surrounded only by Greens, I would now be a murderer. Or perhaps have found the courage to face the consequences of not killing."

"I'm surprised this isn't already widely known," Madeleine said. "Though – I guess I'd..." She paused, considering how she'd instinctively wanted to hide simply the amount of her stain. "What are you going to do?"

Nash hesitated. "It makes most sense to be proactive, to clearly describe the situation and pre-empt any...less calm announcement. We've held back to gauge the environment at Rushcutters."

Now that most of the Greens were up and having opinions. If Madeleine was a Green, she'd probably have an opinion about Nash too. But then there was Tyler.

"Noi and I should be able to support my cousin," she said. "Though I guess he's already managing. We've been working on the relocating plan, in case things get weird, and have keys to enough boats to stage a carnival. Is it okay if I tell her?"

They agreed to that, and left her considering the sketch she'd just completed: Shaun and Nash watching Pan. Would Tyler and Nash be able to feed off normal humans as well, or only Blues and Greens? Would all Blues be seen as dangerous monsters, either destructive or life-stealing?

Before long a car arrived carrying five Blues in their early twenties. More people drifted in while these were running through their tests, a trickle which became a stream, until there were hundreds, Blues and Greens, far more than anyone had expected. Someone had brought a portable stereo, there were picnic baskets, umbrellas. As the day warmed, a handful went east of the lifeguard tower to swim. Then Pan discovered that he could use a partial force field to launch himself into the air, and immediately after frantically found a way to slow his fall with another, splashing down into the surf in a minor explosion of spray.

Madeleine drew. Faces full of excitement, strain, hilarity, irritation, hope, suspicion. People who clumped together, never straying too far from their particular friends. Those who sat apart. The group around Fisher, Shaun and Nash, pontificating at each other. The handful who had decided to jump off the walkway and force shield bomb the sand, and the group who went to lecture them.

Among the small sea of strangers Madeleine spotted Finger Wharf residents, and stopped sketching to talk to Asha, and to meet Mrs Jabbour.

"It is the feeling of taking a positive step," Mrs Jabbour explained, gazing fondly at her husband and daughter as they prepared to test. "Even though we saw that you had more than enough participants, we still wanted to come, to take part."

"Saw?"

With a smile, Mrs Jabbour nodded at the railing above and behind them. "The special news broadcast. Did you not know?"

Madeleine looked, and saw two women with a professional-weight camera. Wincing, she turned away.

"We will be leaving, early tomorrow," Mrs Jabbour went on. "To the house of a cousin on the South Coast. If you and your friends wish to join us, you would be welcome."

"Aren't the roads still closed?"

"The main roads perhaps. We will find a way."

The idea of just getting out of Sydney was tempting, but Madeleine didn't want to go too far from her parents, and explained their situation.

"You, too, have been blessed then." Mrs Jabbour held out her hands as Faliha came bouncing up, glorying in the length of her punch. "Cherish that gift."

Like Madeleine, the Jabbours were rare in not having lost anyone from the very core of their little family. Even Madeleine's grandparents were fine, off up in Armidale.

Reminded of Noi, Madeleine looked about and couldn't spot her. Tucking her sketchbook into her shoulder bag, she climbed the stairs and wandered across to the Bondi Pavilion, a low, square building with galleries and a gelato shop, lockers and showers. No sign of Noi, no response to her tentative call in the toilets.

Not quite concerned, Madeleine headed back toward the beach and stood at the top of the flat series of stairs to the left of the lifeguard tower. Bondi Beach was enormous, large enough for ten thousand, let alone the few hundred clustered around its centre. Noi shouldn't be hard to find.

Far to her left an isolated figure in a sunhat was standing at the very eastern end of the beach. Noi. Madeleine headed in her direction, and Noi must have seen her, starting back.

"I think they're about through," Madeleine said, when she reached the older girl. "The flow of new arrivals has slowed, at any rate. Did you know it's being broadcast?"

"Yeah. Casey and Djella, ABC Sydney's newest – and only – roving reporters. One of them was a sound editor, and the other some kind of junior-league production assistant. They knew a heap of interesting goss. You know the home billeting thing being set up – people volunteering to take in some of the city outflow? Blues and Greens are going to be specifically excluded, no matter what the science types say about there being no sign of person to person transmission. And they want to collect any Blues and Greens who are already outside the city, and not let them stay with uninfected people. Even their own families that they've been staying with for the past week without any sign of passing this on."

"I guess it's too early to be entirely certain we won't start spewing out dust," Madeleine said, far from pleased. "It's only going to get worse when they know there's two types of Blues." She explained briefly about Tyler and Nash.

"Is *that* what's going on with Nash?" Noi produced a low, appreciative whistle. "Just what we didn't need. Damn, I was already looking forward to meeting your cousin. This makes him twice as interesting! Think I can talk him into biting me?"

Madeleine gave Noi a wary look, and realised she was being teased.

"People really did give you a rough time for having Tyler Vaughn as a cousin, huh?" Noi said. "I would have thought they'd be queuing up to ask you to wangle an autograph."

"Some did. But at that point I hadn't seen Tyler for six years. We knew he'd come back to Australia, and then we spotted him guest-starring on *Blood Mirror*. It wasn't until they asked him to come back as a rival love interest, and that whole 'you realise I'm physically male' story was released that most people back home even recognised him. School got very strange after that."

She rubbed her forearm, still able to find a slight lump.

"It wasn't the people objecting to the way he dressed who were my main problem. All his new Biggest Fans were angry at me for not producing him for some kind of show-and-tell session, and then decided to be offended that I didn't refer to him as 'she'."

"'Tyler is Tyler'," Noi murmured, repeating what had become his fan club's catchcry.

"Yeah, this was before he gave that interview about labels, and what he identified as. I got trapped in an argument with a bunch of girls about me not being sensitive or respectful enough and, well, we were at the top of a flight of stairs. I ended up with a broken arm, Mum took me out of school for what was left of the year, and we moved to Sydney."

The two people in school she'd thought her closest friends had been in that group. None of it had been strictly intentional; it had all just escalated into stupidity. At her new school she'd almost gone out of her way to cultivate a stuck up bitch reputation, and had maintained total disinterest in socialising right up until she met Noi's Devonshire tea.

For someone who had been so convinced friends weren't worth it, Madeleine was aware of spending more and more time worrying about Noi. She wanted to find ways to make it easier for her, to relieve the hurt beneath her surface good humour. It was an impulse born of more than just a practical need for allies, or a change in herself to fit a new world. There were some people that you were just meant to be friends with.

"Will you tell me about your family?" she asked tentatively, and saw immediately that it was too soon, adding: "Some time?"

Noi had turned her head so the sun hat hid her face, but she nodded, and increased her pace, weaving through the clusters of people sitting on the east side of the lifeguard tower.

"Here you are!"

It was Emily, fine blond hair tumbling out of its topknot, face strained, a waver in her voice.

"What's up?" Noi sounded startled. "Did something happen?"

"No, I —" The girl stopped in front of them, suddenly shamefaced. "I just didn't know where you were. I'm sorry."

Noi paused, expression quizzical, then her wry smile bloomed. "Don't worry so much. We're not going to run off and leave you. You must have seen that the car's still here."

Patches of red blotched Emily's fine skin, and she told them again she was sorry. "I just kept — I keep thinking I see those guys, and then it isn't them. The thing is, I could have blown holes in windows just as easily as them. I could have blown holes in *walls*. But all I did was what they told me, and wish I could get away, and I don't know if I could ever have stood up to them the way you did, and I feel so stupid and so angry and I just want to *hit* things."

"Millie the Mauler," Noi said, and tugged a lock of Emily's hair. "Don't forget I'm technically the responsible adult around here. I've had more time to practice dealing with dickheads. You're, what, fifteen?"

"Thirteen."

"What?! You are not allowed to be thirteen and taller than me! Between you and Maddie I'm going to get a complex. But even with your unnatural stalkiness, I've still got your back. And you and Maddie have got mine, okay? We're the Three Musketeers – except without swordfights. We can be dashing, and...y'know, I have absolutely no idea what the Three Musketeers did, except it involved swordfights. And hats with feathers."

"The Blue Musketeers. We can rescue people."

Emily took Noi's hand and gave her a look of such unbounded admiration that Madeleine, a step behind them, was struck with an urgent need to get them home so she could paint them.

"Weren't muskets guns?" Noi continued. "Why swordfights?"

Madeleine was about to suggest heading off for an artistic interlude when a woman sitting on the sand a short way ahead glanced in their direction, gaped, and sprang to her feet. She was pointing above and behind them, so of course they stopped and turned, and saw a pale ball of light dropping out of the sky toward them.

A falling star.

Chapter Eight

"Back up," Noi ordered, gripping Emily and Madeleine's arms and drawing them toward the edge of the surf as the watermelon-sized ball slowed to a stop about ten feet above the sand.

All those immediately around the light moved similarly, though others came forward, until there was a large circle of people south-east of the lifeguard tower. Some kept going till they were well distant, and Madeleine spotted the Jabbours pausing near the ramp off the beach, and thought it strange that no-one outright left. They'd surely all seen enough movies where the alien arrives and starts disintegrating the people not sensible enough to run.

Yet she, too, stayed and waited because she wanted to know.

Pan hurried up behind them, and poked his head between Noi and Madeleine. "Is it *singing*?"

"I've heard that before," Madeleine said, frowning. "A couple of times."

"It's like an out of tune radio."

"A theremin," Nash said, leading Gavin and Shaun to stand with them at the edge of the surf. "Or very like."

"Shit, is this thing just some kind of speaker? We come from beyond the stars: it's time for a concert?" Pan started forward, but Nash snagged the back of his shirt and pulled him to a standstill.

"Where's Fish?" Shaun asked, looking about. "He'd hate to miss this."

Nash pointed to Fisher and Nick in the lifeguard tower, watching through the glass. "That makes a good vantage. Let's relocate. Move slowly, so we do not draw its attention."

"But I want to draw—" Pan began, and broke off.

The glowing ball of light was changing shape.

Triangular strips opened out like the petals of an unsymmetrical flower. The shortest triangle pointed up, while two of equal length stretched left and right, with the longest unfurling downward until the ball had become a different form of star, four-pointed, glimmering white. An uneven centre band of dark blue reminded Madeleine vaguely of the body of a butterfly, though it was not actually separate from the rest of the star, merely a concentration of colour which thinned out into a filigree lace of veins.

"An angel!" someone shouted.

Madeleine blinked, but she could see the connection. The central band of blue could almost be a narrow human outline, though one with feet which trailed to a point, and no arms, or arms crossed on the chest. The thing was shaped more like a kite than any angel, a fluidly rippling one without any rigid frame. The weird, oscillating noise came again, louder, and the star-kite moved, a lazy undulation only a foot or so forward, sparking an immediate backward scatter from its audience.

"How are we going to know if it's saying 'take me to your leader'?" Pan asked.

"I agree with Nash," Noi murmured. "Let's–"

The star slid sideways, quick as a piece of paper caught by the wind, turned in a moment and settled across the shoulders of a bulky, sunburned guy, who tried and failed to dodge as it landed. For a moment it looked like a hooded cloak, then it sank out of sight.

"The hell–?" Pan and Noi said in unison.

The sunburned guy stood unmoving, face blank, as the crowd around him drew back. Then he blinked, looked sharply left and right, lifted one hand and closed it, opened it.

"The noises are coming from him now!"

The sunburned guy looked toward the woman who had shouted, and she flinched back, then firmed and asked angrily: "Why have you done this? What do you *want* from us?"

"To–" The man paused, repeated the word, a stutter of sound, frowned then said clearly, in a distinct Western Sydney accent, "To stand still."

"Stand...?"

"Fuck."

Pan pointed, the crowd turned. Then, as one, they ran.

ooOoo

The stars came from the east, dozens, hundreds, dropping out of the sky.

Madeleine raced with Emily directly for the lifeguard tower stairs, but the cross-current of people before her was too thick, and she diverted left, angling for the nearest ramp off the sand. Almost a hundred metres from the shoreline, those who had wisely left early were already jamming onto it, others diverting again for the ramp further west. But Tyler's car was right near the head of the first ramp, and Madeleine took a frantic glance over her shoulder, trying to decide whether to forge into the press or just dash west, and keep running.

The leading edge of stars were unfurling behind her, dropping down onto the shoulders of those slowest to move. And one, distinctly brighter, bluer than the rest, was so close, sliding unmistakably in her direction and she gasped and snatched at Emily's hand and darted left, giving up the ramp in preference for speed. But the things – kites, butterflies, angels – moved faster than any runner.

The lightest touch, the breath of the sun.

A response roared inside her, an instinctive outflow, and she found herself lifted off her feet, sailing forward to plough into the sand. Around her others had been similarly knocked down, and were struggling to their feet.

"Shield!" Gavin shouted, staring back. "You can shield! Shield against them!"

The very blue star which had been chasing Madeleine had curled partially closed and dropped close to the sand. The other stars were clustering toward it, filling the air with their oscillating song. Noi grabbed Emily up and took off, and Madeleine was about to follow when she saw Shaun. One of those she'd knocked down, he was lying unmoving to her left, Nash trying to rouse him.

"Is he—?" With a frantic glance at the star cluster, she grabbed Shaun's arm and tried to lift.

"I think shield paralysis," Nash said. "On two."

With desperate energy they lifted, Nash doing most of the work until Gavin dashed back and helped.

"Can you shield again when they come?" Nash asked, gasping with effort.

"I don't know! I'll try!" Their speed carrying Shaun meant she would have to.

But the stars swooped past them to settle on runners on the ramp. As each runner was embraced they stopped short, and the way was quickly becoming blocked.

"Go back past the lifeguard tower," Gavin panted. "Up the wide stairs."

It was longer to run, but Emily was already standing at the head of the lifeguard tower stair, signalling wildly and pointing east, so they dog-legged back. And the stars passed them.

"They're avoiding us!" Gavin said.

"They might be – tack left."

People were running toward them, some moving slow and hesitant, but others picking up speed. Shaun's rigidity abruptly lapsed, and he groaned and flinched in their hold, sending them stumbling.

"C'n r'n," he groaned, thrashing and gulping.

Remembering the agonies of the pins and needles, Madeleine sincerely doubted it, but he surprised her, managing to at least make it easier for Gavin and Nash to haul him.

Two women ahead were on an intercept course – they wouldn't make it past them.

"Go straight through!" Nash ordered.

Madeleine shuddered, but knew they couldn't risk the delay of a collision and held up one hand. Trying not to think of twisted metal, of tumbled cars, she pushed some of the energy inside her into a punch at the two women.

Their shields were just visible, a protective glimmer which appeared as the punch struck them and sent one tumbling backward. The other was only knocked a little off course, spun onto her knees, but this was enough to get them past and in sight of the stairs. Emily was running along the level above, Fisher trailing behind her, and they met in a group and dashed up the next set of stairs to where Nick was waiting in the white hatchback, Pan and a couple of other boys already crammed into the back seat.

"Noi's...coming..." Emily gasped, and clutched Madeleine, trying to catch her breath as Nash and Gavin helped Shaun into the car.

"Go!" Nash told Nick. "Meet you at Rushies."

"Keep moving," Gavin added, as Nick obediently tore off, narrowly missing a small van trying to get past.

They ran all-out alongside the one-way road in front of Bondi Pavilion, and Madeleine's legs were jelly, rubber bands, not forgiving the energy cost of shields and punches, nor her general disinclination to run long distances. She was falling behind, her breath burning in her throat, but then there was a newly-familiar growl of expensive engine and she straight-out dived into the rear seat of Tyler's car as Noi slowed, then surged forward to collect the others, the car soon over-crammed with panting, gasping escapees.

The undersized rear seat was not a good fit for Madeleine, Fisher and Nash, particularly with Madeleine at the bottom. She wriggled out as Noi came to the end of the long one-way street and slewed right onto the main road.

"Hook a left at Blair," Gavin recommended, balancing Emily on his lap. "Are they coming after us?"

Fisher stared back, his expression closed. "They don't seem able to move as fast as a car," he said slowly. He looked at Madeleine, currently sitting mostly on Nash's lap. "Did you do that on purpose?"

She shook her head.

"I think you hurt it," Gavin said. "They weren't keen to come near you after."

"What do we do now?" Emily's voice was high.

"I don't see any other option than to get out of the city," Noi said. "Even though everyone's going to be totally paranoid about Blues and Greens, and there's a huge chance of getting locked up if we're found. But better locked up than possessed. Did anyone from your school get taken?"

"Chris." Nash glanced at Fisher, but didn't find any answer in Fisher's puzzled expression. "Hammad and Ryan were there as well, but I didn't see what happened to them."

"We've no way of knowing how much they can learn from the people they take over. Language, obviously, but they might know about your school from your friend."

Nash nodded. "We need to warn everyone there – if they don't know already – then grab what we can and go."

"This car has about a quarter of a tank left." Noi pushed down on the accelerator. "But we've been collecting car keys back at Finger Wharf. And boats, though they're probably not much advantage for getting away from flying balls of light."

Emily distracted them then by pulling a bag of coconut ice from the glove box and passing it around. In a car full of Blues this was an immediate silencer, and Madeleine was particularly grateful, shaking as she grabbed a handful of pink and white squares and worked her way through them.

At Noi's speed and with clear roads it was a short trip to Rushcutters Bay, and Gavin directed them through a wide-open iron gate to a small car park surrounded by clipped hedges and many-windowed buildings. The white hatchback was there waiting for them, its occupants clustered around Pan as he stood arguing with a dozen boys holding cricket bats.

"I'm going to turn the car for a quick getaway," Noi said, after a brief survey.

She was speaking to empty seats, as Gavin and Nash were already out and bounding forward. Fisher was slower to move, glancing up into the sky before following.

"What the hell's this, Matt?" Gavin said, striding up to confront a tall, tanned boy with brown hair. "We've got to move, not argue."

"*You've* got to move," the boy, Matt, replied. "All you Blues. We won't stop you going, but there's no way you're staying here when any of you could have one of those things inside you."

"All us Blues?!" Gavin exploded. "What shit are you pulling now?"

"They're not interested in Greens, Gav," a different boy said apologetically. "We were watching on TV, and they ignored all the Greens. They only went for Blues. Matt's right – even if none of you are...whatever, there's too much chance you'll draw them here."

"And in what way are the cricket bats going to help?" Nash asked, his beautiful voice mild yet commanding. "We are only here to warn you – unnecessary as that is – and to get our bags and be gone. I would suggest you do the same."

He walked straight at the heart of the crowd, head high and stride scornful, and they wavered, wilted, and stepped aside.

"Tossers," Pan muttered, following.

"Oh, eat it Rickard." The boy called Matt threw the cricket bat after Pan, which was a mistake since Pan had been waiting for it, and the thick wooden bat bounced spectacularly off his shield and through a window.

Nash whirled protectively to stand by Pan, and the two groups tensed, but further words or action were cut short by Noi, leaning on the horn of Tyler's car.

"Can we save the dick swinging until after we've escaped from the aliens?" she shouted into the silence the horn left behind. "Seriously, Blue, Green, Purple, whatever – now is the time for running and hiding. You think just because those things are only possessing Blues they're going to happily ignore Greens? Go get your stuff, *all* of you, get into cars, and get the hell out of the city!"

They listened. Within moments only Noi, Madeleine and Emily remained in the car park.

"What were they thinking?" Emily asked, close to tears. "A Blue could turn a Green into a smear without even trying."

"They're afraid." Noi sighed, and ran a hand over her eyes. "When you're afraid, sometimes it's easier to be angry."

Madeleine, suffering a raging thirst after her handful of coconut ice, spotted a tap on one side of the car park and fished an empty, dented water bottle out from her well-mashed shoulder bag. She was drinking thirstily when a thin, oscillating sound made her gulp and then desperately try not to cough. Noi pulled Emily behind the nearest hedge and ducked down and Madeleine followed suit, though the hedges near the tap were half the height, forcing her to lie full-length between bush and building to have any hope of concealment.

Eyes streaming from suppressed coughing, Madeleine peered up through dense leaves, trying to track the source of the noise. Was there – yes. Floating lightly over the roof of the building opposite was a ball of light. She pressed down into the dirt and leaf litter, sure she could hear an echo of the thing's song. More than one of them.

The memory of the lightest touch stopped her breath, and she guessed, knew, that it was the same one, the bright, rich blue one which had been so close. It had followed her, and no amount of branch or leaf could hide her.

The song died down as the star moved further into the school, giving no sign it was aware of three Blue girls. Madeleine lifted her head cautiously, but across the car park Noi immediately made a lowering gesture. They would wait.

Boys began appearing. Three Greens, running straight through the gates without even glancing around. One of the younger Blues who'd been at the beach, slipping into the back seat of the white hatchback and crouching down into the foot well, sitting his bag on top of him as partial camouflage. Another group, all Greens, piling into a four wheel drive and gunning the engine, waiting for a final friend before roaring off, swerving around Tyler's empty car.

Pan and Nash emerged from Madeleine's side of the car park, crossed without seeing her and paused beside the two driverless cars until Noi beckoned them over for a hasty, whispered conference. Then, as Shaun, Gavin and Fisher appeared among a large clump of Greens, she signalled a dash for the car.

Tensed for the return of the oscillating song, Madeleine was unprepared for a sudden chorus, louder and yet more distant than the encounter at the beach. It wasn't coming from anything in the school, was strangely pervasive, overwhelming. Ahead of her the group of boys stopped and turned, orienting toward it.

"That's the Spire," Emily said, as Madeleine reached the car.

Noi didn't pause, leaping into the driver's seat and starting the engine. "Care later. Leave now."

Madeleine obediently climbed in back as Pan and Nash headed for the white hatchback.

"Shaun?" Gavin, about to join them, darted back. "C'mon man, we've got to move."

Shaun didn't react, listening intently to the wordless, fluctuating noise.

"He's got the keys," Pan said

With a swift, comprehensive glance at a dozen boys, all Greens, all standing motionless staring in the same direction, Nash reversed course, he and Pan climbing into the sports car. Fisher, who had stowed his bag in the boot, took the front seat and a lap full of Emily.

"Gav! Come on!"

Trying to shake some response out of Shaun, Gavin glanced back and that was the worst of timing because he saw their horrified reaction but not the deep blue kite shape which flowed down from the roof and settled in an embrace around him.

Noi let the clutch out, then stamped immediately on the brakes as the hidden boy erupted from the white hatchback and threw himself across the sports car's back seat, heavy bag thumping against the car door until Pan dragged it in.

The car leaped forward, engine rising from a purr to a roar, and they left the school and a dozen unmoving boys behind them.

Chapter Nine

Staring back, Madeleine could see the lone strawberry blond boy who walked to the gate. Watching them go.

"Gav! Bastard things! We'll get them for this!" Pan writhed under the weight of bags and the boy lying across all three back seat occupants. "Shit. Fuck them all! Shit, shit, shit. Damn it, I need better words."

He took a deep breath, and boiled out with:

"I will do such things, what they are yet I know not, but they shall be the terrors of the Earth! You think I'll weep. No, I'll not weep."

He was shouting, eyes bright and wet, punctuating the sentences with thumps on the legs of the boy lying on top of him.

"I have full cause of weeping, but this heart will break into a hundred thousand fragments before I'll weep! Oh Fool, I shall go mad!"

Noi darted a glance back at him, then at Emily's gasp swore herself and swerved around the three Greens who had left first, standing just around a bend in the road. The boy lying on top, a spiky-haired Asian kid, slid dangerously sideways, and Madeleine and Nash grabbed to stop him zipping over the side.

"Be Shakespearian later," Nash told Pan. "Focus on the fact that he's not dead. For all we know these things hop from person to person, and there's a chance we can get Gav back."

Pan punched the inside of the nearest door, a thump to make them all wince, but he stopped talking.

"We've been terraformed," said the boy in Madeleine's lap, his lightly-accented voice edged with a kind of disbelieving, acid delight. "They made us habitable."

"It's what they've done to the Greens which concerns me," Nash said. "There are so many more Greens than Blues, and they seem to have all been impacted at once. We had best not spend long at the Wharf getting those cars."

"Get out of the city as soon as possible," Emily muttered.

"No." "Perhaps not."

Noi and Fisher, speaking together.

"Why not?" Madeleine asked, startled. "Even if we get locked up, it's better than...that."

"Because of the Greens. Because we don't know nearly enough about what's going on. How far does that sound carry? Is it going to tell them to do anything more than stand gaping?" Noi roared down a wider road. "There're Greens in every direction, in all the surrounding towns."

"We need a solid plan on where to go, and how to get there unseen," Fisher said. He had been very quiet, uncertain, but now seemed to have rediscovered his drive. "The problem is finding a place where we can wait safely and gather information."

"That's taken care of," Noi said. "We had a Plan B."

After the swiftest of trips they hurried up to Tyler's apartment, squashing into one elevator, tensely searching for any sign of other people, straining for an individual voice over the song of the Spire.

"Someone pack the edibles while we grab our stuff," Noi said, scooping up a line of keys.

The TV went on while Madeleine was in Tyler's wardrobe, and when she emerged the screen showed a couple of hundred people, all staring in the same direction.

"All of the world," Nash said. "A simultaneous attack."

Madeleine turned to stick a large note on the fridge: "*T – Don't stay here. They know it. – M*" She printed her mobile number at the bottom, in case he'd lost it, then did a quick tour of the room, collecting stray brushes and the bag of pads and pencils she'd put together while hunting nappies and baby formula. Most of her supplies were already in the bolthole, a piece of forethought she owed to Emily.

"Right." Noi emerged, two bags hooked over her shoulders. "We don't have far to go, but it's critical we go quick, quiet and unseen. Let's head down to the central hall."

They accomplished this without much difficulty, the cloak-and-dagger peering about not even comical when they were all so sick and nervous.

"Good," Noi said, as they emerged from the elevator. "Now–"

"Girls! Wait there!"

Madeleine was not the only one who gasped at the sudden voice from above. The elevator's doors closed behind them and, exchanging glances, they watched it go up.

"Wait," Noi murmured. "If it's an attack, run out to the visitor parking – through the big entryway on the driveway side. I've a key to one of those cars."

"But who is it?" Pan asked, eyeing the descending figure.

"Not a clue," Noi said, as a beautifully-dressed woman – all silk and pearls, her platinum hair perfectly coiffed – stepped out.

She was holding a gift-wrapped box, complete with extravagant, curling bow. "Girls," she said, her voice cultured and assured, "I wanted to give you a small thank you before I left." Smiling, she held out the box, which Noi accepted blankly. "Take care of yourselves."

Without another word she turned and walked back into the elevator, her heels clicking.

"Hello *Twilight Zone*," Pan said, as it descended.

"Have you seen her before?" Noi asked, and Madeleine shook her head.

"Something you can discuss later–" Fisher began, and stopped as Noi suddenly gaped.

"Take Him Away Lady! It has to be! Holy flipping hell."

"You think so?" Madeleine stared at the elevator, but the woman was already out of sight. Could that hoarse, frantic whisper really have come from a person who looked like that?

"Has to be," Noi repeated. "And, yeah, now is not the time." She spun on her heel, craning to look in every direction. "Total fail on quick, quiet and unseen, but we're going to have to risk it. Come on."

They were already near the north end of the long central hall, so it was a short trip to the aerial bridge joining the main building to the smaller block at the very end of the wharf.

"This is called the North Building," Noi said, after they had crossed, and the outside world was safely closed away once again. "When we were doing our check-the-neighbours shtick we didn't find anyone alive in here. Almost all the apartments on the east side didn't have anyone in them at all." She paused as Madeleine unlocked the door of their chosen bolthole. "One advantage of this one is that with the help of a ladder we prepared earlier you can jump the patio fences and dash for either the cars, or the boat moorings. There's comparatively limited entry points, we can move through the whole sub-building without risk of being seen, and there's a good hiding spot if anyone actually comes this far."

"You don't think it too close to where you were before?" Nash asked.

"I think that right now there's very few places where we can get in and out without having an encounter like we just had with the Take Him Away Lady, where there's no-one on the other side of a wall to hear us, where there's no easy line of sight through the windows. We might want to move again, sure, but I'm not driving madly through the city till I have a better idea of what's going on."

"Makes sense," Fisher said.

"Why do you call her the Take Him Away Lady?" Pan asked, and Noi explained as they dumped their bags just past the entry hall.

The apartment was enormous, taking up the eastern half of the ground floor of the North Building, with a spiral staircase leading up to another quarter floor on the level above. Sliding doors led to an expansive patio bordered by potted hedges and a glass safety fence which looked directly out into the harbour. The sprawling lounge, dining and kitchen area which backed on to this was full of sunlight, and the room was dotted with touches which showed that this was a family home: children's drawings stuck to the fridge, clusters of photos, and a stuffed unicorn arranged in one of the chairs. The warm comfort of the place seemed to make the day's losses all the crueller, and they collapsed onto the wide lounges, suddenly depleted.

"Damn it," Pan muttered again.

Nash dropped a hand to his shoulder, but he shrugged it off. The taller boy looked worried, but turned his attention to the room. "This is Min," he said belatedly, while Fisher sorted through a collection of remotes.

"Pleased to escape with you," the younger boy said.

"Welcome, welcome." Noi gestured vaguely around the room, then paused and pulled out her phone, answering it as Fisher managed to turn on the wall-mounted television.

Images of silently-standing Greens were interspersed with scenes of unfurling stars, of fleeing Blues embraced to become abruptly composed and purposeful. The stars had found large groups of Blues everywhere, whether gathered to test their powers, or in the survival communities which had begun to form: swooping into dormitories, share-homes, repurposed hospital wards. One group of stars had even travelled far out beyond the fringes of their city, to a quarantine facility outside the dust zone.

"Hiding mightn't be a plan after all," Pan said restively. "They don't seem to have any problem finding Blues."

"The one at the school passed right by us and didn't stop," Emily said.

"None of these places have been hidden," Fisher pointed out. "Most are Safe Zone sites whose locations have been broadcast. And we could hardly have been more noisy about the testing sessions."

"Aliens who surf the internet." Pan shook his head. "Great."

Noi's fragmentary conversation reminded Madeleine to hunt out her own phone, and she was not surprised to see a half-dozen missed calls from home. The spectacle of Madeleine Cost being thrown to the sands of Bondi Beach had already flashed up twice among the stream of TV images.

Moving to sit on the spiral stair, she tried her home number

"Hi Mum."

"Oh, thank God!" A pause. "It – it is you, isn't it?"

A tiny snort of laughter escaped Madeleine, and then her eyes stung and she felt ill and exhausted. "I don't think the 'phone home' stuff applies to all aliens," she said unevenly.

"Are you safe? Are you hurt?"

"Just a little shaken up. I'm with friends. We'll try to leave the city as soon as we figure out a safe way to do it. Mum, I think you and Dad should go now. Go to Gran's."

"Maddie, we're not leaving without you."

"Please Mum." Her voice had gone tight and high and she struggled to bring it back under control.

There came the sound of the receiver being passed, then: "Maddie."

"Dad, make her go. It'll be... Please. If I know you're out of reach of this, it'll help."

"Where are you?"

"Well hidden. Plenty of food. We haven't decided yet what to do long-term, but for the moment we're set to wait and listen."

Silence, then: "We were so proud of you today, Maddie. When you stopped to help that boy, I could see how afraid you were, and I—" He broke off, and Madeleine had to stand abruptly and go upstairs. Their conversation after that was fractured and full, and she broke down when it was done, and wept for the first time since she'd woken lying in dust.

After some time, Noi came up and handed Madeleine a steaming mug.

"There's a few thousand spoonfuls of sugar in this," she said. "We're all pretty shocky."

"Thanks," Madeleine mumbled, and sipped until her throat had opened, watching Noi as she wandered around the room.

The triple-wide landing at the top of the staircase had been fitted out as a spacious library, with floor to ceiling shelving on all walls, and even above the window seat which looked out over the navy base side of the bay. Most of the shelves were a riotous jumble of spines of all colours and sizes, but one bookcase held nothing but two-tone Penguin classics, and on another serried ranks of leather gleamed. The only furniture beside the window seat was a heavy coffee table, a curve-footed floor globe, and two vivid stained glass lamps. It was perhaps the nicest room Madeleine had ever been in, and she wished she was in a state to appreciate it.

"Who called?" she asked eventually.

"Faliha. They went straight south, didn't come back here for anything. And then, well, her Mum...stopped. Is just sitting in the car, turned toward the Spire. Faliha wanted to ask if we had any information – and to check if we were okay."

"What if the Greens *stay* like that? Just standing, staring, until they starve and die? Shaun and Nick and Mrs Jabbour and..."

"The possessed Blues are gathering near the Spires," Noi went on, deliberately shutting down speculation. "That webcam trained on the Sydney Spire is still working, but only a couple of people have shown up so far." She paused, eyeing Madeleine critically, then went to the top of the stair and called down: "Come up here and I'll show you why this place in particular."

The rest of the escapees came clattering up, exclaiming at the room.

"Because we won't run out of reading matter if the power goes?" Fisher asked, with a faint smile and lifted brows.

"Not even because of the Wonder Woman bedroom," Noi said. "Which I've bagged already, thanks. No, check this out."

She crossed to the leather-bound books and pulled three toward her, producing a muted click. And the entire bookcase moved, swinging out to reveal a pocket-sized office with a safe, a desk and computer in front of a slatted window, and high shelves full of files.

"You can tell it's there if you start looking at room proportions," Noi said. "But I would never have guessed if it wasn't standing open when we showed up."

"Your taste in hideouts is impeccable," Min said. "But that would be comfortable for two or three."

"We'll clean out what we can and deal with it," Noi said, shrugging. "If anyone comes to this building, we're straight up here and the door shut. No waffling, no delay. And we need to do what we can to minimise the 'bunch of people hiding out' ambience we've already achieved. I wanted to hook up some kind of motion sensor alarm for that walkway, but didn't get a chance, so we'll just have to be quiet and keep an ear out."

"If there are other computers in the building, there is every chance one of them has a webcam," Nash suggested. "We can feed it to a monitor in the lounge, and roster some kind of watch."

"Good thought. Maybe we better set that up straight away, and then talk what next."

"And have food," Emily said plaintively, sparking immediate agreement. Blues.

Nash left with Fisher and Min to scout the other apartments for an unobtrusive spot to set a camera, while Pan decided to join the cooking crew.

"Is there really a Wonder Woman bedroom?" he asked.

"And a Supergirl one."

"That's mine," Emily said.

"There's six bedrooms." Noi eyed the pantry stuffed with bulk supplies from the restaurants, then passed it over in favour of the freezer. "Two guest rooms – each with twin beds, luckily – the parents' room and three for the kids, and I think I would really like the people who live here and I have no idea if they're alive or dead, or standing in a street somewhere staring at the Spire."

Her voice, just for a moment, had wavered, then she reached into the freezer and pulled out a Tupperware container. Keeping on. Noi, Madeleine knew, wouldn't break down till no-one could see her.

ooOoo

"So," Noi said, after the first edge of hunger had been dulled, "places to run to. Family homes. Houses belonging to really trusted friends who live outside the city. Where's everyone from?"

"Hong Kong," Min said, with a slight smile. "And I suspect we can rule out Nash's home as well."

"I live in Edgecliff," Fisher said, naming a suburb just east of Rushcutters Bay.

"Marrickville." Noi lifted one shoulder. "I had some rellies up in Brisbane, which is no help."

"Leumeah," Madeleine said. "Out near Campbelltown, still in the dust zone. But my grandmother lives just outside Armidale. My parents – I told my parents to try to get there today. It's on the edge of farmland, kind of open, but it wouldn't be totally obvious if we were there."

"Kogarah," Emily said quietly, and did not mention parents. That was a suburb not much further out than Marrickville.

"Oberon," Pan put in. "In the tablelands, just before Bathurst. Relatives all around the area. A couple of spare rooms."

"Shouldn't you be called Puck, not Pan, if you're from Oberon?" Min asked, eyes lit with sudden delight.

"I've played him as well. But merry trickster junk aside, he spends his time being ordered around. Pirate-taunting's way more my style."

"What I'd give for a straightforward pirate right now," Noi said. "Okay, so either west or up north. Oberon's closer, but might be harder to get to since there's fewer access roads into the mountains. How likely is it that a bunch of us could stay at either place for any measurable amount of time without the entire town knowing?"

Neither Pan nor Madeleine were very hopeful of that happening, and they debated splitting into smaller groups, or whether it was necessarily that bad a thing to be known to be Blue, once you were out of the city.

"Can't we stay and fight?" Emily asked. "We're letting them get away with killing our families, and taking our friends, and our homes! It's not hopeless! Madeleine *hurt* one of them, and they couldn't take her over. We can punch and shield. Can't we at least *try*?"

"At this stage, we can only learn more before acting," Fisher said. He hesitated, then added softly: "I won't pretend I don't want to hurt them. I want – very badly – to bring that Spire down. I'm trying to think of a way. That Madeleine was able to shield..." He gave Madeleine a measured glance, then an apologetic smile as she reacted with not unnatural discomfort. "It gives me hope, but it's hardly an upper hand. We will watch for opportunities to go on the offensive, but we need to prioritise staying...ourselves."

"If nothing else, we can practice shielding and punching," Nash said. "The car park below this North Building will give us a relatively private space, though we won't be able to use anything like full strength. But fine control, learning to shield quickly, it cannot be a bad thing."

"We brought some phones back from the other apartments," Min told them. "Use them and turn your own off. And stay off the ground line. I'll set up a monitor and alarm in the lounge for the webcams – there's a program I can use to make them motion sensitive. It'd also be best to go silent on any web identities, and mask our IP for any family contact."

"You're starting to depress me," Noi said. "But more smart thinking. And I'm sure everyone can resist the temptation to give out details. If you have to tell them something, tell 'em we're out near the zoo."

Without a clear decision on what to do next, they finished up dinner, attention shifting to the television as it showed scenes from earlier in the day – Blues being chased, Blues shooting at balls of light which didn't seem to care about bullets, Blues force-punching and hurting each other far more than their pursuers, and no other instances than Madeleine's of anyone even momentarily saving themselves with a shield.

The gatherings of Blues near the Spires seemed to be breaking up, and there were signs of movement among the Greens, some of whom had at least walked out of range of cameras observing them. Others were still standing, waiting, whiles Greens more than two hundred kilometres from Spires didn't seem impacted at all by the Spire song, even if it was played for them.

Fisher and Nash stacked the dishwasher while everyone else shifted bags and tried to rearrange the pantry so it looked a little less obviously stocked for a siege – difficult given the industrial-sized sacks of sugar and flour. With the boys taking all the downstairs rooms, the parents' room was left for Madeleine. It was decorated in dark wood and another beautiful lamp, but she felt uncomfortable, an intruder.

Folding her clothes into piles in the wardrobe, Madeleine hesitated over her backpack. She'd bestowed most of the packets of condoms on Noi, but had kept a few, vacillating between thinking this very bloodless and unspontaneous, and acknowledging that she was not only keenly attracted to Fisher, but also in a situation where she was more than ordinarily inclined to act on that attraction.

Or not. Shaking her head at the thought of successfully advancing anything with Fisher, she tipped the contents of the backpack into a bedside drawer and went to find Noi.

Pan had done so just before her. "You meant it about the Wonder Woman bedroom!" he was saying, standing in the doorway.

"It's the floor-to-ceiling gaming consoles which put the cherry on the cake," Noi said, nodding at the only wall not papered in an enormous wrap-around mural of Amazon princess against a silhouetted landscape of temples and stars. "This is one little girl who wants to kick ass."

"You or her? But you're pretty much Wonder Woman already," Pan said, stepping forward to examine the array of games available, and missing Noi's sudden, painful flush. Noi had backed off from Pan after learning that he was indeed only fifteen, and even the news that it was his birthday soon hadn't changed her mind. Since Pan didn't seem to have realised Noi had been pursuing him, her decision hadn't made a great deal of difference to their interaction, but moments of vulnerability broke through.

"Did you see the lightsabers?" Madeleine asked, to give Noi longer to recover.

"Wai! Guys! Get down here!"

Min's summons sent them clattering down the stair. On the big television was an Asian woman wearing a strappy top which showed arms with only the occasional patch of non-blue flesh. Her tone was sedately calm, her posture relaxed, and the effect was one of casual conversation. Madeleine guessed the language to be Japanese.

"Why are we excited?" Noi asked.

"It's one of the possessed. They said she–"

The image flickered and jumped back to a point where the woman was just sitting down. She turned to the camera, and a man began translating in voiceover as she spoke.

"Listen now. I am the Core of the Five of what you may call the Clan Taiee. The Taiee are First in this cycle of primacy among the En-Mott. We come to this world to settle primacy for the next cycle, and to conduct business of our own."

The woman smiled warmly. "Meaningless things to you. Deliver up to us all who are Blue, unharmed. Do not interfere with those who are Green. Neither hinder nor disturb us. Those who do not comply will be reprimanded." The idea of reprimand appeared to delight her. "Should insufficient Blues be delivered to us, the Conversion – the dust – will be released until a sufficient measure achieved."

"*Fuck.*" Pan, beyond Shakespeare, sat down heavily.

"Our business will take a matter of two of your years. When it is complete, we will depart."

The translation ended, and the screen switched to a non-stained woman. "Further transmissions have been made from four other Spire cities. São Paulo, Mumbai, Shanghai, and New York."

They crossed to the New York transmission, where a skinny black teenager with a shaved head told them that he was the Core of the Five of Clan Na-uhl, who were Fourth in this cycle of primacy.

"We are so completely screwed," Pan said.

"No leaving the city." Noi exchanged a glance with Fisher and Nash, who both nodded.

"People wouldn't..." Emily began, then shook her head. "I guess they would. I guess...I guess people might even expect us to turn *ourselves* over."

"They can live in hope." Min waved a tablet computer. "These cities aren't quite an exact run-down of the most populated cities in the world, but it's pretty close. And they're the locations of the tallest Spires. This primacy they're talking about – they took over our planet to decide on a new pecking order." He was incredulous, losing the mildly-entertained calm he'd displayed till then.

"And business of their own." Nash ran a hand over his eyes. "How very unspecific."

"Two years." Noi tapped the lid of the box the Take Him Away Lady had given her, then absently began to pull loose the bow.

"If they leave in two years, what happens to the people they've taken over?" Madeleine asked. "Do they keep them? Or unpossess? Dispossess?"

"Not a gamble I'm willing to take." Noi lifted the lid off the box, revealing a colourful array of cupcakes, exquisitely decorated. She held one up, studying piping work so delicate it was like lace. "Well, she knew just the thing to give to a Blue. And it's a nice illustration of our primary problem – we all eat like horses. We've enough food for a few months, particularly if we collect everything in the other North Building apartments, but two years is going to mean a lot of scouting forays."

They debated longer-term options. Staying at Finger Wharf. Finding another location in the city or outer suburbs. Trying to hide in a countryside fearing a second release of dust. Getting out further, to an island, or Spire-free Tasmania. But for now, not knowing the abilities of the things calling themselves En-Mott, or the position the uninfected would take, they could only stay and watch.

Pan reached suddenly and turned the sound up on the television and they all turned to see freckles, strawberry blond hair and blue eyes.

"...the Clan Ul-naa," a familiar voice said. "The Ul-naa are Hundred and Fifth in this cycle of primacy among the En-Mott. We come to this world to settle primacy for..."

Pan muted the sound again, and then threw the remote at the television. It bounced, and the batteries flew free, but no-one made any move to rescue it. Noi's shoulders had hunched, Emily was trembling with anger, Fisher withdrawn, and Min uncertain. Nash—

"Are you okay?"

A grey tinge marred the warmth of Nash's finely cut features, and his usual grace had leached away. Pan turned sharply, and sucked in his breath: "Damn, it was Gav's day, wasn't it? Why didn't you say anything?"

"Testing limits." Nash lifted one hand, failing to hold back a tremor. "It is a pitiful thing, to be so dependent. I would not last a day alone."

"Here."

Pan held out his hand, but Nash moved his own away. "We've already established that two days together is an excellent way to knock you to pieces."

He turned his head toward Fisher, but stopped when Madeleine held out her hand.

"I've nothing if not energy to spare," she said. "Do I need to do anything in particular?"

Nash hesitated, then said: "Not at all. Thank you."

"Shall we go clear more space in the hidden room?" Fisher asked, and led the others away, leaving Madeleine with an uncomfortable impression she was about to do something intimate.

She studied Nash's hand, admiring the clean lines, then suppressed a murmur of surprise at the warm sensation which swept through her.

For some reason she'd expected it to hurt, and on one level it did, but the way running too fast down a hill hurt: a plummeting exhilaration. She was suddenly lit up all over, intensely aware of the roil of power inside her, and a complex passage of strength from her to Nash. And even more aware of him, as if she was in two places at once. She watched his stars growing bright, and trembled.

He fetched her cupcakes and super-sweetened hot chocolate, and carefully ignored her pink-cheeked confusion, and by the time her mug was empty she'd recovered and was able to be amused at how he was energetically striding about, tidying things up.

"You'd probably best take first watch," she said. "You'll never sleep after that."

Nash agreed, and then made sure she was able to get up the spiral staircase without falling over. It wasn't quite yet sunset, but Madeleine was more than done for the day. After a quick shower in her room's en suite, and several futile attempts to reach Tyler, she removed her phone's battery, and dreamt of running.

Chapter Ten

Someone – Noi, most likely – had come into Madeleine's room overnight and arranged a tray of snacks and drinks on the bedside cabinet, so when piercing hunger woke her in the pre-dawn grey she needed only to sit up. Once the first urgency was met she noticed the cold, and escaped to another warm shower and an attempt to manage her hair.

Descending to the main floor, she found the lounge dark except for the glow of the muted television, and the clear, pale note provided by a vast, water-lapped sky. Pan was sitting in the open doorway to the patio, legs curled against his chest, chin resting on his knees, staring out at the water. He looked cold, small and defeated, all his mercurial energy drained.

Quietly putting together two steaming cups of over-sugared tea, Madeleine handed him one, then sat to share the dawn. A seagull was hovering in the distance, the first she'd seen since the dust.

"Gav was captain of the soccer team," Pan said, when tea or company had warmed him a little. "And he could act the socks off half the school. Fantastic at the comedic roles – did a great Bertie Wooster. Really generous on the stage, too, not fiddling about drawing attention to himself during someone else's good lines." Pan tipped the last of his tea into his mouth, and swallowed heavily. "Just before, they were showing...Madrid, I think it was. Spain somewhere. You know how we were wondering if the Moths could body-hop? Go from person to person? They can. They'd caught two Blues and – I guess some of them must shop around for Blues with the most stain? They came out, and moved into the new Blues. The people they'd been in just dropped. Some Greens carried the bodies off."

There was nothing Madeleine could say. She sat turning her empty mug and listening to the sounds the ocean made in a quiet bay. Soft, secret noises, large yet gentle.

"Gav's dead." Pan was barely audible. "He might still be in his head right now – or not. He might walk around being the Core of the whatever the hell clan for the next two years. But he doesn't get to come back."

He sat a little straighter, putting his mug down carefully. "I agree with Emily. Fuck the running and hiding. Let's find a way to fight these things."

"I'm open to suggestions."

"Would you do it?" Pan shot Madeleine a quick glance. "Any plan we come up with is going to involve us hiding behind you and your metal-crushing awesomeness."

"It's not metal I'm worried about crushing," Madeleine said. "Fighting the – are we calling them Moths now? – fighting these things means attacking the people they're inside. Hurting people who've done nothing wrong. I don't know if I could try to hunt down and kill possessed Blues. I think I could maybe fight back if we were attacked, if it meant stopping...to stop the people here from being taken."

"Oh, God, yeah. It's hard enough with Gav. I would have gone spare if they'd gotten Nash."

"Are–" Madeleine hesitated. "Are you two a couple?"

Pan gave her a Look, and she started to stutter an apology, but then he grinned, mischief revived.

"Hah, that's okay. You're just the first person who's ever asked me that outright. Nash is – I met Nash my second year at Rushies, Year Eight. I'm a scholarship student there, and while most of the guys are fine about that, there's always a few, you know? My parents run a petrol station, and you'd think that it was some kind of personal affront the way a couple of twits reacted.

"Year Seven was pretty hellish. I wanted to prove myself. You know, be the underdog who comes in and grabs the lead role. Didn't manage it that year, but I snagged speaking parts in a couple of productions. And kept ending up with black eyes. I was a little squit back then, and it was always an elbow to the face, sorry didn't see you there Rickard, ha ha. Then they'd trip me up on stage, put rubbish in the props I was supposed to use. They'd drive me into a fury, then ask me *Can't you take a joke?* I swear, I have to hold myself back from anyone who says that these days. *Can't you take a joke?* Only complete fuckwits say that.

"Year Eight, they were putting on *Peter Pan* and I knew I'd get the lead if I could get through auditions in one piece. And I also desperately wanted to be on the soccer team. Managed to scrape in as a reserve, and the day before my first chance to play some bright spark had disappeared my shoes. Team members are responsible for their own kit, and if I couldn't get replacement shoes I'd be sitting out the match, and somehow no-one had any my size they could possibly spare. Only got a lecture when I rang home for money.

"Nash was one of six in my dorm room, new that year and kind of a big deal because of his family. His life's been all boarding schools and film sets, and he's met a hell of a lot of industry people. Everyone was trying to cultivate him, and he was being incredibly polite and distant. On the day of the match, he gets a package from his sister – stuff for cricket, a fencing mask. And one pair of soccer shoes which were way too small for him. I didn't figure out for months that he'd simply ordered everything himself that morning, and had it couriered over.

"Then, on my way to the auditions for *Peter Pan* I was shoved into a cupboard and locked in. *Just a joke, Rickard. Can't you take a joke?*" For a moment Pan became the essence of smug mockery, self-satisfied and unassailable. "Nash let me out. I was foaming with rage, wanted to go get myself beaten up trying to black a few eyes. The best revenge was getting the part, of course, but I doubt I would have remembered that without Nash."

"I'm beginning to see why he calls you temper-boy."

"Yeah." Pan grimaced. "I'm not that bad, really. Well, I went to counselling, and I'm not that bad any more. Nash talked me into that. Nash has pretty much saved my life the last couple of years, and no-one could be a better friend. We got gay-boy taunts, of course. Well, I did. Rushies has very strict policies about annoying extra-prestigious international students. Nash *is* gay. He's been working out what that means for him, but it doesn't seem to be me. And I could fill a book about the time April-next-door wore this really loose tank top and from the side you could see this *curve*. I was eleven, and I still react when I see a girl in a yellow top."

He leaned forward, sighing gustily. "I've been sitting here thinking about all the guys in my class who died from the stain, and not being able to get Gav back, and searching for a way to protect Nash. We're all trying to think of ways to protect each other, but not even Fish has come up with anything. It's just too *big*."

"We're still gathering information, remember."

"More information really isn't helping." He reached back and grabbed a tablet computer, tapped through screens and handed it to her. "Watch that. I'm going to get started on breakfast."

He'd brought up a YouTube clip.

"Mom, stop."

An American accent, and a wildly jiggling image which steadied on a tearful boy of ten tugging at the arm of a woman packing a suitcase into a car. Beside them a girl of five sat on the driveway, wailing.

"*Why are you going?*" shouted a different girl – the one holding the camera. "*How can you leave us?*"

"*It's my duty to serve, honey,*" the woman said, her voice soothing, unperturbed by the distress all around her. "*La-Saal needs me.*"

She came back toward the camera to collect another suitcase, and Madeleine saw that she was a Green, though the kids didn't seem to be stained.

"We need you more!" the boy said. "They're monsters, Mom. You gotta stay away from them!"

The woman ignored this, packing the second suitcase into the back seat of the car and slamming the door shut.

"*I won't let you!*" The boy darted forward, snatching something from the front seat before the woman could move, stepping away hands held to his chest. "*You're staying here, Mom. You're supposed to be with us, not them!*"

The woman backhanded him across the face. He spun to the ground as the camera-girl shrieked, then the image bounced dizzyingly as she ran forward, and the camera fell. There wasn't clear vision after that, just sobs and shouts, and the sound of a car starting, and driving away.

"There's a lot more like that," Pan said, cracking eggs in the kitchen. "The Greens are...they're still people, but any of them who were within range of the Spires' song have packed up and headed in to where the possessed Blues are. They just ignore or avoid the uninfected, unless someone tries to stop them."

Madeleine had belatedly processed the morning's silence. "The song's stopped, but they're still–?"

"Yeah, it doesn't conveniently wear off, and it doesn't make any difference if you take them out of range. They respond to some questions, but not very usefully."

"They're not all standing about the Spires are they?"

"I wish. Worst news first: road blocks. They did the main roads, then moved on to all the little streets, driving cars across them. A couple of cities even have footage of Greens talking together, marking off street maps. I don't know if they'll manage to get every street, but we can't hope to simply drive away. Equally bad news: they're searching the cities. Collecting bodies mainly, but also flushing out Blues. We did a lot of brainstorming about what to do if they come here – check the fridge."

A list had been added to the collection of flower and superhero drawings.

> *Everyone – own rooms and en suites.*
> *Pan – TV, walkway monitor.*
> *Min – patio & patio door.*
> *Nash – phones, random belongings.*
> *Emily – kitchen.*
> *Maddie – main bathroom.*
> *Fisher – fresh rubbish.*
> *Noi – this list!*

"It's no good us hiding in that study if the sinks are wet, fresh food is sitting on the table, and there's a handy monitor shrieking 'intruder!'. So orders are to keep rooms we're not in spotless, and don't leave your belongings about. The second the monitor alarm sounds, clear your main room task, check your own room, then straight to the study. Strictly speaking Noi wanted us to not cook for the next few days, because, well, the cheery scent of pancakes is a bit of a giveaway as well." He lifted a sizzling frying pan. "But she also wants to use up the eggs before they go off, so I figure this is early enough in the day to be safe, and we clean up straight away. Wanna help?"

They made enormous stacks of pancakes and were washing up when the others began to drift out of their rooms. Min and Noi paused to talk by the dining table, then went out on the patio together. Min set a small statue of Buddha up against the planters, and they both lit some incense and prayed. Fisher collected pots of jam and honey and laid the table while Emily ran through the available channels on the television, but didn't turn on the sound. They decided to let Nash continue to sleep while they worked through the pancakes, and no-one seemed to want to talk much, even after Pan told them about the body-hopping.

"I didn't realise you were Buddhist, Noi," Madeleine said, after they'd drifted out to sit on the patio. The planter hedges thankfully shielded them from most angles, so they'd decided it was safe to venture.

"Technically, Buddhisty-Catholicy." Noi shrugged. "Usually I'm a bit laid-back about it all, but I'm having a ping-pong of faith at the moment." She gazed in through the patio door at the boys cleaning up plates and putting them away. "It helps me when thinking about the people who are gone, but it's not so comforting when considering the ones still around. Especially Gavin."

"Do you think we have any chance?"

"Every time I look at the TV the odds seem to go down. From what we know now, yes, there's a chance, but the body-hopping is a bad thing. If they're specifically looking for the strongest Blues, well, you and I are some of the strongest Blues in the city. That hidden room is a big bonus, but we don't have much time to get to it after the alarm goes off, and food-hunting is going to be a huge risk. One of the biggest dangers is boredom."

"Boredom?" Madeleine stared. Here in this luxurious home, filled with games and books, half a dozen computers, and multiple televisions screening an alien invasion?

"Yeah, boredom. The longer this goes on, the more we'll struggle – both keeping ourselves ready to hide on short notice, and not taking more risks. Pan particularly – he's the energetic type that finds it hard to just stay put. I'm that way myself. Don't you want to get out, *do* something?"

"I want to paint you and Emily."

"Really? Not Science Boy?"

"Fisher..." Madeleine glanced quickly at the door, but no-one was close. "I need to know him better, understand what it is I'd want to paint. If I had unlimited materials, sure, but I've two canvases and I want to use them well. You and Emily, I could really make something."

A warm tinge deepened Noi's skin, but she frowned. "Anyone coming into the apartment would smell fresh paint."

"If I set the easel by the patio door, and move the canvas to the safe room when I'm not working on it, it shouldn't be an issue. And I'd work on sketches the first couple of days. They're likely to search Finger Wharf early on, aren't they?"

"Given who Sydney's new alien overlord is, yeah."

Without warning she hunched down, motioning Madeleine to do the same. Madeleine slid out of her chair to kneel on the patio deck, then turned to see why they were hiding.

A grey navy ship was easing backward out of the narrow eastern part of the bay. Even though she couldn't see anyone on the deck, Madeleine shifted underneath the edge of the patio table, and Noi joined her, making a shooing motion at Min, who was staring out at them.

"Blues escaping?" Madeleine whispered, though there was no way they could be overheard.

"Green navy waiting at the headlands for anyone sneaking out of the harbour?"

It was the more likely explanation. Madeleine and Noi waited until the ship had gained reasonable distance, then slipped back into the apartment, joining the others in watching through the glass.

"Chances are good they'll have something similar to stop people going up-river," Noi said.

"Not an insurmountable obstacle, however." Nash hadn't slept very late for someone who'd had most of the night watch. "A small, unlit boat in the dark would have a good chance of—"

He broke off as Pan gripped his arm, and they all stared, speechless, at a ribbon of light following the ship.

Snake-like and perhaps the length of three buses, it was widest along the front third, where what seemed to be a dozen layers of diaphanous wings marked a lazy, complicated beat. The wings were shaped like sails, triangles of light which thinned to insubstantiality, just like the long trailing tail of the thing. It swooped, lifted, glided: a dandelion seed of a monster decorating the sky.

"Is there someone *riding* that?"

The distance made it difficult to be sure, but there did seem to be two points of solidity near the very front, before the wings.

They watched until their view was blocked by the eastern headland, then Min said: "So, no going out on the patio except at night?"

"And I was worried they'd have possessed some survivors who knew how to fly helicopters." Noi reluctantly slid the patio door shut. "Until we have some better idea of how often those things will fly over, and whether they happen to have night vision, no going out at all."

Chapter Eleven

Madeleine had taken to biting her nails, unable to settle to anything, shifting from room to room, scouring the internet for news then not wanting to read it. She had a most wondrous portrait boiling inside her and couldn't let herself progress now the sketch was transferred, couldn't immerse herself in paint and escape the new world. Pan wasn't much better, debating plans of action with Min, who seemed to delight in pointing out problems with every idea, their squabbles getting on Madeleine's nerves until she realised that Pan was less edgy after these minor spats.

The television delivered a constant stream of bad news. Stain appearing anywhere and everywhere, infection blown on the wind. Families on the fringes of dust zones where there'd been no rain, gambling with their lives when food supplies ran low. Millions of displaced overwhelming non-Spire cities. Fights over food, water, face masks. Glimpses of Moths making themselves at home while Greens buried bodies and restored services, even travelling out of their cities on errands. New religions, and established ones grown strange and angry, calling disaster a judgment, a test. Very occasionally a sighting of a creature of light, every description different from the last.

To Madeleine's surprise, not a single government, pre-existing or hastily formed, agreed to obey the Moths' demand for Blues. Officially. But Blues were handed over all the same: countless quiet betrayals.

Once, a spectacular battle on the fringes of Buenos Aires had been streamed. Two girls running from, then fighting back against a group who'd been discreetly drugging and delivering up local Blues. The girls had shield-paralysed most of them, and killed one, before stumbling into an army detachment. No-one seemed able to decide who should go to jail.

The phrase "the greater good" reached fingernails-on-chalkboard frequency, and the fourth day after the attack at the beach the robotic *Warning! Warning!* of Min's walkway alarm came almost as a relief.

Madeleine, sitting on the rug near the closed patio door, glanced at the laptop set on an ottoman next to the television, but whatever had triggered the alarm was already out of camera range, in the small foyer where they would have a choice of doors, an elevator, or stairs.

"Go! Go!"

Nash, voice sharp and low, was already scouring the room, while Pan turned off the television and bent to mute the walkway monitor and switch the laptop to camera mode before tucking it out of sight. Madeleine grabbed her big sketchbook and dashed to the main floor bathroom.

They'd made it a rule to wipe down the shower after use, and by the middle of the day it had had time to dry thoroughly. It was quick work to swipe a handtowel around the sink, and glance to ensure nothing looked out of the ordinary. Then a race for her bedroom, trying not to pound the metal of the circular stair, to double-check her en suite, and close the wardrobe doors before heading to the quickly-filling study.

She'd managed to be second-last, Fisher following her through the door with the garbage bag of kitchen scraps, which he tucked into a pre-cleared file drawer after pulling the bookshelf door closed. And then they settled in, Noi sitting next to the computer, Pan underneath the desk, and Emily perched on top of the filing cabinet. Min, Nash, Fisher and Madeleine sat on the floor, legs in a tangle because there really was no room – they'd had to remove the chair after the first practice run so they could all fit in.

The computer was already set split-screen between the walkway and lounge room webcams. Neither showed movement, and there was a frustrating wait while they all wished they'd dared risk more cameras, and wondered if it had been a false alarm. Minutes ticked by with no sign of movement.

Pan, playing with a laptop and headphones, suddenly sat upright, knocking his skull against the underside of the desk. The noise wasn't truly loud, but in the strained silence it felt like a shout.

Rather than apologetic, Pan looked excited, waving the laptop in response to frowns. Nash made a 'get on with it' gesture, and Pan paused a moment to launch a word-processor and type:

ALIEN OVERLORD SINGING ON YOUTUBE

He waited till they had all had a chance to be properly incredulous, then switched windows to show the Japanese Blue, the Core of Taiee. She seemed to just be standing, smiling cheerfully at the camera, but when Pan passed the headphone ear buds around they could all hear the oscillating song which was presumed to be the aliens' language.

Noi snagged a notepad and pen from the desk and scribbled: *What's the text say? Googletrans plz.*

A few clicks later they could see the clip was titled: "First" and the text below, posted by "Taiee", said: "First challenge call: Lot-nak".

This was hyperlinked, and Pan followed it to a site – a blog entry which was in Japanese but proved to also say "First challenge call: Lot-nak" above a time and date, a map of a golf course with a line drawn around its borders, a hyperlink to the video, and last a picture of a small glowing ball which had just a suggestion of paws and trailing ears.

"That's tomorrow?" Nash asked, then made an apologetic face.

Noi held up her pad: Why are they using the internet? Can't they use their ships to talk to each other?

Min took the pad from her: Must have same limitations we do – without satellites, can't communicate on other side of planet. Makes sense to use our tech, especially since they're in human bodies.

Maybe they can't use their ships while in human form? Pan suggested.

Fisher, a warm presence at Madeleine's side, had been browsing a tablet computer, and wrote: *This place is in Manila. The Philippines Spire is there.*

She said they've come to settle primacy. They're holding a competition and this is round one.

Pad held high, Noi frowned because everyone's attention had shifted to the computer monitor beside her. Four people had crossed the walkway, coming from the main building. Then, just at the edge of the screen, movement in their apartment. Someone heading up the spiral stair.

They sat frozen, not daring even to scribble notes, unsure whether this was simply part of the Greens' search for bodies, or if their presence was suspected, looked for.

A creak, not a metre away, and they held their breath as a heavy step moved toward the master bedroom. Madeleine felt inexplicably invaded, even though it was not her home, not truly her room. She hunched down unhappily, and then Fisher shifted at her side, leaned a little closer. That was all, but it distracted her from the person in her room.

The steps returned, heading toward the two superhero rooms, but the pace was brisk, and after only enough time to glance in the doors the person moved for the stair, and down. It was a search for bodies then, not hidden Blues. They could relax, and wait it out.

There was no sign of anyone leaving the building, but Noi guessed that it would be easier to remove bodies via the garage level rather than take them over the walkway stairs, and so decided on a two hour delay before emerging, in hopes that would be long enough for any lingerers to make their presence obvious. Everyone had brought something to do, and once staring at the Manila Golf Course had lost its early attractions they settled to their separate entertainments. Madeleine, of course, had planned to sketch, but it was hard to drag her mind from the canvas she planned for Noi and Emily, propped against the wall beside the desk, ready for paint.

Fisher was reading the first book of *The Lord of the Rings*, despite the movie marathon of the trilogy and prequels they'd held yesterday in an attempt to take their minds off aliens. Madeleine liked him a great deal when he was wearing his glasses and had that absorbed expression, so she began, through sideways glances, to capture a small portrait which pleased her. She moved on to fill the page with her companions, lingering over Emily cross-legged on the filing cabinet reading the copy of *The Three Musketeers* she had discovered with great excitement in the apartment library.

A study of each of them finished, and nearly an hour to go, she was hesitating over what to work on next when Fisher held out his hand for her pencil. She'd been aware that he'd stopped reading to watch her draw and, warmed by his interest, she'd been working to do her absolute best. It was inordinately difficult to not react to the faint brush of his arm against hers.

In tiny, precise letters he wrote: *Draw Emily as a Musketeer.*

Usually she didn't like bright suggestions about what she should draw, but this one sparked a response. She'd need a reference, though, so pointed at his abandoned tablet, using it to look up clothing, sabres, stances. But then, as a different picture crept into her thoughts, she switched the tablet to camera mode and held it above and a little before her, triggering the photo button with difficulty from the angle. After a miscalculation which captured only half her face, she managed a satisfactory shot of herself staring upward, and handed the tablet to Fisher, gesturing for him to do the same.

He photographed himself obediently, paused to look at the result and shook his head with a wry lift to the corner of his mouth. But handed the tablet over to her.

After some pantomime and a little stifled giggling, she had seven photographs, and began to outline, covering the whole of a page in her large sketchbook with faint circles and lines, roughing out proportions and angles. It was a challenging picture, a circle of seven seen from above, each with a sabre raised to a central point, some faces smiling, some grave beneath their broad-brimmed hats and curling feathers.

"That's two hours," Noi said softly, breaking Madeleine's concentration. "I think we can risk sending a scout now, but first I'm dying to see what the hell it is you've been drawing Maddie."

Madeline passed the sketchbook around, and felt oddly breathless, not at their pleased reactions, but at the implications of that picture. Blue Musketeers, united and bold.

She, too, agreed with Emily.

Chapter Twelve

"Will it bother you if I watch you paint?"

In the middle of setting out her first palette, Madeleine turned to find Fisher watching with an open interest which pleased and daunted her. Since they'd run from the beach Fisher had buried himself in one of the laptops, searching for any scrap of data he could use to fight back – pausing occasionally for meals or discussions, but usually to be found in the library window seat on a shadow-eyed quest for answers. She wasn't sure why they all held on to the hope he'd find a way to fight back, beyond that he hadn't given up yet.

"Not if you stay quiet." She tried to keep her tone casual. "I usually tune distractions out when I'm working."

"I noticed that yesterday." His smile was slow and warm. "I'll set a chair over here if that's okay with you."

Madeleine shrugged, and avoided Noi's eye as she finished preparations, then stood before her easel entirely focused on Fisher instead of her subjects. But she was longing to finish this painting, the light was good, and Noi had agreed that the faint scent of acrylics weren't that big a risk now that the building had been cleared. Even Fisher wasn't enough to keep her from becoming completely absorbed.

Together on a couch set by the patio entrance, Emily and Noi were a study of contrasts. Fine blond hair drifting beside foaming black curls. Slender height; compact curves. Shy pleasure at being painted against entertained interest in Madeleine's awareness of Fisher. Below it all, never going entirely away: anger, hurt.

Madeleine blocked in colours, not pushing herself so frantically this time, spending more effort on consciously analysing shadow tones before beginning to detail the two figures. Emily and Noi chatted and read, and watched the television behind Madeleine, keeping roughly to their original positions but accepting Madeleine's assurance that she did not need them to sit stiff and frozen except when she was working on specific detail. She released them a little before two, in part because the light had begun to shift, but also because the "First Challenge" was due to start at midday in Manila.

Fisher helped carry her used brushes, jars and palettes to the laundry, and had made a good start on cleaning them by the time she returned from stowing the paints and canvas in the study.

"Thanks," she said, and took one of the palettes.

"Will you have enough paint to complete the portrait?"

"I should. But not for the third canvas. When we toured the other North Building apartments this morning I saw a computer with a graphics tablet, and I was thinking of teaching myself how to properly use a digital art program. I don't think I could talk Noi into the importance of art supplies to my continued existence."

"They are, though, aren't they?" He was watching her face in his deliberate, considered way. "It's so central to you. I sometimes wish I was so focused."

"You mean you can't decide what you want to do?"

"I wanted to study astrophysics. And biochemistry. And archaeology. And words, and a great many things said with them. Year Ten was when we started seriously choosing courses, and I had to face that I couldn't sign up for every unit, that–"

"There's never going to be enough time," Madeleine finished. "Oh, I know how that feels. There's so many things to try, to perfect, so many different techniques and media and–" She lifted her hands at the enormity of her hoped-for future, and shared a look of mutual comprehension with Fisher. "Does the fact that you said astrophysics first mean that's what you'd chosen to do?"

He shrugged. "The Sciences are where I've started – I've been allowed to study ahead for a few different courses. I can hope to self-study the Arts, at least to a basic understanding, but Science tends to require a little more equipment."

"You were seriously going to try to study them all?"

"Eventually. Those and more." Fisher paused, then added: "To try to be a Renaissance man."

"Renaissance man?" He wasn't talking time travel.

"Someone who has multiple areas of expertise. Think da Vinci – mathematician, artist, inventor – so many things. The ideal of the Renaissance man is to be a fully rounded person – to embrace the Arts and Sciences, languages, society, sport. Knowledge both broad and deep." The tips of his ears had gone red, and he smiled with self-conscious amusement. "I don't usually talk about this – it makes me sound so greedy."

"Not really," Madeleine protested. "Intimidating maybe." Which was not what she'd meant to say, and she wished she had a quarter of Noi's ability to joke and tease, but pressed on gamely: "Did they have Renaissance women?"

"Some. A Greek philosopher called Hypatia is the earliest known example. One of my mother's heroines – my mother was a mathematician, an architect, cellist, linguist. She's the ideal I measure myself against."

"I'm sorry," Madeleine said, and his dark brows swept down – puzzlement, not anger. Then they lifted and he shook his head.

"My parents died when I was ten. Though I'm sorry too. Did yours make it to Armidale?"

"Day before yesterday. They want me to try to make a break for it, but people recognised me from the beach broadcast and are, well, paying attention to see if I show up."

She realised they were both rinsing perfectly clean brushes, and with a murmur of thanks shook water out of the last of them and went back upstairs to stash them away. And wash her face.

When she returned she helped Fisher bring the 'portrait couch' forward to fill its original position in the semi-circle before the screen, feeling distinctly like they were giving everyone a bit of extra entertainment to go with the alien dominance challenges.

"Just in time," Noi said. "There weren't any good cameras on the Manila Spire, but webcams on other Spires are picking up movement."

Min handed over one of the laptops, which showed the Sydney Spire via a webcam set in St Marys Cathedral, giving a clear view of where the Spire had risen through St James Station and then the fountain at the north end of Hyde Park. One of the fountain's bronze statues was visible, resting in a tumbled tree: Apollo inverted.

The fountain was named for the same person who had established the Archibald Prize. Madeleine stared at the tumbled remnant, thinking of all the hours she'd spent planning to win, then turned her attention to the handful of people gathered by the Spire. They were too far for details, but appeared to be casually chatting while waiting. She gave the laptop to Fisher and glanced at the presenter on the muted television.

"He looks excited."

"Yeah, it's a sporting commentator feel, which is totally the wrong tone to take." Pan frowned at the screen. "But he's not the only one like that. Just this past day I've noticed it. Most are still aching to hit out, but the non-infected...well, they've got this end date now. Stay out of it for a couple of years and you get your world back."

"Once people work out what these challenges mean, they'll start betting on them. Guarantee it." Min, smiling cynic, sat back as if the idea pleased him.

"Two years until we get our world back too," Emily pointed out, more in defiance than certainty.

"That's what we're aiming for Millie." Noi changed channels, then restored sound.

A terse voice told them they were looking at a view of the Mumbai Spire, which had one of the closest webcams available. A dozen Blues were standing together, holding umbrellas to keep off heavy rain, and someone at the broadcaster was drawing lines on the image pointing out the Core, who was a slim man in his early twenties. The image looked slightly off, and that was because the Blues held themselves in an attitude of conversation, but didn't move their mouths. Speaking Moth.

Two of the Blues handed their umbrellas to a Green standing to one side, and then turned and walked into the Spire. Seamlessly, without an opening or a ripple, as if the star-studded darkness truly was the night sky, and they had been swallowed by it.

Nash had already been sitting unhappily upright at the appearance of his home city, but at this he turned to Fisher: "Could it be they brought their shield down? Have they just shown us an opportunity?"

"Possibly." Fisher was reserved, not ready to be drawn.

"Still, these challenges could mean a missile at the right moment—"

"We're cutting to a broadcast direct from Manila," the presenter said, as the image changed to a different Spire, surrounded by many more people, with more arriving, walking out of the darkness of the Spire to spread over closely maintained grass. The presenter helpfully pointed out what Madeleine had already seen: the two Blues who had walked into the Spire at Mumbai had emerged a few moments later in Manila.

Noi, sounding annoyed, said: "Okay, so either the Spires have teleportation devices...or they aren't ships at all. They're gates. Great big pointy wormholes."

"It felt like stone when I touched ours," Madeleine reminded her.

"Either you weren't at the In point, or it has an on and off mode." As alien song began to sound an accompaniment to the images Noi glared at the screen, then slowly let out her breath. "Guess we get to watch the Olympics after all. I just...seriously, have they really half-wrecked our world for a pissing contest? They couldn't decide their primacy shit on their own world?"

"They said 'and business of our own'." Min had risen to his feet to approach the screen, but glanced back at Noi. "I've a bet of my own – this other business is nothing we're going to like. Maybe when they leave they take all our water, or our sun or something."

He turned back to the screen and pointed to a tanned Blue at the edge of the ever-widening crowd. "I remember this guy from Bondi."

It was the woman standing beside the tanned man who had Madeleine's attention. Short-cropped blond hair and a lovely line of neck and shoulder.

"Asha." She exchanged a glance with Noi, then added for the benefit of the room: "One of the people we met going through Finger Wharf. We cooked dinner together."

"Every country – every Spire is sending two people to compete?" Emily asked. "What was the little glowing animal picture for?"

"I guess we're about to find out."

The flow had stopped, the crowd forming into a loose circle around the Spire. The weather in Manila was a step up from Mumbai: only overcast and drizzling, and most of the Blues moved with an eager, alert step, though some must come from time zones when they'd normally be well asleep. The air filled with oscillating song, and Madeleine wondered if they were just saying hello, or were sledging each other, or boasting about their stolen bodies.

She glanced at Fisher, sitting attentively, and could almost feel the roil of anger swelling in him. The room was thick with it, with resentment, and worry, and over it all, helplessness. Was this how it would be? They would spend two years hiding and watching, feeling as though their faces were being rubbed in their loss? The cheerful excitement of the Manila crowd, and the wash of language impossible for humans to understand, seemed to declare the irrelevance of any audience but the Moths. They had co-opted cities, people, technology, and would use them as they pleased.

The chorus of song died away, and one Blue outside the circle climbed onto a rock, raising a single thin warble.

"Speeches?" Min said. "Skip to the good stuff."

Quite as if she'd heard, the Blue standing on the rock raised one hand, and produced three short notes.

Fireworks. All around the circumference of the Spire, about twenty feet from the ground, balls of light burst out in unison. But instead of popping, or arcing to the ground, these zigzagged away, leaving a suggestion of a trail behind.

The circle of Blues gave chase, the sudden intensity of movement wholly at odds with their light-hearted cheer of moments before. One woman, particularly quick to react, leapt impossibly high into the air to intercept the nearest ball.

"Shield jump!" Pan cried, while the ball curled at the woman's touch, no longer trying to move.

A second Blue had followed the woman into the air, aiming not for the ball, but for her. He hadn't quite connected when another woman punched at him from the ground, clipping him so that he spun away then tumbled down, slowing at the last moment as the grass and dirt bellied out below him beneath the cushion of a shield.

"Are they wearing any flags or colours to tell which team they're on?" Min asked, frowning at the screen.

"I guess all they'd need to know is their partner. Everyone else is on another team." As the two women sprinted for the Spire, Pan leaned back, visibly resisting being caught up in the competition. "And maybe they can see something we can't."

A different pair were trying to intercept the sprinters, gouging a channel into the bright green grass with a punch which knocked both women sideways. The one holding the light animal – dangling it by its ears – somehow angled her landing so that her shield bounced her toward the Spire. With a stumble, she ran into starry darkness.

At the end of the muddy gouge her companion lay broken. She had been a short woman, maybe twenty, with dark braided hair and bronzed skin which set off the blue of the stain. The fine drizzle dewed her skin, and glimmered in the light of blooming wings.

The Moth lifted, a slow undulation, and swam through the rain into the stars.

"There's a leader board," Fisher said, and tilted the laptop so Madeleine could see a web page where a name had appeared in two different scripts, with the number 2 beside it. "That's the São Paulo clan." He paused, looking across at Noi, who was grey, lips set, and added: "You don't have to stay."

"Yes, we do," she said. "They're showing us their limits. Their attacks."

Madeleine stared at the screen, as the image shifted to another part of the golf course in Manila, to another group of Blues chasing long-eared balls of light. The second time a Blue died, the Moth seemed to be fatally wounded as well, emerging only to slump to the wet grass, colour leaching from its blue pattern. Other Blues were merely injured, and limped or were carried away, helped by Greens stationed near the cameras.

The chase for the long-eared balls of light was quick, brutal and efficient. There were many more teams than balls, and soon the losers were returning to their home Spires, to face the widely varied reaction of their Cores. Two dozen corpses remained, human and alien, but it wasn't particularly comforting that most of the Moths had died with their hosts.

"The garage," Madeleine said stiffly, when it seemed they were done. "Practice? If we use a look-out?"

They looked at each other, then at the screen at another crumpled, discarded shell which had been a person, and nodded.

Chapter Thirteen

"You do not understand me, gentlemen," Pan said, throwing his head back. "I asked to be excused in case I should not be able to discharge my debt to all three; for Monsieur Athos has the right to kill me first, which must much diminish the face-value of your bill, Monsieur Porthos, and render yours almost null, Monsieur Aramis. And now, gentlemen, I repeat, excuse me, but on that account only, and—on guard!"

Min made a by-play of drawing a sword, and wincing as if his shoulder was injured, but said: "*When you please, monsieur,*" and then skipped backward as Pan feinted, fist out. Extra layers of clothing bulking their figures, they circled each other, throwing out finger-punches, and then firmer blows, not full strength, but enough that they had to set their feet or be knocked backward by their smoothly responsive shields.

"*The cardinal's Guards!*" Emily called suddenly, and Min and Pan spun toward Madeleine and punched with dual force, and though Madeleine's shield automatically reacted to the punches, there was no way to keep her footing and she struggled to bring up a second shield at the right strength before she collided with one of the support pillars.

Bouncing forward, she stumbled and dropped to padded knees, but managed to counter-punch at Min and Pan both, since they'd foolishly clumped together. Min dived to one side, leaving only Pan to be slammed into a car door. The glass had been smashed in an earlier bout, but this time metal crumpled.

"All right, Pan?" Nash asked from the east lookout post, as Madeleine held her hands out in the 'no attack' signal.

"Yeah." Pan stepped out of the concave imprint he'd made. "I managed not to bounce! Though I'm not sure if I can claim credit, or if I just hit the right point between too hard and too soft. You weren't holding back as much that time, Maddie."

"Meant to only step up a notch," Madeleine said, shakily. "But I think I'm getting a little better at judging." Hopefully she'd improve before accidentally killing someone.

"Rest and then we'll swap to Emily and Fisher for a final bout," Noi said from the west lookout, and Madeleine obediently plopped down near the entry gate. Min plucked an invisible hat from his head, dipping into an elaborate, hat-twirling bow, and joined her.

It was the fourth practice session. The garage under the North Building was suitably isolated, entirely separate from the main apartment, with only one perforated metal entry gate and a few ventilation shutters offering anyone a chance of seeing what was happening. And for that they would need to walk most of the way down the wharf and peer into the gloom of the garage.

The first day, upset and angry, they'd done little more than peck at each other, limited by the unforgiving concrete and steel environment, and recognising an added hurdle: for all its privacy, the garage was cramped by a half dozen cars – and their alarms. But as dusk came on, they risked moving several out to the visitor parking between the two buildings, and disconnected the batteries of the remainder, disabling the alarms.

During the second session Pan had started turning their attempts to learn into a game, switching through an endless stream of fight scenes – *Hamlet*, *The Princess Bride*, *The Empire Strikes Back*, *Monty Python* – and falling frequently back on an evolving Blue Musketeer persona. It wasn't till the third session that Madeleine realised that Pan was as intent on distracting everyone else as he was trying to make himself feel better. They were all facing the gap between their current abilities and those displayed during the Manila challenge, and trying to believe they had some hope.

"We're getting better at blocking physical impacts, at least," she said, loud enough for the two lookouts to hear. "And not paralysing ourselves when we try to shield-stun someone else."

"I wish we could practice in a park," Emily said. "So we didn't have to keep worrying about bouncing into the ceiling."

"Or through it." Pan grinned up at a circular impact mark. "Too much pixie dust, Tink."

"I think I'll nap before the next challenge," Madeleine added. "And take the late night watch."

"I'll take early–" Nash began.

"Down! Move!"

Noi, eyes wide, hurled herself from her lookout position at the westernmost ventilation shutter. They scrambled to their feet, hurrying for shelter behind pillars and cars.

Too late, and pointless beside. The glowing thing which leapt against the entry gate clearly knew exactly where they were. It made a huffing noise which had something of the whine of a jet engine to it, and the metal bars shuddered

"The Hell is that?" Pan asked, abandoning attempts to hide.

The thing huffed again, and scrabbled. It stood a little taller than a person, the head long, tapering and bony, topped with two trailing streamers of light which suggested ears. At the front it had streamer-fluffed claws, but its rear was elongated, and curled on itself: a sea serpent's tail.

"Let it in," Fisher said.

"Have you lost your mind?!" Min asked, backing rapidly away from the gate. "We can't let that thing in here!"

"We can't let it go away either."

"He's right," Noi said. "Maddie, brace yourself against the rear wall so it sees you first. Everyone else to either side. Try not to force punch wildly or we'll have the building down. Nash, close the gate after it, then stay back."

Nash, nearest the controls, gave Fisher and Noi a sharp look, then pressed the manual release.

"Oh damn," Pan said, then ducked to one side as the gate tried to lift, and slowed as it hit the glowing creature outside. "I don't think we're ready for this."

Madeleine was sure she wasn't, but seeing no other option she dashed to the rear wall of the garage, and set her back to it. She'd barely turned before the gate had lifted enough for the thing to duck under. It raced straight at her, a galloping motion made strange by the twining tail, which undulated above the ground as if it swam through water. She hastily brought up her shield, unwilling to rely on any automatic response, struggling for control. This was impossibly different to mock duelling with Blue Musketeers.

As it neared her the thing reared, mouth gaping, then pounced forward, the impact driving her into the concrete even as the shield bounced it away. Immediately it surged at her again, at a slower speed which didn't produce the bounce reaction, and she gasped at the weight of it, pressing both the shield and her into the wall.

"Try knocking it down with shields while it's occupied with Maddie," Pan said, racing up.

Fitting action to words, he immediately shield-smashed the glowing creature, but rebounded from the contact. Then the coiling tail lashed toward him, a crunching slam only avoided by frantic rolling.

"Everyone stand to this side of it," Min said. "Then all low-level punch at once. That might do it without sending it through a wall."

"Hold fast, Maddie," Noi called, as they scrambled. "If it gets too much, try to knock it back."

Maintaining the shield for a long period required concentration, and Madeleine was starting out tired from training, but at least its interest in her gave everyone a chance to gather together out of tail-lashing distance.

"Get ready to move if this doesn't work," Fisher said. "Go."

All the punches together made a whomping noise, and the creature did seem to feel it, twisting sideways. But then, glowing brighter than ever, it leaped back at Madeleine, its jet engine howl increasing in intensity.

"I think you made it stronger!" Madeleine gasped, as she was again slammed backward into the wall, not daring to cushion with a shield in case it bounced her forward. Unable to stand the weight, she pushed out with the front shield, glad she'd put a lot of practice into not paralysing herself, and took a relieved breath when she succeeded in jolting the glow-monster a few feet away.

"If shields cause rebound when struck quickly, move in slow," Fisher said rapidly.

"Surround it and all press in," Noi agreed.

"Nash, come when we have it pinned," Fisher added, and Madeleine couldn't understand why, but had to focus on keeping her shield up as the glow-monster came at her again.

It seemed to be trying to knock her to the ground and with its increased strength Madeleine was not only being pushed into the wall, but she could feel the glow-monster getting closer, making gradual progress through her shield.

"Set your feet," Min warned, and then rocked backward as his attempt to pin the thing's tail was only partially successful.

Nash ran up. Madeleine still hadn't understood what he was expected to do, since, while he could shield and punch a little, he was vastly weaker, and tended to collapse almost immediately. He couldn't use the precious energy he drew from them to fight.

But that, of course, was the answer, and Nash had thought through Fisher's reasoning quicker than Madeleine. Squeezing between Noi and Pan, he set both hands to the thing's heaving side.

The reaction was immediate: frantic thrashing threatening to hurl them in every direction. Fisher and Pan, the weakest among them, stumbled, but pressed in again.

"Hold firm," Noi gasped as the thing's howling cry scaled up to painful intensity, enough to make them want to stop everything in favour of covering ears.

"Too much." Nash was blazing, his palms and the stars which covered the back of his neck burning pinpoints.

"Vent," Fisher told him tersely. "Go outside and punch over the water."

Nash ran, the necessity of re-opening the garage door slowing him down. But once he was out, he had a clear shot east.

"Hurry!" Pan called, as the glow-monster heaved back from Madeleine, trying to escape, to push against the weakest shields. Emily and Min fell, and the tail lashed, swiping Fisher, who ricocheted into the nearest car, and Madeleine gasped aloud, but saw he'd managed to shield himself against the impact.

Noi and Pan dived on the tail, pinning it to the ground between them, but they weren't usefully braced. They'd been able to keep it in place when it had her against the wall and they'd surrounded it and pushed in, but now that it was loose there was no way any of them could hold it without being knocked away.

"Push down on it and use another shield against the ceiling!" Min was already attempting to put his words into action, but it was definitely something easier said than done. With a startled shout, he ended up bouncing sideways, and water began spraying from the fire sprinklers.

Not trusting herself with such a difficult manoeuvre, Madeleine ran for Nash, barely beating the glow-monster's attempt to run right over him. With no time for explanations, she simply spun and shield-punched the thing toward the car with the Pan-sized dint in its side, the impact catapulting her backward.

"Pin it! Pin it!" Pan ran forward, and the others joined him, holding the creature against the car so Nash could risk approaching. Madeleine ran to join them, keeping it still as it frantically tried to escape Nash's touch.

It collapsed.

The transition was so swift that most of them went down with it, falling to puffing heaps around a thing which now glowed no more than a paper lantern. A lantern the size of a small car.

"Is – is it properly dead?" Emily whispered.

"I think so." Nash, stars bright, pressed his hand against the thing's neck, then started back when his fingers sank into the glowing surface. "It doesn't have – it's like it's turned to mud. Less than that. Fog."

"It looks like a dead jellyfish," Pan said. "Which is a step down from the 'mermaid called Rover' thing it started with." He grimaced, and wiped at the water running into his eyes. "We beat one of these things. We know now that we can fight back. Why the hell aren't I cheering?"

"We don't even know what this is," Min pointed out. "Our problem is the Moths. Whole different ball game."

"It's familiar in an odd way," Madeleine said. "I know I've never seen it before, but I felt like I had."

"The balls with ears from the first challenge," Noi said, using Pan's shoulder to lever herself to her feet. "Come on, we can't just sit here in a puddle. Nash, go see if you can spot anyone coming down the wharf. Everyone else, there have to be controls to shut these sprinklers off."

Fisher, next to his feet, held a hand down for Madeleine, and waited to check she could stay up. Then they paused to stare at the thing they'd just killed. It did remind Madeleine a little of the targets from the Manila challenge, but a car-sized doggy mermaid was a long way from a soccer ball with ears and paws. Related species? Parent? She puzzled over it while they hunted for a way to shut down the broken sprinkler system without cutting off water to the entire building.

"No sign of any movement on either side," Nash said, jogging back to the garage entrance just as they succeeded in stopping the flow. "Why alone? It seemed to know where we were."

"Maybe it's some kind of Blue tracker," Min suggested. "Able to smell us or hear us or something."

"Doesn't explain why they'd let it gallop off to leap on us alone," Noi said, then shivered and shook her head, a few drops of water spraying from damp curls. "Speculate later. Right now we have a big glowing corpse, no obvious Moths, and a huge decision."

"Stay or leave." Fisher said.

"At sunset, while cold and wet. When the only one of us not exhausted is Nash." Noi ticked the obstacles off. "Not necessarily insurmountable. We've talked about Goat Island as a possibility. We have boats and have downloaded harbour charts, and it's a straightforward enough trip. We could probably get there in the dark without running into anything. But for all we know Goat

Island is where they keep their flying snake, so condition unknown. And it's one of the few largish islands in the harbour, so a bit obvious as a hiding place. That's the question of leaving – what about staying?"

"The gamble is whether they have another Rover," Min said. "If, that is, the thing really could track us. They obviously haven't been able to before now, or our pyjama party would have been over days ago. If we're to believe the internet chatter, the Moths don't know when Blues are hiding nearby. This building has been cleared already, and the hidden room and webcams are seriously hard to give up, so long as we think this Rover is the only Rover. The problem with staying is that." He nodded at the corpse, large and obvious in the fading light. "We could risk using the garage because it's dim and sheltered and there's little chance anyone will go in it to notice any damage. The glow from that thing is a neon sign marking the start point of any hunt."

"Staying or leaving, we need to get rid of it," Fisher said.

"True enough." Noi's stomach growled, announcing another issue they needed to deal with, and soon. "Right. Fisher, grab the laptop and see if you can dig up any other sightings of Rovers. Nash, Pan, take lookout either side. We'll try to push it into the water."

The yielding, insubstantial mass would only shift when thumped with a shield, and by the time they had knocked it out of the garage and then chivvied it to the navy base side of the wharf, all Madeleine could think of was food and rest.

The lantern glow of monster sank below the surface, and they went inside to eat and decide what next.

Chapter Fourteen

A chorus of breathing in a room lit only by the flicker of computer screens. Madeleine shifted, warm beneath a blanket, bracketed by sleeping people. Her back hurt.

With no sign of Moths following Rover, and everyone but Nash close to dropping where they stood, the decision to stay or leave had been a forgone conclusion. As a precaution they were all spending the night in the hidden study. While his fellow Musketeers filled their stomachs, Nash had shifted the computer to the top of the filing cabinet and removed the simple desk, creating a little more room. Then he'd been stuck with a lot of cleaning up, as everyone else focused on getting warm and dry before curling up to sleep and digest. The extremes of the Blue metabolism.

Madeleine had gone to sleep propped between Noi and Emily, but, drifting awake, she could see Nash sitting beneath the window with a laptop, and Noi curled next to the sprawling pile which was Min and Pan. The shoulder she was tucked against belonged to Fisher.

Noi had most likely contrived the swap during a bathroom excursion, and Madeleine decided to be grateful, to enjoy the moment. Fisher had continued to provide a fascinated audience during the portrait sittings, helping her clean up afterwards. Today – yesterday – they'd spent all of the time between the sitting and late afternoon training chatting. He'd avoided talking about himself, instead drawing her out on what still needed to be done on the new portrait, and the chances of a young unknown winning the Archibald Prize, and all her hopes for being able to study full time, to not need to compromise between what she wanted to do and what was likely to earn her a living. About scholarships, and the gaps in her portfolio. She hadn't meant to talk so much, but Fisher was a good listener, and so interested.

The question was whether his interest was in her, or her art. And if he was pretending to be interested in her painting as a way to get closer to her. She wasn't sure she would be able to forgive that.

But she still filled a small secret sketchpad with images of him, and worried about how little sleep he got, and wondered whether it would be stupid to suggest they surely had enough time for him to rest occasionally. Her private challenge was to capture how he would pause sometimes to be amused at himself, and it discomforted her, in reviewing these attempts, to see just how much of her own emotions the pictures revealed.

Nash had noticed she was awake, and was smiling at her, at the way she was trying to look at Fisher's face without moving from his shoulder. Her sketchbooks really weren't going to tell anybody anything they didn't already know.

"What's the time?" she whispered.

"Twenty to one." Nash's voice was particularly delicious when he kept it low, and she regretted being unable to find a way to express the sound of him. "I promised to wake everyone to watch the challenge, but it can wait till there's something to see." He removed the power cord from his laptop and leaned forward to hold it and the headphones toward her. "Here is something you will be glad of."

Reluctantly abandoning her comfortable contact with Fisher, Madeleine stretched to take it. The screen showed the ABC website, an article with a headline of "Shocking Survival" below a video image of a woman with a soft brown bob and sun damaged skin.

Researchers from James Cook University have reported a breakthrough in the treatment of Blue-Green. Earlier this evening, a representative of the School of Biomedical Sciences made the first announcement of this critical discovery.

"Our preliminary results show a dramatic increase in the survival rate of the infected if they are shocked with shield paralysis as soon as possible after exposure to the Blue-Green Conversion," Dr Jennifer Elliman said. "A healthy subject, even among smaller mammals where mortality has been nearly one hundred per cent, has in the area of a fifty per cent survival rate with Green stain, and thirty per cent with Blue."

Madeleine skimmed the rest of the article, then played the video and listened to the woman answering questions, and insisting that it was early days for absolutes, and that this was by no means a cure, only a treatment method.

She'd felt Fisher shift while she was watching, and when she removed the headphones he said: "This will provide a counter-motive for those so eager to hand over Blues."

"Perhaps," Nash said. "But only so far as keeping one or two on hand. I still would not risk putting ourselves in another's power."

Madeleine closed the browser window, and found a second open page, headed: *Leech Blues: Inevitable Murderers?* Her eyes met Fisher's, and he reached unhurriedly to brush the trackpad, closing the window.

"How is your back?"

"Sore," Madeleine admitted. "I couldn't tell if it was bruised or not. Peering over my shoulder at the mirror isn't effective when everything is blue." She suddenly remembered him circling her taking pictures and had to look away. "I'll get Noi to check later," she added hurriedly, and saw that Noi was awake, watching with unabashed interest. "Or maybe now. It's nearly time for the challenge."

"And past time for midnight snacks," Noi said, stretching. "Even normal practice sessions make it hard to get through the night without getting up to eat, let alone yesterday's extravaganza."

She poked the pile of boy next to her while Madeleine woke Emily, and then they opened the door to let in a wash of chilly air. Nash offered to cook something, and Noi took Madeleine into the master bedroom en suite to examine her back.

"I should have suggested doing this tomorrow," Madeleine said, shirtless and shivering. "It's definitely getting to the end of Autumn."

"Yeah, pity we can't risk turning on the heating in this place. As it is I've been wondering if we'll end up having the power cut off by some automated you-haven't-paid-your-bill system." She poked Madeleine's shoulder blade gently. "Hurts here, right?"

"Yes. You can see bruises then?"

"I can see where the stars aren't. The only thing I know to do for bruises is put ice on them."

Madeleine shuddered at the idea. "Definitely not bad enough for that."

"Okay then. Look at me for a moment." Noi was standing, arms folded, eyebrows raised, lips lightly curved. "See me here, visibly restraining myself."

"Is that what you call that?"

"Did I mention I took photos? Didn't even wait till he was asleep." Noi paused to fully appreciate Madeleine's reaction. "He laughed. That makes him a keeper in my book."

"Noi..."

"I was going to point out that we could have died yesterday afternoon, that we could die today, or tomorrow. After all, we're not talking wear clean underwear because you might get hit by a bus – we're talking glowing flying buses hunting us down and trying to hump our legs. But, seriously, it's way too much fun watching you two dancing around each other with no idea what to do next. It surprises me, since Fisher's really very confident and assured for a Science Boy. I'm having to revise my stereotypes."

"We only met eleven...twelve days ago," Madeleine protested, pulling on her Singlet and tracksuit jacket.

"I guess so. Seems like much longer. Seems like centuries."

All the liveliness drained from Noi's face, and this time Madeleine didn't hesitate, but turned and wrapped her arms around the shorter girl. Noi started to pull away, but then leaned into Madeleine's hold, breath turning to gulps.

"We were so close to being lost, Maddie. All of us, any of us. There's no way we can make it through two years of this, and I'm just so – everyone's gone, Maddie. I can't stand it. They're all gone."

Madeleine wondered if the reason Noi had stopped pursuing Pan had less to do with his age than it did Noi's fear and grief. There was still nothing she could say which would make Noi's loss easier, though she told her she was sorry, and stroked her back as she struggled with her tears. After yesterday's fight, it wasn't surprising that Noi's control had frayed: Madeleine was only surprised that the lot of them hadn't kicked each other awake having nightmares.

"You don't have to be the strong one all the time, you know," she said, when the storm had begun to pass.

"Don't I?" Noi took a deep breath and straightened. "How will Millie cope if I'm having dramas all over the place? She's just a baby. How will it help anyone if I sit in a corner rocking back and forth?" Turning away, she dashed water into her face, firming her mouth.

"Does it have to be one extreme or another?" Madeleine paused, then added: "We made a good team yesterday. I don't know if it's enough to get us through this, and I don't like to think about how I now have a bunch of people that matter. I know I rely on you a bit much – I don't think ahead in the same way – but you don't need to..." Madeleine stopped. Who was she to dictate how Noi coped? "Anyway, I'm here if you need anything. And you can email me those photos."

That brought back Noi's smile, and then the scent of cooking drew them downstairs. Madeleine let herself be the entertainment by sitting next to Fisher so she could peek at what he was typing. Surviving the next two years wasn't just a matter of successfully hiding: it was being brave without losing your head, and squabbling a bit but not too much, and having two people around not managing to hide that they liked each other, because watching that was a happy thing.

"Do you think they're being deliberately dickish?" Pan was eyeing the television, which had switched from thousands of people gathered in a candlelight prayer vigil to a sunny parkland, and another gathering of Moths.

"Is that some kind of trick question?" Min asked, derisive. "What is *not* dickish about invading someone's planet so you can play games?"

"Yeah, yeah." Pan threw a mock-punch. "I just mean picking a religious icon for this challenge. Are they going to go for the Spring Temple Buddha next, or play chasies in a mosque?"

"Given they started with a golf course..." Min said.

"That was the Manila Moths," Pan said. "These are the Rio Moths. We know not all Moths act the same because of the way some go out of their way to destroy any webcams in their areas, while others don't care. The London ones wave when they pass. Maybe the Rio ones are trying to make a point today, rubbing our faces in how we just have to sit here and watch."

"Or maybe the Rio Moths were trying to decide on a challenge, looked about and saw a great big statue on a hill?" Min's acid tone was leavened by a grin. "How about, you do my next turn at the washing up if I'm right and they don't destroy the thing?"

Pan held his hands in a warding-off gesture. "I'll pass. You've already got me doing your laundry and cleaning your room."

The great big statue was called Christ the Redeemer and its appearance on the challenge website had caused a new wave of upset, at least among Christians, who were convinced that the goal of the challenge was to destroy the statue.

"Do you think they're going to destroy it?" she asked Fisher.

"I don't believe they'll care if they do." He stopped typing to glance at the television, where the Mothed Blues were lining up near a long row of cars, then turned the laptop toward her. "There's been another Rover sighting. Again it's a city which gained points during the first challenge. But look at it."

He started a video, and within a minute everyone was hanging over his shoulder having him replay it. The Rover they'd killed had stood as tall as a human, but wider, and its tail had extended a couple of metres. The video, an elevated street view, showed a Rover which was taller than the size of an ordinary door, so that it had to crouch and crawl to get inside the building it was trying to enter, its curling tail trailing behind like a swimming snake's. Several Blues followed it in.

"Who filmed this?" Nash asked.

"A Green who returned to Berlin after the Spire stopped singing. She's been documenting Blue activities."

"Damn. Above and beyond." Pan shook his head respectfully. "What've you been saying?"

Fisher paged down the comments, where his new net identity, 'Theo', had been making suggestions about fighting Rovers. "I don't dare outright say what worked for us," he explained. "Too big a flag. But I tell enough. Important, since the Rovers do appear to be tracking Blues."

"I'm not sure we could fight one that big," Madeleine said.

"There's every chance we won't have to." Fisher flipped through the mixture of photographs and drawings he'd collected in the short time before and after urgent rest. "The first sighting of a Rover is soon after the Manila challenge, and if we look at the progression of sightings, each larger than the previous, it's not unreasonable to conclude that the Rovers were some form of prize. That suggests a scarcity."

"With Nash, we have a chance against these glowing things," Noi said. "I'm more worried about what we do if Blues come after us. Greens we can shield paralyse and run. Blues – Mothed Blues fight far better than we can, and if Nash drains them, well, from what we've seen that will probably kill the host as well as the Moth. Are we all willing to do that to people? Are we willing to do that to Gavin?"

Silence.

"Ho-*ly* shit!"

Pan almost catapulted himself into Fisher's lap, gaping at the muted television, though by the time Madeleine looked there was only an image of three fighter jets, moving into formation as they streaked away over a tree-dotted city.

"They shot a Spire! They shot a Spire!" Pan said. "Turn on the sound!"

Min dived for the remote and a woman's gasping voice said: "*...there an impact?*"

"Get higher," a second woman said. "In case they're coming back."

The image dipped and bounced as whoever was filming ran, and there followed a confused jumble of stairs and biohazard suits.

"I didn't see any explosion," Pan said.

Noi had an iron grip on Madeleine's shoulder. "Let it work," she breathed.

"But why would they think–?" Madeleine paused. "Of course. The Moths bring the shields down to go through for the challenges."

The camerawoman had reached a roof and provided a shot of a placidly unperturbed Spire standing in the middle of a very long, straight park.

"The Spire which rose under the Washington Monument," Fisher said.

His tone and expression were no more than thoughtful, but sitting beside him Madeleine could feel the tension behind the relaxed appearance. She touched the back of his hand, and he looked at her blankly, then managed a semblance of a smile. "The most likely result is that they just bombed Rio de Janeiro."

"Damn, Fish is right," Pan said. "No sign of any damage on the Spire, anyway. Does anyone have the Moth transmission still up? Any explosions?"

"Wherever those missiles went, it wasn't to Rio," Min said, holding up a tablet. "The Moths aren't acting like they've even noticed."

"*Here they come!*" gasped one of the rooftop women.

The image jumped sideways, then focused on the three jets, approaching in a tight triangular formation. A giant tower made an easy target, and each jet fired and peeled off in rapid succession.

"Shield's back."

Noi, voice flat, let go of Madeleine's shoulder as the blooms of fire died.

"And now we find out if they meant it about 'reprimands'," Min said, trying for his usual caustically delighted tone, but lacking the enthusiasm for it.

Madeleine drew her feet up, wishing she'd brought a blanket down, and then murmured gratefully as Nash handed her a bowl of steaming pasta shells. The television divided its time between the video uploaded by the two uninfected women, and the challenge in Rio de Janeiro, which seemed to involve several hundred people scrambling for the nearest vehicle and racing off. A full stomach and not enough sleep combined to make this a lullaby, until Fisher woke her to a room darkened and emptying.

"We're going to finish the night in the study," he said. "Now that the challenge is over, it's possible the local Moths will pick up any search for their Rover."

She sat up, neck stiff, rubbing at her eyes and glancing at Pan and Nash tidying in the kitchen. Fisher gauged her winces as she straightened.

"I'll get you an icepack," he said. "We shouldn't have left your back untreated."

Ice was no less revolting a concept than when Noi had suggested it, and so Madeleine had to smile at herself obediently taking off her jacket, turning it to cover her front and slipping her arms back through the sleeves. She was sore, but more interested in an opportunity for another small step forward into something new. She felt increasingly certain, too, that Fisher was finding chances to take them as well.

"Shoulder blades primarily?" He'd brought two folded tea towels, and prodded her gently to lean forward so he could rest them both against her back. Cold seeped through her Singlet, and she shivered.

"Not that giving you a chill is ideal," he said, lifting and turning the packs. "After a couple of days you're at least able to switch to hot packs."

"What happened with the challenge?"

"It was a straightforward race. The base of the statue was simply the end point."

"It all seems so petty." Races and competitions – played with a distinct lack of care for the possessed hosts, but still games which hardly seemed worth the immensity of death which preceded them. "And the attack in Washington?"

"No sign of any immediate response." Fisher's voice was composed, but the pressure on her back momentarily increased, and she knew that if their positions were reversed she would feel the roil of frustrated energy in him.

"You and Noi are so alike."

"Noi?" he repeated, startled, then stopped and gave the idea some thought before saying: "I don't see it."

"You're both always trying to hide how really worried or upset you are. All stressed and pressured, as if you were responsible for looking after the rest of us, and so can't show when you're overwhelmed. You must know we're not so unfair as to expect you to produce some miraculous solution."

She couldn't catch any response. The icepacks remained steady, and the only sound was Pan and Nash putting dishes away.

"I expect that of me, though," Fisher said finally, voice almost too low for her to hear. "Call it ego, or...I had so much I wanted to do, and it's been taken away from me, and I seethe and grind my teeth and *shake* with this need to sow vengeance and regret."

He paused, took an audible breath, then said: "For that we need to bring down the Spires. I have ideas on how to find a way to do that, but I keep coming up against what it will take to gain the information we need. And my courage fails me."

It was an admission, weary and subdued. Madeleine wished she could see his expression, but resisted the impulse to turn, instead asking: "Did you feel that way in the first days after the dust, when you were trying to identify the best way to treat Greens?"

He turned the icepacks again. "I knew I would kill people." A simple statement of fact. "Dividing up boys of about the same condition, and giving one group sugar water and one saline sounds innocuous, but what if the Conversion was more efficient with an infusion of electrolytes? What amount of energy did their bodies need to survive? Raise their temperature or lower it? Keep them active, keep them still? When one option appeared more promising,

I couldn't just switch them all to it immediately, had to keep a control group in case it was a false positive. I had constant nightmares about the data I was accumulating, this logic puzzle of life and death written in permanent ink, with no option to erase it all and start over. I will never forget the faces of those in the groups where treatment clearly wasn't helping. Never. But the knowledge that that was just the first wave, those exposed in the first hours, drove me on. Doing nothing was the worst option.

"With the Spires, doing anything could result in another release of dust or...or anything else the Moths consider a suitable 'reprimand'. Endangering hundreds of thousands of people who only need to wait two years to be safe. And every time I hear Pan or Emily say 'All for one, and one for all' I wonder how that will work if one of us is possessed. Everyone here wants to do something in the abstract, but to get anywhere, to find a way to fight them, we're going to have to gamble everything."

"Have you stopped trying to find a way, then?" Madeleine asked softly.

"No."

"Are we ready to actually do anything?"

"No."

She shook her head. "I've been around Pan too much, and all his dramatic speeches – it makes me want to try one. I feel so strange and unlike myself, possibly the least social person on the planet suddenly part of this group of people which can seriously consider the Three Musketeers' motto as something which fits us. But yesterday none of us ran. We all held together and fought, because we are...we've become more than just people in the same place, trapped by circumstance. If any of us comes up with a plan, we'll think hard about what we mean to do, and then we'll all face the consequences of fighting back."

"Together." He sounded sad, exhausted. Then briskly stood, lifting the icepacks away. "That should be enough. I'll go kick a few people out of the way so you have room to lie on your stomach."

He went upstairs, and Madeleine trailed up to change her shirt, wondering if she'd helped at all. And if her imagination was running overtime or, as he turned away, he'd brushed a finger across the nape of her neck, just below the knot of her hair.

Chapter Fifteen

Sinuous bodies wove a mid-air ballet, so beautiful and strange that Madeleine could not help but sit spellbound as the pair of dandelion dragons twined a pas de deux between bridges and skyscrapers.

Machine gun fire rose, a rat-tat accompaniment which sparked a new form of dance. Dipping, twisting, wildly joyous: driven by countless wings in a madcap obstacle race mere handbreadths above rooftops, from air-conditioning plant to scaffolding and fire escape. It was so obviously a gleeful game, exultant and playful, that its culmination in a tumbling human figure made her gasp in protest.

"Where is it this time?"

Madeleine started. At nearly two in the morning, she still had an hour to go on intruder watch. Judging by his hair-on-end, rumpled and cross appearance, Min had simply given up trying to sleep.

"Pittsburgh," she said, as a rifle began firing.

"Pointless." Min sniffed disparagingly at the gunshot punctuation.

"They did hurt one once."

"And what did that achieve? A glowing thing spitting up its load of dust in the middle of the street." He shook his head, then crossed to the patio door and slid it open despite the chill, kneeling in the entrance to light incense before the statue he'd placed just outside.

The reprimand had begun the day after the Rio de Janeiro challenge, late night Sydney time, and dawn on the east coast of the United States. The many-winged flying serpents which served as air transport for Mothed Blues had appeared in numbers, and flown riderless to the non-Spire towns and cities nearest to Washington. The first sighting had been at a large hall housing Washington refugees, where one dandelion dragon simply thrust its enormous head through upper windows and vomited a great gout of dust over hundreds of sleeping families.

Two weeks after the appearance of the Spires, small outbreaks of stain had occurred in countless non-Spire towns and cities, and breathing masks were ubiquitous, some even managing to sleep in them. But it had been established that the Conversion could infect through contact with eyes, and masks could only do so much for those who woke coated in dust. Even when people stayed home, when there were no convenient large groups for the dragons to target, the increased concentration of dust had soon led to thousands of new cases of Blue-Green. The sheer manoeuvrability of the dragons, and their relative indifference to sprays of bullets, made them almost impossible to stop.

"I think we can safely say that the chances of anyone else trying to shoot a Spire have dropped into the not worth betting on range," Min said, standing and sliding the door shut. "There been any let-up in numbers?"

"No." Almost thirty hours in, a new attack was still being reported roughly every hour.

"Coffee? Damn, this milk is still solid." Min thumped down the carton Madeleine had taken out of the freezer an hour ago, making dishes rattle, then sighed. "Green tea?"

"No thanks. I guess I should go to bed," Madeleine said, but didn't move, wondering if she should be worried. Min was usually very even-tempered. "Would it offend you if I asked what you pray for each morning?"

"Mostly for my brothers to be reborn as slugs in a salt mine," Min said flatly. "Oh, they deserve it, don't worry. I'm virtuous by comparison. Normal." He gave her a sardonic look. "The contrast works the other way here, among you would-be heroes trying to do the right thing, all caution and common sense. No-one's even gotten into the liquor cabinet. Noi's planning this surprise birthday party for Pan, yet thinks it's a bad idea for us to cut loose."

"Alien invasions aren't exactly the time to get drunk."

"If there was ever a time to get drunk, alien invasions are it. We could lock ourselves in the study first, and let Millie play lookout. But you all insist on being so dull and supportive with your musketeers and your stick-together attitude. I keep expecting to find the lot of you sitting around a campfire singing *Kumbaya*."

"You've been singing along with us, Porthos," Madeleine pointed out, relieved because Min's tone had lightened, growing amused rather than acidic.

"Just humouring the natives," he said, but smiled. "I started at Rushies with no interest whatsoever in acting. But it's hard not to get caught up, and a little addicting playing Spy, Turncoat, Hero. Very elaborate lies, just my kind of thing. You, however, are totally transparent, especially when trying to cheer people up. Go to bed."

Uncurling, she headed upstairs to the lamp-lit library. Fisher's favourite place was the window seat, and she wasn't surprised to see him still awake, but it was unusual for him to be gazing steadily out the window instead of reading.

"Is there something out there?"

He turned his head, making one of his unhurried studies of her.

"Take a look."

It was an unremarkable exchange, but Madeleine instantly filled with a total awareness of him, tucked snugly in a corner of the seat, a book set on one raised knee, posture relaxed, weary smudges beneath his glasses. She would have to lean across him to see in the direction he'd been looking, and the way he kept his attention on her as she hesitated, and then slowly approached, made her extraordinarily conscious of her hair falling loose from its usual knot, and the cheap, rumpled tracksuit hiding almost all her stars.

One knee on the edge of the seat, she rested a hand on the sill, leaned forward and saw...light. A pathway dancing across the black sheet of the bay, leading to a low, heavy moon sinking into the horizon.

"Beautiful."

"Very."

There was a hint of laughter to the word, and she turned her head to see the scene reflected in his glasses, twin moons which obscured but did not hide eyes focused on her face. A charged moment, chained lightning. Then Madeleine decided she was tired of small steps and took a big one, dropping her head to press her mouth to his.

Barely a kiss, simple contact. He exhaled as she drew back, and she felt the feather-touch of his breath. They stared at each other, then uncertainty turned into forward motion, and this time they both moved, found lips, discovered the tingle of tongues entwined.

Technicalities. What felt right, what didn't. A stop-start exploration of reaction, then relaxation into sheer enjoyment. Madeleine shifted her hand from the sill to his shoulder, and Fisher moved his to her waist. As their kisses grew deeper, he pulled her forward, and she slid into his lap.

Like all Blues, Fisher's palms were covered with stain, though most of his fingers were free of it. Breath coming faster, he slid both hands from her waist to the small of her back, where her tracksuit top and the shirt below had ridden up. The contrast of sensation, velvet and flesh, made her shiver and tighten arms around his neck. Encouraged, he moved further up her back.

Sitting as she was, Madeleine was completely clear about the effect she was having on him. This was no longer merely a big step, was becoming an outright leap, and she found she was fine with that, though maybe not on the library window seat. She slowed her kisses, then drew back, and the small noise he made was all about her weight shifting.

She had to smile, because his glasses had steamed up, and he looked ruffled and owl-like, but when she lifted them carefully away his cinnamon-brown gaze transfixed her. He took the glasses, put them on the windowsill, then, slowly, constantly monitoring her reaction, reached for the zipper-pull of her tracksuit top, and drew it down.

Her shirt, form-fitting and dark green, had been rucked up by his exploration of her back, and the very tips of his fingers brushed glimmering skin.

Moth song.

They both leapt as if struck, Fisher so violently that Madeleine would have been propelled into a nosedive if he hadn't caught at her arm. She staggered to her feet, ready to run, to hide, and was turning toward the study when she recognised a quality of distance.

"It's the Spire."

Only the second time the Spire had sung. The Moths mightn't be near, but this suggested a change, perhaps new instructions for the Greens. Muffled, hurried footsteps on the floor below revealed Min's reaction, and down the hall the door to the Wonder Woman room was wrenched open, though Noi had slowed to a less urgent place by the time she reached the library.

"Well that was better than an alarm clock," she said, looking at them both standing by the window. "Do we dive for the study yet again?"

Fisher was frowning ferociously, head cocked to one side, but responded after a pause with a quick headshake. "Prepare for it, perhaps. I'll see if I can spot anything on the city webcams." He went into the study, mouth set in a grim line.

"I was feeling peckish anyway," Noi remarked, and tugged Madeleine's shirt down.

ooOoo

Most of Sydney's webcams were set in uselessly scenic places. They had two views of the skyline, three of the Bridge, one of Bondi, a couple in Circular Quay, but around Hyde Park where the Moths were most active, only the hastily-rigged cam pointing at the Spire. At night, that didn't tell them anything.

Dawn added little.

When the Spire stopped singing mid-morning, Madeleine went to bed, too tired to care anymore. She woke sour-mouthed and headachy in the late afternoon, feeling cheated of something she'd wanted. A long shower eased her temper, and she dressed with care, nothing out of the ordinary, but neatly. The Spire's interruption had thoroughly shattered the moment for her and Fisher, but the step had still been taken. As often as she'd looked at him since, she'd found him looking back, and Madeleine was surprised at the comfortable acceptance she felt. Mutual liking thoroughly acknowledged, action postponed.

She had tried to think about the situation in wider terms, with words like love and belonging. But it was difficult to look beyond the now of allies facing an incredible situation. Too soon and too strange to be sure of more than wanting there to be another moment.

Stomach rumbling, she headed downstairs. The buzz of a newsreader's voice was the only sound, and everyone was gathered around the television. No surprise – it was around the time when, if they stuck to schedule, the Moths announced the details of the next challenge. Which city would be their next plaything.

Everyone was so still. Statues, faces stiff with shock, staring at the screen. Only Emily looked around, and she jumped to her a feet with a cry and rushed to throw her arms around Madeleine's waist. But by then Madeleine had joined the others in being frozen, staring at the newsreader, and the over the shoulder graphic clearly labelled "SYDNEY CHALLENGE".

The image was the figure of a girl, cut off at neck level. A noodle-like figure in short shorts and a crochet halter neck top, and all the rest of her, stars.

Chapter Sixteen

"Okay, enough freaking out. We need to think this through."

They had responded to the announcement as Blues: with a massive injection of sugar pretending to be hot tea. Madeleine had been firmly sat down on the couch, a steaming mug pushed into her hands, with Emily curled comfortingly along one side, and Fisher a more restrained support on the other.

"At minimum, one hundred and fifty-five Moths," Noi went on, eyeing Madeleine with open concern. "About sixty of them with Rovers, if they're allowed to bring them along. Maybe the dragons as well, for better coverage. Given the first Rover found us at the garage, I think the wharf party's over guys. Time to run."

"But," Nash said.

Noi looked at him, sitting tensely upright on the opposite couch, and sighed. "Yeah, big bloody but. I think we can guess what the Spire was singing about last night."

"A cordon."

"They'd be mad to announce a Blue hunt without putting up a fence first. You slept through it, Maddie, but another of the big Navy ships moved out around lunchtime."

"There's no way there's enough Blues and Greens in Sydney to guard every possible route," Pan said. "We've just got to pick the right direction to run."

"They've had days to drive cars across every back street," Min pointed out. "Along with that they just need spotters, and that dragon. If I were them I'd have spent the day setting up my own webcam network. At least given Greens a number to call and told them to lurk at all the through-streets."

"Why do they even think Maddie's still in the city?" Pan asked. "Gav thought we were leaving. We all thought we were leaving."

"The film from the beach." Fisher reached for one of the laptops, and began typing in a search. "The discussion of Madeleine fending off one of the Moths has never completely died down. The uninfected are doing the Moths' job for them." He turned the computer so Madeleine could see her name on the screen. "My fault, ultimately, for posting the Subject M data."

He moved one hand to brush against her back, a gesture of apology or reassurance.

"Still a big assumption to base one of their challenges on," Noi said. "Though I guess they might consider Maddie prime suspect in Reasons Rover Didn't Come Home."

"I should go."

The words were faint, finding their way out of Madeleine's throat almost against her will. She made herself continue, facing up to the impossibility of any other choice.

"If I'm there, if I'm – if there's no need to hunt me, then they won't hunt you. I have to go."

During the chorus of protest which followed, Emily burrowed into Madeleine's side, murmuring something. The words were indistinct, but it was sure to be some variation of 'all for one'. Then Min tossed a screwed-up piece of paper at Madeleine, bouncing it off her forehead.

"Sorry to rain on your self-sacrifice parade, but if you give yourself up, you're giving the rest of us up at the same time. As soon as you're possessed they'll know where we are. Can the melodrama and drink your damn tea. You're in shock."

"Minnow, you make the *best* speeches," Pan said, wrapping his arms around Min's neck. Min shoved him away, and they wrestled briefly, a flurry which had more relief than anger in it. It lightened the atmosphere, and Madeleine made herself sip obediently, then remembered her hunger and drank thirstily.

"Under no circumstances."

Fisher breathed the words into her ear as she lowered the mug, and when she looked at him a great many thoughts which fit neither time nor place rushed to the forefront of her mind. She had no idea what her face showed, but the betraying colour of Fisher's ears revealed his mind had followed a similar course.

"Right, as I was saying," Noi said, too serious for more than the faintest smile in their direction. "Running away. Anyone have any arguments against it?"

"It's the most dangerous option," Fisher said, firmly. "Don't underestimate the difficulty of finding a route unseen when we're the only cars moving, and every Green is primed to expect an escape. I'm not certain we could even drive off this Wharf without setting off the first alert. And if we get out of the city centre, it won't only be the stained we're hiding from. The whole of Australia will now be highly aware of the probability of Madeleine running, and as soon as she's spotted it's almost inevitable that someone in their excitement will tweet or post or share the news in some way."

"We could use that," Nash pointed out. "Create accounts. Post and tweet sightings. Very likely there are already false reports, errors of identity. Add to that to send Moths running in every direction."

"Good idea." Fisher looked approving. "We should do that anyway. But camera phones will highlight the true trail even if we manage to break the cordon. We have a head start, but we've also had a demonstration of the dragons' capabilities."

"I don't see how that's more dangerous than staying in Sydney with a hundred and fifty-five hunters and their Blue-sniffing glow dogs," Noi said.

"We've confirmed the Rovers are used to track. It's a reasonable assumption to believe they home in some way on the energy Blues create. That gives us three options: gain distance, obscure like with like, or containment."

Fisher paused, and they all looked at the television, where Madeleine's face was displayed, circled, on her last class photograph.

"Distance is the option the Moths will have prepared for, and thus where we will face the greatest opposition. But if they track the energy we produce, moving as close as possible to the largest energy source around, a place where a large number of Blues will be gathered, may have the effect of hiding a lamp by placing it in a room full of chandeliers."

"You mean sitting next to the Spire?" Noi's brows lifted. "Somehow standing around Hyde Park doesn't strike me as – oh, I get you. Maddie came out of the rail tunnels from St James, so we know we can access the Spire that way. You want to trace her path back, and sit beneath the Moths' feet while they run around in circles."

"St James even has dead-end tunnels concealed behind false walls," Fisher said. "It's a gamble, of course. The energy created by a free Blue may be distinctive enough to distinguish despite proximity to the Spire and Mothed Blues. Or they may be guarding the tunnels."

"And containment would be, what, putting ourselves in a box? Something sturdier than the study?"

"Walk-in refrigerators," Fisher said. "Air-tight, insulated, offering an all-round metal shield. What few escape stories there's been from still-free Blues in Rover cities have all shared a shielding factor – those deep in subways, someone hiding in the back of a container truck. But again a gamble, and it would be too great a risk to use those at the Wharf restaurants, even if they're large enough, since the local Blues and Greens will link you to Finger Wharf. Size is a major factor, more than a question of how many of us can fit. We'll need sufficient oxygen for at minimum twelve hours, if not twenty-four. The previous two challenges don't give us enough information to know if there's a time limit, but it is clear that the Moths have a territorial, hierarchical culture. The whole challenge appears to be an attempt to steal a..." He paused. "...to steal a highly desirable Blue from a clan which hasn't yet claimed her."

"Hot property?" Min offered Madeleine a sympathetic grimace. "I'd ask how it feels to be a penthouse on The Peak, but your impersonation of a Green says it all."

"There is no guarantee containment will block the trackers, and we would need to reach a suitable place which isn't occupied by Moths," Fisher continued. "I have a possibility in mind outside the area they've been using – that new hotel which was due to open at Barangaroo on the fifteenth. Like Circular Quay, it's accessible from the waterfront."

"Well, we're not going anywhere while it's daylight, so we don't have to decide right away," Noi said, rubbing her forehead. "Driving off the Wharf would be a huge risk, so we'll strongly consider the boat option first. Pack what you can easily carry and stash anything we can't take with us into the study. Nash, can you take the binoculars and search for movement while it's still light, particularly any sign of those navy ships? And also look over our boating prospects?"

When Nash nodded, she went on: "Fisher, if you, Millie and Min can scare up any images on the public webcams of any of the directions we might head, that will help with our choices. Pan, when it hits early dusk, not dark, go out and see if you can finger-punch the lights over the north end of the marina."

"Mindless vandalism is my forte," Pan said, his spirits recovering with the prospect of action. "Guess we'd better wait till after midnight for the great escape? Let the Greens get sleepy?"

"After three," Fisher said. He glanced at Madeleine. "After the moon has set."

Would they ever have another moment in the moonlight? "I'll help with the cooking," Madeleine said, scarcely feeling real.

"First check the apartments for gloves, hats, anything which looks useful for a boating trip in this weather. Right. Let's get started."

Fisher rose with the rest, but only to sit on the coffee table in front of Madeleine, brows drawn together in concentration. Madeleine, half out of her seat, dropped back down, and looked at him uncertainly.

"I wish I could make you promises," Fisher said. "But I don't want to downplay the danger we're in. I'd like you to make a promise to me, however."

"What is it?"

"Fight. Always fight. No matter how impossible the odds, no matter who you've lost, how you've been hurt. If there doesn't seem to be a way out, look for one. If you seem to have come to an end, start afresh. Never, ever give up."

She stared at him, startled by the anger, the complex swell of emotion in his voice.

"You don't think your plan has a chance?"

Fisher looked away. "The Cores will almost certainly participate. Those of the higher ranked clans are sure to be stronger than the Moths we've previously encountered. And tomorrow is just one day of two years. It's what comes after which frightens me most of all."

He still wouldn't look at her, was watching Noi heading upstairs.

"It makes it easier for me," he added, voice muted, "to know that you won't falter. Can you promise to try?"

Madeleine promised.

ooOoo

"What are you writing?"

"Thank you note for the owners of the house," Noi said, frowning as she read it over. "Miss Manners totally needs to add a chapter on squatting during an apocalypse. I wish we didn't have to leave your painting behind, Maddie."

"I'll come back for it."

"That's the spirit. A big improvement over yesterday afternoon."

"I'm trying to keep focused on how glad I was to survive St James," Madeleine said. "I was convinced the dust would kill me, and I concentrated everything I had on getting out, and painting the picture I'd been waiting months to start. I got to do that, by going on step by step, not giving up. And then I met you, and we got through Bondi, and the seven of us have really..."

She gazed out the patio doors, to the moon being swallowed by the sea.

"I've spent years thinking I was so self-sufficient, that I had all I needed. My art is always going to be the most important thing for me, but this place has been...good for me. I'm really proud of the portrait of Tyler, and I think the one of you and Emily might be the best thing I've ever done. They have something my usual work lacks. And–" She smiled. "And I want to paint Fisher. When that Spire's no longer in Sydney, and I can do something so indulgent as hit the nearest art supplies store, I *will* paint him."

"Preferably nude."

"Maybe." Madeleine refused to be embarrassed. "We better get downstairs. Two years of this still seems a near-impossibility, so I'm focusing on the current step."

Noi nodded, folded her note in half, and stuck it in the middle of the children's drawings on the fridge. "I'll miss this place," she said, then tugged a scavenged beanie over her riot of curls, and picked up her backpack.

They turned out the last of the lights, and rode the elevator down to the garage, stepping into chill, pitchy dark. The open service door was a grey square of illumination, and cubes of windshield glass crunched underfoot as they edged their way toward the three shadows which interrupted the thin light.

"Won't be long," Pan murmured. "They're aiming for the slip closest to the near entrance."

"I'll head down to check," Min said. "If I don't come back, they're ready. Or I've fallen in."

"We'll listen for the splash, Minnow." As soon as the younger boy had gone, Pan took and let out several long breaths. "I'm so wired. Makes me want to shriek, and jump about."

"Tempting." Noi shifted the spare bag of food she was carrying. "When all this is over, I think some full-throated yelling while running down the middle of the nearest street will be in order."

"Works for me."

"You'll join in, won't you Millie? Maddie?"

"Through Hyde Park," Emily said, firmly, and after a moment they agreed to that, then Noi led Emily out and down the Wharf to the northern gate of the marina.

"I can't believe, with all the millions of dollars of high-powered luxury boating stretched before us, this is the plan we've come up with," Pan said. "There's something inherently deflating about the words 'utility dinghy'."

"Rowing four kilometres in the dark," Madeleine said. "Racing dawn. Smuggling ourselves right beneath the noses of the Moths."

"Stop trying to make it sound awesome. Utility Dinghy. Utility Dinghy."

"Let's go." Lifting her allotted share of the food, Madeleine stepped out of the garage, and waited while Pan pulled the service door gently shut behind them. They crossed to the corner of the main building and peered down the Wharf, all shadows and moonlit edges, and then the soft glow of lampposts beyond the area where Pan had punched out the lights. No sign of movement. They slid around the corner, keeping close to the high patio fences which hid the view into the lower apartments, and moved as quietly as they could, straining their eyes to spot the gate to the marina.

"I think it's here," Pan said, barely audible.

Finger Wharf didn't have safety railings, the edge a shin-high wooden board punctuated by the occasional pylon. The marina gate was transparent, opening onto a ramp leading down to the floating dock, which had no rim at all. Even though they'd given their eyes plenty of time to adjust, Madeleine still didn't dare do more than inch forward, searching with her free hand. They'd timed their departure to use the last of the moonlight to get around the dock without torches, and she was able to make out shapes, but couldn't force herself to move any faster.

"It's here."

The words were accompanied by the faintest metallic noise, as Pan turned the key left by their advance boat-seekers, then pulled it free. The ramp at least had railings, and Madeleine followed it down until there was nothing left to guide her, and she stood clutching the end, trying to adjust to the faint bob of the dock.

"Directly left, Maddie," breathed the night. "It's only a metre or so, so take one step forward, then kneel and pass me your bags."

Nash whispered similar instructions to Pan from the next slip over. Obedient to Noi's command, Madeleine stepped, knelt, and held out the food bag, then her overstuffed backpack, and by the time that was done she was more sure of what was in front of her, could just make out Noi, Fisher and Min. Then it was a matter of lowering herself, guided firmly by Noi, until she was sitting in the back of a small boat, shivering more from nerves than the chill lifting from the water.

"Put this on."

A bulky shape with confusing straps. Madeleine fumbled it over her head, and found parts which clicked together. By the time this was done, the moon was no more than a fading memory.

"All clear," Noi said, a fraction louder.

"Lift off."

There was a gurgle of water to accompany Nash's response, and then another as Noi pushed the boat away from the dock, and Fisher and Min used their oars to prod them out the rest of the way.

Rowing lessons had been the highlight of the wait for moonset. Boats made of couch cushions, and brooms for oars, with Nash patiently drilling them with the motions despite the spurts of giggles born of a long night's tension. Madeleine felt little urge to laugh now, as they eased clear of the slip and began to turn, with water making blooping noises off the oars, and a faint creak from the oarlocks. Unlikely to be heard no matter how well sound carried over water, but she still stared back over her shoulder at the long bulk of the Wharf, searching for movement. There would be no outrunning anything in a dinghy, but sailing at night with a crew of total amateurs would have been suicidal, and any engine a trumpet call in the hushed city, so no-one had been able to argue against using the small boats. Nash had been confident that the trip could be made well before dawn, even with inexperienced rowers, and there was little chance of them being spotted so long as they kept away from the shore.

As they picked up speed, passing the North Building, Madeleine began to relax. There was nothing but parkland on their left, and a long gap to the navy base on the far side of the Wharf. The Bay had few sources of light, and they were leaving those behind, scudding along beneath a cloak of stars, invisible.

"Destination: North Pole," Noi muttered, and squeezed Madeleine's hand.

Webcams had ruled out other choices. Circular Quay seemed to be a hive of Moth activity, while a beach cam had provided glimpses of smaller craft moving near Watson's Bay, making it clear that a speedboat dash past the headlands and out of the Harbour would not merely be a matter of avoiding two very large, weapon-festooned ships. Finally, representing the uninfected portion of Australia, some isolation-suited reporters had settled down with long-range cameras to watch Greens stationed at roadblocks, broadcasting through the night and incidentally making it even harder for free Blues to sneak out of the city. So the Musketeers were gambling on refrigerating themselves.

Three hours till dawn. Four kilometres to row. Sydney's city heart was shaped like a partially unfolded fan, with the Spire in Hyde Park located on the lower right edge of the narrower southern end. Woolloomooloo Bay sat just east of the fan's top right stretch of parkland, and they were aiming to row out of the Bay and curve around the cove-notched upper edge, keeping to a central point between the north and south shore until they'd passed beneath the Harbour Bridge and could turn down the western side of the fan to the newly-developed waterfront area called Barangaroo.

It had seemed a vast distance when they were poring over maps, but caught up in the sensation of floating through blackness, Madeleine found their arrival in the open water of the harbour came disconcertingly quickly, their narrowed view opening up to the shimmering golden sweep of the North Shore. Constellations of abandoned apartment blocks, and suburban nebulae: terrestrial stars which spun and bobbed as the dinghies hit the swell outside the shelter of the bay.

Facing the wrong direction to appreciate the vista, Fisher said: "The current's not too bad. Tell me when we reach the turn point."

The turn point was halfway to a small island called Fort Denison, helpfully furnished with a squat lighthouse. When Noi gave the word, Fisher and Min backed their oars, slowing forward motion.

In the relative quiet which followed, they could clearly make out the creak and splosh of the second dinghy, and Noi called softly: "Duk-duk! Duk-duk!" A nonsense sound, their chosen signal to try to orient the two boats in the dark. Their theory was that the noise could be mistaken for a bird, and Madeleine supposed it was mildly less obvious than "Over here!", but it did sound silly, and Emily's stifled giggle in response came to them clearly over the shush of the ocean.

Nash and Pan succeeded in following the sound, and Madeleine's straining eyes caught the shape of them just before a thin, wet rope smacked her in the face. She managed to catch it, and with a small amount of manoeuvring the two boats were soon side-by-side, temporarily lashed together.

"Any sign?" Nash asked, serious, but with a measure of exultation lighting his voice. Desperate and dangerous as this might be, the Harbour was transcendent.

"No movement to the west," Fisher replied.

Noi had the binoculars, and was peering as far down to the Harbour entrance as the angle would permit. "I think those lights belong to one of the big ships," she said. "It must have moved in from the Heads, but doesn't seem to be coming any closer. You four fine to go on after a couple of minutes' rest, or do you want to try swapping about?"

"It's easier than I expected," Min said. "Not that I won't complain about it later, but I shouldn't have problems with the full run."

"My only worry is I don't want to stop," Pan said. "This is the most incredible thing I've ever done. I feel like I'm flying." He went on, whispering, but his stage-trained voice lifting irresistibly:

"Take him and cut him out in little stars,

And he will make the face of heaven so fine

That all the world will be in love with night

And pay – oof!"

"Enough, Juliet," Nash said, sitting ready to bop the shorter boy again. "You can give us a command performance in the refrigerator."

"Somehow, I don't think that'll have quite the same atmosphere." Pan heaved a great sigh, a combination of regret and sheer delight, but didn't argue further.

"After the challenge," Noi said, a smile in her voice. "We'll find a stage and you can perform for all of us. Right now, everyone take a few breaths. We need to calm down."

They drifted slowly, giving themselves another few moments to enjoy their surroundings, then separated the dinghies and returned to the business of escape. Madeleine's role as a non-rower was both lookout and defender, should they encounter anything. The fact that a well-aimed punch could scupper a boat had been part of the arguments both for and against trying to make a dash out through the headlands, and there'd also been an amusing discussion on whether shields could be used as a form of propulsion, or would merely be a spectacular way to overturn.

The long dark stretch of the Royal Botanic Gardens gave way to curving white shells lit by spotlights. Madeleine wondered if the lights were automatic, or if the Moths or Greens were turning them on. Perhaps they, too, were reciting Shakespeare or, more likely, singing in their oscillating language. The world knew so little of what the Moths were like, what they were doing with their hosts, whether glowing balls of light had any interest in the words, the music, the pictures to be found in the cities they had stolen. There had been indications – Greens sent to obtain fresh milk and meat – that the Moths were at least interested in Earth's food, but given the Blue hunger drive that was hardly surprising.

It wasn't until the dinghy was almost past the Opera House that they had a good view into the rectangular notch of Sydney Cove, with the ferry docks and train station at its southern end. Noi, peering through the binoculars, murmured that there was no sign of anyone, but Fisher and Min still increased their pace as they approached Dawes Point and the sweep of well-lit bridge above. The Harbour Bridge was such a focal point, and at some angles the passage of even a low boat might be visible against the lights of the North Shore, so they'd planned to get through the area as quickly as possible. Madeleine found herself holding her breath, especially when she spotted Nash's boat well ahead, tiny wake shattering golden reflections. Passing beneath the huge span, they were so small, and yet seemed so obvious.

Panting, Min and Fisher scudded after them, and Madeleine forced herself to strain for any glimpse of movement on the shoreline rather than gaze up and up at the bar across the sky. They turned directly after passing beneath, and drew the dinghy to a stop in the shadow of the first of the Walsh Bay piers.

The map had shown a hotel at this location, so they didn't dare speak, simply waited till the two rowers had their breathing under control, then pushed back out of the bay and pressed on toward the turning point marked by Barangaroo's northern park.

"Duk-duk! Duk-duk!"

Something had gone wrong. Min and Fisher stopped rowing, though they didn't back paddle, allowing the dinghy to continue slowly onward. They could hear the dip and creak of oars ahead of them, coming closer, and after a long hesitation Noi responded, and the two dinghies found each other north of Walsh Bay's central pier.

"What is it?"

Noi sounded as sick as Madeleine felt. They'd taken less time to cross the Harbour than expected, but they had few contingency plans, none of them ideal.

"There's something in the water off Headland Park."

Nash's whisper was calm, unhurried, and Emily better summed up the situation by adding: "Glowing eyes. There's glowing eyes, looking."

"Did it spot you?" Noi gazed anxiously past them.

"Don't think so," Pan replied. "We didn't get close, saw it as we started around the curve. Scurried away like mice."

"It's not visible from the near corner of the park?"

"We didn't spot it till we were past the initial bump of the sea wall."

Noi lifted the binoculars and peered into the gold-striped dark. Barangaroo was broken into three sections grouped into a north-south rectangle. The north was covered in trees, sandstone blocks rising out of the sea to a grassy hill. The south was crowded with apartments and skyscrapers under construction. The middle, separated from the other sections by two small coves, was a mixture of garden and cultural sites – Madeleine had visited it the previous year to see an open-air sculpture exhibition – but several large buildings sat on its southern edge, including the enormous Southern Sky Hotel, a 6 Star extravagance which, before the Spires interrupted, had been in final preparations for a grandiose opening gala. The plan had been to row down to the cove nearest the Hotel, risking only the briefest amount of time travelling by foot.

After a tense wait, Noi lowered the glasses. "It doesn't seem to be following you. Is it feasible at all to get into the park without going into its line of sight?"

"Yes. Easily." Nash paused, then added: "It is more a question of what we will encounter in the park, given that there is already one creature on guard."

"I'm for risking that," Noi said. "Anyone against?"

No-one spoke.

"Right. We'd better do this without any chatter. We unload, and push the boats out. Even with the path lights, it's probably a bad idea to go stumbling through the trees, so walk along the inner path all the way down the east edge to the car park entrance. If the hotel looks like a no-go, we break into the nearest apartments and get keys, cars. If we're split up, we're split up, and will either meet in Plan B City or...we won't. Nash, lead the way."

The nearest edge of the park was an inlet sheltered in all directions except north across the harbour, with more than enough room for both dinghies. They bumped against stepped blocks of stone, and Madeleine was not the only one to wet her feet in the process of getting out. A lamppost stood above them, marking the path's location, and they took their time dumping their life jackets, pushing the boats out, and then climbing, a hands and knees progress, constantly reaching to confirm each other's location, passing the food bags up, angling to avoid the light.

Moving at a pace just short of a trot along the path through the trees, they hesitated at the inlet at the southern edge of North Barangaroo, then darted from shadow to shadow in the more open Central section. The hotel loomed above, a monolith of glimmering blue glass, and they approached it at a tangent, following the road down to the gates of the underground car park.

Firmly sealed.

Chapter Seventeen

"Who takes the time to lock up in the middle of an alien invasion?" Pan deposited his food bag on the traffic island dividing the in and out lanes. "Want me to go try the front?"

"Not yet." Noi tugged experimentally at the service door to the right of the main gates. "Even if this isn't wired with an alarm, punching it open will leave an obvious sign someone's broken in."

"Shall I look down here?" Nash unslung his bags and headed down a branch of the entry drive, Pan at his heels.

Madeleine added her food bag to the growing pile, and peered through the mesh of the gate. This hurdle had not been unanticipated, but even though the garage entry was lower than street level, she felt painfully exposed beneath the cold fluorescent lighting. Not long till dawn. Just over six hours before the world would come hunting.

"We could try to finger punch just the lock," Emily suggested, peering over Noi's shoulder.

"Because only breaking it a little would be less likely to set off any alarms?" Min asked. The sharper than usual edge in his voice brought a warning glance from Noi, and he made a gesture of apology, then sat down on the traffic island, examining reddened palms.

"In a hotel this size there will be a dozen entry points," Fisher said. "After the panic of the arrival day, the chances of every single one being firmly sealed is low." But he glanced toward the eastern sky.

"Guys, check this out."

Pan, beckoning from the junction of the drive. They followed him past a "Staff Only" sign, to another set of metal gates. Nash was peering through the one on the right, and pointed as they came up: "A solution."

Standing two metres inside the gate was a machine sporting a big green button, a gate release meant to be hit by departing drivers.

"All it needs is a finger punch, at just the right strength to push the button, but not so strong we smash the machine." Pan looked around. "Who thinks they have the best control?"

Knowing her limits, Madeleine opted to fetch the food bags, and returned just as the gate whirred upward. The elevator obliged them by not requiring any keys to access the ground floor, and then they were standing at a spacious junction directly before a door marked 'Reception'.

"Kitchen," Pan said, and went right. By the time they followed him into an enormous rectangular room of shining stainless steel, he was pulling open a heavy-duty door. A wave of chill flowed over them. "Freezer. And this would be – damn, I've seen houses smaller than this refrigerator. We should all fit in here."

"No." Fisher walked into the rack-lined space and paced out an estimate of its boundaries, stepping around pallets of boxes set on the floor. "Four, no, three people at most. It's not the oxygen; it's the carbon dioxide build-up which is going to be the problem. Depending on the length of the challenge, we may need to risk even opening the doors at least once. Unless..." He glanced around the kitchen. "With big enough containers we could try to rig some kind of crude carbon sink. That may help a little."

"Then where do the rest of us go?" Emily asked, stepping closer to Noi.

"There's four restaurants in this hotel – we'll need to spread between them if we want to survive twenty-four hours." He pulled the freezer door open again and considered its size. "Plenty of space here, which is good since one of us will probably need to use it. We can adjust the temperature to the highest setting."

Madeleine shivered at the mere idea, and looked around at worn, shadow-eyed faces. Some of them had tried to sleep during the gap between the challenge announcement and leaving, but the attempts hadn't been very successful, and after a pre-dawn row and a park excursion with wet feet, the idea of even the refrigerator made her feel ill.

"Right." Noi dumped her food bag on the nearest work surface. "Iced Blues it is. But first snacks, hot showers, a warm meal, and then we'll see what we can do about making a freezer habitable.

ooOoo

An elbow to her ribs. Madeleine started awake, and came close to falling off the edge of the triple-stack of mattresses set in the centre of the refrigerator. Emily, beside her, shifted and groaned until Noi, on her far side, turned to rub the girl's arm.

"She's trying so hard," Noi murmured. "She's not even thirteen-going-on-fourteen, has only just stopped being twelve. I don't know how to convince her that she's allowed to be overwhelmed and frightened sometimes. Just like the rest of us."

Madeleine blinked in the orange glow of the emergency exit button. "I spend half of each day being overwhelmed. What's the time?"

"Ten minutes till midnight. How's your breathing? Feeling headachy? Stifled?"

"I feel like I'm in a refrigerator," Madeleine said, tucking the quilt back under her side, then contemplating the metal ceiling. "I guess it worked, then."

"Yeah, looks like Science Boy was right. I had my doubts, I admit it."

"I think he did too," Madeleine said, remembering Fisher's expression as he asked for her promise.

"Twenty minutes before we get to check what's going on. Distract me by describing exactly what you're going to do to Science Boy first opportunity you get."

"I think I'll leave that to your imagination." Madeleine's own imagination caught her up, and she paused to enjoy it before adding: "The rooms in this place are–"

"Yeah. Lap of luxury, fallen into it. And did you see the big room half done up in decorations? We'll be able to use them for Pan's party."

"Much as I liked that apartment, there are some definite advantages to this move. And we have enough food to last us maybe for the rest of the year."

"Pity we'll be leaving it behind." At Madeleine's confused look, Noi continued: "Once the fuss from this hunt dies down, we really need to get out of this city. No matter the problems we'll have dealing with the uninfected, it's clear that you – all of us really, but you particularly – are way too interesting to the Moths. We need to get out of dragon range."

"But can we do that without anyone helpfully pointing me out while I'm still within reach?"

"If Nash's sister has come through, then the Moths will have been flooded with sightings – a few more won't hurt. Though a judicious makeover is probably a good idea. A tub of peroxide should dent your serious arty girl look."

Emily's voice rose, small but defiant: "How can we fight if we run away?"

Noi blinked as the girl turned to her, then said: "Leaving doesn't stop us from returning. To fight, we need to both learn to confidently control all these fancy new powers, and come up with a plan. Getting out of the city will buy us the time and freedom to do that."

"If we leave, we won't come back." Emily spoke with a furious certainty. "We'll be like the rest of them, cowards waiting two years for it to be safe again. Don't you *want* to make the Moths pay?"

"You know I do." Noi was a rock against the tide of Emily's anger. "I want it enough to not run shouting at them before I'm ready. They've taken everything that was precious to me away, and I will find a way to hurt them for that. I know you miss your family, Mil–"

"No!" Their mounded quilts were pulled away as Emily sat up, her slender body rigid with ever-increasing anger. "I don't miss them! You think they're dead, don't you?"

After a swift, astonished glance at each other, Noi and Madeleine struggled into sitting positions. Noi reached out, hesitated, then changed direction to take Emily's gloved hands in her own.

"I did," she said. "They're not?"

"They left." Two words and a world of emotion. "When the dust started, they went straight to my brothers' school and then out of the city. I couldn't even get home – a girl from school took me to her house. My parents are the worst people in the world."

The tears came, bringing with them violent, wrenching sobs, and Madeleine and Noi could only clasp Emily between them until the storm had eased.

"Emily." Madeleine shied away from asking if the girl's parents even knew she was alive. "You know that, whatever happens, we won't leave you behind. We'll come for you."

"No you won't." The words had an exhausted, bitter certainty. "I know it's all a lie, just play-acting to make each other feel better. The Moths will get us one by one, just like they got Gavin, and we can't do anything at all."

"You're underestimating us there." Noi spoke with quiet assurance. "We know that we can fight. I'm sure we could hurt some of them. It's just a matter of hurting them effectively which we've yet to figure out." She stroked Emily hair. "I think you're not being quite fair to your parents as well."

"They *left*."

Noi took a deep breath. "Millie, when the dust came, my Dad was up at Kellyville, well away from the cloud. He drove back in. The traffic was madness, people driving the wrong way down the roads, and it took him hours, but he got home. My Mum, and my Nonna, and all his brothers, they yelled at him, called him stupid, but he said he wanted to be with us, whatever was going to happen.

"I guess maybe it helped Mum, him being there. And because he got sick later than the rest of us, he was able to look after everyone, for a little while. And, with Mum and all his brothers and all of our family gone, maybe he would have preferred to not have to be around afterwards. But me, I'd rather still have a Dad."

"Th-that's different."

"If you say so. And it's different again to get ourselves out of the reach of the Moths until we can find a way to hurt them. Nor is it just play-acting to give it your best shot. And that's what we're going to do. I'm not going to guarantee that we'll win, but I promise you we'll try." She paused, studying the stubborn set of Emily's shoulders. "About time for breakfast, don't you think? Ah, and check-in time – almost missed it." She fished a tablet computer out of one of the bags set alongside the mattresses.

Keeping devices off was more about preserving battery life than the possibility of being tracked, but it still gave Madeleine an uneasy feeling as Noi, complaining about the poor signal, slid off the bed and held the tablet toward the door.

"Pass me the thermos?" Madeleine said to Emily, and was pleased to find the tea clinging to a lukewarm state. They set out a miniature feast as Noi reported that the challenge was still underway.

"Next check-in time at seven," Noi said, returning to accept a cup. "Science Boy says if it goes much past that we might have to risk opening the doors to try and cycle the air, and we're to keep alert for any headaches, muscle twitches, or turning new and original colours. Anything to report?"

"Just cold," Madeleine said, around an oatmeal biscuit. "I'd hate to be in Pan and Nash's shoes."

While the Southern Sky had four restaurants, it had proven to own only three walk-in refrigerators, with both ground floor restaurants catered out of the same kitchen. Fisher was in the top floor restaurant's refrigerator, and Min in the one on the Mezzanine level, while Pan and Nash were stuck with the biggest freezer at its warmest temperature setting. Since the warmest temperature setting of the refrigerator was still making Madeleine wish for another hot shower, she hated to think how they were coping with the long night.

"Do you feel sleepy?" Noi asked. "I'm tired, but it might be because I kept waking up and stressing."

"Not sleepy," Emily murmured.

"Cold aside, I'm fine," Madeleine said. "Energetic, even. I usually wake up feeling good after feeding Nash. Don't know why."

She dusted away crumbs, and they packed their leftovers, then took turns using one of the large lidded buckets Noi had found and emptied during their hurried preparations. For all they'd thought they would have plenty of time between arriving and their deadline of an hour before the challenge, they'd barely been ready. With no password for the hotel's computers they'd been unable to code the card-keys to access the higher floors, and had been limited in their movements until the discovery of an unlocked security room on the Mezzanine level which, along with master keys, had provided camera views of much of the hotel.

Fisher's hunt for wheelie bins and caustic soda had taken even longer, and dumping entire containers of bathroom cleaner in after they'd been filled had produced an eye-stinging reek, which thankfully had lost its edge by the time they'd rearranged their hiding places enough to fit both the bins and mattresses hauled down from the hotel rooms, along with some wilting pot plants from the foyer. How much difference the bins would make to carbon dioxide levels was something Fisher hadn't been willing to guess, beyond insisting that in theory they should help.

She'd wanted to kiss him before they locked themselves away. She'd planned on it. And hadn't even managed an exchange of meaningful glances, though she'd known it could well be the last time she would see him. Too tired after the long night, and having Nash drain off much of her energy. Too new at all this to seize the right moment.

"Noi," she said, after they settled back down under their quilts, "did you see if any other Sydney Blues had been captured?"

"I figured looking at that can wait till we're out of here."

Madeleine sighed, and curled against Emily, working hard at not feeling guilty. Unless they'd gambled wrong about the length of the challenge, it looked as if she would have another chance to see Fisher.

How many chances had she stolen from other Sydney Blues?

Chapter Eighteen

The clunk-clack of the latch broke through the refrigerator's steady hum.

Emily, quickest to react, flung quilts back in time to throw a force punch at the door as it opened. There was a gasp, and Madeleine caught a glimpse of Fisher as he was knocked backward by the impact against his shield.

"Someone not a morning person?" Min said, poking his head cautiously around the side of the doorway.

"What are you–?" Noi began, then stopped. "It's over."

"The time limit seems to have been dawn," Fisher said, from his new horizontal position on the floor. "They were all gone by the time the sun touched the horizon, but I gave it another half hour."

"I'm sorry!" Emily struggled to her feet. "Did I hurt you?"

"My fault," Fisher said, sitting up. "It would have been sensible to knock first." He moved arms and legs gingerly, then smiled. "Not to mention polite."

"Let's see if polite works on Nash and Pan," Min said, and rapped on the freezer door. "We should have thought up some kind of secret knock."

"That'd only be useful if none of us were taken," Noi said, and crossed to pull the freezer door open. Worried, Madeleine realised, as they probably should all be.

Nash and Pan did not force punch at the door, or shift on their mattress pile, though they did stir in response to Noi's urgent shaking. Flushed and lethargic, they were slow to sit up, blinking with confusion.

"Let's get them to the foyer," Fisher said. "Without an oxygen mask, all we can do is give them space."

Out in the soaring, glass-and-excessive water features foyer, Madeleine found herself analysing the changes to Nash and Pan's skin tones, struggled with herself for a moment, then accepted. This was part of who she was, and she could only be relieved that the shift she was watching was a return to healthy shades of brown and pink.

"Were any Blues captured?" she asked Fisher, noting that he, too, was returning to a normal colour, though for different reasons. Would he have nightmares about Nash and Pan, a plan almost gone wrong?

"Yes." He met her eyes directly, not cushioning the statement. "From the leader board changes, just over thirty."

"Thirty!" Noi spilled some of the water she was offering Nash. "There were thirty Blues still free in Sydney?"

"In and around it. It was a good decision to let Madeleine warn her parents. At least five dragons were sighted in the Armidale area."

With a news channel unhelpfully broadcasting their location, speculating on whether she was hiding with them, Madeleine had insisted on emailing her Mum and Dad. Thankfully they must have taken her grandmother and gone in time. But thirty other people had paid the price for this hunt.

"So, what now?" Min asked.

"Errol Flynn marathon."

They all stared at Pan, propping himself against the legs of a low chair.

"One of the symptoms of CO2 poisoning is delusions, right?" Min picked up a brochure and used it to fan in Pan's direction. "More oxygen required."

"If you'd read that brochure you'd know there's suites with mini-theatres." Pan was working on a wall-to-wall grin. "Not to mention a gym, three swimming pools, spa baths in the suites, huge vats of ice cream, and a chocolatier. We just outsmarted our alien invaders, people! We've learned more about what they *can't* do, we've kept our hides our own, we've lived to fight another day. Time to celebrate with some quality swashbuckling and strangely sped-up repartee."

Min wrinkled his nose. "Couldn't we at least watch something released this century?"

"Without a password to the hotel computer system, chances are we won't be watching anything at all," Noi said, her eyes giving away the smile she was trying to suppress.

"Some drip always writes their passwords down." Pan waved a hand airily at the glassy grandeur of the foyer. "There's sure to be an administrative office with some actual paper files, or a post-it note stuck to the bottom of a drawer, or a computer left on when they all ran away in the dust."

"That would be on level two," Nash murmured. He was not recovering as quickly as Pan, but his finely-moulded features had lit with quiet amusement. "A two-day celebration, I think. Today for living, tomorrow a not-fully-surprising birthday, and then we will be serious again."

"Hey, you told them!" Pan only succeeded in looking gratified. "Do I get cake? Can we dress up?"

His enthusiasm bubbled over them, and though they decided partying would need to be postponed until they'd established escape routes, checked for ways to detect and avoid any alarms, and seen to preserving their food supply, it was hard not to enjoy the idea of a 6 star hotel as a hideout.

As they discussed what needed to be done, Madeleine spent her time watching Fisher, who was watching her in return. A silent shared awareness of a first step already taken, of something which had moved on to a question of when.

Later.

ooOoo

Two men fought, the music flaring into dramatic highlights as they danced across the deck of a ship under sail. Madeleine watched with vague interest, studying poses, but most of her attention captured by the warm fingers tangled with her own.

A strange dissonance cut through the music and Fisher's hand tightened, then let her go. "Spire song."

"Stupid Moths." Pan fumbled for the controls and paused his movie mid swordfight so they could better hear the eerie sound, distant yet penetrating. "What are they up to now?"

"Sending the Greens back to whatever they were doing before the Challenge, I guess." Noi stood and stretched. "Let's see if we can spot any movement, and finish the movie after dinner. Maybe it will have shut up by then."

After some debate about the wisdom of taking rooms close enough to the ground to be able to shield-jump out the windows, they'd given in to the view and settled into the most palatial suites, high on the Harbour side of the hotel. These not only offered tiny cinemas where a world of movies could be dialled on demand, they could be opened up into a single, enormous apartment by the unlocking of cleverly concealed sliding walls. One floor down from *Open Sky*, the top floor restaurant, they had plentiful food, carefully planned escape routes, and a number of rules about turning lights on and off at night. An added sense of security had been provided by the discovery of the keys to the fire escapes and elevators, giving them in effect a drawbridge to raise when they went to bed.

It was late afternoon, and sunset crept up while they pitched in to prepare their meal, so they chose a table to best take advantage of the spectacular vista. But despite a view which stretched from Darling Harbour across the sweep of the North Shore, and past the Bridge to glimpses of the Opera House, Madeleine found she didn't like eating in the restaurant, where the array of empty tables only served to remind her of a city quietly rotting.

"Crimson skies and thunderclouds on the horizon." Noi stared out to toward the headlands, but there was no sign of the navy ships. "I could wish it had rained on them yesterday, but even then I have to think of their hosts, and whether they feel everything the Moths do."

"Yeah." Pan's smile had faded. "It takes the fun out of planning to smash their faces in."

The pervasive song of the Spire filled every gap in the conversation, eerie and oppressive, but they pressed on, forcing bright chatter, watching the approaching storm as the colour faded from the sky.

As they were constructing elaborate ice cream sundaes, Fisher disappeared downstairs and returned holding the binoculars. "Come look at this."

"Movement?" Noi crossed quickly to stand with him at the windows.

"Not quite. Look at the hull of that overturned yacht just off Headland Park."

Frowning, Noi obeyed, seemed only puzzled as she peered into the growing twilight, then suddenly snorted. She waved the binoculars. "Millie, check this out."

The younger girl's reaction to this mystery view was to gasp and say: "Oh, it can't be! I don't believe it."

"Will you lot quit with the commentary and just tell us what you're looking at?" Min asked, exasperated.

"Glowing eyes," Noi said. "There's eyes painted on the hull. Must be some kind of phosphorescent paint."

"We ran away from a boat?" Pan grabbed the binoculars and, after a pause, burst out laughing. "Shit, I feel like such a dick."

This discovery provided a counterbalance to the song of the Spire, and they were able to revive the light good humour they'd been so deliberately maintaining, to talk party plans over their dessert, to clean up in good humour and take pleasure in their return to their enormous suite.

"Guess we can check the news while we wait for the Spire to shut up," Pan said, and they clustered toward one of the lounge areas. Madeleine, struggling with the weight of the continued song, excused herself and headed to her room on the far left of the interconnected set of suites to run a bath.

During their explorations they'd discovered storage rooms full of items intended for the suites, from robes and kettles to some very up-market varieties of miniature soap, bath salts, and hair product. Madeleine programmed the room's stereo system with a selection of her favourite jazz singers and Ella Fitzgerald began to croon, the music loud enough that the Spire song was drowned. Stars blurred by steaming, scented water, Madeleine could finally allow herself to think of thirty people who had paid the price of her freedom. Guilt over the actions of the Moths was stupid, but that wouldn't stop her.

The Spire song faded before her fingers had turned to prunes and, clean and warmly wrapped in one of the robes, she drifted out to the lamp-lit lounge room and stood finger-combing her damp hair, listening to the stereo and watching rain beat against the windows.

"Feeling better?"

"Now that it's stopped." She turned as Fisher rose from one of the chairs and crossed to her. He'd obviously bathed as well, and his dark mop was damp and almost tamed, while his expression was the closest to anxious she'd ever seen from him. "My cousin – the last time I spoke to him, just before we went to Bondi – was talking about wordplay, bad puns on song titles. I was just thinking that I'm feeling Blue right now. Not sad, just...particularly when I've had a bath or shower I end up extremely aware of the velvety sensation. It makes me feel like I don't belong in my own skin."

"If it's any help, I think the velvet is a kind of field." His gaze dropped to the point where the robe crossed beneath the start of the stain on her chest and the tips of his ears gave away the line of his thoughts, but he forged on in his most neutral tone. "Your skin isn't velvet at all. But it's storing or generating power. Imagine touching a million microscopic lightning bolts. Or how it feels holding the like polarities of two magnets together. It's a sensation not inherent in the object, but produced by what is generated from it."

Giving up on talking, he lifted a hand, fingers hovering just before the patch around her eye, then brushed his thumb delicately over the unstained skin below. When was becoming now, and Madeleine caught at his hand as he lowered it, clasped it firmly, then moved toward her room

Eyes wide but sure, Fisher followed, then hesitated at the door. "Protection," he murmured, looking in the direction of his own room.

"Bedside drawer." Later she would have to thank Noi for insisting on practicality.

He pushed the door closed behind them, the room lit only by the light spilling from the bathroom, and there was an awkward moment, so she filled it by reaching up to kiss him. Tentative at first, with soft touches of hands to his back. He was wearing loose sports pants and a T-shirt and as their kisses deepened she found herself bold with impatience and drew back to lift the shirt over his head.

Coat-hanger shoulders, and a chest still filling out, striped like a barber's pole with bright diagonal streaks of stars.

"You've got comets."

He made a face, said: "Please, I'm feeling awkward enough," and self-consciously shucked his pants and underwear, becoming a naked boy gleaming with light, lifting his eyes to meet hers.

He was already partially erect, and later perhaps she would be amused that his penis was striped as well, and that he visibly swelled as she pulled loose the cord of her robe, letting it gape open. Stepping forward, he raised hands to her shoulders and smoothed them back so the robe fell around her feet, and then, breathing deeply, he took his time looking at her, bringing back to her years of feeling inadequate, of needing a bra to give herself breasts rather than hold them up, and never would she have thought someone would gaze down at her barely A-cups so reverently, or shake as he slid his hands forward and down to cover them.

Madeleine inhaled sharply, the sensation surpassing anything she'd anticipated, and she found she was standing up straighter, pushing into his touch. She had no idea how much the velvet of the stain was contributing to what she felt, though there was definitely an added tingle created by the shift between the stained and unstained skin of his palms as he slid his hands down further, exploring with his fingers.

The kiss which followed was clumsy, Fisher losing a great deal of his poise to eagerness, and they pressed together, exploring with hands and mouths, hard erection prodding her. He became urgent, steering her to the bed, fumbling for the box of condoms and tearing it open only to sprinkle packets in every direction. Madeleine opened one and, remembering the thoughtful instruction of many a glossy magazine, tentatively moved to try and put it on him.

He took it off her with a gusty cough of laughter. "You're seriously overestimating my self-control."

"Sorry."

He smiled, and kissed her, but she had lost some of her certainty, felt tense and nervous as he moved over her. She tried to relax by touching his face and hair, and took small, uncertain breaths as they fumbled themselves into alignment. Fisher was shaking with effort, trying to hold himself to the slowest of paces, checking her reaction as he moved forward. The motion brought a little stinging at the very start, but a surprising lack of pain.

"Velvet," Fisher gasped, and lost his careful restraint entirely, plunging against her, a rushed, spasmodic motion which bounced them on the well-sprung mattress. Overwhelmed, Madeleine clutched at his shoulders, but already he was collapsing, his weight heavy on her, breath hot against her throat.

"Hell." He moved, shifted to lay beside her. "I didn't – sorry, I didn't think I'd be quite that pathetic." He propped himself up and looked at her worriedly, his hair ruffled, face flushed. "Did I hurt you?"

"No." Feeling less overcome, Madeleine touched his shoulder. "It's okay. Though I'd like it if you spent some more time doing things to my breasts. They've never felt quite so real before."

He spluttered into laughter, and they held each other and shook, helpless hilarity. That turned to enthusiastic kissing, pressed together, legs tangling, then relaxing back to take a breath.

"I had pictured this very romantic," Fisher said. "Slow, and measured and...well, lasting longer. Magical, not farcical." Chagrin competed with amusement. "I would be very glad to continue to prove the existence of your breasts. And I am, if nothing else, an extremely good study."

ooOoo

Madeleine slid out of the bed and paused to move a couple of condom wrappers from the floor to the bin, adding to the detritus of a night's diligent practice. Glancing out floor-to-ceiling windows at early morning sun and the grand curve of the Bridge, she picked Tyler's koi robe off the back of a chair and slipped it on. Her Blue metabolism worked against long, lazy sleep-ins, and she followed the call of her stomach to the plentiful supply of snacks she'd stocked yesterday morning. Once the edge of her hunger had been dulled, and she'd cleaned herself up and managed to unknot her hair a little, she returned to look at the boy sleeping in her bed.

Comets. Stars which streaked across ribs, a bellybutton which glimmered above a trail of dark hair leading down to a thicker swatch. Long arms and legs, their impression of length increased by his overall skinniness. Head resting at an angle, tangled half-curls swept back from the brow, wide mouth relaxed. The position of his hands was somehow graceful, one bony wrist exposed, and she entirely forgot her intention to fetch them a hot breakfast and instead positioned a chair to take advantage of the light, fetched her biggest sketchpad and backing board, and lost herself in capturing him.

She'd moved on from the main figure to work on the fall of the sheeting to the floor when a peaceful voice said: "Is it okay for me to get up?"

"Mm. Try not to mess the line of the sheets."

After he'd carefully rolled off the bed and crossed to look at the sketch, it filtered through to her that this was probably not the most lover-like way to act on their first morning together. Blushing, she looked up, but he kissed her on the forehead and said, "I love the way you are when you draw. And you really should sketch how you look right now because it's definitely something worth waking up to."

"A little impracticable," she said, but Fisher simply smiled and moved a standing mirror from the far side of the bed, then headed into the bathroom while she studied her reflection.

He was right. Sitting with one foot tucked up, sketchbook balanced on her lap, the gold and black of the koi robe spilling around blue and stars, the slight curve of one breast, a length of glimmering thigh, crinkling brown hair waving loose. She turned to a new page and began outlining, and when Fisher emerged, damp and wrapped in a towel, said: "Can you get the case of coloured pencils from that table?"

He did more, moving the café-style table within her reach, and lifting out the trays of pencils before rescuing his clothes from the pile by the door, hanging up her bathrobe, and heading out to the main room of the suite. She had made a great deal of progress before his return, enough that when a sweet, spicy scent forced itself on her notice she was willing to look at the bowls and cups he was fitting into the gaps of the table. Steaming porridge sprinkled with nuts, dried fruit and brown sugar.

"Did you make this?" Hunger abruptly triumphed over art, and she reached for a bowl.

"With considerable guidance from Noi. I've never really had much occasion to cook."

"Was she very entertained?"

"If today wasn't Pan's birthday, it probably wouldn't be safe for us to venture out." He slipped her sketchbook from her lap and studied the picture while she began to eat. "What do you do with your sketches? And the paintings."

"Keep them in my room. I used to scan them and post them on an art site, but I took them all down last year. Being hypercritical. Not wanting to be known for work I no longer considered my best." She sighed, then glanced at his face, absorbed as he continued to study the picture. "You can have that one," she added softly. "When I've finished it."

His open pleasure made her feel light-headed, and as soon as she'd finished her meal she took him back to bed. Still plenty to learn. But curled with him afterwards, thirty people crept into her thoughts. This was an interlude which could not last.

"Do you think we should try to get out of the city like Noi wants?"

"Getting out of the city is likely to be considerably harder than Noi wants to believe. More to the point, that dragon's range and speed means out of the city isn't any guarantee of safety. But I don't think we'll last two years here, either." He hesitated. "I know it seems like we've made no progress, but it's only when we have a full understanding of what we can do that we can hope to mount any kind of attack. I do think I've found a third ability, though a practical use for it isn't immediately obvious."

"A third ability? What?"

He didn't reply immediately, shifting to lie staring at the ceiling. "Think over what it feels like to feed Nash," he said at last, almost too low for her to hear.

Everyone tended to shy away from discussing the heady warmth Nash could conjure. It wasn't quite a sexual thing, but it was very pleasurable, like an intangible massage. It usually left Madeleine a little tired, yet feeling good.

"Now think about what it feels like to punch, and to shield. The sensation is not the same. Although Nash is clearly drawing on that punch power reservoir, it is—"

"There's something else involved." The more she thought about it, the more convinced she was Fisher had a point. "When I feed Nash, I really feel like I'm, well...almost like I'm sitting next to myself. I don't get that sensation at all when I shield or punch."

"I've been focusing on that," Fisher said, still speaking very low. "Isolating the sensation, trying to work with it. This is..." He stopped, frowning fiercely at the ceiling. "Close your eyes."

She studied his profile, then settled herself more comfortably and obeyed.

"I'm going to reach for you," he continued. "I'm not certain how..." He paused again. "Tell me to stop right away if I hurt you, and try not to shield-stun me."

Madeleine realised that part of the reason for the hint of reserve in his voice was an unspoken: "Or mash me into paste".

"Okay," she said, deciding to postpone some serious thought on a life of being uncomfortably dangerous.

Warmth. A delicate thread which was somehow a thing to capture all her attention and make her want to shy away, to push back, but also light her up, a spark to a bonfire. It wasn't simple heat, was a presence, a piercing tenderness, underlaid by anger and fear.

"It's like I'm *breathing* you."

The warmth faded, and Fisher moved so he could tangle fingers with hers. "Did it hurt?"

"N-no." Pain was the wrong word, but she didn't have any proper equivalent. "Like drowning, but not," she tried. The sense of his presence as a thing additional to the physical was fading, leaving her as alertly roused as a jolt of caffeine.

"Try it on me. As lightly as you can."

This was far from simple. The power she used to shield and punch was something tangible to her, and her awareness of containing it was strong. Trying to locate and manipulate something presumably intrinsic to herself – perhaps literally her own self – was a bit like attempting to look at the colour of her own eyes. But in a way Fisher had held up a mirror.

He drew in his breath, hand tightening on hers, and she faltered, then reigned back the outpouring of self to a thread as delicate as gossamer, a thistledown spiritual embrace. Fisher reached back with a thread of his own, and that was something new again, fragile and overwhelming.

They couldn't sustain it, and drew back, panting like runners. Not tired, like feeding Nash would leave them, but instead feeling powerfully alive.

"There's no way I'm practicing that with a group," she said when she could speak, and he laughed, but the sound had a bereft note to it, so she kissed him and that was an easier, more familiar path to follow, but made different again by their intense, lingering awareness of each other.

Madeleine wondered if this was something non-Blues would be able to do, something related to the spirit or the soul, or if it was merely another newly discovered difference to make her less human. And whether she could possibly cope with the way she was feeling about this boy she'd known a bare few weeks.

"What are you thinking?"

She didn't answer, shifting against him.

"Tell me. You're bothered by something."

"I was wondering," she said, very slowly, "if we would have gotten together if all this hadn't happened."

"No."

The answer was immediate, unhesitating, and she shrank a little. His arms tightened around her.

"We would never have met," he explained, voice dropping to a husky note. "I would have gone about my life and not thought I was missing anything. You would have – you would have painted obsessively, all those transformative images, and I would be someone unimagined and unknown, and I cannot decide whether it would be trite to call that a tragedy or if I should resent you for making this – all this *death* – somehow bearable, tolerable for the tenuous joy I have gained. You steal my anger and leave me dazed."

He stopped, took a shaking breath, then laughed.

"I sound like Pan's understudy, failing to channel Shakespeare. There's no way to do more than guess what would have happened if Fisher Charteris and Madeleine Cost met one day in a world which had never feared dust, any more than we can be certain of surviving two years, or two days. I can't speak to what-ifs, but I know I will always be glad to have been here in this moment with you."

Chapter Nineteen

"When I'm having an apocalypse, I always insist on six star accommodation." Noi waved a gloved hand languidly, and turned so the skirt of her dress coiled and swirled. She considered herself in the mirrored wall dominating one side of the store. "Maybe a little too Grande Dame?"

"Try the yellow one," Madeleine suggested.

"All I can think when I see that is Fire Hazard."

"Which makes it a good thing the cooking's all but done. And, plus, aprons."

"There's not going to be any winning of arguments with you today, is there?" Noi's smile was indulgent, and she disappeared into the dressing room with the fringe-covered yellow dress just as Emily emerged in a ruffled satin gown. "No, Millie, absolutely not," she said, before tugging the curtain across.

Emily eyed herself in the mirror and evidently agreed, selecting a white dress from the store's limited range of evening wear and retreating once again.

The day had already been full. Madeleine and Fisher had emerged in time to help decorate the small function room chosen for the night's festivities, and only smiled at teasing looks and comments. After lunch there had been swimming, and then a group effort at preparing an evening feast, Pan insisting on joining in because: "What fun is there in sitting by myself while you're all off together?"

With only a few things needing last-minute heating, they'd separated to clean up and take advantage of finally locating the security codes to the foyer's selection of expensive stores. Party clothes.

"Pity there isn't a shoe place," Noi said, emerging to eye herself doubtfully. The yellow dress, a tight-fitting sheath covered in tiers of gold-shot fringes, shimmered with every tiny movement, emphasising her curves. "But I can live with barefoot in sheer silk stockings."

Madeleine looked down at her legs, glimmering blue through the semi-transparent skirt of the icy flapper-style dress she'd fallen for on sight. "I'm not sure stockings work for me any more."

"Mm. You've got a point. Shall I take the time to point out that you're suddenly no longer trying to hide every inch of your starry starry skin?"

"Would there be any way to stop you?" Madeleine asked, and wondered how Noi would react if Madeleine shared her discovery that breasts were like tickling: a concept not fully appreciated until someone else was involved.

Noi took a few dancing steps, watching the fringes at her hips shimmer, then plumped down beside Madeleine.

"Okay, less teasing, more congratulations. You think you'll work out? Long term?"

"Maybe." Madeleine had to admit to wanting there to be a long term. "If the Moths give us the chance. I...I think I fell in love with him this morning."

"What, not till then? Not that I'm arguing against try before you buy, mind you, but it took him all the way till morning to impress you?"

"Before, I knew I really liked him. A lot. But this morning when he woke up I was drawing him, and he asked if it was okay to move. And then fetched me stuff, instead of expecting me to stop. Most people, when they meet me, it's completely obvious to them that drawing is important to me. But Fisher, he treats my drawing as important. The way that makes me feel..."

"Are you looking for a boyfriend or a groupie?"

"I'm not sure I could really...belong with someone who treated my drawing the way my mother does – a nice little hobby, admirable enough, but always to be put aside in favour of everything someone else thinks is important." Madeleine sighed, then gave Noi a steady look. "And are you ever going to give Pan a chance?"

Noi lifted brows in exaggerated surprise. "What, you think I'm falling over for want of someone warm to hold? You don't get trapped with a small group of people and have one of them just happen to be your one true love. Or–" She broke off, and gave Madeleine an apologetic grin. "Well, the odds are against it, and I think you've used all the good luck up. Pan's just a nice kid."

"Noi."

A single word to add cherry tones to Noi's warm brown skin. The shorter girl looked away.

"The way I am about him, it's not me," she went on, the words low and rushed. "I'm usually the together, lightly-invested one. But, hell, all I want to do is throw myself at his feet and beg to be the Tink to his Peter. I want to do flighty, charming things which make him break out into speeches, and then I want to do...everything. He treats me like his *Mum*."

"No, like Wonder Woman, remember? He thinks you're awesome."

Shoulders hunched, studying her toes, Noi shook her head. "It's all because of the Spires, the disaster. I can't trust the way I feel right now. I wouldn't have looked at him twice, in the real world. Well, I'd have looked, but I sure as hell would never have wanted to find myself a green mini-dress and a pair of wings."

"Tinker Bell's an inch tall. I don't think she'd be much use for...everything. Wouldn't you be better off being the Noi to his Lee? Pan can hardly be the right role for him today, not on his birthday. And he really admires you."

"That's not helpful." Noi was recovering, and shook her head so her curls bounced. "Enough. The whole world doesn't have to fall in love just because you have. This is the day for fun, not serious talk."

She climbed to her feet in time to inspect Emily, shyly emerging in a delicate white shift. Approving this enthusiastically, Noi bustled them off to see to hair, and regret the lack of makeup. They decided not to risk the jewellery shop, the contents of which were locked away behind an extra level of security.

"But in a way I like the whole mix of formal and underdressed," Noi said as she led the way to the menswear store, patting the upswept Grecian style into which she'd wrestled her curls. "It's a bit like a beach wedding."

She took several dancing steps, fringes flaring as she spun: a lively girl of eighteen more than a little tired of running and hiding and being sensible. Nash, the only one of the four boys visible in the store, turned to look at her, smiled, and then bowed and held out a hand. Noi dipped in return, and they waltzed over marble: Nash tall and fine in a dark suit, black hair swept back, wearing black socks and no shoes; Noi vibrant and shimmering, barefoot.

"Man, Noi is totally in Goddess mode tonight." Pan had emerged, knotting a blue-black tie. "Told you Nash could dance."

Madeleine studied him carefully, but decided to shelve the question of what kind of admiration was bright in his eyes. "Enjoying your birthday?"

"Unbelievably. And I refuse to be guilty about it. Tonight we live!"

He grabbed her hands and, head tipped back in abandoned laughter, spun her into a child's whirl across the marble, then fumbled for more formal movements. Fisher, in crisp shirtsleeves, offered Emily his hand, and stepped her carefully through the basic movements of the waltz until Min, with a James Bond air in a suit a little too long for him, dryly recommended they fool around somewhere other than in full sight of the glass entry doors.

Furnished with coats to protect their finery, they made a quick detour to the kitchen, heating and bringing down the last of the dishes to where most of the feast was already laid out in a small room off the dance floor on the Mezzanine level. Nash opened and poured champagne, which was Fisher's suggestion to resolve Noi and Min's positions on cutting loose during alien invasions. They would start their meal with a glass of champagne, close the evening with a single cocktail, and otherwise stick strictly to juice and soft drink. Fisher had volunteered to be 'designated driver', steering them away from any sudden impulses to play chicken with Moths.

The meal was despatched with Blue gusto, Madeleine sampling parmesan-dusted gnocchi, handmade personal pizza, and sweet potato frittata before sitting back with a sigh and deciding she was glad they'd planned a gap before any desserts.

"Gift-giving time?" Nash suggested.

"Wait, you guys went shopping?" Pan pretended amazement. "Or have the Moths started a home delivery service?"

"If you'd shut up for more than five seconds at a time you might find out," Min said, swiping casually at Pan's head. Pan ducked, but they didn't launch into their usual mock-fight since Emily was stepping up with the first present.

"This is from me and Min," she said, presenting a stuffed pillow case serving as wrapping paper.

"Thank you, Tink," Pan said, twinkling at her. "I'd say you shouldn't have, but really, a daily shower of gifts would be most..." He paused as a mass of folded black cloth spilled out of the case. "Sheet set? Caftan?" His eyes widened as he held it up, then with a delighted grin he swept it around him, a black cloak with an ornate golden fastening, and leaped up to stand on his chair. He preened and posed until Nash threw a bread roll at him, then leaped down to hug Emily.

"Totally awesome, Tink. Where the hell did you find it?"

"It really is sheets. We made it. Min did most of the work."

"Really?" Pan held out a hand, and shook Min's firmly. "Thanks, man. Appreciated."

The departure from teasing imp obviously startled Min, but he recovered and shrugged. "Something to do while sitting up on watch."

Madeleine, after careful questioning of Nash, had drawn Pan in a fictional rehearsal scene of *Henry V*, and offered it up to earn herself an appreciative hug.

"Someone's been spilling all my ambitions," he said, with a muted grin in Nash's direction. "You guys are too much."

Nash simply produced another pillowcase and watched with characteristic quiet enjoyment as Pan drew a slim stack of paper out and frowned down at lines of type fresh from the hotel's office printer.

"This is...?" Pan flushed bright pink, turned pages and looked up at Nash in disbelief, his cocksure edge lost to wonder. "You wrote this?"

"With a great deal of input from Fisher. It's only the first act, but something to go on with."

"The Blue Musketeers: A Play by Avinash Sharma."

Pan's voice was reverent, and it was only with difficulty that he could be distracted from an immediate read-through. Nash had inserted a Moth invasion into the plot of Dumas' adventure, tailoring the role of D'Artagnan for Pan. He admitted that he couldn't face writing anything set in the modern day.

During the chatter Noi disappeared and returned wheeling a sweet-laden trolley topped by a two-tier candlelit cake.

"I haven't anything so impressive as a play," she said, "but it's as chocolate as you asked for."

Noi was underselling herself: she'd worked on the cake in the Mezzanine floor kitchen, and produced a glossy triumph of confectionary. Pan immediately put down the script and gave the cake its due, declaring his need for an urgent injection of chocolate, bowing and flourishing his cloak as they sung to him, and lustily bellowing '*Happy Birthday to ME*' before blowing out the candles.

"Thimbles all round!" he cried, and gave Noi theatrical air-kisses on each cheek, then worked his way through everyone else. He was as much Puck as Pan that evening, a breath short of wild, repaying their gift of a birthday with indefatigable high spirits, insisting on charades after cake and, when those had collapsed into helpless laughter, coaxing them all onto the dance floor to attempt the Charleston. They began to wind down after that, and moved to the restaurant so Min could create drinks with names like Tom Collins, Mint Julep and El Presidente. Emily was given a Fuzzy Navel, which Min promised had barely enough peach schnapps to taste. Madeleine sampled each, an experiment which left her pleasantly detached as they conscientiously returned to clear away the remains of their meal.

"I'll turn off the music," she said as the others pushed away laden serving trolleys, but a song she liked shuffled into play as she approached the control screen, so she turned it up instead, and revolved to slow, mournful words on the part-lit dance floor, watching for glimpses of her stars in mirrored sections of wall.

"Enjoying yourself?"

Holding out her hands to Fisher, she drew him close so they could turn together. "Yes. Though I think I'll stick to the mostly fruit juice drinks in future. I don't think I could shoot straight right now. Let alone avoid shield-paralysis."

Fisher smiled, though his eyes were grave and serious. "What about the third power? Do you think you could use that at the moment?"

A bubble of laughter escaped her. "Science Boy," she said, full of a boundless affection for him. Snuggled against his chest she made a valiant attempt, but it was like building a tower of mud. "Results of experiment: negative."

His arms tightened, then he tried himself, a fine thread of Fisher which made her gasp and stumble, so intense was the flood of warmth, desire, and tender concern. Underlying it were darker emotions: an ever-present note of anger and dread.

Letting the thread of connection die away, he kissed the side of her throat, voice a breathy sigh as he said: "I wish I could do more to protect you."

"I get to protect you, remember? Or try to. Super-strong."

When he didn't say anything she drew back and saw his mood wasn't one which was going to respond to spirit-fuelled quips.

"I know we're slow-dancing in the eye of the storm," she told him. "I'll remember my promise. But I'm...very happy right now Fisher."

His expression fractured, glad of her, yet somehow wounded. "I didn't want to waste a moment of this day on gloom," he said huskily.

"Then don't waste any more." She kissed him, and this time summoned fire, a response so strongly passionate she felt lucky he was holding her up.

"Maddie? Fish? You two still—? Ah." Pan stood in the doorway, trying not to look too highly entertained. "Sorry. Just came to say we're heading up, and the centre elevator's unlocked. Night."

"Lee."

Pan paused, offering Madeleine a look of polite enquiry which passed over the fact that Fisher had managed to unzip her dress and slide the straps over her shoulders to the point where it was necessary to use him as a screen.

"Noi likes you, you know."

A puzzled partial shrug in response.

"*Really* likes you."

His smile faded and he looked disbelieving. "You sure?"

"Very."

He blinked twice, then looked down and away, face completely blank. Lee Rickard, lost for words. Then the tiniest involuntary curling of the corners of his mouth, a smile trying to happen despite any attempt at control, twitching back whenever he tried to erase it. He looked up at them, eyes very wide, drew a deep breath, then let it out, and simply said: "Anyway, g'night," before leaving.

"Matchmaking?" Fisher asked.

"I wondered if perhaps it had simply never occurred to him that she would consider him."

"Because Lee Rickard is not, beneath it all, the eternally cocksure Pan?"

"Exactly. I hope it wasn't a mistake. I'd hate to make this harder for either of them."

Out on the Mezzanine balcony a stage-trained voice lifted, strong enough to be clearly heard over the music. "Cock-a-DOOdle-doo!"

Fisher laughed. "Don't worry too hard."

She smiled, and tightened her arms around him. "I've never really been part of a group. Not even before I had trouble at school. The teachers were always telling my parents I need to be taken out of myself. They thought I was hiding in my drawing."

"Too busy doing important things, no time for people. All very familiar." He stroked a loose curl away from her eyes. "I think I'm a good deal more like you than like Noi. And I'm enjoying all the complications of people far more than I could ever have expected. Tonight – tonight makes it easier to face tomorrow."

Madeleine couldn't help but agree. Birthday parties, charades, and slow-dancing with someone whose eyes turned bright when he looked at her. Things which, like her painting, could give her the strength to run or to fight or to just keep going.

ooOoo

A climb to any height almost seems to invite calamity, and it was with a sense of the inevitable that Madeleine woke to oscillating song.

So close! She heaved out of the bed, an immediate, instinctive reaction, then stumbled in scant dawn light at the absence of Fisher. There was no time for guessing. Madeleine snatched at clothes, shoved feet into shoes. A glance showed the en suite was empty. Grabbing her bag, with only a fraction of thought spare to regret how little she'd kept packed, she bolted from the room.

"Maddie! Thank God."

Noi snatched Madeleine's hand and reversed direction, pulling her into the next suite.

"I can't find Fisher," Madeleine said, struggling to keep the words low, searching the thin shadows.

"He knows the plan."

Moth song again, sounding like it was right outside the door of the room, and Madeleine gulped and hoped a plan would be enough, racing with Noi through the series of interconnected suites. The others had already collected in the furthest, poised by the entry door.

"Did you and Fish leave the elevator unlocked?" Pan asked.

"No!" Madeleine was absolutely certain of that.

"Questions later." Noi pushed them toward the door. "Go."

The floors of the hotel tower were shaped like a segment of rainbow, with the suites all along the outside, accessed via a single corridor which bracketed the smaller inner curve containing the lifts and service areas. Fire escapes were located at either end, and the plan for escape was to run to the fire escape furthest from any intruding Moths and go down two levels to one of the lifts which had deliberately been parked away from their sleeping floor. Of course, it was a plan based on the assumption that the Moths would have to approach their floor by climbing and punching their way out of one of the fire escapes, that they would be guessing as to which floor the Musketeers were on, and would have tripped one of the alarms getting into the building in the first place. Instead of five steps ahead, the Musketeers were four behind, and all they could do was scramble.

They barrelled through the door into unfurling wings.

Momentum carrying her forward, crowded on all sides, Madeleine didn't dare shield-punch, and dived left, trying to avoid the Moth while still heading in the direction of the fire escape. She lost her footing, found Emily on her knees beside her and grabbed her hand.

"Go! Don't wait!" Noi urged, catching up Emily's other hand as the boys hesitated a step down the corridor.

Madeleine staggered to her feet. Emily's hand tightened in hers, and the girl let out a startled little sound. And stopped still. Nearly falling again, Madeleine stared back at Emily's calm face, and tried to let go of a hand which suddenly held firm to hers.

"*No.*" Noi, caught on Emily's other side, pulled her hand free, but did not run. "Millie..."

"Noi." A mocking tone, accompanied by a thin smile which did not fit Emily's young face. "Just wait there."

"For pity's sake, look up!" Min grabbed Noi's arm and swung her aside, then ducked himself, but not quick enough. A second Moth settled around his shoulders, and sank beneath his skin.

With a wordless, sobbing cry Noi snatched at Madeleine's hand and pulled her free, and they ran with Nash and Pan as another ball of light drifted into view, and behind them two boys, one strawberry blond and the other sandy-haired.

"Fish!"

At Pan's exclamation Madeleine looked ahead. They'd rounded enough of the corridor's curve to see the fire exit door, and Fisher waiting beside it, and the relief was so strong she stumbled, but then found the strength for a burst of speed, catching up with Nash as Fisher took a step or two in their direction.

Their speed undid them. The quiet determination of Fisher's expression, the way he moved away from the fire exit instead of opening the door, stopping to rest a hand against the wall and lift the other, it was all clearly wrong, but they processed this too late to not run straight into the shield he raised.

Madeleine's own shield reacted automatically, saving her from paralysis while bouncing her violently backward. She had barely wit enough to create a shield to protect her head from smashing into the ceiling, but this had the effect of slam-dunking her to the carpeted corridor floor.

Wind knocked out of her, sight hazed with wriggling grey, she lay stunned for vital seconds, struggling to breathe. Time enough for the strawberry blond boy who had once been Gavin to take hold of her arm and pull back the sleeve, for the prick of a needle to add to her confusion. She tried to pull away, managing to catch a glimpse of Pan floundering to his feet above a paralysed Nash, trying to shield against the Moth which danced around him.

Noi, least-impaired, punched at Gavin, but the sandy-haired boy was between them, planting his feet, shield shimmering to visibility as it absorbed the energy.

"Not bad," he said, and then collapsed.

The sandy-haired boy's body landed beside Madeleine, as a deeply blue-veined Moth lifted out of him. She gasped and tried to make heavy limbs move, staring into the boy's green eyes, glazed and empty. It was so hard to lift her head. She heard Noi cry out, a shout of rage and despair, and then, nothing.

Chapter Twenty

Cotton-headed, mouth dry, driven to consciousness by a Blue's hunger, Madeleine cracked eyelids and winced at the assault of unrelenting sunlight. Then the full unpleasantness of memory intruded, and she bolted upright.

There was no-one near her. Not a sound, or any hint of movement. The strangeness of her location took her attention. She was on a single bed in an enormous curving room, bare except for carpet. Floor to ceiling curtains formed distant makeshift walls in both directions. The narrower curve of inner wall displayed signs for toilets. Behind her, nothing but windows.

Staring out – and down – over Sydney, Madeleine realised where she had to be. Sydney Tower, the tallest building in the city. Four doughnut-shaped floors which from the outside looked like a gold ice bucket balanced on a pole, crowned by a thick cylinder and antenna. The bed was out of place: this wasn't somewhere people slept, it was a tourist site with restaurants and observation decks.

Her backpack and a spare bag of clothing were sitting a short distance away. She was still wearing the clothes she'd snatched on at dawn: sneakers, track suit pants and a white dress shirt held together by two misplaced buttons. Looking down at the shirt, Madeleine began to shiver in the warm sunlight, rubbing her arm as she realised the significance of the needle. She was too strong for the leader of clan Ul-naa to possess. The Moths had taken the others, and drugged the prize they could not use, yet would not give up.

A black balloon swelled in her chest. Fisher...Fisher must have gone downstairs and met a roaming Moth, then simply led others to where a clutch of free Blues slept. To the people who had become her comrades in arms, her friends. They were all gone. Arms wrapped across her face, curled protectively over her head, Madeleine wept in suffocated abandon. She had failed every one of them. All for one had become the only one.

Fight. Always fight. No matter how impossible the odds, no matter who you've lost, how you've been hurt. If there doesn't seem to be a way out, look for one. If you seem to have come to an end, start afresh. Never, ever give up.

Fisher had been so insistent that Madeleine particularly had to go on, had foreseen with his usual clarity that her strength would set her apart. But being difficult to possess didn't give her a path forward. These bare two weeks as part of a team had left her all too aware of her deficiencies. She needed Fisher to gather information, Noi to come up with a plan and three backups. Emily's determination to fight, Pan's madly inspired suggestions, and Min to poke holes in them until Nash mediated a resolution. They were supposed to have stood together, and found a way to win.

If she fought, these would be the people she killed.

No-one, human or alien, interrupted her tears. When she had sobbed her way to numb exhaustion the curving room was as still as when she'd woken, nothing but drowsy sunlight and dust motes, offering no guide to how to face what next. Madeleine could pretend that she found renewed determination, that her promise to Fisher spurred her to seek information, some plan or solution. But it was the Blue's imperative appetite which got her off the bed.

It must be the same day, perhaps very early afternoon. A full day without eating would have left her single-mindedly focused on filling her stomach, a hair's breadth from licking the floor. What she'd be like going without food for more than a day was something she'd never care to find out.

The presence of her backpack made the food hunt simple. Emergency cinnamon fudge, safely tucked in the front pocket beneath her clean underwear stash. She munched steadily through it, staring out the window at Hyde Park and the black rise of Spire, no less featureless despite her elevated view. No sign of movement. Pressing against the glass she tried to see the top of it, this thing which had brought so much death.

It was not true to say she felt numb. She felt hate. But it was formless, a resentment which had no sharp edges, stymied against acting by the consequences. If she stopped caring about the people they were wearing, Madeleine suspected that she would be able to kill at least a few Moths by swinging full-strength punches. She wanted something far more difficult: her friends, free, together, undamaged. Something she had no idea how to achieve.

If you want B, first do A. Which was great advice, but what she wanted was more like M – or X – when she didn't know what the letters of the alphabet were, let alone in what order they lined up. But the thought helped. Instead of stumbling over how to do everything, all at once, she would step back from the big picture. Neither X nor Z – the destruction of the Spire – seemed at all possible for her to achieve alone, but if she first did A, perhaps she could find a way to B and to C.

A was simple. A was looking around.

She began to explore, heading for one set of the curtains which shut away the rest of the doughnut-shaped room. Pulling them back she found herself standing beside a flight of stairs leading back and up. Beyond them, the inner wall was filled by a bar, all shining glassware, with a row of tall round tables and barstools set against the windows opposite. The shelves meant to hold bottles were empty, but there was a tray set out and waiting with a handful of muesli bars and a rectangular carton of long life milk.

The milk was open, the carton cool. Madeleine sniffed it suspiciously, then took a wineglass, poured out a sample and tasted it. Honey. She drank, and ate a muesli bar, and was glad of the emergency fudge, which allowed her to put two of the bars away for later. A carton of sweetened milk and a few muesli bars was not a generous serving for a high-stain Blue, and she thought through the implications of that as she moved on toward a line of elevator doors, and a spiral staircase descending.

None of the elevators worked. Unsurprised, Madeleine completed her circuit of the mostly bare floor, then worked her way through the other three before returning to her bed to make an inventory of the contents of her bags. Clothes, her sketchpads and various pencil collections. The two mobiles – her own and one looted from the North Building – were missing.

The tower was bare of both people and food. She found the entrance to a rooftop skywalk, and some small machinery rooms in the squat cylinder set on top of the 'ice bucket' of the larger floors. A gift shop on the top main floor offered an array of key rings and magnets. The restaurants filling the lower two floors held endless potential kitchen utensil weapons, and water. No telephones. There were touch screen computers for tourists which would only tell her about Sydney landmarks, and drink machines which had been broken open and emptied. The Moths had gone to the effort of removing everything edible or useful for communication, turned all the lifts off, and left her to sit.

If they wanted her alive, they'd have to come up to feed her. That would be an opportunity. First, however, there were fire escapes.

Simply walking out of the tower seemed unlikely. Perhaps the Moths had left a guard down the bottom, and rigged an alarm to let them know she was on her way. That would mean a fight, but during her explorations the main thing she'd discovered was a quiet determination to find step B, and then step C. Pulling on a reorganised backpack, she found the nearest fire exit and pushed it open.

Stairs. Well lit, no movement or suspicious noises. She slipped through to the landing and eased the door shut on a gift shop toy placed as a block, then stood listening, looking. If there were traps or cameras she could not detect them. The plentiful supply of tourist information had let her know there were 1500 stairs and it would be a struggle to stay strictly alert all that way. Which was no reason not to try.

Five flights down, Madeleine stopped to gauge a change to the quality of light. The flat white had taken on a tinge of blue. A Moth? A Rover? She doubted one of the dandelion dragons would fit in a stairwell, but nor was it likely she'd seen all of the Moths' bestiary. The question was whether the best move was to fight, here in the narrow support shaft of a building unlikely to cope with holes being punched in walls.

She eased forward, pausing at every turn to steal glances around corners, the blue tinge growing stronger, dominant, until the stairwell took on an underwater air. And then it was ahead of her, no dragon or mermaid-dog, but...goo.

Wall to wall electric blue jelly. It completely blocked the flight of stairs below her, every gap sealed with luminous glop. There was no visible reaction to her approach, no tentacles lifting from the surface or sudden pulsing, just a steadily glowing barrier.

The fight with the Rover had taught Madeleine enough to not simply try to power her way through it. A very cautious finger punch suggested that it would absorb energy in much the same way the Rover had. A light tap with her shield nearly bounced her into the wall. The goo had defences.

Gritting her teeth, Madeleine considered the problem, then climbed back up to the nearest kitchen and returned with a jug of hot water and a knife. The hot water produced no response, while the knife...

The goo's shield punch threw her up the stairwell. Rapid shielding bounced her straight back down to ricochet again off the glowing barrier, and only frantic easing of her shield prevented madcap ping-ponging. She collapsed on the landing above the goo and lay shaking, trying not to let her head fill with imagined injuries, only to have them replaced by guesses as to what was happening to Noi, to Emily, while she failed to get down a flight of stairs. What were the Moths doing with their stolen Musketeers?

Taking deep breaths to calm herself, Madeleine began to reassemble her fragmented determination, to force herself look at the moment as an achievement. Easing shields to control ricochet had been something they'd only begun to explore during their combat practice sessions. Watching the possessed Blues fight had made clear the Moths' ability to control much of the shield bouncing, and the Musketeers had been attempting to modulate the intensity of the shielding to cushion an impact rather than rebound. Madeleine had struggled to make any progress. She could manifest the shielding on just one side rather than all around her, which meant she no longer paralysed herself when swiping to shield-punch, but her skill level was a rough equivalent of doing embroidery while wearing gauntlets.

Step B was obviously shield practice.

ooOoo

Twenty-four hours later, Madeleine's plans and ambitions had contracted to a singular focus: food.

The Moths had not come to feed her. It didn't make a great deal of sense, since if they'd wanted to kill her there would be no need to go to the time and effort to clear out two entire restaurants, including cleaning away any plates and glasses in use on the day of the Spire's arrival. It would have taken a team of people – Greens most likely – to have so thoroughly removed everything edible.

Madeleine's hunt had so far won her a tomato sauce squeeze packet. She scanned the compact, curving kitchen, searching for missed possibilities, her gaze settling on an industrial-sized toaster. A quick examination located a sliding crumb tray, specked and dotted with charred bounty. Madeleine shook everything loose into the palm of her hand, licked that clean, then began dotting crumbs with a finger which trembled.

All but black scrapings remained when, disgusted, she threw down the tray and dashed out of the kitchen. She did not want to be this. What would come next? Rats? But, no, all the warm-blooded animals in the region had been finished off by the dust. It would be cockroaches.

Pounding up the stairs to the third level, she ran along the curve of windows, intent on the grandly mature gesture of throwing herself onto her bed. And stopped so quickly she fell to her hands and knees. On the bar counter a new tray, another carton of milk, three muesli bars.

One part of Madeleine was incandescently furious. It was a pitiful serving for a Blue. Even before the stain it would have been an inadequate day's meal, and the idea that this was all she would have to combat stain-fuelled hunger made her want to yell and throw things, left her frightened for what state she'd be in after another day. The rest of her wasted no time on anything but gulping down milk.

Honey-sweetened again, this time with a trace of butterscotch which, even when that sounded a note of caution, was not enough to stop her draining most of the carton before coming up for air. As she gauged the dregs, a sledgehammer of heat hit her squarely, providing a full and unavoidable explanation for the additional flavour. Spiked.

For long moments Madeleine simply stood, breathing deeply as the alcohol surged through her, but then she snatched up the muesli bars and headed around the curve of the floor toward her vastly empty bedroom. An awareness that there had to be a reason to spike the milk filled her with panic. At minimum, when drunk her ability to control her punches and shield would be near non-existent. Already the world had tilted.

Stumbling past her bed, she headed to one of the curtains which divided the circular level into segments, and pulled it all the way to the inner wall. Then she slid to the floor behind it, a makeshift hiding place. Tucking herself in, fumbling with the cloth in hopes of making it appear its fall was uninterrupted, she tried to still her shaking.

It occurred to her that she could have tried to make herself vomit. The alcohol had hit her almost immediately, but expelling most of it would surely lead to a quicker recovery. But then she would be back to licking toasters.

Determinedly she ate one of the muesli bars and drank the rest of the milk, placing her energy needs above the problem of even more alcohol. Should she fight, when the Moths came? Shields would be too risky, punches more a question of how much she was willing to damage her eyrie prison. She might get lucky and hurt them, but lashing out wildly would not get her friends back. Unless she was on the verge of being completely lost, she would have to restrain herself, try to learn more.

The tower felt like it was swaying.

Fingers tangled in her hair, hauling her from behind the curtain. Jolted from a doze, Madeleine cried out in pain, twisting to see her attacker. Gavin. Or, rather, the Core of the Five of the Ul-naa.

She tried pulling away, but her hair provided far too good a handhold, and he wrenched it agonisingly, slinging her forward so that she tumbled to the blank expanse of floor by the windows. Head spinning, she found herself face-to-face with an enormous, streamlined muzzle. A dandelion dragon, multi-layered wings fanning slowly, the bulk of it apparently draped over the roof of the main tower turret as it dangled over the side peering in at them.

"In future, you will not hide," said the Moth, and she shifted to face him. "You will drink and you will wait here."

His tone was curtly assured, allowing for no possibility of anything but obedience. He clearly believed he could dictate her behaviour. The words 'in future' lit her attention.

Dizzy, and on the verge of being sick, she refused to cower, attempting a little of Noi's blunt defiance: "Go to hell."

The Core slapped her. A light, casual backhand as if he were cuffing a misbehaving dog. "There are no choices here."

Face stinging, increasingly angry that this alien so clearly did not consider her a person, Madeleine worked to speak without slurring: "I'm not killing you right now because I liked the boy you're wearing. But you're making it very difficult."

It got under his skin, just a little: she could see the suppressed annoyance. Then he straightened, and she gasped as that annoyance hammered down on her: a cascade, a torrent. It hurt, was suffocation with needles, and she collapsed down, a small part of her recognising the sensation, though her brief experiments with Fisher had as much resemblance to this as a brush stroke had to nail gun fire. The third power, turned to an onslaught of prickling anger. She could feel his vicious enjoyment of her reaction, and his triumph, a barrage of gloating elation, increasing as Madeleine tried to make herself as small as possible, to curl into a ball, to find some way to keep him out.

Unable to summon any defence, she retreated into darkness.

ooOoo

Madeleine woke, warm beneath the bed's quilt, still herself.

It was not quite a surprise. There would have been no reason to speak of where she should wait in future if the Core had been on the verge of taking complete control, though she was full of a certainty that that...bombardment of identity was the beginning of a process which would leave her a shell, a vehicle driven by alien will. Instead of all at once, he – it – would possess her by degrees.

Almost, she could still feel him. As if the air itself could taste of triumph gone stale, of emotion, soul, self, spirit, turned to some tangible substance which could rain down on a person and hurt and hurt–

Madeleine shuddered, again curling protectively, then forced herself to shift, to sit up. Outside the tower it was dark, the curving array of windows showing city lights and stars. She had been put to bed and left till next time.

Inevitably, she was hungry.

Feeling fragile, and terribly alone, Madeleine tried to imagine how the Musketeers would deal with this situation. Fisher would point out the link between her experiments with him and the use of alcohol. The Core had learned of this and starved her, then set out spiked milk to interfere with her control.

Right, Noi would say. So all we need to do is not take the bait next time, and then slam the bastard when he shows up.

Steal his dragon! Pan would suggest.

Like that's going to work, Min would put in. Besides, he knew Maddie had taken the bait. There must be cameras.

So we get the old carton, fill it with water, and have it ready to fool them. Noi would give a little nod, confirming the plan.

If they wait long enough, I won't be able to do that, Madeleine thought. I won't care if it's spiked, I'll just care that it's food.

You can. Emily would take her hand, and give her a look of tremulous faith.

Then Nash would offer an understanding smile. You have two muesli bars left, he would point out, and have yet to exhaust the possibilities of the kitchens.

But does that mean I'm willing to kill Gavin? She had no answer, nor did she know what she would do about the dragon, if she did manage to fight off the Core.

"I'm having imaginary conversations with my friends, because my friends are all possessed," she said out loud, and made herself get off the bed.

Step C was beginning to resolve. She would assume there were cameras – at the very least where she slept, and the bar where they left the food. She would hide and conserve her muesli bars as long as possible, and hunt for any scrap which had been missed in the clearing out of the kitchens. She would do her best not to fall for spiked milk traps in future. When the Core came again...hopefully by then, she'd have some idea what step D might be.

Scanning the ceiling, Madeleine failed to spot cameras, and headed into the bathroom to clean up and change clothes. If she was going to use the old milk carton to fake drinking spiked milk, she'd need to smuggle it into place. There would surely be somewhere she could hide it behind the bar.

Heading around the curve to check, Madeleine stopped short, confused. There was a new tray, mounded high with packages. Did this mean they weren't going to starve her? Surely the Moths didn't expect her to obediently get drunk on command?

She approached the bar cautiously, scanning for traps, cameras. There was enough food for days: a stack of frozen pizza, pasta, a box of meat pies, cake. The cardboard was damp, everything well on its way to defrosting. There must be some kind of time constraint to the identity assault. The Core couldn't do that to her every day.

At first insensibly relieved, Madeleine moved on to unhappily wondering how many days this food was meant to cover. This would give her more of a chance to practice shields, but if it, for instance, was supposed to last her for a week, she could still be brought to a state of driving hunger. Common caution led her to prepare a relatively small portion of the frozen gnocchi, and stash everything else in the second floor kitchen freezer. Then she went back to her bed, and debated whether it was worth blasting holes in the ceiling in the hope of destroying any cameras. Sydney Tower really was an excellent choice for a prison – she was tremendously wary of damaging it.

After thinking the problem through, she simply alternately pushed and dragged the bed around the curve of carpet, to the far side of a dividing curtain. Drawing the curtain halfway, she hoped that would put her at the wrong angle for any cameras. Then she fetched her backpack and surreptitiously tucked the muesli bars into the front pocket.

Her sketchpads and pencils took up half the space in the backpack. She touched the spine of one, but didn't take it out, hadn't opened any of them since she'd woken in the tower. Looking at images of friends found and lost would be unbearable.

Someone coughed.

In the still isolation of the tower, that faint, distinct sound was a clarion call. Madeleine sat frozen, listening for more, trying to gauge direction. She thought, perhaps, above. It wasn't close. Standing, she circled to the elevators as quietly and rapidly as she could manage, to jab the buttons. Nothing.

Moving back to the bar, she picked up the long knife she'd abandoned after her attempt on the goo, and forced herself to slow, deliberate movements, up the straight stair to the fourth floor, pausing at its head to survey. The fourth floor was less clear than the third, with a raised inner section, an information booth, gift store, touchscreens, even an area with lockers for people heading out on the rooftop Skywalk. It was not until Madeleine had left the head of the stair and started clockwise around the circle that she saw him. Fisher.

In a chair moved from the locker area and set so he could gaze in the direction of the Spire, he sat legs stretched out, posture weary. His glasses were folded on a closed book on the floor beside him, and she could see his face reflected in the window: brows drawn together in one of those frowns which made him look furious. So familiar, and so wrong.

What could she do, to get back the person who was so incredibly precious to her?

"The knife seems a little redundant."

Madeleine started, and saw that he – the Moth controlling Fisher – was watching her in the thin reflection in the window. She looked down at the knife, decided that she was more likely to hurt herself with it than him, and put it on a nearby counter.

"I don't have a key to the lift," the Moth added helpfully. He hadn't turned, had straightened in the chair, but continued to watch her via the reflection. He held himself so like Fisher, had that quality of attentive contemplation.

Her mouth so dry she could barely speak, Madeleine asked: "Why are you here?"

"Oh, I have various threats and ultimatums to deliver," he said, with a faded hint of amusement. "The theory being that you're less likely to attack me. But before we go on, there's something you should know."

"What?"

In the reflection his eyes met hers, inexplicably sad.

"You've never met Fisher."

Chapter Twenty-One

"I don't *believe* you."

Hoarse, whispered protest, but Madeleine had to grab the nearby counter to keep herself upright. Because the expression was his. The way he held himself. She'd known on some level even before he spoke. This was the person who had watched her paint. The person she had danced with. The one who had held her, kissed her, become a new sun in her sky.

"It doesn't make sense. You helped us hide! You...ever since the stair? But why?"

"Initially my role was forward scout," the Moth who was not Fisher said. "To locate Blues sufficiently stained for the Five's purposes. And, if possible, assemble Blues for the initial dispersal. That practically arranged itself. You, of course, I had marked for the Core." Still watching her in the glass, a reflected boy with a steady gaze. "I don't know if it was due to your sheer strength, or your initial contact with the Spire, but you were able to instinctively defend yourself, and injured the Core badly. My orders changed: to keep you within reach until the Core was able to claim you."

"They knew where we were the whole time?" All that hiding, a futile game?

He nodded. "What better way to stop you running than to let you think yourself hidden? The North Building would likely not have remained unoccupied without orders to stay away. Unfortunately your existence was known to the other clans: that Rover's attack was almost certainly an embedded command. And then the challenge, which made it necessary to properly hide you."

Effortless manipulation. Tiny touches, never pushing. Supporting decisions to stay, to fight. Playing Musketeer while searching out holes in her defences, gaining her trust. Throat tight, muscles rigidly locked, Madeleine faced all which had been said and done between them. She could barely force the question through her lips.

"It was all an act?"

"No."

Those reflected eyes were fierce, his mouth a set line, firm and absolute. Then he looked away, drawing in a deep breath.

"There's a great deal I can't discuss. Most outside the Fives are barred from speaking at all to the Untaken. I have minor exemptions, but critical subjects can't even be broached, and I've lost some of the leeway I had. Do you remember what I said, the first time we spoke?"

A boy with a head injury, newly possessed, glaring at the Spire with concentrated hatred. *All this useless death. Don't you want to tear that down and stamp on the pieces?*

"That was true? But...why? You still – you told them where we were, didn't you? Unlocked the elevator."

"You've never met a hierarchy like the En-Mott," he said, then winced, as if something had poked him. "I can't explain in any detail. I can't directly act. I've done all I can to...to line up dominos. Time, place, opportunity. The pieces of information you need." He frowned at the window. "Let me get these threats out of the way. You understand what the Core intends to do to you?"

"Take me over slowly, instead of all at once."

"Your strength makes that a dangerous process. You cannot be kept permanently asleep – it requires a conscious mind. Each time, you need to be made safe to approach, prevented from attacking. You might choose to harm yourself. You might even manage to escape. And if you do any of those things, the Core will hunt down your parents." At her sharp look he shook his head. "He does not have them yet, though the Press very helpfully traced them to Bathurst. Tell them to move, the first chance you have."

What was he suggesting? Did he intend to help her escape? Madeleine stared, but he was no longer looking at her reflection, was gazing down toward Hyde Park. She didn't know how to feel. It would be stupid to trust someone who had lied to her from the day they'd met. There was no way to simply step back into absolute certainty. But something about the way he held himself, shoulders tight as if braced for a blow...

"Do you have a name?"

His eyes came back to her reflection with a jerk. Startled. Had he expected her to keep calling him Fisher? Then, a thin, wobbling note, a sound she would struggle to describe, and certainly couldn't reproduce. The name of a Moth.

"Call me Théoden," he said, with a shrug. "He was only possessed in the movie, but it seems appropriate enough."

After a blank moment she realised he was talking about a character from *The Lord of the Rings*. A fictional name, to emphasise the falsity of the person she had known, telling her Fisher's hopes and dreams while carrying out the Core's orders. And behind it, an agenda of his own. She had been utterly taken in, never for a moment suspecting.

"You act very–" She stopped, finding herself stupidly embarrassed. "Nash and Pan, the others. No-one from the school noticed any difference?"

"Why would they?" Her question had conjured the ghost of a smile. "I'm not sitting in a little control room in Fisher's head pulling levers. He is...a layer of knowledge and reaction, a filter through which I experience this world. Of course I would act human."

His reflected gaze was unwavering, saying things words did not. Madeleine wanted to look away, to deny any kind of response, but she could not. Everything about this was wrong, based on five kinds of lie, and still her heart raced looking into his eyes. This was a person who had connected with her on a level no-one else had, and the air between them thrummed.

Beyond Théoden, a ribbon of light curled across the sky. He looked away from her reflection to watch it twine once around the Spire, then dive and disappear.

"Time to start," he said, in a voice which sounded short of breath. He stood, and Madeleine was unable to stop herself from taking a step back, but if Théoden noticed he gave no sign. "Go to this point on the floor below."

Madeleine hesitated, then obeyed, perhaps because he was walking toward her and she was not sure if she could deal with him any closer. Her mind raced as she headed down the stair, keeping well ahead while she tried to guess his plans. When she reached the window there was no sign of movement in the park below, and so she watched the reflection of a boy walking up behind her, stopping perhaps two metres away.

"Is it time for another of the challenges?" she asked, mouth dry.

"Buenos Aires. The Core and two others of the Five will be gone till dawn. Think about how Nash survives."

She frowned at this apparent non sequitur, and behind her the boy who was not Fisher held out a hand as if to brush fingers against the back of her neck. He'd stopped too far away to make this possible, but the angle of reflection made it seem that they'd touched. She could not begin to describe his expression.

I'm going to push," he said, barely audible. "You will react. But I am glad, Madeleine. Thank you for the courage to do this."

Turning sharply, Madeleine drew breath to speak, and let it out in a gasp as a hammer-blow of emotion struck her. Grim determination. Fear. Fury. And wound through it all a fine, cutting thread of concern.

"S-stop!" This was not like the Core's assault. She was not drunk, defenceless. The storm of identity collided with roiling strength, and it took everything Madeleine had to hold back an automatic blow. "Th–!"

He struck again, intensifying the assault, and the roil of power Madeleine contained hit back. Not tangled with a shield, as had happened on the beach, but a blast of pure will, of self, and it was like a starburst, a sudden blooming of white and blue, and for a moment before her stood a boy, and above him a Moth.

Then the light went out of them both, and they crumpled to the floor.

"Stop," Madeleine repeated, and dropped to her knees.

Fisher lay on his back, eyes open, blank. The Moth – Théoden – was just behind him, a crumpled kite. She'd killed them both.

The tower was silent. Neither Moth nor boy moved. Madeleine knelt, at a complete loss, unable to understand why Théoden would tell her to think of Nash, then–

Groaning, she scrambled forward on hands and knees. When a Moth left a Blue, the Blue died. There'd been no stories of a Blue living through the end of possession. But when had any Moth tried to revive one? CPR was an obvious thing to attempt, but Madeleine had a better example. A leech Blue, needing a daily dose of energy to survive. Théoden had all but drawn a map.

How much? A thread? A jolt? Surely not the crushing blow which had struck them down. She pressed her hands together on his chest, and measured out a dose of desperation and panic, channelling it into him, the whole of his body shifting in response, as if he were a balloon inflating.

Lifting her hands, Madeleine scanned him anxiously for any sign of change. His eyes had shut, but he was so still. Should she try again, flood him with energy, or shift to CPR? But then his head turned, just a little, and his eyelids cracked. His chest rose as he drew in a slow breath, life returning as gently as waking.

Madeleine drew back, suddenly unable to touch this boy she had undressed, this stranger she had kissed so thoroughly. She looked instead at the crumpled creature behind him. A flattened paper lantern.

Easing over to kneel beside that alien shape, Madeleine studied the network of fading blue lines which suggested an almost humanoid figure. But it was a pattern on a kite, no true body. No eyes, no limbs, no heart. She held out her hands anyway, placed them over a central point. Her palm sank into a chill surface, and she drew it back. Then, trying to keep to the very surface, Madeleine sent out a measure of confusion and regret. With it came gratitude, and a deep note of stronger emotion. Briefly the blue lines took on a brighter hue, which almost immediately faded.

Tears wouldn't come. The need for them was a tight pressure in her head, her chest, but Madeleine was at the bottom of a well, and everything was distant. To her right Fisher lifted a hand, turned it to study the palm, opened and closed it.

"What did you do with that food?" he asked, still lying on his back.

"...second floor freezer."

The words came out tiny, squeezed past the lump in her throat, but he seemed to have managed to hear her, sitting up, then standing in a single, fluid motion. He didn't turn, paused only a moment to stare out at the Spire, then circled left along the outer wall of windows.

Everything inside Madeleine had snarled into a tight, vicious-edged lump, knotted beyond untangling. She watched the colour fade out of Théoden until, after what was probably a long time, or moments, Fisher returned. He stood very still, looking at the creature which had stolen his body then given it back.

Without comment he moved to Madeleine and held down to her a plate. Once-frozen chocolate cake, microwaved until the icing had melted and run. She had never felt less inclined to eat, barely turning her head enough to see what it was. Fisher hesitated, then took the plate over to the window, set it on the sill, and sat beside it.

"I know this is extremely hard for you..." he began, then stopped. Long seconds ticked by, and when he spoke again his voice was halting. "I have no idea how to feel about you. There is...I have a great deal of emotion for you, but I don't know how much of it is mine. I suppose you – I – " He paused again, then changed tacks completely, becoming crisp and businesslike: "In around five hours the Core will return. There's a great deal to do before that. Although it's possible for me to manage it without you, the chances of success are much lower."

It made it easier to have him focus on the larger issues, to not go anywhere near how either of them might feel. And through the barbed wire wasteland which filled her, Madeleine had discovered a direction.

"I could do that for Noi, and the others, couldn't I?"

"Yes." His relief at her response was obvious. "In fact Noi is the crux of the plan, since she's been taken by one of the Five."

"Does this plan include some way to get out of this tower?"

"We jump off."

That was enough to make her turn to him, and she suspected it had been intended to. He was frowning at her, that angry expression she'd learned could mean whole layers of emotion. As soon as she let herself see him, this tall, skinny, very smart boy she'd found herself adoring, her wire-wrapped heart thumped and bled and she had to drop her eyes. She couldn't do it, couldn't face how much he remembered, how he felt, dared not let herself study him for differences, similarities. She would not look again.

"Tell me what to do."

ooOoo

Circling the upper turret of Sydney Tower was a walkway which led to two glass-bottomed platforms projecting over the edge of the main floors. The Skywalk. Madeleine and Fisher stood on the platform facing south-east, a light breeze exploring the vulnerabilities of their jackets.

"That hotel," Fisher said, pointing left and almost directly below. It sat on Elizabeth Street: two sets of terraced balconies joined by a rectangular main building, all with an uninterrupted view to Hyde Park and the Spire. An immense distance down. "Noi is in the section on our right. We'll be going in through an access door from the roof. Aim for the left of the central building, beside that pool. The shape you practiced should give good control of speed and direction, but if you miss, head to ground level and meet me at the corner of Market and Elizabeth."

Even in her bruised and locked-down state, Madeleine could not simply jump off a building. Clutching the straps of her backpack, she peered at the array of roofs doubtfully.

"I'll be going first." Fisher bent to study the beams below the glass floor. "Looks like this will be structurally sound without the railing, but stand back while I make a gap."

"I'll do it."

Fisher hesitated, then moved away, silently acknowledging the power differential between them. He would need to save his strength.

The vertical sections of metal railing were thick and solid, but a couple of well-aimed finger punches easily took care of the narrow horizontal bar joining them. A tiny piece of metal remained connecting the bar, and bent easily as she pulled it inward. Then, stepping to one side, she held her arm over the railing and punched the clear main panel inward.

"Practice again," Fisher said, still maintaining the crisp, businesslike tone which made it bearable to be near him. "Get a feel for it at full size."

On another day, even with the two upright posts to hold, standing on the edge of such a drop would have had Madeleine gulping, trying to convince herself the floor wasn't tilting. But this night, in sight of the Spire, she was only allowing herself to think of her friends, of Noi down there needing rescue. And of carrying out the plan Théoden had died to set in motion.

Narrowing her eyes, she raised a shield a few metres in front of her, then began to thin and shape it, so it became a massive curve facing away from her, hopefully matching the form Fisher claimed would help her control direction. It was difficult to be sure: she had never tried anything like this with her shields, and its near-invisibility made the process a kind of mental sculpture, theoretically producing a combination between a sled and an oversized paraglider. The wind tugged at her, the tiny gust suddenly immensely powerful, so she hastily released the shield and moved back.

"Okay," she said.

"Because of the size, your descent should be slow, allowing you time to experiment with steering. It can be more responsive than a parachute, given you'll be on top, and can alter it at will. Do you think you can change the shape quickly?"

"Maybe." This still involved jumping off a building.

"If you find this too difficult to control, try shifting to the more triangular glider shape I showed you. Even if you panic and let the shield drop, just make another, as large as possible as fast as you can. It doesn't need to be complex – anything large will give you the drag to slow down." He paused. "If you can't do it, signal once I've landed, and I'll get the lift key and come for you."

She almost looked at him, then made the tiniest negative motion with her head. "I can manage."

"I'll see you down there, then," he said, voice momentarily flattening. He stepped into the gap, holding the upright supports tightly. Wind ruffled his mop of hair, and with barely a pause he tipped forward, and vanished.

Catching her breath, Madeleine clutched the railing, and in the night-time shadows spotted him only because he was falling, slowing as she watched. He must not have spread the shield till he was well on his way. Conserving his strength. He curved toward the hotel, the movement controlled, effortless. She lost sight of him in the gloom as he circled, then saw a tiny shape pass over the lighted rectangle of the rooftop pool.

Seeing how quickly and easily Fisher had managed somehow made it worse for Madeleine. There was no way she could swoop down like that. Jump off a building and work out how to fly, all in an easy two-step process? Maintain a shaped shield while falling? No matter how strong she was, that was beyond any reasonable learning curve. She'd end up slamming into the support shaft of Sydney Tower, or zooming off toward the Spire. Or dropping like a stone.

Her hands on the cold railing felt slick and damp, and she shivered in the late autumn chill. Impossible. Beyond impossible.

Noi. She repeated the name out loud. Noi down there, possessed by one of the Five. The need to bring her back was a rock-hard certainty, a promise never quite spoken. Noi, and Emily, Min, Nash, Pan. Lee Rickard would certainly have something to say about being able to fly beneath the stars.

She raised her shield, working quickly, having learned the power of even a tiny wind. The possibility of being dragged off her feet helped, because it meant she could not keep standing there, clutching the railing uprights.

"*Straight on till morning,*" she breathed, and tilted forward.

Chapter Twenty-Two

There was no plunge. Madeleine glided with soap bubble ease, the sensation almost that of sliding over ice, the shield beneath her far more responsive than she'd anticipated. She shifted it a degree, as easily as moving a mental arm, and the glide became a leisurely swoop toward Central Station.

Glorious!

Unhurriedly, for she was still very high, Madeleine attempted to follow Fisher's instructions, and made a minor adjustment to the shape, a curling of one corner, taking care to keep her changes small. She curved to the left, circling over the Anzac Memorial at the southern end of Hyde Park, and drifted back. The hotel was a good place to aim for, with its distinctive terraces and long upper roof. Still too far below to hope to land, but if she went south again and lined herself up as if for a runway, she would have plenty of opportunity to correct her height, and face far less risk of overshooting.

The city spun below her, reduced to blockish shapes and streaking lights. The Spire was a slim shadow ahead to her right, Sydney Tower a shorter rival to the left. Blobbish lumps below were all she could make out of Hyde Park's trees, which were far too low to pose any danger of collision, and provided a simple line to use as a guide. The hotel's long roof was not entirely flat, had some kind of air-conditioning plant on top, but that was long and flat as well, and she dropped to a mere leg-breaking distance as the near edge of the long centre building approached. Passing above four large fans, she lifted a little to barely clear a white circular projection, then swooped down the last few feet to the surface of the roof, contracting her shield so that her landing was a little fast, but obligingly bouncy.

Done. Face-down on concrete, arms spread wide, safe. She rolled onto her back and stared up at a foreshortened view of two towers. Had he known how that flight would make her feel? Lined up this domino, knowing she would desperately need to be uplifted? It had helped, so much. Théoden, all that she felt, was still a roil of confusion and grief, but the barbed wire had rusted through. It was gratitude which blurred the stars.

The recollection that she was lying on the roof of a hotel full of possessed Blues prodded her to movement. She scrambled to her feet and padded softly to the north end of the section of roof. The curve of the pool room roof was a lighted jewel below, and Fisher waited just before it, a so-familiar silhouette. Kneeling, she reversed, dangled and dropped down off the plant level, noticing deep scrapes in the concrete as she let go. The Core must land his dragon up there.

Another drop and she was beside the pool, Fisher turning as if to take her arm, then stopping short. But Madeleine had found the strength to keep herself focused on her goals, and was not thrown by the near touch.

"Were there cameras monitoring me?" she whispered. "Will the Moths know what's happened?"

"There were cameras, just not enough. They can't see the place where Théoden is, and will only know that you have gone up on the roof with what they will think is him. They can tell a possessed Blue from a non-possessed, but not through a camera image."

"So they'll know right away when they see you?"

"Yes. Every Blue we encounter, you will need to spirit punch immediately. Most of the Moths will die." The clipped tone wavered for a moment, then resumed. "If there's multiple Moths, I'll try to revive the fallen Blues while you fight, and it will be easier as we progress because our numbers will grow. However, the strongest Moths, particularly the Five, can survive separation from the host. That's why, before we go for Noi, we need Nash."

"To drain, like he did the Rover." Some of what needed to be done was obvious. Dominos, falling into place.

"Nash won't be possessed – he's being held for much the same reason you were. Any Greens will need to be shield-paralysed and locked up. Ideally, we want to collect Nash and free Noi as quickly and quietly as possible. If an alarm is raised – well, that will involve running, and passing on the information we have before the united strength of the En-Mott clans descends on us."

He led her to an access door and eased it open. Glancing down as they stepped inside, Madeleine saw that folded paper had been wadded into the gap in the jamb. Another domino. How had Théoden felt, this last day, putting in place all the things which needed to happen after she killed him?

Madeleine took deep, calming breaths, trying to prepare herself. Going into battle, a thing which she'd technically accepted back when the Musketeers had been practicing combat, now meant facing the probability of killing another Moth like Théoden. There was no way of knowing.

But she would do it. The consequences of hesitating were too large.

ooOoo

The next domino had been a card key, tucked behind a picture frame in the first hallway.

"The elevators are monitored," Fisher said as he collected it. "The cameras are in the far right corners. Put your hood up and look down and to your left as we walk in, then turn and straighten. There should be no problem with anyone seeing me on camera – perhaps a little heightened attention, but not the full alert you would inspire. The security room is on the same level as Nash, so we'll take it out first. It's usually manned by Greens, so in this case I'll shield-stun first, and you spirit punch anyone who doesn't fall down. Ready?"

Madeleine tugged her hood well forward. "Is it only Noi and Nash in this building? Do you know where the others are?"

"Min and Pan will be here. Emily is part of the sub-group led by another of the Five, based in the hotel next to this one."

"Okay."

The clarity of Fisher's knowledge made it obvious he remembered every detail of the time he was possessed, and she could not let herself think about that too much, could not spend time going over all the things she'd said and done. But it was no easier to think of killing people. Glad of the shadow of her hood, she followed him to an elevator, and did her best to move casually, bending her head as if she was glancing at Fisher's shoes, turning unhurriedly.

They travelled more than a dozen floors down, and strode with casual confidence to knock on and open a door, quite as if they belonged. The room beyond was lit by a grid of screens, images of corridors, rooms, the hotel entrance. Heart thumping triple time, Madeleine barely saw the people sitting before them, dark shapes turning, one getting to her feet. Fisher was quick, all three of the figures jolting from a blow, but the one standing was still moving, the tiniest fragment of Moth song lifting, and Madeleine punched, panicked by the idea of dozens of possessed people running in response to an alarm. In the compact room, the sudden bloom of Moth above Blue seemed blinding, the alien too close, giant.

Then it fell, becoming Madeleine's second kill that night, and she recognised with sick certainty that she would keep a count, and remember it always. But the Blue, a woman, had dropped back on the chair, limp and wrong, and Madeleine had to make certain that the count didn't jump immediately to three. Rushing forward, she pressed hands above heart and pushed out a frightened little spurt of worry.

"Good." Fisher sounded as breathless as she felt, but he was already moving, turning on the room's light and closing the door. "I'm going to grab gear to tie them up," he said, bending over the two Greens and searching pockets, removing mobile phones. "Paralyse them again if they begin to revive before I'm back. Is she breathing?"

"Yes." The woman had blinked, and tears were now welling in brown eyes. Behind her, the limp corpse of the Moth slid off the room's wrap-around counter to take up too much space on the floor.

"I won't be long," Fisher said, dragging one of the Greens into the corner furthest from any buttons. "Check the monitors for an indication of how many Moths are active."

He pulled the second Green across to the first, gave her a quick, sharp glance which she caught out of the corner of her eye, and then left. Madeleine turned to watch him stride into one of the elevators on screen and stand, hands in pockets, head bowed. Tense, strained, and already looking tired. They'd only just started. How could they possibly prepare for the Core's return in a scant few hours?

"Thank you. So much."

The Blue she'd freed reached out deeply stained hands, only occasional patches of brown visible. When Madeleine offered hers in automatic response, the woman gripped and squeezed them painfully tight, then let go and began to explore her own face.

"I can't hardly believe..." She swept her hands slowly over softly curling hair, squeezed shut her eyes, causing tears to break loose from lashes. "Me again. At last."

"Welcome back..." Madeleine said uncertainly.

"Sarah," the woman said, making the name a release, a triumph. "Sarah Jeteneru."

"I'm –"

The woman widened her eyes, a momentary laughing expression. "You're Madeleine Cost. Do you think there's any of us in this city who doesn't know the Core's great prize? And, oh, he's reached too far, hasn't he? You're here to bring him down."

"We're here to try," Madeleine said, startled and impressed by the woman's rapid shift toward self-command. She surveyed the wall of monitors, wondering how many Moths were in the hotel. A central screen was flicking between images, and Madeleine caught her breath, staring at a person sitting cross-legged on a bed.

The picture changed to Nash, standing at a window, but a furtive sound demanded Madeleine's attention, and she turned to find one of the stunned Greens trying to overcome post-paralysis pins and needles and get to the door. By the time the Green had been stunned and stashed back with his companion, Fisher had arrived, wearing a backpack and hauling heavily loaded Eco-shopping bags.

"Eat," he recommended, putting down four bags brimming with blocks of chocolate, boxes of muesli bars, bags of dried fruit. He slid his backpack to the ground, produced a mobile phone which he passed to her, then pulled out a large roll of duct tape, turning purposefully to the Greens.

"This is Sarah," Madeleine said, opting to stock her backpack first. She refused to contemplate crumb trays ever again.

"Fisher," he said, with a preoccupied nod. "How many people are up and about in the hotel?"

"Up, quite a number, watching the Buenos Aires Challenge." Sarah glanced toward a laptop, where images of an arena were being streamed, then pulled a keyboard into reach and tapped out commands. "Most in their rooms, but there's a cluster in a guest lounge, and another group in with the North."

"The North?" Madeleine asked.

"One of the Five. There's no English word – no Earth word – which fits what they call the four who support the Core, so they use North, South, East and West. The four quarters. The South and the North are watching together," she added to Fisher, who paused, frowning, then briskly resumed his taping efforts.

"We'll need greater numbers before we go up, then," he said. "But first the leech Blues. Any obstacles?"

"One guard, at the beginning of their corridor," Sarah said, and when the Greens were thoroughly wrapped led Madeleine and Fisher directly to a row of rooms which had been roughly reinforced with the kind of security screens usually seen on the front doors of houses. The first in the row, by contrast, had had its door removed, making it difficult to get past unseen, so Madeleine simply ran straight into the open room, the man inside not even facing her when she spirit punched. Too easy, but already she was feeling a pinch of strain.

"I'm not sure how many of these I can do in a row," she said, as she knelt over the fallen Blue. "I'll be okay for a handful more, but..."

"No, you need to rest for when we go for Noi. With this third freed Blue, we can safely take all but the strongest without you, and punching duty can pass on to each new Blue to limit exhaustion."

"Have you posted how to free people?" Sarah asked from the door. "We need to get something out there, tell the world how to do this."

"Is right..." The man lying on the floor beside Madeleine groaned, then tried to lever himself too quickly upright. "Can't delay–!"

"We'll prepare a time-delayed post after we have the leech Blues," Fisher said shortly. "Failure insurance. But we can't go public yet. Not everything's in place."

He too was thinking in terms of dominos. Of course he would, following the memory of Théoden's plans, and that idea started to bring too much to the surface, so Madeleine turned to help the newly freed Blue to his feet. He wobbled unsteadily, told her to call him Kiwi Joe, then gathered her up in a huge hug. Since he was a big, solidly built man, this was more than a little overwhelming, but then he, like Sarah, took himself in hand, producing the keys to the makeshift prisons, asking Fisher questions about what next.

They shared out keys, unlocked the screens, and then Madeleine jumped back with a stifled squeak as Nash cannoned out of the room she'd opened, a broken chair leg swung like a sword, missing her head only because he pulled up at the last moment.

"Not possessed!" she said hastily, but he'd already worked that out, probably because Moths weren't given to squeaking.

"The others–?" he asked.

"Soon," Madeleine said, but suddenly Nash wasn't looking at her, was staring past her down the hall, the tense determination vanishing from his face, replaced by stunned disbelief.

"Leina?"

Madeleine had known, had seen him on the monitors, but still that husky, once-familiar voice broke something in her, and she whirled and flung herself into a startled Tyler's arms.

Chapter Twenty-Three

Tyler's soothing, barely audible hum took Madeleine back to the summer when she was five, an inconstant moon in Tyler's orbit as he strolled the back pastures of a neighbouring farm. She would dart off to follow a butterfly, examine a flower, bring back a seed pod to offer him. At twelve he had seemed impossibly tall and distant, holding his sun hat against the wind. But when there were nettles, scrapes, bruised knees, he would drop down to her height, open his arms, and hum just as he did now as he gave her a tiny squeeze.

"Are you rescuing me, or am I rescuing you?" he asked, as completely self-possessed as Tyler always managed to be.

"Both?" Madeleine gave a shaky little laugh and made herself let him go. "I think it's supposed to be more we're mustering forces to save the world."

"What's that supposed to mean?" Another of the leech Blues stepped forward, a short, ivory-skinned woman with a bruised face partially hidden by streaming red hair. "We don't have a hope of fighting these things."

"Let's not discuss this in a corridor," Fisher said, and herded them back to the security room, where they could talk while keeping an eye on the monitors – and the Greens who had inched across the floor and were trying to lever themselves in reach of a desk phone. The question of Greens bothered Madeleine immensely, since there wasn't a Moth to remove to make them themselves again.

Ten people and a jellyfish corpse made for an extremely crowded room. Madeleine and Tyler tucked themselves onto a corner of the wrap-around desk, and since Sarah was partially shielding her, Madeleine took the opportunity to let herself look at Fisher, who was giving them all a survey in return, betraying a hint of impatience.

"In a little over four hours, the Core and two others of the Ul-naa Five will return from the Buenos Aires Challenge," he said. "And discover that Blues have been freed and revived, which is the most forbidden act among their people. Freed Blues retain the information they experienced. Not a lifetime's memories, but everything including the Moth's thoughts during the period of possession. This is such a serious thing that the clans will unite with a single purpose: to kill us."

The redhead looked doubtful. "What do you know that's so important?"

"Isn't knowing how to kill Moths, and free and revive Blues enough?" Joe asked.

"After what happened because of Washington? Shit no." The last leech Blue, an Asian teen with an impressive collection of piercings, moved restlessly, limited by the crowded space. "Not that I'm sorry you busted me out, but unless you found a way to stop them dusting any more cities, you got to be ready to kill a lot of people to save a few Blues."

"Are you volunteering to be locked back up?" Fisher leavened the question with a tired hint of smile. "I don't have enough information, yet. What I need to do is free a Blue possessed by one of the Ul-naa Five, gambling that one of the Reborn – one of the Fives – will know of a way for us to bring down the Spire. If there isn't..." He hesitated.

"I will not turn my back on the possibility of ridding ourselves of the Moths," Nash said firmly. "And for the moment, we cannot do a great deal more harm by trying to find out if there is a way. If there is not, then we can discuss the risk of another dust attack, and whether we allow that threat to keep us from fighting. Until then, there are friends I must find."

"Hear hear," Tyler said, his voice soft, but carrying effortlessly. Nash immediately lost his poise, his glance at the cramped corner uncertain.

"But *how* do we fight?" the redhead asked. "They feed us just enough to stay upright. It's all I can do to stand here so close to you lot, not draining you dry."

Madeleine couldn't see the woman's expression as Nash explained the Rover fight, but her stance shifted enough to be a response in itself.

"All right," the woman said. "I can't say I want to do this. And I can't say that I'll go willingly back to that room, threats of more dust or not. But I'll help to a point."

"Until we know more," the Asian boy conceded.

Fisher simply nodded, already focusing on the next step. "We have just over four hours."

ooOoo

"Your remodelling job on my bathroom was impressive."

The words were only teasing, but Madeleine still shifted in embarrassment and glanced across at the redhead, Claire, who was watching the monitors for progress of the 'collection team' Fisher had led off to free reinforcements.

"I didn't realise you reached the apartment."

"Oh, yes. I'd just found your Mysterious Note when, well, aliens, and my two friends became very curt types who bundled me up and delivered me here. It sounds like you've been having a far more adventurous time."

"I guess. I–"

A great roil of emotion swelled, blocking Madeleine's throat, filling her eyes. Tyler glanced at her, then tucked her against his side.

"The edges become less raw," he said, conversationally. "Big hurts never really go away, but you can contain them, build up scar tissue to stop them cutting so deep. The question for you here, given that it's apparently so important you rest for this fight, is whether it will help you to cry about it now, or put it off till later."

Madeleine leaned her head against Tyler's shoulder and let his warmth seep into her, borrowing the strength to push back breaking down a little longer.

She was far from the only person who had lost someone, and the thing to do was focus on freeing Noi, not so much to save the world, but because it was Noi.

"Did you see the painting?"

"It was there?"

"On the wall in your bedroom."

"I didn't get that far. Will I like it?"

"No. But I do."

"And that's what matters?" The door opened as Tyler laughed, that rich, throaty burble, and Pan, leading the way in, stopped dead, a delighted grin consuming his face.

"Maddie, you seriously held out on us," he said, stepping aside as Fisher, Nash, and the fourth leech Blue, Quan, bunched up behind him. "I'd tweak your nose for it, but I'm so damn glad you figured out a way to free us I'll let you off this once."

It was a brave show, and Pan almost succeeded in behaving just as usual, though his eyes gave lie to his smile. Full of sympathy, and awareness of the length of Fisher's possession. Mercifully, he transferred his attention to Tyler, crossing to hold out his hand. "I'm Lee, and I give you fair warning that I am going to fangasm over you at some point when we're not saving the planet."

"I'll look forward to that," Tyler said with perfect gravity, shaking the proffered hand.

"I didn't figure out how to free you," Madeleine began, then caught Fisher's expression. A clear 'later', which she understood and accepted while hating the idea of receiving thanks which belonged to Théoden. "Do we have enough to go get Noi?" she asked instead, glancing at the crowd outside the door and feeling a little better to see Min among them.

Fisher gave her a brief, grateful smile, surely not intended to pierce her heart so thoroughly, and said: "Yes. A quick parcelling out of targets and we'll go up."

A woman called Jannika was left behind as monitor room guard, and the now dozen freed Blues and four leech Blues crammed into the nearest emptied hotel room, to assign each leech Blue a protector, and divide everyone else into attacker or reviver with the recommendation to "adapt as necessary". This piece of advice became the whole of the plan after they split into two groups, and the elevator Madeleine rode up in arrived at its destination floor and opened its doors on two surprised Blues.

Min punched and one of the Blues fell beside a limp possessor, but Moth song rose piercing and urgent from the other. The freed Blues spilled out into the lift foyer, Fisher punching, Pan dropping to his knees to revive the first Blue. The second Moth bloomed, but did not fall. It was the worst moment possible for a Moth to survive separation, filling the air with song, and Madeleine thrust herself forward, raising a shield. Instead of attacking the Moth flitted sideways, and off down the corridor.

"Heading toward our target!" Fisher said, and they raced after it even as answering song rose from surrounding rooms.

The Moth's path lay through the foyer of the second elevator, and it was that which saved the moment. The other group stepped out, and Sarah reacted to a Moth flying directly at her by shield-punching it into the ceiling. Claire, confused but willing – or hungry – reached up and pressed her hands to the single trailing tip in her reach, and the song abruptly died.

"Clear the rooms we've passed?" Pan asked urgently, and at a nod from Fisher reversed direction and headed toward a door just as it opened.

Madeleine scrambled with the rest, using the security master key taken from the monitor room, and ran through the next door only to be blasted by a force punch which knocked her on her behind. The Blues on the far side of the room were the youngest she'd seen, but clearly strong and too far away for her to comfortably spirit punch. Hating the idea of injuring children, she snapped a light force punch in their direction to keep them occupied – blowing out wooden shutters and glass from the windows behind them – and staggered into a run at them.

The taller one – a skinny boy with a blue stripe down his chin – punched her again, but she was expecting it this time and set her feet so she wasn't bounced when her shield absorbed, then spirit punched, both at the same time. A wave of dizziness swept through her, and she fell against the foot of the bed as twin Moths projected back through the gaping windows.

"Leina?" Tyler, following her about according to instructions, lifted her more or less upright.

"Help me over," she said urgently, and fed two still little figures energy despite the dizziness. She stayed kneeling by them because there was no way she could leave without being sure she hadn't just killed two children, even if she could stand up.

She could hear the progress of the fight in neighbouring rooms, flurries of sound, brief outbursts of Moth song. It seemed to spread and spread, and then when Madeleine thought she had to go help no matter how dizzy, it all died away. By then one of the children, a girl around ten, had her eyes open, all her attention on the boy, who was slower to revive. They both looked to be of African descent, might even be brother and sister, and a knot gripped Madeleine's stomach then relaxed as his eyelashes fluttered.

"Always sleeping in," the girl said, and promptly put her head down on his chest and began to cry.

"Where did–?" Pan came through the door at a trot. "Maddie, we're going for Noi straight away – there's too much chance they heard something. You good?"

The dizziness had faded enough that she could stand, so she nodded and followed along, grateful when Tyler slipped a supportive arm through hers. The group of freed Blues had grown in size yet again, and there was a milling confusion of people gathering in the nearer lift foyer.

Sarah, low-voiced, was making brief explanations, but an urgent trill of Moth song interrupted her and it started all over again, but this time the figure they were chasing down was Emily, who wasn't even supposed to be there, and no convenient third group emerged to intercept her as she ran straight for their target suite, song spiralling.

"Go! Go!" Madeleine didn't even recognise the person who shouted, but sprinted, hand-in-hand with Tyler. Someone ahead punched straight through the door closing in their face, and they streamed inside, a frantic mass, but Madeleine checked at a glimpse of a fallen tangle with blond hair.

Min, panting but bright-eyed, was there before her. "I'll look after her. Get Noi."

No choice, the crowd surging, flooding into a spacious lounge area, so many that Madeleine couldn't be sure which were the possessed Blues. Then Fisher yelled "Balcony!" and she turned to see a familiar figure heading over the railing.

Far too far to spirit punch, but Madeleine did it anyway, a desperate move which sent her ploughing into carpet, feeling like she'd shield-stunned herself except with an absence of sensation which was more frightening. But the punch worked, blue and white blazing out, Noi left hanging like abandoned laundry. The Moth rose, and only Nash was even close, his full speed run turning into a hop, a leap off the top of the railing to grab a trailing edge of white before it could escape. He landed like a gymnast, balanced on the crossbeam, dragging his captive down. Tyler and Quan, following, raced to stretch and press hands to light.

It died quickly, a candle flicker compared to the Rover.

Nash's pose on the railing – and Noi's position hanging over it – were not so perilous at second glance. The balconies were merely sectioned off portions of the roof of the tier below, with a broad expanse of concrete beyond. Still Madeleine desperately tried to lever herself off the carpet because there were only leech Blues near Noi, and the attention of the room had been drawn to the fight with the 'South' of the Five.

But from two lone escapees their numbers had grown exponentially, each freed Blue quick to put to use the skills and knowledge gained during their possession. It was two skinny kids who hopped over the top of Madeleine and ran to the rescue. And Madeleine managed to stay awake long enough to see Noi, precious for many more reasons than perhaps knowing how to bring down the Spire, lift her head.

Another domino.

ooOoo

Madeleine was resting her eyes, with occasional interruptions. The first had been Tyler, prodding her to drink lukewarm soup. Next, a relative hush in a room which had been humming with voices. Then a question.

"Is it possible?"

"Yes."

Not Noi, but the lightly accented voice of the former South, a Malaysian man in his late twenties named Haron. Madeleine opened her eyes to look at him, the focus of a room crowded with forty or so freed Blues.

"It is a faint chance," he went on, apologetically. "When the Spire's shield is down, but it is no longer functioning as a portal – as it will be in the moments immediately after the Core returns – the Spire is vulnerable. A pulse, an application of carefully timed blows of force, will paralyse it, preventing the raising of the shield. If this is followed by a continued attack, there is a chance we could kill it, but more likely it will withdraw."

"Kill it?" That was Nash, startled. "It's alive?"

"The Spires – all the Spires – are a single, living construct. A grander creature than the Hunters and the Aerials, but sharing the same origin."

Only the leech Blues reacted with surprise. Curled in a corner of one of the room's couches, Madeleine considered the faces of the Musketeers among the crowd of freed Blues. Pan, Min, Noi, and Emily, each having looked through a window at an alien world and culture. The knowledge alone would always separate them, and the experience had marked them in other ways. They were all so bruised. Pan tried to disguise it with his usual frenetic energy, but drooped when there was no-one to bounce off. Emily hadn't spoken, not once, while Min's few words had been sharp, full of edges. Noi's eyes were shadowed.

Three days since they had danced barefoot. Every one of them silently wounded.

Madeleine glanced at Fisher, who did not drop his eyes quite quickly enough to hide that he'd been watching her. His face was drawn, the lids drooping with exhaustion, and despite her determination to not deal with her feelings until after the coming battle, she had to check an impulse to wait until he looked again. He continued to take a deliberately businesslike tone to everything, giving her little chance to gain a sense of him, but already there'd been glimpses of a different person to the one she'd known. A hint of impatience, a touch of sarcasm. More often brief glances rather than those calm, unhurried surveys. The connection, the rapport she'd thought she had with Fisher – had it all been Théoden?

Too much noise to think. Forty freed Blues, each with their own opinions, making it impossible to simply issue peremptory commands without explanation. Madeleine closed her eyes on the debate, then opened them to check again on Noi, subdued and contained, holding an icepack to Emily's shoulder. Now that all the Musketeers were free, Madeleine had lost her immediate drive. Incapable of celebrating, unable to mourn.

She shifted so she could see Tyler's profile. Always distant in his own way, yet conjuring a sense of comfort, safety, the certainty of family. He would always be her cousin, no matter what happened. But even with Tyler she could not find any way to explain her confusion, or her need to have Théoden's sacrifice acknowledged, could only tell herself over and over that now was the wrong time. Everyone had their own hurts, their own struggle with the coming battle. She shut her eyes again, trying to listen without feeling.

The crux of the debate was the consequences of failure. If the Spire remained functional, then the united clan response would mean the deaths of most, if not all the freed Blues who had mustered to fight, followed by a release of dust to create more Blues around Sydney. Even if they succeeded, they would be facing the Core and two Quarters – and a dragon.

"Eight years."

Noi hadn't raised her voice, but her flat tone still managed to cut through the noise.

"The gap before the next cycle of primacy will be eight Earth years," she continued. "Why are we even discussing this? You mightn't have been hosting one of the Reborn, but it still must be obvious to you all that there's no question of passing up this chance, or of making sure the information we have is spread as far and wide as possible."

"A cycle." Nash had straightened in dismay. "Of course. That has always been there, right in front of us. A cycle suggests repetition."

"They'll come back," Noi said. "Until there's not enough people left on Earth to make it worth their while. And then they'll skip our planet for a few cycles, until we've built up a big enough population for them to care. Over, and over, and again. Unless we stop them."

There was no argument after that.

Chapter Twenty-Four

A small 'command group' – primarily the Musketeers and the leech Blues – woke Madeleine a third time, returning to the North's suite for a strategy meeting after the rest of the hotel had been cleared. Of the three hundred and fifty-odd possessed Blues in Sydney, they had now freed a hundred and eight. There were as many Greens in the building, posing such a technical difficulty for the freed Blues that any suggestion of rescuing Blues in other hotels was quickly shut down.

"It will have to wait until after we've faced the Core. If the Spire withdraws, the Greens will recover themselves in..." Noi shrugged, her eyes still flat and dark. "The North didn't know the exact timing. A day or a week – long enough that we'll be either fighting, avoiding, or have our hands full helping them. The most we can do beforehand is try to limit Green involvement with the initial battle, and then deal with them after, along with any Moths which attack us."

"Any guesses how many will?" Nash asked.

"While the Spire stands, and the Core's alive, all of them will come. That's not an option for them. The longer the battle lasts, the more we'll have to fight." Noi nodded at the television, where an endless series of battles between possessed Blues was being waged. "Less than two hours till dawn, and we'll want to be in place well before, in case that wraps up early. Let's get this recording done."

"I'll wake Fish," Pan said, picking up one of a pair of compact video cameras Fisher had produced from his backpack.

"No, we'll do the technical sections first." Noi glanced at Madeleine, not Fisher collapsed on the couch opposite. "Everyone should get as much rest as they can."

Drowsy, but no longer numbingly exhausted, Madeleine stayed curled up, watching as Noi explained the process of freeing and reviving Blues, and the best techniques for fighting Moths and their creatures. Then Haron set out the plan to bring down the Spires, in the hopes that if they failed another city would be able to carry it out.

While they talked, Madeleine watched Fisher sleep. The mouth she had kissed, the hands which had touched her. Beneath the jacket and shirt, comets. She squeezed shut her eyes, and when she opened them again he was looking back, and did not shift away. Half the room between them, and identical unhappy expressions.

Haron finished, and Noi grimly checked the time on the television. "Ready to do the history, Fisher?"

He nodded and sat up, pausing to run his fingers through his hair, trying to tame sleep-born excesses.

"You want me to hunt you out a comb?" Pan asked, still determinedly upbeat in defiance of the subdued focus which had settled on everyone else. "A mirror? How about some cucumber slices for the circles under your eyes?"

"Maybe later." Fisher's gaze was level. "You'll want to save your primping for yourself – you'll be doing a closing recording."

"Me? Why?"

"If we bring down the Spires, the Moths will be furious, desperate. Worse, if we fail, and the Moths are alertly on guard, holding the threat of dust over their cities, any free Blues are going to be facing tremendous hurdles. We've had the advantage of surprise. Picture trying to work out how to spirit punch, then heading into Moth territory hoping to free a possessed Blue, with the knowledge that the response might be the deaths of thousands of uninfected. We need an Agincourt speech."

"And you expect one from me?" Pan held the camera before him in protest. "You write me something and I'll perform it, but I'm no good with my own words."

"You always did want to play Henry Fifth," Nash said, clearly entertained.

"Yeah, I'll tell the world it's Saint Crispian's Day, that'll help. Or yell fuck a few million times, which is about my level of improv. Or–" His gaze settled on Tyler, sitting quietly at the end of Madeleine's couch. "Or, hey, world famous actor! That would make much more sense."

"But very poor casting." Tyler crossed one leg elegantly over the other, and said, in a smoky, musing voice: "'*From this day to the ending of the world, But we in it shall be remembered*'. You'd pass that up? You don't want to make that moment your own? To have aspirant actors, centuries from now, vying to play you?"

Pan was clearly much struck, but shook his head. "Now I *really* can't think of anything good enough to say."

"Don't try for good enough." Noi crossed to take the camera off him. "It's not the words that matter. It's the emotion. I'll film Fisher's intro, and you can think about how you feel about the Moths."

Pan wavered, then mischief crept into his expression. "I'll give it a shot for a thimble," he said, presenting his cheek.

"You and your thimbles." Noi leaned forward, but Pan, eyes wide, turned his head so that their lips met, the briefest touch before she started back. Looking close to angry, she shook her head. "You better come up with something good for that."

"I'm sure as hell feeling inspired."

It was the complete lack of imp, of any hint of joking, which brought the blush to her face. Visibly at a loss, but suddenly much more like her normal self, Noi looked down at the camera, then raised it as a shield. "Ready when you are, Fisher."

Fisher, hair almost tame, moved a few steps, waited for Noi's nod, then spoke.

"We are here because of a Moth." The words were crisp, clear. "The name he chose to use was Théoden, and he died so we could be free."

Fisher had gained the total attention of the dozen people in the suite, but he didn't react to their surprise, gazing past the camera to Madeleine.

"It is true enough that the En-Mott will leave in two years. A timeframe is useful, the first time they visit a planet, to minimise attacks. It is equally true that they will return. Their driving reason is not their ruling order, but their own survival.

"The En-Mott were once the Mottash, a tired race on a tired world. Not too different from us – warm-blooded, oxygen breathing – facing a depleted future. They were searching for ways to leave their world, and instead they left themselves. The Conversion – a two-step process, the first part of which we have experienced – was considered a triumph. Lack of water, failing crops: what did it matter if the world turned to dust if you could live on light? And the newly created En-Mott would survive centuries.

"Still, they could die, and did. A slow attrition of numbers. Reproduction of a sort was possible, a slow and deliberate division which weakened the parent, hastened death. The En-Mott had set themselves on a path to extinction.

"They turned to the Spires for a solution. One of the planetary travel methods under development before the Conversion, it had matured to the point where it could be used to look for and reach inhabited worlds. A partial conversion of a warm-blooded host gave the En-Mott access to energy reserves, enough to increase in strength, to breed without death. For the first time in centuries their numbers rose."

Fisher glanced toward the master bedroom, where the corpses of a half-dozen Moths had been chivvied out of the way.

"Their solution had trapped them in flesh, since leaving the host was dangerous, often fatal even when energy levels were high. But then a handful discovered a use for faulty conversions – the leech Blues – and the Reborn came to be. Leech Blues lack the ability to produce some of the energies which form the substance of the En-Mott, and cannot be directly possessed. But the Reborn are able to slowly transfer their...selves to them, to complete what is missing. This act, unlike their fission reproduction, increases the strength of the Moth instead of depleting it."

Madeleine sat up, and slid along the couch so she could sit shoulder to shoulder with Tyler. Her cousin, as usual, looked no more than coolly interested in proceedings, but if he had had a fortnight of assaults like the one Madeleine had experienced, what he was demonstrating was his self-control. Nash, Claire and Quan's expressions were all variations of suppressed revulsion.

"In each clan there are five Reborn. Most of the rest are the offspring of the last cycle of primacy. When the cycle ends, they are ordered to leave their hosts, and, because the Reborn do not give them time to recover strength, with a tiny number of exceptions who are strong enough, they die."

"Why?" The redhead, Claire, was staring in disbelief. "You mean they kill themselves? Why would they not just stay?"

Noi made a query signal whether they should start over, but Fisher shook his head and went on.

"They're not given a choice. The Moths' reproduction, the splitting off of part of their self, leaves their offspring bound to them – and to their progenitors. Every single Moth is in a direct line of descent from the Cores of the thirty most powerful clans, and subject to their commands. Even the Cores of lesser clans can only partially mitigate the orders of those originals, and some edicts – such as the ban against reviving discarded Blues – are absolute. Every cycle the overall number of En-Mott increases, but the cycle's pace is dictated by the needs of the Reborn, who sacrifice each generation in turn to increase their own strength.

"The only hope for a member of a new generation is to grow strong enough to survive separation, and the Reborn facilitate this by rewarding the most loyal with exemptions from reproduction, which greatly increases their chances – and can even lead to joining the Reborn. To describe what this does to the En-Mott – born with a potential life-span of centuries, and told to kill themselves within one or two decades, with a vicious competition to gain an exemption, to become one of this privileged class... A whole race driven by a combination of hate and hope. Hatred for the Reborn. Hope that they might join their ranks."

Fisher's frown had grown heavier with every word, and he stopped to take a deep breath, visibly upset. Looking directly at Madeleine, he forged on.

"Théoden, the Moth who possessed me, loathed the cycles of death. There is very little each new generation can do about their situation, and it was not until the Ul-naa Core was injured by a Blue strong enough to instinctively defend against possession that Théoden saw any way forward. While ostensibly searching for a way for the Core to overcome that instinctive defence, he worked to create an opening, a chance to end the cycles. For his apparent success in finding a way to disarm that Blue, he was rewarded with an exemption by the Core. Perhaps in other circumstances he would have taken it, despite his fury and disgust. He did so very much want to live."

Expression easing, Fisher took a moment to meet the eyes of each of the Musketeers in turn.

"But during the time Théoden spent carrying out the Core's task he found a source of strength. A cause is a cold thing to die for. To die to protect the people you count as friends, people you have laughed with, and grown to cherish, that is a gift.

"In an hour it will be dawn, and we will try to bring down the Spires. We have recorded separately the methods of fighting. There are countless selfish and obvious reasons for the people of Earth to fight back against the Reborn. But another reason is for that one person who found a way, who put our future above his own. We mattered to him, and so he bought us this chance. Honour him."

Turning abruptly away, Fisher walked back to the opposite couch and sat down, looking as drained as Madeleine felt. Noi lowered the camera, and the room sat absolutely still. Then Emily uncurled from the ball she'd maintained since she'd been freed, and crossed to tuck herself by Madeleine.

Pan broke the silence. "You expect me to follow that?"

Fisher gave him a dry glance. "You've never been short of something to say. Why start now?"

"Ha. Hell." Pan scrubbed his hand through his hair. "Okay. Make sure you get my best side, Noi. Nash, stop me if I start ranting."

With a shamefaced grin, he stood, studied his feet, then momentarily was the exact image of the sketch Madeleine had given him: Lee Rickard as Henry the Fifth. The young King. Then just as quickly he was a less grand figure, a boy with the face of an imp, but no smile.

"So we're about to go try to bring down the Spires, and if we fail, someone else gets to have to do it. Even if we succeed, there's going to be a lot of fighting ahead. After all the people who have died, all the friends I've lost, the last thing I want to do, really, is risk any more. I'm betting most of you feel the same way.

"For the Blues out there: we've a lot of advantages you probably won't have. Strong people, smart people, a team. It makes such a difference when you know someone's got your back, who'll try to bring you up when you're down, or tell you to stop when you're going the wrong way. There might be hardly any free Blues in your city. You might be alone. But we're passing on Théoden's gift. Take the knowledge, make the opportunity. Find your strongest Blue, your tactician, your strategist. Rescue your leeches. And stand together and try. Even if the first attempt fails, even if they take you, don't lose hope. Someone else will come for you, will bring you back like I was brought back.

"For those of you who aren't infected, those who are going to say, no, we can't fight, they'll release more dust, they'll attack us, that it's better to wait it out like a bad storm. Let me remind you: they come back. They'll take all us Blues, and use us up, and throw us away, and then they'll have a little breather and start all over again. No-one can think that's a good idea. This is a war. And they tricked you into not fighting."

He darted a quick look at Fisher, and took a deep breath.

"Moths. Because I'm only talking to you thanks to Théoden, I want to make an offer to others like him, those Moths who don't want, never wanted this...slaughter. We are going to hunt you down. Those bodies you're wearing belong to someone else. But if you turn yourself in, if you surrender to us and take that huge risk of dying so that the Blue you're riding can be free, then we won't attack if you survive. I don't know what the hell we'll do with you after − put you on an island? But...anyway."

His chin jerked up, as if he was still unravelling the implications of his offer. Then his stance shifted, not the king returning, nor Pan, cocksure and defiant, but a cold, angry declaration.

"Finally, for those of you who did this to us, for the Remade. Fuck you.

We'll dance on your graves."

Chapter Twenty-Five

Half an hour before dawn Madeleine was trying not to break her ankle. Even though they'd circled around to the relatively clear eastern side of the park, entering from College Street, the debris of the Spire's arrival formed a black obstacle course of tree trunks and torn earth, to be navigated by touch and hope.

"Team Dragon and Defenders, stop around here," Noi called in a carrying whisper. "Spire Squad, you get into position first, then the Defenders will shift into place around you. Good luck."

Madeleine's searching hands encountered a metal face, and she bit back a gasp even as she realised it had to be one of the statues from the Archibald Fountain. She slid down to sit in a small depression behind it, glad to be out of the rising wind. Sydney nights in early May were jacket weather, cool not icy, but her fits of sleep hadn't fully balanced excessive spirit punching, and the urge to curl into a ball and sob was rising.

During the last half hour Fisher and Noi had worked rapidly through endless pre-battle issues which would never have occurred to Madeleine. Release timers and mirror-sites for the four videos, drawing on Nash, Min and others to write quick introductions in multiple languages, asking viewers to redistribute and subtitle. Choosing the north-east corner of the park because it was not bordered by residential buildings, and the bulk of the Spire would hide them from early risers in the hotels. Escape routes for those staying on Green guard duty, and transport strategies for the fighters, should running become the only option. Distribution of laptops to watch the progress of the challenge, and spotters with torches to signal if the Core came through from the south-west side. Rope, for those standing at the edge of what would become a huge pit. The need to remove the webcam in Saint Marys Cathedral.

Haron was in charge of the Spire Squad: fifty Blues who were going to try to give an alien tower a heart attack. The Defenders, led by Sarah, would do everything they could to keep attacking Blues and Greens away from Haron's team. A trio with varying levels of medical knowledge waited with first aid kits out on the footpath, and there was even a pair optimistically cooking up enormous vats of soup back at the hotel. The Musketeers and leech Blues, forming the majority of Team Dragon, would try to deal with the returning Core and his large glowing mount.

Emily, who had been following close behind, tucked in beside Madeleine in the shelter of the statue, and whispered: "I'm sorry for being angry with you."

Having completely missed Emily being angry, Madeleine shifted in confusion, then shrugged mentally and curled an arm around the girl's waist. "I'm sorry for making you angry." She also wished she could send Emily off to safety. Thirteen was so young. But there was a drive in the girl to fight which held little of bravado, had a level of necessity.

"I think it's a bad idea, what Pan said," the girl added. "Letting any of them live. E-even if there are a couple of nice ones, how will we know? It could be one of the horrible ones, just trying to get away with it."

"Their – the Blues would be able to tell us that, wouldn't they?" Madeleine had been dismayed by Pan's offer of amnesty, and yet glad of it. "So far it's been very rare for any of the non-Reborn to survive separation, anyway."

A scrambling noise rescued Madeleine from a subject she wasn't certain she could face, and Noi, only a few feet away, said: "Any problems?"

"Do stubbed toes count?" Min, who had been sent to take care of the webcam, eased into a spot near Madeleine and Emily. "I just shifted the angle upward, rather than turning it off. Can't guarantee those two kids will stay there though. It's mad the number of people round here who want to play hero."

"You say that, but I remember you running back trying to rescue me," Noi pointed out.

"Heat of the moment," Min's voice was dismissive. "And not exactly effective."

"Does that make a difference? I hope those two stay put – maybe we should send someone back in there to keep an eye on them."

Ari and Tia, their youngest Blues, had been assigned camera duties, filming the battle in the hopes of passing on dragon-fighting techniques – and keeping the pair out of a fight they were keen to join. Madeleine's primary feeling about her own involvement in the coming battle was dread combined with resignation, and an impatience for it to be done. To know whether the Spires would fall, and what that victory would cost them.

"Challenge is finishing up," Noi said tersely. "They'll keep to the pecking order heading back, so we're on schedule. Millie, come keep an eye on the feed for me."

Emily clambered over to the shielded hollow Noi was using to hide the glow of the laptop. Once she was there, Noi balanced on top of a fallen tree trunk, and held a torch high, turning it on and off three times in rapid succession. After a pause, she jumped down.

"Haron's team's in place. Defenders are heading in. Count off the entries that you see, Millie, and let me know when you get to fifty, and then eighty. And everyone eat something."

The Ul-naa were hundred and fifth in the primacy. That was a lot of dragons to fly on home, and Madeleine doubted Sydney's Core would return before dawn. She sighed, and tucked her hands into her armpits as Noi curled down beside her.

"I said eat."

"I have been. Everyone keeps trying to feed me."

"Yeah. Well." Noi evidently chose not to point out that Madeleine had spent most of the last few hours either unconscious or trying to hide in her cousin's armpit.

"Why was Emily angry with me?"

"Because it didn't happen to you. Because you escaped it."

The certainty of Noi's answer meant she'd probably already discussed this with Emily. Or perhaps felt the same way.

"Was – was it very bad?"

Noi didn't answer immediately, and Madeleine again felt the new gulf between them.

"It hurt all the time." The words came slowly, each an obvious effort. "Almost like shield-paralysis combined with the pins and needles afterwards. Not so sharp, but never ending. This – this constant, swooping distress of trying to move, to speak, and nothing. And suffocated by *its* presence. Sat on. That without even considering what your *it* is like, and what it's doing with you."

Regretting asking, Madeleine slid closer, and Noi leaned against her, shaking. But then, in an exhibition of sheer determination, the shorter girl's breathing eased, and she straightened, taking Madeleine's hand instead.

"Fifty," Emily said, and all around them came the faintest rustle of anticipation. Soon. Fighting, killing.

"Do you think Pan was wrong?" Madeleine asked. "To offer amnesty?"

"No. I hate the idea, but the alternative is..."

Genocide. A hard word to link to your own goals.

"Pan says his Moth was mostly frightened," Noi went on. "Not someone who'd put anyone before himself, just a scared squit trying to keep his head down. I'd still kill every single one of them to free the Blues they're riding, but...well...there's a bit more nuance to my attitude thanks to Fisher's little speech."

Fisher's recording had left Madeleine struggling to hide tears, grateful but perhaps even less able to deal with the tangle between them. At least he seemed to share her immediate need for avoidance, staying at a careful distance.

"He is distinctly different, isn't he?" Noi added, tone low, edged with sympathy. "I asked Nash and Pan how they could not notice he was possessed. They thought he'd gone suddenly polite wanting to impress you."

Not knowing how to respond, Madeleine simply hunched her shoulders, and after a pause Noi said quietly: "I owe you an apology."

"What for?"

"I did kind of encourage you into bed with him."

"Oh." It was like a jab to a wound, sudden and shocking for all they'd been talking around the subject. "No, don't be sorry. I'm not, not for that." She recognised a truth spoken, even though her throat immediately locked with unshed tears. "I was so happy," she said, struggling to get the words out. "It fell into a flaming heap, and I want to crawl under a rock, but I can't regret it. I'd never been happier in my life."

Noi's hand tightened on hers, then relaxed, and they sat connected by loosely linked fingers, waiting out the slow degrees of dawn. The Cathedral roof became a black silhouette against a pale sky, and, faintly, Nash murmured a Hindu prayer.

"Eighty."

"Right." Noi stood, and signalled again with her torch. "Keep counting, Millie, and let us know when you hit a hundred, but from this point on we're assuming it could be any moment."

Noi wasn't quite able to keep a hint of breathlessness from her voice, an awareness of how critical the moment was, and the consequences of failure. Madeleine stood as well, and tried to look at the Spire. South-west, its base was little more than an impression of depth, though its upper reaches stood out spear-sharp. Even on its own it was a difficult thing to encompass, and she struggled to frame the whole truth of it – not a ship, not a building, but a kind of spike or tentacle of a creature so vast it must look like a mountain range, clawing an alien sky.

Feeling cold and wobbly, she searched through the increasingly visible shapes around her until she found Tyler, incongruously seated on a park bench which had survived and remained upright. It rocked a little as she sat beside him, but it was a good place to collect herself. Lost in his own thoughts Tyler didn't speak, but gave her a small smile, and Madeleine recognised that even after years of having little to do with her cousin they retained the simple acceptance of family. Noi, along with so many millions of people, had lost that completely.

"Hey, Maddie, what's the name of that statue?" Pan, poking his head over her shoulder, pointed at the bronze figure Noi was leaning against. The gloom had lifted enough to reveal a woman armed with a bow, kneeling beside the mashed remains of a stag.

"It's the Roman goddess, Diana."

That imp's grin lit up the morning. "Thought so." He bounced across to Noi. "You know, Wonder Woman's real name is Diana. I'd call that a sign."

Noi almost visibly dragged her thoughts out from under the shadow of the Spire. "If that means spandex in our near future, I want a different sign."

Pan took Noi's hand and swung it gently. "You don't need a costume to be super."

"One hundred."

Noi flashed the torch again, and everyone held their breath. Madeleine found herself looking away from the Spire, at her feet, at Tyler, at the faces of the Musketeers. Fisher.

"Now!"

The shout was scattered, a dozen different voices. Madeleine stood and immediately spotted the ribbon of light, a dandelion dragon come home with the dawn, but it was impossible see whether Haron's squad had succeeded.

Whether they'd taken those few moments when the shield was down to press forward, thrust their hands against the Spire and blast it, a united punch intended to stun a mountain.

"Work," Noi muttered. "Work, work, wo—"

The Spire screamed. There was no other word for it. Electronic dissonance at a thousand decibels. Madeleine, hands over her ears, was moving back to the statue, all her attention focused on the curling ribbon of light swooping in a tight circle over the southern section of the park, and then coming to a near-halt, dozens of gossamer wings fanning. It was too far for her to clearly see the riders, but she could just make out the shape of them. Three people, one of whom was Gavin, who had driven to her rescue in his apple-green car.

The attackers' position in the north-east corner bought them time, with the Spire blocking the Core's view of those closest to its base, and the more widely scattered attackers sticking close to their chosen pieces of rubble. But already the dragon was moving, a swift arc north along Elizabeth Street, and then a slow drift toward the Spire from the park's north-west corner, approaching the double line of Blues pulsing measured punches into the velvety surface.

"Get ready," Noi said, barely audible over the continuing unearthly scream.

Madeleine nodded, resting her hands on the statue's outstretched arm, tracking the glowing creature's movements. The tactics Noi and Haron had recommended for dragon slaying were not greatly different to the Rover fight. The dragon had some shielding, and would gain strength from force punches. They needed to keep it still long enough for the leech Blues to drain it. Quite a task when it was currently drifting about sixty metres above the ground, searching the shadows. Stopping the attack on the Spire would be the Core's first priority, and a great deal depended on what he chose to do when he spotted the Spire Squad. The best option for the freed Blues would be for the Core to pick up speed and circle the Spire, returning to sweep through the people at the base. But he might drop immediately down toward them, or try to blast them with punches from dragon-back.

"All for one, guys," Pan shouted over the scream of the Spire, hopping up to balance on the mashed stag.

"All for one!" the Musketeers responded, quite as if they'd rehearsed it. One of the figures on the dragon's back looked toward them.

Around them, others picked up the cry, a scattered echo across the park which united and became a chant, a roar.

"All for one!"

"All For One!"

"ALL FOR ONE!"

For Théoden, Madeleine told herself as layers of gauzy wing beat into a faster pace, and the dragon whisked into a diving curve, crossing directly between the Musketeers and the Spire.

Madeleine punched. Full force, everything she had.

Her target was not the dragon's body, but below it, into the downbeat of its wings. The weakest point, with the least capacity for shielding or absorption. Diaphanous sails shredded into fragments of light, and the punch continued onward to strike the Spire, one more blow against the mountain. The dragon's swift arc spun out of control, and it zagged suddenly left, dropping into trees to the south.

Madeleine sagged, hooking her arm around the statue's in order to keep upright, while all around her there was an immediate scramble after their target.

"Stick with your partners!" Noi yelled. "Don't rush in – regroup on the road." She paused to grab Madeleine's shoulder. "Follow when you can." Then she was gone.

Alone in the pre-dawn twilight, Madeleine staggered back to Tyler's bench and flopped down, nearly overturning it in the process. The sudden decrease of the great roil of power within left her feeling chilled and vulnerable. Her hands were shaking.

The Spire continued to scream, shredding nerves exposed by cold, but she made herself ignore it, to take deep, even breaths until she felt that she could walk without falling. She didn't feel ready to fight, but she could get closer to her friends, in reach so she could act when spots stopped swimming before her eyes.

Although she could now see almost clearly, it took care and effort to cross the uneven ground to the road, and she sat down in the gutter for a little while, searching anxiously down the road for signs of her friends. She couldn't even make out the light of the dragon, and with the noise the Spire was making she was struggling to hear anything of use. Even the small medical team had vanished.

Standing, she checked back to the base of the Spire, and saw that on the far side of the park there was already fighting. Just a handful of people so far, but more streaming from one of the hotels, racing down Elizabeth Street. Gritting her teeth, she started trotting in the opposite direction, down College Street, searching the trees ahead for signs of battle. A dragon shouldn't be so hard to spot.

Passing the far end of the Cathedral, she glanced to her left across the paved forecourt and over the eastern suburbs. The first gleam of gold had touched the horizon. How long could the Spire Squad keep pounding the mountain? Were they feeling as drained as she? Haron hadn't been sure how long it would take, or how quickly the Spire would recover if they failed to bring it down.

Turning, Madeleine met the eyes of a familiar, strawberry blond boy skirting the edge of the trees.

She drew breath – to shout, or take some action – but he was too quick for her, force punching immediately. Her automatic shield kept her whole, but the blow was so strong she was blasted off her feet, too stunned to bring up a second shield as a cushion as she tumbled down a short, flat flight of stairs leading to the main forecourt.

Caught in that moment between being injured and knowing exactly what hurt, Madeleine levered herself to knees and one elbow, but another force punch hit her square in the back and she went down. Her shield was strong enough to keep the punch itself from breaking her to pieces, but not to prevent bruising impact with granite pavers. A third punch hit her, and the stone around her cracked.

"STOP IT!"

Emily's voice. Horrified, Madeleine jerked her head up, just in time to see Emily launch herself physically at the Core's stolen boy. Girl and alien overlord went down in a tangle of legs.

No time for recovery. Emily was a strong Blue, but the Core was stronger. Madeleine hurled herself to her feet, staggered, and sat down abruptly. Above her, she could just see Emily, punching at the Core beneath her, only to be blasted upward, more than ten metres into the air. The girl twisted like a cat, and came bouncing down, almost succeeding in slamming into the Core. He punched her again, and this time she tumbled out of Madeleine's sight, across the street.

There was so little Madeleine could do. She didn't have the strength to force punch or even attack the Core physically. Her only advantage was the power of her spirit punch, and that she didn't dare to do because there were no leech Blues nearby. Pushing the Core out of Gavin wouldn't kill it, and there was all too great a chance that, in her weakened state, it would simply possess her instead.

Whatever came after, the first thing was standing up. Madeleine rose carefully this time, discovering on the way that her left arm hurt when she put any weight on it. Five granite steps, broad and low. Then a short stagger out to the footpath, to find Emily still holding her own, if only just.

Putting what was left of her strength into her voice, Madeleine shouted.

"Shouldn't you be more worried about the Spire?" She walked unsteadily forward as the Core turned sharply toward her. "While you're wasting your time trying to squash us, we're winning this war."

The last thing Madeleine wanted was the Core to go attack the Spire Squad. She needed to unbalance and distract him, long enough to get closer.

"I think you've given him a black eye, Millie," she added. "But I expect Gavin will forgive you. Look after him." Another few steps.

The Core glanced toward the Spire, still standing, still screaming, but was not so easily diverted. His arm started to lift, and Madeleine dived forward, not trying to reach him, just closing the distance so that she didn't need to stretch herself beyond endurance.

She slammed into the footpath, hollow, a doll. Empty, as if only a scrap of her self remained. But light had bloomed. Madeleine rolled painfully onto her back and stared up at the deeply Blue Core as it moved toward her.

Hands, rough and hasty, grabbed her by the armpits and pulled her backward. Fisher. Blackly frowning, hair wild.

"I'm sure you have some perfectly reasonable explanation for not waiting for the leeches," he said, panting as he reversed them both rapidly away, "but right now it's escaping me."

"Delaying manoeuvre." Madeleine hadn't heard him running up. "I figured I'm such a temptation to the Core, it couldn't resist." She was hurting, dizzy, but feeling more herself purely because of the huge swell of emotion any contact with Fisher brought her. "Possessing someone who can hardly stand up would have to be a tactical error."

Fisher let out a startled laugh, and shook his head. "Dangerous logic."

A heavy round bin served as a useful prop, with Fisher positioning himself in front of her, a lone figure almost as tired as she. But already there were pounding feet behind them, and a cry of "*Once more unto the breach, dear friends!*" to herald a sudden crowd, a city's defenders arrayed before her.

The Core, far from stupid, immediately flitted in the other direction, and a Moth's speed may well have led to an escape, but for a grim figure which rose into its path.

"No cutting out on your death scene," Gavin said, perhaps trying to achieve a lightly chiding tone, but with such a harsh undernote of anger that he sounded totally unlike himself as he hit out with a shield.

Knocked backward, the Core failed to evade reaching hands – Nash, Tyler, Claire and Quan – all of them crowding forward. The Core lasted only a few moments longer than Noi's Moth, and then it was nothing, a collapsing jellyfish.

"May you rot."

Gavin stepped forward, and for a moment seemed about to spit, but shook his head instead and turned his back. And then they were all looking around at each other, eyes large.

"You finished the dragon–?" Madeleine asked.

Pan turned, checking. "Nah, it's still galumphing up the road behind us, but the Core was the primary target. Time to snicker-snack, ev–"

The Spire stopped screaming.

Madeleine found enough energy to slew around with the rest, to stare across Hyde Park at a familiar skyline, where Sydney Tower was the tallest building, and no midnight spear stabbed the dawn.

Then, as cheering rose all across the park, the dragon reached them.

Chapter Twenty-Six

A neutrally-decorated guest bedroom dominated by a four poster bed. Sunlight streamed through French doors, danced with dust motes, and kept Madeleine, tucked beneath a quilt, toasty-warm. Inertia pinned her in place.

"I've bad news if you're planning to stay in here permanently. All your little playmates are talking about leaving town."

Madeleine shifted gingerly, moving from her side to her back. "Noi told me," she said. "Did you find your friends?"

"Only Eliza. She thinks Josh is still Plus One." Tyler put down a carry bag and sat on the side of the bed, rearranging the long skirt of his dress before surveying Madeleine judicially, from her scraped and bruised face to her tightly wrapped left arm. "Malingering, or genuinely can't cope?"

"Both?" There had been a patch, when she'd woken early in the evening after the battle of the Spire, where it had all slammed down on her and she'd wept herself numb, barely responsive even to her Blue's hunger. The next day she'd slept when she no longer needed it, and struggled to have anything to say to Noi and Emily when they brought her food and news. "I just...don't know how to be."

"Would it help if I mentioned that burning first loves rarely look quite so eternal from the perspective of a couple of years? Or weeks. No?"

"Has saying that ever helped anyone?"

"Probably not." Tyler shifted so he could see through the French doors to the long sweep of sunlit garden outside. "I will concede that this is deliciously complicated. You're not sure if you were in love with the alien, or the boy, or a pastiche which was neither of them. What do you think would have happened if your Théoden had settled on a different host? The practical Noi, for instance?"

Tyler could be unsparing. Madeleine tried to picture a Noi who was Théoden, but it was impossible, so she dived into a different subject.

"Was the fight with the dragon bad?"

"No, highly entertaining." Tyler accepted the redirection without comment. "You chose a terrible moment to pass out, and missed a most impressive exhibition of bronco riding from our junior acting squad. Though with the Spire and the Core gone, I'm fairly sure the thing was only trying to run away. All I had to do was provide suitable applause." He caught Madeleine's change of expression and gave a tiny shake of his head. "Yes, I am aware of the massive crush. Sixteen. Not going to happen."

Madeleine wondered if she was sorry, and sighed. "I've missed you, Tyler. You never walk on eggshells."

He laughed, that beautiful, warm chuckle. "You have a most lowering opinion of me, judging from that excoriation on my bedroom wall. How unsparing, Leina." But his smile faded, and he touched her strapped arm, which she'd been told was likely only a hairline fracture. "Did you blame me?"

"No. A bit. I blamed everyone. But I didn't really care whose fault anything was – I just wanted to get away, not have to see any of those people again."

Tyler waited, humming softly.

"That's not what I'm doing now."

"It mightn't be what you want, but it is what you're doing. Not that I haven't gone out of my way to avoid an awkward conversation or two in my time. Do you really want to not have this one?"

The thought of talking to Fisher, sitting down and properly trying to work out where they stood... She squeezed her eyes shut.

"Things worth having are rarely easy, kiddo. There are worse responses than deciding how you want things to be, and doing everything you can to make that what is. Here." Tyler plopped the carry bag onto her lap. "If nothing else, get out of this room, sit in the sun a while. Your complicated beau is off having discussions with a crowd of military types who showed up this morning, so you'll have an hour or two to lose your nerve. If it all ends up being too much, my couch is always available. Oh, and I've spoken to your parents, but you might want to call them."

Dropping a kiss on her forehead, Tyler left Madeleine to inspect the carry bag, which held a pile of unused sketch pads. She still felt absolutely no impulse to put them to use, but supposed she could at least open these without fear of coming across drawings she couldn't bear to look at.

Madeleine's eventual reason for getting up had more to do with not liking the extra burden she was putting on everyone. The two days since the fall of the Spires had spared the Musketeers little time for victory parties. Around a third of the Blues in the city were still possessed, and for the first day both they and the Greens had continued to either attack or hide. The second day the Greens had stopped, like run down toys, which was not a better situation, but after several hours of emptiness they'd started to show signs of reacting. And new Blues and Greens were returning to Sydney, helping to lighten the load of people who'd started out damaged and exhausted.

Two possessed Blues had surrendered themselves, but both Moths had died at separation.

It hurt to walk about, but it hurt to lie down, so there was no real reason to stay in bed. Noi had left her a choice of painkillers in the en suite, so Madeleine first took a fresh dose, then went through her bags until she found her original phone. A little reassembly, and a brief charge while she washed and dressed, and then she was listening to a stream of voicemail. Her parents had called every day, despite her warning that she wasn't using her phone, just to leave a message, to let her know where they were. Her own call was met by a busy signal, so she sent a text and email.

Then, taking a sketchbook and pencils, she went outside.

The backyard was long, with a central gazebo, a number of blazing Japanese maples, and a wisteria arbour winding to a tennis court hidden by hedges. A tall sandstone fence, a shade darker than the walls of the house, kept it private, a little world of its own. Madeleine liked it very much, exploring with interest, then sitting on the rear stairs of the gazebo.

The house was Fisher's. With half the Musketeers in various states of collapse, he'd suggested it as an alternative to the hectic confusion of the Elizabeth Street hotels. Because it was away from the centre of the fighting, and wasn't known to others, they'd been able to use it as a retreat, moderately confident of not being attacked. Noi had told Madeleine this carefully, as if she'd half expected Madeleine to immediately try to escape out of the window. But the place didn't bother Madeleine, just the prospect of talking to Fisher and finding someone unrecognisable.

Almost everything Théoden had told her had to be Fisher's past and Fisher's opinions. A smart, incisive boy, layered over with a quiet consideration which didn't match up to the Fisher Pan had first described. It had not been Fisher's deep anger and black fear, nor Fisher who would stop and be amused at himself. How many times had she tried to draw that expression?

Madeleine found herself impatient, wanting to get it all over with, to face the fact that she'd killed the person she loved. A conversation as a burial, a wake, and then perhaps she could find the strength to not keep pushing everyone else away. Lacking a necessary participant for the conversation, she opened the sketchpad and balanced it on her knee. If nothing else, not wanting to sketch people would give her a chance to improve her non-figurative work.

"You're drawing again. I'm glad."

Working on a study of the arbour had helped immensely, and Madeleine felt only a sense of inevitability as she looked up at Fisher. But there in front of her was the beloved shape of him, the face she had kissed, that direct gaze. She turned all her attention back to the page, to gnarled cords of wisteria, and the slight problem of perspective she'd been trying to correct.

After a pause, Fisher sat down on the opposite side of the gazebo stairs, where he would have to reach to touch her.

"Hello," he said, and held out his hand. "My name is Fisher."

Madeleine stared at the pad, entirely focused on her peripheral vision. She understood the gesture, but could not bring herself to move. He sat with hand held out, waiting long after the moment had become awkward. A stretched eternity, and his arm shook a little, reaching the point where muscles would be longing for release.

The pencil Madeleine was holding snapped, and she looked down at the faint suggestion of marks on her blue palm, wondering at herself. Had she always been this person, completely unable to cope with any private crisis? The tightly-wound paralysis was familiar, was, as Tyler had pointed out, very like her reaction when she'd been knocked down a flight of stairs for having a cousin.

Carefully she put the pencil on the wooden boards beside her and felt ill and alive to take the hand which a spare few days ago she had reached for with complete confidence.

"Madeleine."

The hand clasping hers tightened in a way which was achingly familiar, then let go.

"Why does your cousin call you Leina?"

The casual, neutral question helped. Perhaps it was real, this introduction. Strangers who had just met. She could deal with that if she didn't look at him. And tried not to react to his voice.

"When I was, oh, five I think, I lost my temper at something at the family Christmas party. My uncle – Tyler's Dad – told me I was a 'real little Maddie' and teased me a tiny bit during lunch. My family had always called me Maddie, but I had no idea the word meant anything but 'me'. I spent the afternoon – and much of the next few months – insisting that people call me 'Leina' instead. Tyler was the only one who did. Everyone else thought it tremendously funny."

"Why not introduce yourself as Leina, then?"

"I prefer Madeleine. And I've gotten over caring about being called Maddie. Leina's just become Tyler's name for me."

Fisher was looking at her sketch, and she checked a ridiculous impulse to hide it, lowering her hands to her sides.

"I wouldn't have reacted to your painting in the same way," he said then, with the air of a confession, and beneath that something like a challenge. "I'm interested in art, and I think I would have enjoyed watching you paint, but it's difficult to imagine – imagine the me before this – sitting for hours, so singularly absorbed. I would have at least read a book at the same time."

Madeleine glanced at him, uncertain. To start by making that clear...

"The others are talking over Melbourne and Brisbane," he went on. "The Sydney situation is stable enough we could leave tomorrow, perhaps splitting into two groups." He took a deep breath. "I had such a...visceral reaction to the idea. That I didn't care what group, which city. The only absolute was that I go with you."

She sat frozen, found that he was waiting for a response. "You said you thought those feelings weren't real."

"I said I don't know how much of these feelings are mine. I wasn't in control, but I was there, for all of it, every moment. The pretence that we just met falls down straight away, because every time I look at you I'm slammed in the gut. It's not possible to start fresh, to go back. Feelings so strong and deep they make you stop and catch your breath don't need rediscovery. They need decisions."

He rose, but to her relief paced a few steps away, and stood with his back to her. His voice was crisp and almost combative when he went on.

"I'm not the same person. I would not have behaved as Théoden did. I would have admired your painting, your talent, but I would not have sat and watched you. I would never have made so much interest clear, or told you half the things he did, things that I don't admit. I would have put up walls against you because I've spent years being bored by people, finding them an annoyance or untrustworthy. I'm not bored by you. I can hardly breathe when you're in the same room."

He paused, turning just enough for her to see his profile.

"I also refuse to be the kind of person who follows you around making you flinch. So, I'm not going to follow you. I'm choosing Melbourne. If you want time, or want to never think about the parts of the past few days which involve me, go to Brisbane. If you want to find out–" He broke off, and summoned a wry, self-mocking expression which faded as he glanced at her. "I sound like I'm throwing down a gauntlet. Perhaps I am. I want you to come to Melbourne, to let yourself find out if any of what you felt was for me."

Without giving her any chance to respond, he turned on one heel and strode off, back to the house.

Madeleine looked down at clenched hands, then slowly opened the right to inspect the tiny scratch which marred her view of her stars. There had been a lot of pride in that speech, and hurt. Had she really been flinching from him? She'd been trying not to.

She had to admit he had immediately attracted her on a physical level, and she'd been intrigued by things which couldn't possibly be Théoden. A boy who couldn't draw but wanted to be da Vinci. Whose mother had been his ideal. Who hadn't faltered from necessity in the days after the Spire's arrival, then had had nightmares about the people he'd failed to save. Driven, time-poor, prone to putting people last outside of emergencies. Very like her. And, if that conversation was anything to go by, just as shielded and defensive as she, for all his clear self-confidence.

It mattered a great deal that he'd made sure the entire world knew the debt they owed to the Moth who had possessed him. And he'd seen that the first thing she'd needed to know was how he felt about her art. But how could she go with him, constantly seeing only that he was different from the boy she loved? That would only hurt them both more, a long spiral of comparisons and disappointments she didn't have the strength to face.

Fight. Always fight. No matter how impossible the odds, no matter who you've lost, how you've been hurt. If there doesn't seem to be a way out, look for one. If you seem to have come to an end, start afresh. Never, ever give up.

Had Théoden foreseen this choice? Unable to settle her thoughts, Madeleine walked up to the house, to wash her face and follow the noise of discussion to a crowded lounge room. Musketeers dishing out food and talking over what to do next. They greeted her cheerfully, entirely as if she hadn't been curled up in her room for the past two days, and shuffled about to make a space for her to sit. Madeleine tucked in beside Emily so she could thank her for a timely rescue, remarked on Gavin's impressive black eye, and accepted a piled plate from Nash. Pan grinned at her from the floor beside Noi's feet, then turned his attention back to a sniper war of paper balls with Min.

Acceptance washed over her, a sense of care and belonging, a certainty of place. Whatever happened, they would support her, pick her up if she fell, cover her weaknesses and be glad of her presence. She ate, and found herself almost smiling, and when Noi asked which city Madeleine thought they should go to, she looked across at a closed, expressionless face and said:

"Melbourne."

Epilogue

A perfect autumn day. By ten the streets were already filling, crowds flooding from the train tunnels, walking from the bus drop sites, meandering down the centre of the closed roads, gaping at the crest of white visible above the trees. Most wore dust-catchers: broad-brimmed hats supporting elbow-length veils, reminiscent of beekeeper garb but with a dense, silky weave. A few – the elderly, the very young – were clumsy in Hazmat gear. Bareheaded among them were Blues and Greens, or the foolhardy percentage who gambled that the Conversion would make them heroes, not corpses.

Many crossed the southern portion of Hyde Park on their way to the ceremony, some glancing at the young woman seated on the stair of the Anzac Memorial, none coming close enough to see the deep stain of her hands, or the patch on her face hidden by an unnecessary dust-catcher. She watched them on their way to commemorate a different war, and occasionally glanced at a worn paperback while fielding a stream of text messages. As midday approached, the flow of people tapered off, but by that time the northern half of the park and surrounds were a solid mass, even spilling across the dividing street into the southern park. The mood was celebratory. It was a day to mark a return to some semblance of normalcy, to gather at the point of invasion, no longer a gaping hole leaking toxic dust, or the churned scar which had plugged it, but a park once again, with a functioning train station beneath. To proclaim relief, sorrow, triumph, and a move forward. The dust-catchers silently, unavoidably, underlined that there was no going back.

The white noise of chatter died away to echoing speeches. Then applause, more speeches, more applause. Finally, inevitably, a united chant which thousands of voices turned into a roar, thunder.

"All for one! All For One! ALL FOR ONE!"

By two o'clock the park had nearly emptied, thousands streaming over to The Domain, where food stalls and a sound stage had been set up for an afternoon concert. Music thumped. The performance was in full swing when a curvy young woman wearing a white dress and blue headband crossed into the southern half of Hyde Park, followed the length of the reflecting pool, and climbed the Memorial stair.

"Not sketching?"

"Not stupid."

"I guess it would be a bit of a giveaway."

They hugged, and as ever Madeleine was immediately warmed. It was if a year's separation had never happened.

"How was the ceremony?"

"Blah blah blah, then a few thousand people in tears. Ready to go down?"

Madeleine glanced at the time on her phone and nodded.

"I should have grown some sense and skipped out too," Noi said, as they headed north. "I'm so jetlagged I can't think straight."

"Do you want to put off dinner? Change it to tomorrow?"

"Hell no. I'll nap for an hour or two while everyone's gabbing, then I'll be good to go. Besides, I've been dying to meet Millie's girlfriend. What's she like?"

"Zoe? Clever, a bit of a joker. Tries to be cool, but absolutely hero-worships Millie. Wait till you see them in their uniforms."

"A potential portrait?"

"Maybe. I've done a few studies." She caught Noi's frown and smiled through the veil. "I think the police thing is working out. Millie's breezing through the training, and she's so happy even her parents are starting to accept."

"Mm. I still regret talking her into calling them. All that fuss and drama."

They'd been in Mumbai at the time, six months after the fall of the Spires, and the Wrights' discovery their daughter was still alive had led to a stream of accusations and demands. Though it gave Madeleine a headache just to remember, she thought that it had worked out better for Emily in the long run. Her parents so clearly adored her.

"How's casting going?"

"All the major roles are set. The rest we'll work through next week, which should be fun and a half. At least now Tyler's signed Nash can go back to being himself, instead of the Walking Tower of Stress."

Madeleine laughed. "Why was he stressing? Tyler really wants to play Milady." Reshaping the villainess of *The Three Musketeers* into a loyalty-torn heroine had produced a particularly juicy role, and Tyler was far from the only Big Name who'd been keen to win it.

"Oh, just a small matter of Undying Devotion. Besides, TBM is not exactly a major-league production company, even with Saashi on board."

They crossed Park Street speculating on the chances of Nash winning Tyler, which at least had shifted into the realms of possibility now he was twenty-one instead of sixteen.

"Do you think you'll finally settle for a while?"

"Hey, you've gadded about almost as much as we have – is there a city you two haven't studied in? But, yeah, we're thinking of basing TBM in Sydney even after the film's done. I'm going to have to slow down anyway." She touched her stomach, and nodded at Madeleine's questioning glance. "Not a hundred per cent planned, but we'd been talking about it. We both like the idea of a big family."

Delighted, Madeleine paused to hug Noi again. "I'm not sure I should congratulate you though – TBM's going to have it rough without you keeping everyone organised."

"I'll be keeping my finger in the pie, don't worry about that. Just not baking them for a crew of fifty for a while."

"So does this mean you're going to schedule the wedding at long last?" Madeleine asked as they made their way through a mix of towering fig trees and recently-planted saplings.

"Yeah, time to make it official, and devastate Lee's more rabid fans. I think I might ask Min to do the dress – he's so wasted as our costume department."

"Wasted as in still loving every minute while pretending the world annoys him?"

"That about covers it. Be warned, I'm ready and able to rope you in to paint the backdrops again, if and when we move to another stage production."

"Good. I learned a lot last time."

The prolonged stay in India had been due to a combination of circumstance and choice. Attempting to leave Sydney, they'd been co-opted by the Australian Army, which at least had solved transport problems. Particularly when they'd decided on Tokyo as the next stop after Melbourne, joining the effort to weed out the most powerful of the Moth clans. From there they'd been shuttled to Mumbai, just in time for the local forces to declare victory. With most cities well on the same path, they'd been able to cut loose from the military so Nash could meet up with Saashi. But that had effectively stranded the Musketeers, since civilian air travel wasn't exactly happening. They'd turned the situation into a hands-on apprenticeship in film-making, as Nash's powerhouse sister put them all to work helping her document some of the thousands of stories of the invasion. The combination of interviews and 'mini-play' dramatisations had won Saashi a great deal of notice, and kept the company which had been her parents' ticking along while the world tried to sort out if it had an economy.

TBM – The Blue Musketeer Production Company – had evolved from this experience, and Nash, Pan, Min and Noi had worked steadily toward gaining the reputation and knowledge to film *The Blue Musketeers* to the standard it deserved. Of course, it helped immensely that the Musketeers were world-famous, and even more that Saashi had agreed to direct and provide experienced crew members.

"Do you think they regret asking you to submit a design?" Noi asked, as they emerged from the screening trees and stopped, gazing up at the replacement for the Archibald Fountain.

"Maybe. I did sometimes, during the fuss. But there were a lot of other submissions, and they decided by public vote."

"Beautiful and terrible," Noi murmured. "I can almost look at it without cringing."

The statue rose twenty metres, a graceful curve of white shot with central veins of blue clustered into a semblance of a human figure. The base was suspended in a clear block, giving it some necessary stability, and beneath was a patterned non-slip grid to drain the water which fell in a single sheet from the outstretched, kite-like wings. On hot days children would be able to play in the near-mist of the fall.

"He liked water," Madeleine said.

They walked on in silence, ignoring the small scatter of people who recognised Noi and looked closely at her companion. In the mist, tiny rainbows were visible, shimmering in the fine liquid sheet.

Arms slid around Madeleine's waist, warm and familiar, and Fisher rested his forehead wearily on her shoulder. "What mad impulse made me agree to be a speaker?"

Madeleine leaned back, knowing perfectly well he'd done it to make it easier for her to refuse. "When are they bringing them?" she asked instead.

"Just after dawn."

"What's this?" Noi asked. "Bringing who? Oh, wait – do you mean the Goat Island crowd? Seriously?"

"It seems to be important to them." Fisher tightened his arms briefly, then shifted to Madeleine's side, catching hold of her hand. "And kept absolutely quiet for obvious reasons."

In Australia twenty-seven Moths had survived a choice to surrender. After interminable debate the Government had recognised Pan's offer of amnesty and collected them all on Goat Island. Not every country followed suit – some were still struggling to form a stable enough government to make a ruling – but there were still several hundred En-Mott around the world. And, of course, endless rumours that this or that prominent Blue was really an undiscovered Moth.

Fisher didn't work directly with the team which had spent years creating a way to communicate with the remaining Moths, but occasionally he was drawn into issues surrounding them, just as he had been all through the months immediately following the fall of the Spires. The En-Mott would ask for him, because Théoden had become as much a hero to them as he was to the Blues he'd saved. Every time, the discussions gave Fisher nightmares, and he would seek Madeleine out and start talking – about art, about whatever he was studying at the moment, or the latest book he'd read. Talking until the knots relaxed, and the tension flowed out of him.

A shout summoned attention, and it was time to greet long-absent friends, be introduced to new, and ignore the people taking photos of the rare sight of the original Blue Musketeers all in one place. After the initial excitement had eased, Madeleine broke away from the crowd and drifted with Fisher to a simple plaque set in the paving right on the edge of the mist.

His profile as he gazed at the curve of blue and white above took all her attention, and she was immediately distracted into planning a canvas. "Will you sit for another portrait?"

The expression he wore when he looked down at her became another that she urgently wanted to capture, stealing her breath with its intensity. "Do you remember what I said the first time you asked me that?"

"I'm not likely to forget." He'd said 'Always', voice shaking, and kissed her immediately afterward.

"It meant you'd started seeing me. You asked that question and I —" He paused, glancing at the audience behind them, and offered her a faint, wry smile. "For you to see me, ME, was everything."

"Now I feel bad because I was simply glad that I'd finally figured out how to paint you."

His smile became sardonic. "By that point I'd noticed you draw a great many people, but only seem to urgently want to paint those who matter to you."

She'd not thought of it that way, but it was true enough, making another similarity between them, since he spared time from his studies only for people he considered important. There had been times, even after Tokyo, when she'd struggled not to give in to divided feelings, but she'd never regretted choosing to go to Melbourne. And had been rewarded by a slow return of the total confidence she'd felt when she first held her hand out to a boy more complicated than anyone guessed.

"I wonder if Noi and Lee would be interested in a double wedding?" she asked, standing beneath mist and rainbows.

Fisher's hand tightened on hers. "Are you proposing to me?"

"I think I must be." The dust-catcher was a mercy, her face surely crimson. "I can't imagine ever not wanting to paint you."

Fisher gave her his response silently and completely, turning to take her free hand, every line of him shouting joy as the mist-fine fall drifted around him. She was glad this had happened here, the place where it had begun and ended, and wasn't even annoyed by the faint awareness of camera shutters whirring. The Musketeers had helped her along by maintaining to a very interested world that "Fisher and Maddie got together in Tokyo", but she wasn't ashamed of what she'd felt for Théoden. He had given her many gifts, and it felt right to share this with him.

Keeping a firm clasp of Fisher's hands, she looked up at rainbows, then down at the stone plaque they stood before.

"Théoden," it read.

Beneath the name, three words:

ONE FOR ALL

Musketeers

Avinash (Nash) Sharma
Emily (Millie) Wright
Fisher Charteris
Lee (Pan) Rickard
Madeleine Cost
Min Liang
NaengNoi (Noi) Lauro

Quotation Sources

Henry V, William Shakespeare
King Lear, William Shakespeare
Peter Pan and Wendy, JM Barrie
Romeo and Juliet, William Shakespeare
The Three Musketeers, Alexandre Dumas